# Moondogs

# Moondogs A NOVEL

## ALEXANDER YATES

*Doubleday*

NEW YORK  LONDON  TORONTO  SYDNEY  AUCKLAND

**DOUBLEDAY**

All rights reserved. Published in the United States by Doubleday, a division of Random House, Inc., New York, and in Canada by Random House of Canada Limited, Toronto.

www.doubleday.com

DOUBLEDAY and the DD colophon are registered trademarks of Random House, Inc.

*Chapter icons courtesy of Rebecca Cullers*
*Woodcuts by Emily Bender*
*Jacket design by Michael J. Windsor*

LIBRARY OF CONGRESS CATALOGING-IN-PUBLICATION DATA
Yates, Alexander, 1982–
    Moondogs : a novel / Alexander Yates. — 1st ed.
        p. cm.
    1. Fathers and sons—Fiction. 2. Americans—Philippines—Fiction. 3. Kidnapping—Fiction. 4. Insurgency—Philippines—Fiction. 5. Philippines—Fiction. I. Title.
    PS3625.A74M66 2010
    813'.6—dc22
                                2010007947

ISBN 978-0-385-53378-2

PRINTED IN THE UNITED STATES OF AMERICA

10 9 8 7 6 5 4 3 2 1

First Edition

*for Terhi*

HORATIO: O day and night, but this is wondrous strange!
HAMLET: And therefore as a stranger give it welcome.
  —*Hamlet*, Act I: Sc 5
  William Shakespeare


HURLEY: Back home, I'm known as something of a
  warrior myself.
  —"All the Best Cowboys Have Daddy Issues"
    *Lost*, Season 1, Episode 11
    Javier Grillo-Marxuach

## ACKNOWLEDGMENTS

My deepest thanks to Arthur Flowers; George Saunders; Melissa Danaczko; Alanna Ramirez; Brett Finlayson; Tracey Levine; Tami Monsod and Toby Monsod; David Beaty; Rebecca Cullers; the Syracuse University Creative Writing Program and Summer Literary Seminars, Russia.

Thanks above all to my wife, Terhi Majanen.

# Moondogs

BOOK ONE *Departures*

*Chapter 1*

## MR. ORANGE

A man and a rooster exit a taxi idling on a crowded street. The man is short and thin, and the rooster is green, and the rooster belongs to him. The taxi belongs to him as well. He's wearing a fresh shirt, the blood all washed out, and his polyester slacks shine a little in the afternoon light. He's too young to be balding, but is. His mouth is a rotten mess, owing to bad hygiene and a shabu habit. His name is Ignacio. He and the rooster are villains.

Ignacio grips the open taxi door and stretches his legs. It feels good to be standing. The drive south from Manila should have taken only an hour, but he demanded that Littleboy—his idiot brother—make wrong turns so they'd be harder to follow. He'd barked instructions from the backseat, where he and Kelog pored over a soggy map and planned intricate double-backs. Kelog is the rooster. He's named Kelog because he's green, with red and orange in his tail, and a blood-red comb, like the rooster on the cereal. He used to be a fighting cock. He still would be, if not for the onset of blindness. He's retired now.

Littleboy stays in the family taxi, drumming his fingers on the wheel and singing along to the SexBomb Girls on the radio. Littleboy loves the family taxi. He never minds picking up Ignacio's shifts, and people tip him better, because he's a safer driver and doesn't look so scary. He looks big and soft. When the song ends he leans out the window and calls over to his brother.

"Is this it, Iggy? Are we there yet?"

"Not so loud, dummy!" Ignacio shouts. "What did I tell you?"

Littleboy looks embarrassed and squints. He hadn't been loud at all.

Ignacio holds Kelog tight and releases the open taxi door like a mother's hand. He steps into the after-lunch foot traffic, searches out a number above the shops and checks it with the address he'd written on his palm the night before. They're in the right spot—or close to it at least. They'll walk the final distance on side streets, just to be safe.

"Go park the car," Ignacio says. "I'll make sure we're alone."

"Be careful," Littleboy says, thumbing the scented Virgin Mother statuette on the dashboard. Ignacio watches him courteously reenter the slow moving traffic and then signal—*who signals?*—at the intersection ahead. He again thinks that maybe his brother isn't up to today's challenge. On a whole bunch of levels. Like maybe he's too softhearted. Or maybe he doesn't have sense enough to know he should be scared. Ignacio sure has sense enough. He's terrified. He appreciates the seriousness of the shit he's starting.

Ignacio shifts Kelog to his other arm, leans against the concrete wall of a store selling toilets and bathtubs and tries his utmost to look nonchalant. He scans the noisy street, all bathed in sweat from an unusually hot mid-May, even for the Philippines. Power lines sag dangerously low over speeding buses and jeepneys. Women hawk cool juice and duck eggs from tin kiosks, while men in a repair shop fold up their shirts to air out their guts. Two children chase a scalded cat down the sidewalk, but they get distracted by Kelog, and the cat escapes. "Is that a fighting cock, mister?" they ask. Kelog eyes the general area of the children with hungry disdain, and Ignacio tells them to beat it.

"Who are you talking to, pussy?" the smaller one says in a high, lovely voice. "This isn't your neighborhood, *Manileño!*"

The boys goose their crotches, spit near his shoes and run down the gravel sidewalk laughing. Ignacio presses himself into the shop wall and watches them go. He knows he looks out of place. But he's on the lookout for people even more out of place—scanning the street for the Americans that he's sure are following him. Men in suits ill-suited to the climate, peering out from behind menus in the karaoke bar and the buko pie shop. Pale men or maybe black men with sunglasses on their eyes and wireless earpiece-things in their ears. Blond freckled athlete virgins hiding in the lengthening shadows of stop signs; ready to pounce, ready to pull him into an SUV with diplomatic plates and tinted windows and take him somewhere dark and dress him in something bright and deprive him of sleep, ready to drag him screaming to ocean-distant rooms of electrified genitals and nudity-near-dogs, ready to lock him up with the real hardcore types at Guantanamo Bay, ready to laugh and eat pastries as they watch him get ass-raped through one-way glass. He's afraid of those Guantanamo types—his maybe future cellmates—the most. He isn't hardcore. And they'll know it in a second.

"How far is the mosque from here?" Littleboy's voice startles him so much that he drops Kelog, whose fighting spur—attached today for the first time in years—makes an ugly noise against the gravel.

"Idiot," Ignacio says as he reaches down to recover Kelog and coo to him. "Don't say that. Keep your mouth shut."

Littleboy shuts his mouth and breathes through his whistling nostrils. He takes obvious glances over each shoulder and then puts on what he must think is a nonconspiratorial expression. He looks like he's trying to pass something so big it hurts a little. He makes Ignacio sick.

"Come on," he says. "Walk behind me, and don't say anything to anybody."

Without another word, they make their way along the street. Ignacio slips down the first pedestrian alley they come to and walks the labyrinthine footpaths in the general direction of their destination: the Blue Mosque. He's not happy to be getting so many curious glances from passersby, and his hands shake, his long nails scraping audibly on his cheap slacks. The paranoia and the shabu have kept him awake for days now. The bags under his eyes are swollen so dark it looks like he's weeping tar. People avoid him in the narrow corridors between shanty walls; sometimes stepping in sewage to do so, as though they're afraid what he's got might be catching. When they pass Littleboy—dutifully a few steps behind—they've got no choice but to keep hugging the walls. He's almost as big across as Ignacio is tall, his head large as a breadfruit. He's got to duck every few steps to avoid do-it-yourself power lines, stolen cable and jagged aluminum siding.

But of the three of them, Kelog by far gets the most attention. Ignacio expected this—bringing him along is a calculated risk. He's conspicuous, but if shit goes down he'll be needed for protection. Even in retirement he's an impressive bird. His comb stands erect as a crown, the plume of his tail is thick and his talons are solid as a fat kid's fingers. Back in his heyday he put larger opponents away in the first round, leaving them open and disgorged like fancy unpacked handbags on the arena floor. He has thirty-three wins to his name, which may as well be thirty-three thousand considering the lifespan of your average working gamecock. If he hadn't started going blind he'd still be at it. And Ignacio would still be spending his earnings unwisely. And he wouldn't be doing something as dumb, and risky, as this.

The alleys widen as the villains get farther from the main road. Palms compete with makeshift antennas for canopy space, each a perch for sooty pigeons and wild sparrows still dyed red and green from the holidays. Shanty windows breathe talk radio in the heat, their corrugated roofs shimmering like skillets. The squat buildings seem more solid out here, built of concrete masonry blocks and insulated with mortar and foam. Some have fenced-in gardens; sunny resting places for chained dogs or old men chained by gravity to rattan lounge chairs. The old men heckle passersby as though it's charming.

"Hey!" one of them says, noticing the spur fastened to Kelog's foot. "You're going the wrong way, pal. The arena is *that way*." He points.

Ignacio quickens his pace. He can see a blue-capped minaret ahead and it's all he can do to keep from gawking. The alley opens further and they come abruptly to a white outer wall with a sprawling low dome beyond. The area around the mosque is quiet, save for a pair of shirt-less teenagers in black-and-white crocheted caps playing basketball on the pounded dirt. The one with the ball freezes mid-pivot to look at the strangers and then, as though he's deemed them boring, shoots against the plywood backboard.

Ignacio and Littleboy walk along the wall to the arched entrance. It is trimmed with indigo and a vein of stone-inlaid Arabic script. "You'd better wait here," Ignacio says. "Don't come in unless you hear me yell-ing. Or, if I don't come out for a long time, then you can come in."

Littleboy bites his bottom lip and it quivers under his front teeth. His eyes glisten.

"Don't do that," Ignacio says as he hands Kelog over. "I'll be just fine. But if I'm not, then don't you dare run away. Come in and help me."

Littleboy gravely tries to shake Ignacio's hand, but Ignacio pulls away. He walks through the mosque entrance and finds himself in an empty courtyard surrounded on all sides by a white colonnade made featureless and bright in the midday sun. Dark arched doorways lie at irregular intervals beyond the columns, some of them open and others closed. Ignacio peeks inside one and sees a pair of concrete tubs filled to the brim with water, ringed by shallow troughs and drains. A young man in reading glasses sits on a stool beside one of the tubs, running water from a spigot over his bare feet. He looks up at Ignacio and smiles warmly. Hoping to look like he knows what he's doing, Ignacio stumbles into the room. He dips his hands into one of the tubs and washes them. He wets his forearms and his face and the back of his neck. He exits, dripping, and hears the young man behind him chuckle.

Ignacio peeks through arched doorways until he finds the large prayer room—confident that the Imam should be in there. He kicks off his shoes, grabs a knit cap from an empty desk by the doorway and walks inside. The carpet is the color of sand and feels good against his feet. It bunches up, here and there, around several white pillars garlanded with strands of beads. "Hello?" Ignacio calls. The prayer room replies with quiet. He looks about the walls and sees more beads, some prayer mats and unintelligible script running upward in a continuing frieze. It's nothing like the church in his old seminary, where the wooden eyes of the saints and Mary and baby Jesus and grownup Jesus were everywhere to stare you down. As frightening as he's always found them, the absence of faces here disturbs him even more.

"That was a quick ablution," someone says. "Are you in a rush?"

Ignacio spins to see a figure framed by sunlight in the doorway. It's the young man from the washroom—fully laced and dressed in a crisp white shirt. His slacks are ironed and wisps of a goatish beard cling to his chin.

"I'm sorry . . ." Ignacio looks down at his toes, and as he does a few greasy droplets of water drip from his head and spatter the carpet. "Am I doing something wrong?"

"It's all right. Come on out, why don't you?" The young man steps aside so Ignacio can exit the prayer room. He accepts the cap back from him and drops it on the desk, slightly apart from the other caps. Ignacio is jarred by the realization that this young man is the Imam he's come to meet, and he takes a moment to recover. He'd expected a transplant from the savage south; a bearded asskicker streaked with gray like molten stone. But this young man has a coffee-shop softness. He looks even more like a Manileño than Ignacio does.

"My name is Joey," the Imam says.

Joey? Ignacio thinks. Joey?

They shake hands and look at each other for many moments.

"You don't wish to tell me who you are?" the Imam asks.

"You can call me Mr. Orange."

The Imam smiles. "I love that movie, too," he says.

Ignacio sputters. "I telephoned you," he says. "I telephoned you. Yesterday. About that thing. The thing I'm selling?"

"Oh." The young Imam looks let down, disappointed in his new friend. "I said on the phone I wasn't interested."

"That's because you don't understand what it is."

"Even so. Even if I wanted it, this isn't a place to sell anything." The Imam begins walking through the bright courtyard, back to the washroom. "Please leave," he says without looking back.

Ignacio chases after him, the courtyard tile burning his bare soles. "Wait!" he calls. "Just take a *look.*"

"No, thank you." The Imam makes to close the heavy washroom door but Ignacio jabs his naked foot through the frame. "Please go away," he says in an angry voice.

The door presses—not too hard—against Ignacio's foot, and he panics at the thought of having taken so many risks only to fuck this up now. He fumbles in his pockets, grabs a small rigid card and shoves it through the door so the Imam can see it. The pressure on his foot ebbs. The Imam is silent behind the door. When he finally speaks his voice echoes pleasingly against the tile walls and floor.

"What is this?"

Ignacio feels a brief flutter of confidence. He asks the Imam what it looks like.

The door opens slowly and the Imam plucks the card from Ignacio's fingers. It's an Illinois driver's license, three years past expiration, picturing an overweight white man with glasses and a full head of sandy hair. The Imam backs into the washroom and sits again on the wooden stool. He looks from the license back up to Ignacio.

"I told you that you'd be interested." Ignacio slips inside and sits on the wide rim of one of the concrete tubs—acting cool and awkward.

"I don't know what this is," the Imam says.

"Of course you don't." Ignacio winks. He taps the side of his nose twice, significantly. He kicks the washroom door closed and seals them both in hot half-darkness.

"No." The Imam drops the license on the tile between his feet. "I really don't know what this is."

Ignacio stares at him. He can hear Kelog crowing impatiently outside. The chain net jingles as the teenagers shoot hoops. Engines rumble distantly on the main road.

"I have that," Ignacio says, pointing down at the license.

"You have what?"

Ignacio puffs his cheeks in frustration. For all he knows, there is a team assembling on the corrugated rooftops outside. They'll be waiting by the exit with a bag for his head and shackles for his wrists and legs. He doesn't have time for these games. Ignacio scoops the license up and mashes his finger into the white man's face. "That!" he yells. "This! *Him*!"

"You have the person?"

Ignacio nods.

"I understand," the Imam says, in a crackly voice. The crackly voice encourages Ignacio. He's caught him off guard, and that's always a good position to bargain from.

"So I was thinking, that, you know, you, being who you are . . . I watch the news. I have subscriptions. I follow what's going on. It wasn't a leap for me to imagine that someone like you would be interested," Ignacio says.

The Imam puts his head in his hands, as though thinking. Ignacio, on a roll, can't stop talking.

"Because I'm not stupid. I've seen enough movies to know that if I try and do the whole . . . that, you know, if I call up his *family*. If I say meet me at such-and-such with this much money. That shit *never* ends well. And I know plenty about you guys and those guys. I mean, there's a war on, am I right? They call it a war. They call it that on their websites. And you do too—don't argue. I don't judge. I don't have a dog in the fight. I'm just here to check if you want him. Or if you know folks who'll want him. You know who I'm talking about. Abu Sayyaf. MILF. Jemaah Islamiyah—don't think I haven't looked into this. I've done my research. They've paddled all the way to Malaysia to kidnap tourists. I'm making it easy on them. And on you."

Joey the Imam looks up from his hands. "So you're here to ask if I want this person?"

"I'm here to ask if you want to buy this person. *Buy*." Ignacio leans back and nearly tips into the tub. He adjusts his weight and tries to look comfortable.

The Imam says nothing for a long time. Then he stands and opens the washroom door, once again flooding the small space with sunlight. He disappears without a word. He returns some moments later, flanked by the shirtless teenagers who were playing basketball outside the mosque. They've taken their caps off, and their heads and chests glisten with sweat. They look larger in the confined space of the washroom. Not boys, but soldiers. Older, in a way, than Ignacio himself.

"We need to talk about this," the Imam says. "You have proof he's still alive? Proof he's well?"

Ignacio nods, trying to restrain his grin. He doesn't want to over-play his hand. Joey the Imam closes the door and approaches with the teenagers. They all stand around Ignacio. He feels their breath on his skin even before he opens his mouth to speak.

*Chapter 2*

## AFTER THE FUNERAL

Benicio Bridgewater left the main building of Montebello High, crossed the parking lot and sat at one of the carved-up picnic tables. He pulled a paperback history of the Philippines from his bag, found the dog-eared page he'd bent over at the end of lunch and picked up again where he'd left off—Bataan had just fallen to the Japanese. Americans were rounded up while hundreds of their Filipino allies were made to dig their own graves. Japanese soldiers saved bullets by executing their prisoners with ceremonial blades. Cut off from the mainland, soldiers on Corregidor Island prepared to mount a final defense against the Imperial Army. The authors of the history didn't attempt to sustain tension or drama—they made it clear from the beginning that the little island was doomed.

Benicio's father had sent him the book a few months ago. It arrived in an oversized package stuffed with styrofoam peanuts and bubble wrap, covered with bright stamps and postmarked on the same day that Benicio finally agreed to spend the summer with him in Manila. He wasn't sure exactly what route mail took to travel from the Philippines to Charlottesville, but his father's package seemed to have had a rough trip. It arrived looking rained-on and dropped, the book inside warped and brittle. His father's note on the cover page was so smeared it was almost illegible. *Benny*, it said, *I finished this a few weeks ago and couldn't believe I'd lived here so long without knowing some of this stuff. Think you'll enjoy it. I mean the book, and the country. So glad you're coming!* Below that, in a different color of ink, his father had added, *Thanks again for what you said at the funeral. I'm really so sorry Benny. About all of it. I can't wait to see you.*

Reading the history, like talking one-on-one with his father for the first time in almost five years, had been kind of a chore at first. The book started off with dry descriptions of trade and migrations, broken up only occasionally by colorless maps and arrows. But things picked up after the Spanish arrived, and more so when the Japanese did. Now Benicio could hardly put it down. He glanced at his watch, hoping to get to Corregidor's surrender before his girlfriend locked up her classroom and came out to meet him. Alice taught ninth- and tenth-grade English at Montebello High and spent afternoons tutoring captive audiences in detention. The next time he peeked over his book he saw Alice emerging from the front door of the school. She waved to him and he stood and waved back. She glanced around, and when she saw that no one was looking, flipped him the bird. He sent one right back and gave her an ugly face.

"My love," she said as she pecked him on the cheek—as much affection as either of them ever showed on school grounds—and snatched his book from him. "How's the war going?" she asked.

"Not well." He kept his hand on her hip as they walked to her truck. "Not at all. Those poor guys are fucked."

"That's unfortunate." She pulled her keys from her purse and threw them in the air. Benicio caught them.

"We need to make a stop on the way home," he said. "The shop called—my gear's good to go."

"If we must," Alice said, a slight grin marring her put-on pout. She had one of those rare faces that looked much prettier up close than it did from far away, and when she got playful like this he found it down-right irresistible. Closing the truck doors behind them, Benicio leaned into her for a real kiss, longer and deeper than usual.

"I'm going to miss you, too," he said.

"Too? I'm not going to miss anybody."

And there was that grin again. Benicio returned it, gamely. He put the key in the ignition. "Yes, you are. You're going to be lonely, and sad. But don't worry. It'll be a short trip."

"Oh yeah?" Alice shifted in her seat and threw her leg over the hand brake. "How short, would you say? Because I've got affairs and trysts and whatnot to plan."

He put his hand on her knee, caressing it for a moment before mov-ing it aside and lifting the brake. He started the engine, shifted into first and brought them out of the lot. "Stay this shitty, and I might not come back."

"You'll come back," she said. "I'm the best thing you've got going for you."

And no question about it, she was right.

THEY'D MET WHEN BENICIO was in his third year as an undergrad at the University of Virginia, the same school where Alice was finishing up a master's in secondary education. They were little more than casual acquaintances—just familiar enough to exchange smiles and hellos—and only began dating as the result of a drunken hookup, embarrassing only for how utterly typical it was. Benicio had just graduated, and for a while they both seemed happy enough to treat their relationship with the lightness its beginning seemed to warrant. But that changed when he got a job at the same school where Alice worked. It later became a point of contention as to whether he'd found the vacancy announce-ment on his own, or if she'd pointed it out. He'd asked her permission before applying, they both agreed on that, and she'd given it in an offhand, careless way.

And so, for the last year Benicio had worked as a systems administrator for Montebello High. It wasn't even a partial lie when he told friends and family that he enjoyed the job. He was in charge of managing the local network and user accounts, maintaining each of the workstations and doing technical assistance as needed for the faculty and staff. He may not have felt especially passionate about it, but the pay was good and it usually kept him interested. Moreover, it was comprised of tasks that were straightforward and none too challenging, but that seemed impenetrable to everyone else he worked with. He loved the way older teachers and administrators would gawk at the simplest of his daily tasks, the way they'd try to escape a conversation at the mere mention of firewalls, IP switches or routers. He got a kind of pleasure from this, similar to the pleasure he felt when speaking a language that the people around him couldn't. Like on his childhood visits to his mother's old home in Costa Rica, teaching his beaming cousins absurd English phrases that in retrospect weren't nearly as naughty as he'd thought. Or the exclusivity he'd felt as a teenager in their Chicago townhouse, walking through the living room where his father was watching the news, speaking to a friend on the phone in side-slung Spanish that—as far as his father could tell—flowed out effortlessly and without the slightest trace of an accent.

But that had been awhile ago. Benicio hadn't spoken Spanish, nor heard it in the mouth of a real live person, since his mother's funeral in January. He'd been the de-facto translator and guide for the members of her family who'd managed to get visas in time to attend the service. That included communicating with their hotel for them, shepherding the ill-prepared aunts to Macy's so they could buy winter coats and ferrying them from the funeral home to the church. When they all boarded a flight back to San José they took Benicio's Spanish with them. They even took it from his dreams, which were now like silent movies that lacked even a piano soundtrack. Since then Benicio had only uttered a word of Spanish if Alice asked him to. The two of them would be on the couch, Alice flipping channels while Benicio stroked her pale, round knees. She'd linger on Telemundo sometimes and ask him to repeat what the announcer was saying. There were words that she liked the sound of, especially in Benicio's Spanish voice, which she insisted was different from his English voice. Like a whole different person speaking. "Moribundo," he'd say. She'd have him repeat it a few times before trying to sound it out with him. Festividades. Sueño. Pico de gallo. Nieve. Sabado Gigante.

The dive shop on Barracks Road was small and packed with more gear than should have reasonably been able to fit through the door. Each of the walls was lined with multicolored wetsuits hanging from racks above deep bins of gloves, booties, mask and snorkel sets, dive lights and fins. Regulators and buoyancy control vests dangled from big plastic hangers suspended from the ceiling and Benicio had to navigate between pyramids of empty dive tanks and rusty magazine racks just to get to the service desk. Alice began to follow him but became distracted by a big fish identification chart stapled to the only scrap of bare wall space. Benicio watched her as she ran her fingers over the laminated names and fins of moorish idols and triggerfish.

"Pickup or drop off?" the silver-haired man behind the service desk asked.

"Pickup." Benicio handed over a crumpled receipt. "For Bridgewater."

The man scrutinized the paper and disappeared through a door behind the service desk. He emerged a moment later, his arms laden with the tubes, hoses and chrome of Benicio's gear. "The old Oceanic," he said as he laid the gear out on the desk. He wrapped his fingers around one of the regulator's hoses and traced it down to combination depth gauge and dive computer at the end. "Haven't seen this model in years. An oldie but a goodie. Got it used, I'm guessing?"

Benicio shook his head. "I've just owned it for a while."

The man seemed pleased by this. "Good for you. Well, she takes a round six-volt. I had to mail away to a third-party in Singapore just to get it. Came in this morning." The man patted the back of the device with affection and handed it to Benicio for his approval. Benicio felt the almost forgotten heft of it in his hand. He pressed the round black button below the screen and numbers sprang to life. His depth was zero and his pressure was zero. His nitrogen level was safe. "Go often?" the man asked.

"Not really, no." He became aware of the fact that Alice was standing very close behind him and glanced back to see her staring at the jumbled mess that was his gear. "It hasn't been too long, though."

"Well, the battery should last your next trip, probably a few more after that. But if I'm in your shoes, I consider an upgrade. Especially if you're serious about returning to our sport." The man stepped sideways to an ancient-looking cash register. He continued speaking as his two bent index fingers worked ponderously over the numbers. Apparently the direct feed—which ferried air from the tank to the buoyancy control vest—was corroded and needed replacing, as well as his regulator's dust cap and all of its O-rings. The final price came out much higher than the quote he'd gotten over the phone, but Benicio didn't doubt it was fair given the admittedly shabby state of his gear. He paid the man—including a few extra bucks for a bottle of Sea Drops for his mask and a tube of silicone jelly for his rusted dive knife—and collected his gear to leave.

Back outside Alice helped him hoist everything onto the bed of her pickup. "So," she said, her voice a little thin, "it's been how long since you did this?"

"Just about five years," he said. "I took my last trip the summer before I moved down here."

"And, you still know how? You're not getting in over your head?" Alice laughed a bit as she said it.

"Getting in over your head is kind of the point." He took a light hold of her arm, just above her elbow. "There's nothing to worry about."

"Who's worried? I'm just trying to keep my options open. What with the affairs and trysts."

He released her arm and closed the back of the truck. "I'm done playing for today," he said. "It's safe. And we'll take it slow. Dad hates current and he gets seasick on overnight boats, so nothing but easy, shallow dives for us all summer."

"Your father dives also?"

"I didn't mention it?" Benicio knew of course that he hadn't. In the year that they'd been dating he'd mentioned very little to Alice about his father. "Yes, he does. I mean, he used to." He opened the door and got back into the passenger seat. "We used to do it together."

ALICE HAD ONLY MET HIS FATHER ONCE, on the day of his mother's funeral in Chicago. She accompanied Benicio to O'Hare, and while they waited in the torn leather chairs of the arrivals lounge he gave her the bare bones. His father's name was Howard and he was in the hotel business, work that kept him on the road most of the time. It used to be he worked mostly in Costa Rica, but as Benicio grew older his father's interests began to expand to higher-end resorts in Southeast Asia. His firm provided boutique-style management services for locally owned hotel franchises. Howard even owned a few establishments himself— some sushi bar in Bangkok, as well as a little wine lounge in Manila. "Quiet little places," his father called them, on the rare occasions that he brought them up at all.

Howard started spending a lot less time in the States after Benicio graduated high school. He didn't tell Alice that was also the summer they'd stopped talking. Benicio was always cordial—he acted like nothing was wrong when the family was together at home—but he stopped making calls to his father or taking them from him. He stopped sending letters and e-mails, and he returned the ones he received without reading them. Given the amount of time that Howard spent abroad, there was about a seventy-thirty chance that he'd be gone if something tragic ever happened. The higher odds won out, and when Benicio dialed his father's number for the first time in almost five years it was to sob and say that his mother had been crushed between a Dodge and a brick wall on her way back from the hairdresser—a humiliatingly flamboyant, stupid way to die. Howard was so shocked to hear his son's voice that it took him a while to understand the words. But when he did understand he began to sob as well. And that's how it ended. Five years of silence, and then the two of them, on the phone, weeping.

It was a change that persisted after the funeral. Their grievances—

or rather Benicio's grievance, as the silence was largely one-way—were not forgotten, but they began talking again. Before Howard returned to the Philippines they even made a vague promise to see one another in the coming months, though neither suggested when or where. It was a slow correspondence, at first. Howard began sending postcards, and in late February Benicio received a slim package that contained an odd-looking eggshell shirt that went down to his thighs when he tried it on. *Benny*, the note inside said, *I sent one of these a year ago, but I guess you didn't get it.* Guess? Benicio had sent it back. *This is called a barong. It's formalwear here in the Philippines, made from banana fiber. A good one can cost hundreds of dollars. Don't worry though, this isn't a very good one. I've got a few that I have to wear to events sometimes, and in case you're wondering, yes, I do look pretty stupid in them. Thought you might find it interesting.* Benicio hung the barong up with his work shirts and left the closet door open so that he could sit on the end of his bed and look at it. He did find it interesting.

A few days later Benicio got a cell phone call at work. The reception was so bad at first that he almost hung up, but then through the static he recognized his father's voice.

"Ben, can you hear me?"

"Yes," he said. For a while there was nothing but popping and tearing sounds. "Yes," he said again much louder, leaving the hum of servers in his little office and stepping out into the hallway. "Hi Dad. Can you hear me?"

"Yeah." Even through the static Benicio could tell that his father was excited about something. "I'm sorry to call while you're at work. Is this a bad time, Ben?"

"Not really." Benicio wasn't being polite—if it had been a bad time he would have said so.

"Great." The static flared up and his father's next words came through garbled. They sounded like: *guess who I am.*

"What?" Benicio turned down the hallway, pushed open the front doors and walked out into the parking lot where the reception was better.

"Guess where I am," his father repeated.

"I don't know . . . business trip? Home?"

"No." The static died down. "No, I'm on the beach! I'm still in the Philippines and I'm on the beach. Ben, the most amazing thing is happening. There's all this . . . I don't know how to describe it. The moon is out, but it's cloudy and dark, and there's all this stuff out. This plankton. The waves are just washing it up. It's glowing Ben. Bright greenish, in a thick band all along the sand. It's just amazing."

Benicio didn't really know what to say, so he settled for "wow."

"Listen Benny," his father continued, "I've been thinking, for a while, that it might be really nice if you came out here. You know, for a month or so, maybe early summer?" He paused for a long time and left a silence that Benicio didn't fill. "You could stay in the same hotel as me. It's really . . . it's really a beautiful country. I could take you around, or you could do a little exploring on your own, if you prefer. We could do the rice terraces or fly down to the chocolate hills. I mean, if you got here in May we'd beat most of the rain, and could even hit up Boracay Island. Or, there's always plenty to do in Manila."

Benicio watched the enormous shadows of his feet as he took slow steps through the sunny lot. "I'll think about it," he said. The line went silent and he wondered if the connection had dropped.

"Hey," his father finally said, "hey. That's wonderful Benny."

"I just said I would think about it. It's kind of short notice for a big trip."

"I know. I know. But you're welcome here. I'd love to have you. And you know . . . they have some good diving. I mean, some world-famous diving."

"I know that."

"It's been awhile, but I could dust off my old fins. We could do a dive trip or two, just like we used to." His father's voice went rigid and Benicio's back did the same thing.

"Just like old times," he said.

"No." It wasn't just the reception; his father's voice was also cracking. "No, I promise. Nothing like old times."

"That's good," Benicio said.

• • •

HE AND ALICE GOT BACK TO HIS APARTMENT a little before six. They unloaded his gear and laid it out carefully over the bed. He went into the kitchen and started on dinner, while she lingered in the bedroom, ostensibly to change for the gym—by *gym* she meant the elliptical and incomplete set of free weights in the communal basement. But he could hear her futzing around with his gear as he started prep; laying out fish to defrost, rinsing and quartering baby potatoes, setting salted water to boil. And when he turned away from the stove he saw her standing in the kitchen doorway. She wore nothing on top but his buoyancy control vest. The straps covered her breasts but left a line of bare flesh that ran from her collarbones to her abdomen, broken only by the small frayed buckle. She stood there, one hand gripping the doorframe, the other toying with the direct feed hose of the vest.

"Jesus." Benicio dried his hands on his shirt. Though an incomplete surprise, this was pleasant.

"I don't think I'm wearing this right," Alice said. She tried to twist the direct feed so it would reach her mouth. "What part am I supposed to breathe out of?"

"You don't breathe out of anything." He stepped toward her. "There's a whole other piece for breathing."

His telephone erupted into loud, insistent chirping and Alice gave him her cutest, coyest look. He took the phone out of his pocket and set it on the counter beside the sliced potatoes. It rang for what felt like a minute before finally dying down to silence. Benicio moved toward Alice and she took a step back as though she were about to run. He grabbed her before she could and they stumbled back into the bedroom. Alice tried to get out of the buoyancy control vest but the buckle was caught so she just loosened it and opened the straps wide. Together they collapsed atop the hard tubes of his regulator and the rubbery foam of his full-length wetsuit.

"I can't believe it," he said. "I can't believe how much I love you."

"Bite me," Alice said, unbuckling his belt with her left hand. "You're too good for that Hallmark crap."

"No," he said, "I'm not." He pushed aside the coarse fabric of the vest and went right for her nipple, just as he'd been scolded not to, giving it a too-hard pinch between thumb and forefinger. "That's all I've got. That's me being honest."

"It's not funny," she said as she got his pants open and moved her hands inside.

"The worst part is, I mean it. I—"

She kissed him deep, to shut him up. "You're foul," she said. "You're rotten."

THIS WAS A GAME THEY PLAYED OFTEN, and the rules of it were simple—though Benicio wasn't really sure he could describe them. Surprise had a lot to do with it, along with the shock of mock aggression like cold water in the shower. Obscenities were important, as was obvious lying. It was a way of counteracting the creeping suspicion that they were too young to be living this way. It started after graduation, when their friends scattered to jobs, internships and parents' basements, and the two of them were left alone together. Not yet in their mid-twenties and they'd backed into what felt like a domestic, almost middle-aged life. They used the game to balance things. To lighten the feeling of playing house. It was how they reminded each other that they were, maybe, not so serious. They were still young. They had options.

But it was more complicated than that, because at the same time they really *were* getting much more serious—especially since his mother had died. Their relationship took on more passion, and a strange, formal weight. Benicio said "I love you" for the first time a few days after they got back from Chicago. It slipped out, embarrassingly, while they had sex. That drove Alice wild and made their first fuck after the funeral—even more embarrassingly—the best they'd ever had. And it wasn't just a fluke. Sex became consistently more intense and more frequent. So did arguments. Actually, arguments were what they used to have—the occasional sharp-toned conversation that might end with Alice crossing her arms tight over her chest and someone leaving the room. These were knock-down, drag-out screamfests. It was as though

their relationship became a kind of Hollywood sequel of its old self—
built on the same premise as the original, but with a bigger effects budget. They still hadn't gone to Ikea to replace what they'd broken during
their last fight. They'd been eating dinner a week ago, plates squeezed
onto the little coffee table in front of the television. Alice scanned
channels until she landed on a telenovela. She turned the volume up on
high. A mustachioed actor was confiding something serious to a wrinkled crone played by a young woman in heavy latex makeup, and Alice
repeated everything he said, word for belabored word.

"La ot-tra no-che . . . tu-ve unna pesa . . . pesadilya. Cre-yo que Pab-lo
no es mi hi-ho."

"Hijo." He corrected her. "Pesadilla."

"Translation?" She watched him chew for a while. "Translation?" He
kept chewing. "Hello?"

Benicio swallowed. He picked up the remote and changed the channel to something in English.

"Hey," she said, "hey, look at me." He looked at her. "There's no reason to be an asshole," she said. She looked hurt, but he knew she wasn't.
She was at bat, waiting for him, on the mound.

He set down his fork. "How are you not sick of this?" he asked.

"Sick of you?"

"Nice. No. Sick of your own bullshit. You don't want to learn a word
of Spanish. What are you, afraid I'll forget it now? Will that make me
less interesting?"

Alice stood, and on the way up her knee struck her dinner plate and
sent it somersaulting off the coffee table, crashing on the floor. Both
of them looked at the shattered mess. Alice made a move as though
she was going to start collecting the shards of plate and rounding up
stray green beans, but she seemed to decide against it midstream. She
took his plate from him and threw it down on the floor as well. "Fuck
you," she said, lingering on the word, stretching it out—not wasting it
the way they did when they were playing. "Don't project your shit on
me." She went into the bathroom, slammed the door shut and locked it
behind her.

They exchanged obscenities as he cleaned up the mess. When he finally cooled off he sat in front of the bathroom, concentrated on the chipped paint on the door and apologized. Alice didn't say anything back, but after a while she slid her forefinger under the locked door and let it rest on the tile. Benicio reached down to give it a squeeze and the finger squeezed back.

THEY CAUGHT THEIR BREATH atop the tangle of dive gear. She went to the bathroom to clean up and he stayed in bed, shifting this way and that to make himself more comfortable. He began to doze off and was soon in a light sleep, dreaming about Corregidor Island—that little rock that he'd been reading about earlier in the day. It was night on the island, and very hot. Above him stretched the dark silhouettes of palm trees and the barrels of heavy artillery guns. The guns looked old, like they hadn't been used in a lifetime. He found a path leading up a little hill and decided to follow it, picking his way through bramble that thickened into a dense jungle. Then an odd thing happened. It began to snow. Thick, angular snowflakes fell like bits of paper down through the palm fronds. They blanketed his hair, his shoulders and the wooded floor. He was alone, and certain that he would die.

Benicio was awoken by the sound of a telephone and Alice's voice, shouting: "It's yours!" from the bathroom. He took his time getting up and walked into kitchen, where he saw on the cell screen that it was the same number that had called earlier. It went silent just a moment before he opened it. "Who was it?" she asked.

"No one." Benicio said. He snapped the phone shut again and put it back on the counter. "Just my father."

*Chapter 3*

## RAINY SEASON

Monique woke to the sputter and hum of her air conditioner—a tremendous window unit that she and her husband bought last year, just two days after moving to the Philippines. It sounded like a minivan idling in a covered garage, but there was no sleeping without it. She blinked in the darkness and slid her hand toward Joseph's half of the bed. It was cool. He wasn't there. What a lousy way to start the day. For both of them.

Monique propped herself up on her elbows and looked around. The wall facing her was mostly glass, and from the fifteenth story she had an incredible view. Filmy dawn lit the horizon, bleeding into the fluorescent nightglow of the city. Joseph stood there, a lean silhouette among the towers. He wore silk pajama bottoms and pressed one hand against the glass, as though for balance. His other hand massaged his own long neck. Pale light brightened wisps of gray hair about his ears. "Don't tell me." Monique was too sleepy to hide the frustration in her voice.

"Morning." Joseph turned around. His eyes were so bleary she couldn't tell if he was looking right at her or not.

"All night, again?"

"Not quite. I got an hour or so on the couch in the den."

She pulled back the undisturbed blankets on his half and beckoned him over. Joseph climbed in, threw an arm across her chest and pressed his face into her. His insomnia had never been this bad before.

"We should talk to the doctor again." She felt his lashes against her neck. "It can't be good for you. I'll set something up at Seafront today."

He shook his head, which tickled a little. Just two weeks ago he'd given up on his fifth prescription. The embassy doctor insisted it was the last reliable brand you could get locally, and their hopes were high when he rode the first dose almost to dawn. But it didn't last, and by the third night he was pacing again. He got so mad he took the nearly full bottle up to the rooftop helipad and chucked it off. Monique told him it was a stupid thing to do, but she didn't needle him about it. She was angry, too.

"Early shuttle today?" he asked. She nodded, letting him change the subject. Every day the American Embassy sent a light armored van to pick her up and ferry her to the walled-off chancery by the bay. It always arrived at a different time and always took a slightly different route. Monique had this month's schedule pasted over last month's schedule on the inside of her closet. The variation was supposed to make her unpredictable, which was supposed to make her hard to follow, which was supposed to make her safe. But Monique didn't feel unpredictable. Having no routine was sort of a routine in and of itself. Every weekday morning she got up $x$ number of minutes earlier or later than the day before, hid her access badges under her beaded blouse and snuck out the side exit like an unfaithful spouse.

"Hey." Joseph's voice was suddenly animated, and too loud in her ear. Monique pulled back. "Do you know what today is?"

"Wednesday."

"That is true. But this morning is also the twelve-day mark. Just twelve more mornings like this and we will be out of this hot, disgusting, traffic-congested city and on our way back home." Mandatory leave was just around the corner—five whole weeks of vacation back in D.C. He already had the suitcases laid out on the bedroom floor, open and ready for packing. "Just twelve more mornings until the end of soot on the windowsills. No more 'sorry sir, out of stock.' No more spoiled brats treating the kids like pets. No more food that is cooked in vinegar and soy sauce. No more spaghetti with sugar and hotdogs. No more crowds at the mall and on the street and at the movies and in the—"

"So we're doing this every morning, now?"

Joseph sat up and looked old as he closed his bloodshot eyes and pinched the bridge of his nose. "You know you are as eager as I am."

Monique put a hand on his cool, damp back. "There's still a year to go after we get back. It'd be nice to know this isn't torture for you."

He was silent. He worked his back into the heel of her palm and she started rubbing it, bouncing up and down the depressions between his ribs. They both turned their heads when a loud crash erupted from the kitchen—likely a cast iron skillet falling onto the already chipped countertop. Amartina, their maid. Monique felt a chuckle thrum through Joseph's trunk.

He turned back to look at her with a half smile. "I suppose you are going to miss her, then? Her heavy, greasy food? Her banana ketchup?"

Monique quit rubbing. She sat up so they were shoulder to shoulder. "Never having to scrub mildew. The kids' laundry always washed and folded. Coming home to a meal."

"I never begged for those things. If she were not here, I would gladly do them myself. It would help fill up the day. We both know that is something I could use."

They'd had this fight so often that it didn't feel like a fight anymore. Monique got out of bed and stripped off her nightgown. She walked to the master bath, paused in the doorway and spoke without looking back. "So I take it you're not coming into work today?"

"That isn't work."

"The people who do it would argue."

"The people who do it are wrong. Or desperate. Escorting janitors, watching them empty dustbins and water the ambassador's ficus, is not work."

Monique closed the bathroom door on him. He was right—most of the jobs available to trailing spouses weren't real work. But neither was staying at home, sleeping on the sofa, lamenting the lack of nearby universities with Composition and Cultural Rhetoric programs, English instruction, and vacancies. Not much she could do about any of those things, other than take the man on his vacation.

She leaned in close to the mirror and examined her pores, which seemed bigger every month in this weather. The master bath shared thin walls with the den and kitchen, and from where she stood she could hear almost everything. Joseph had turned off the air-conditioning and was back at the window, tapping his fingernails on the glass the way he did when he couldn't sleep. Shawn had the television on and epileptic Japanese cartoons—dubbed into a mix of Tagalog and English—fought their way through the den. Music played from Leila's bedroom computer and Monique guessed that she was online, chatting with old friends back home about new friends that she hadn't yet made in one year of living here. And Amartina was still clattering about in the kitchen, making breakfast. Monique could smell fried Tabasco-Spam and eggs, and her stomach did a slow roll. She hauled herself into the shower. The pressure was strong, and the water was very hot.

SHE'D EXPECTED HER FAMILY to resist—even hate—the idea of moving to the Philippines, but they surprised her. She sounded Joseph out first, one evening while they were up late watching coverage of the invasion of Baghdad. He didn't say anything for a while, his face lit green by night-vision scenes. He muted the television and turned to her.

"What kind of commitment would we be talking about?"

"A two-year tour is the standard minimum. We could do more. If we wanted."

He nodded. "Why didn't you tell me you had passed?"

She took a breath. Her Foreign Service exam results had sat in her office inbox for weeks. "I'm sorry. I wanted to be sure how I felt about it. But now they're scheduling me for orals, and I don't want to attend if it's not something we're interested in." She paused and watched him. Explosions brightened the walls. "I've looked into it, and it shouldn't take too long to transfer from Civil to Foreign. I've already done the paperwork for the higher clearance I'll need. We could be in Manila by the fall."

"I thought that you didn't get to choose your post."

She paused. "I don't. I'll have to do a whole bid list. But with my Tagalog, Manila is likely. Also the admin councilor knows me from when I was at RM, and she's ready to request me. They have a junior slot opening up at American Citizen Services."

Joseph nodded some more. He turned the television off and Monique lost sight of his face. It was already going better than expected, and for that she credited her timing. Joe was having a rough year. He'd been turned down for a tenure track spot at Georgetown after almost a month of interviews, and American University halved his teaching load for the spring semester. On top of that was the incident at the faculty Christmas party. The department chair, who'd had a few too many cocktails, jabbed a pen in Joseph's mouth like a tongue-depressor and diagnosed him with Adjunctivitus. Joe said something ugly about the clumsy art that the chair's teenage son had pasted all over the kitchen door. Monique believed him when he said he didn't know the kid was retarded—a word Joseph scolded her for even using—but no one else seemed to.

"You must really miss it there." His voice was disembodied in the dark room.

"I do, sometimes," she said. And it was true, what she remembered of the Philippines she missed intensely.

The kiss on her left cheek surprised her. "Congratulations. Whether we go or not, you should be very proud of yourself." He kissed her again on the corner of the mouth, and again on her bottom lip. He lay on his side and didn't say another word. Monique's eyes adjusted to the dark and she watched him fall asleep. He always used to fall asleep first.

The next morning Joseph acted as though the decision were already made. Toothbrush poised before his mouth, he extolled the virtues of relocating to Manila. It was the perfect time to move the kids. With Shawn in sixth grade and Leila in eighth, they would both have to change schools next year anyway. And moreover it was responsible parenting. Asia was an emerging player—his exact words—and personal experience in that part of the world would be invaluable for a young person. It would broaden their perspectives like it had broadened Monique's. He gesticulated, flecking the mirror with foamy blue paste.

Later that week she brought home the Manila Post Report and laid it out on the kitchen table. Glossy and laminated, it had pictures of the skyline, maps highlighting beaches and dive resorts and lists of restaurants and outlet stores available near embassy apartments. The children leafed through the book excitedly. They paused at a picture of the old U.S. naval base at Subic Bay. It was taken from the air on a clear day, Mount Pinatubo shimmering in the distance.

"Hey Mom," Shawn asked, "isn't this where you're from?"

"Not really," she said. "It's where I was born."

MONIQUE DRIED AND DRESSED ALONE. Looking good in her navy herringbone skirt suit was not overly important to her, but she was glad she did. She went light on the makeup, just some lipstick and a dusting of powder to keep from shining when she went outside and started sweating. No meetings scheduled for today so she slipped on a comfy pair of flats with gel insoles and walked out into the den. The television was still on, screaming at empty couches. The door to Shawn's room was open, which meant he definitely wasn't in there. He'd left his lights and air conditioner on, and from where Monique stood she could see slithering movement in his bedside aquarium. His spotted gecko pressed itself against the glass looking emaciated and intensely unsympathetic. It was one of two replacement pets, bought shortly after the family cat arrived dead in her carrier. It had been upsetting for everybody. Leila chose an African lovebird.

Monique turned off the television and went into the kitchen. Her whole family was there, sitting around a square table and eating meat and eggs on piles of thick, crusty pancakes. Amartina was at the sink washing the skillet and pretending not to eavesdrop. Monique said good morning to the room at large and sat down between her children. Leila responded with a vague greeting directed mostly at her breakfast and Shawn said nothing at all. The kids looked so much alike, and nothing like their parents. They were brown, which in racial shorthand could be called black, while Monique and Joseph were more Irish sunburned pink. This confused new acquaintances. Their reaction was always the same, rippling under their faces like brail. Did she say son? Oh. Oh. *Adoption.* Good for them.

"Good morning, Shawn." Monique looked right at him and he looked right at the wall. He hadn't spoken a word to her since she forbade his going to the prom. Not hello, or good night, or can I please have so-and-so. The worst part was that she'd said yes at first—she'd assumed it was the local counterpart of one of Leila's middle-school dances back home. Awkward and harmless, as long as the chaperones stayed on their toes. But a few days later Shawn came home with a rock in his ear. It was a gift from his date, the seventeen-year-old who was going to take him to the *senior* prom. Monique took away the earring and her permission faster than it took to slam a door, and by dinnertime she'd gotten hold of the girl's home number and had an angry conversation with her father. Shawn said she was intentionally trying to humiliate him and she laughed. That made things worse. The hole in Shawn's earlobe still hadn't healed. It had been joined by a fuzzy top lip and tightly braided cornrows that Joseph wouldn't dare say he hated. Wouldn't dare, on account of the fact that Shawn and Leila were, as far as their parents could tell, the darkest children in their new, private school. And Joseph suspected an eagerness on the part of all those rich kids to engage in racial caricature. Such a matter, he insisted, had to be broached delicately. If at all.

"Good morning, Shawn." Still nothing. "You left everything on in your room. It's wasting electricity. And that lizard of yours looks like it needs to be fed."

Joseph swallowed hastily so he wouldn't have to talk with his mouth full. "And don't forget, son, that you still need to find someone to look after it when we go back home."

"I'm not going."

"You're going," they said in near unison. Joseph leaned over his breakfast. The fluorescent kitchen light brought out the red in his eyes and the loose way his translucent skin seemed to hang. "You are going."

"Nope."

Monique sipped her coffee and held the mug up, pretending to look at it. "Lights. Air conditioner. Crickets for the lizard. Now." She put the mug down hard and some coffee sloshed onto the plastic tabletop. Shawn nodded almost immediately. Then he poured himself more juice. He did this as though it had all been one motion and the nod was happenstance. He drank his juice slowly, got up and walked out to the den.

Joseph and Leila continued eating in silence. Monique took a bite of pancake and wished she hadn't. They were thick and slightly hard, another attempt at what Amartina clearly thought was an American breakfast. Dinners were the same story. Over-salted pork medallions and grease-dripping fried chicken, usually served alongside mashed baking potatoes. Monique would have been happy enough with tapsilog for breakfast, and a sour soup or pancit at night, but her family vetoed Filipino food. She made up for it by taking lunch breaks at the embassy gym, but a year of this cooking was starting to show on the kids, especially Leila. It wasn't that she'd gotten fat, but she still insisted on buying outfits for the year-ago version of herself. Monique walked in on her more than once taking apart some piece of clothing with a pair of art scissors. "That wasn't free," she said when she caught Leila destroying the elastic waist of a miniskirt. "You could just as well be cutting up the shopping money we give you." Leila responded coolly that the skirt cost less than a dollar at Landmark, and that her mother could "bill her." Monique played this conversation over and over in her mind. Sometimes she imagined slapping Leila, hard. But the Leila in her mind always slapped back, and things got terrible after that.

Out in the den the telephone rang. Shawn yelled that he would get it and appeared in the kitchen a moment later looking put out. He placed the cordless on the table and left again, tossing "It's for Monique" over his shoulder.

She picked up the phone. The voice on the other end was familiar. "Are you as horny as I am right now?" he asked. "Or are you hornier?"

"Sure thing, Chuck. I've got it in my bag." She stood and walked calmly through the den and into her bedroom.

"Chuck? That's hot. Let's incorporate that. Are you dressed for work yet?"

"No." Monique closed the bedroom door. "Just socks."

"You are very good to me."

"I've got to go."

"I need to see you before you leave. How does a king-size at the Dusit sound?"

"Can't. Nowhere in Makati, the kids spend half their time there.

Besides, you had your chance. I was at that goddamned bar for two hours last night."

"I'm still in Davao. A friend of mine had an accident."

"I'm sorry."

"He'll be all right. I won't be if I don't see you."

"I'll try."

"Hard?"

"Don't call on this line anymore. Next time I'll just hang up."

"That's what you said last time."

Monique hung up. He always, always did this. Flowers delivered to the apartment with ambiguous notes. Singing telegrams, which apparently still existed in the Philippines. E-mails to her state.gov address with *From Your Lover* in the subject line. Joseph was none the wiser, thank God, but Monique thought that deep down he might be fostering a kind of proto-suspicion. Not in his heart of hearts, more in his ego of egos. As though he was righteously primed—ready to be the injured party. And in this case, he would be. Monique, for her part, threatened to break it off if her lover didn't quit with the risky games. He called her bluff.

She washed her face, reapplied her makeup and collected her things. With briefcase in hand she left the bedroom. Leila was on the couch in the den, doing homework that should have been finished already. Shawn's door was closed and from behind it Monique heard his humming air conditioner and the horrible chirping sound his gecko made at mealtimes. Joseph dozed in the kitchen while Amartina cleared the table. Monique shook him awake. "I'm heading out. Are you sure you don't want to come to work? There's a construction crew in the annex and Jeff needs all the escorts he can get. You probably have time if you get dressed right now."

"I told you. That's not work."

She was running out of things to say to this. "It might keep you up. Give you a better chance of sleeping tonight."

"I can keep myself up. I'll pack."

"All right." She kissed him on the mouth.

"Just twelve more mornings."

"I know."

MONIQUE BYPASSED THE LOBBY and descended a concrete ramp
to the loading dock. The boxy beige minivan was late, which would
have been early yesterday. She put her weight into opening the heavy
armored door, said good morning to everybody and climbed aboard.
Jeff, the regional security officer, rode shotgun. He turned in his seat
and glared at her, jabbing a thumb at his chest. Monique looked down
and saw that her badge was dangling there for everybody to see. She
pinched open her blouse and dropped the badge inside. Jeff grinned
and gave her a thumbs-up. "No Joe today?"

"Nope." Instead of giving the tired *errands* excuse, or the more
legitimate *packing* excuse, she just let the word hang.

Traffic was worse than usual. McKinley Road, EDSA and Roxas Boulevard were all stop-and-go. She stared out the window as they passed
boarded-up nightclubs, girly bars and the tall, sooty looking Department of Foreign Affairs. The bay was calm beyond the concrete promenade. The fishing boats looked almost beautiful as they trembled in
early light. She could see the embassy up ahead—a big patch of green,
conspicuous among pastel high-rises. When they got closer she made
out high walls and an armored jeep with a roof-mounted machine-gun
trained on the street. Beyond the walls was a stretch of wet grass, weeping yellow trees and a flagpole still pockmarked with Imperial Japanese
bullets. The main building, the chancery, was long and white like a plantation house. Everything else on Roxas Boulevard looked out, toward
the sea, but the embassy faced inland, as though arriving from it.

The shuttle pulled up to the high walls and was surrounded by
private guards. One gazed into the windows to check faces. Two more
looked under the hood while a fourth circled them with a mirror on
wheels, looking for bombs in the undercarriage and rims. More guards,
as well as Filipino soldiers, stood behind the high electronic gates. The
chancery itself had bulletproof glass, blast doors and a small detach-
ment of U.S. Marines. It all made Monique uneasy.

"So," Jeff's booming voice startled her. "I assume you heard about Chuckie?" Chuck—her boss at American Citizen Services. And no, she hadn't heard. "Ain't that a bitch, after going through all the trouble to get an easy post like this?"

"Sorry?"

"Temporary duty yonder—they're sending the poor boy to Kabul for the whole summer. Only gave him a week to get ready!" This information meant more than it seemed to. "I mean, my question is, why do you need someone from ACS in Afghanistan? The local YMCA needs a consultant?" Jeff grinned. He either didn't notice or ignored her expression, and kept talking. The shuttle drove through the final gate and then up to the chancery steps. Monique looked out at the bay again. She knew at that moment, without being told, that her vacation was off. She'd be in Manila through May, and straight through to the rainy season.

*Chapter 4*

## THE BOXER BOYS

Efrem Khalid Bakkar is asleep. He's in his bunk, in a big tent, north of Davao City. It's where he's supposed to be. Skinny Vincent, his bunkmate, isn't there. He's had the shits ever since the division left Basilan, and they boil up worst between midnight and dawn. The sickness leaves Skinny hollow, and grumpy, but Efrem doesn't mind. He enjoys the extra privacy, and though Skinny is his friend, they aren't that close. Efrem isn't that close with anybody.

So he's asleep, and happy, getting the bunk all to himself. But then someone shouts. More than one someone. Not yet dawn and goddamn Manileño officers are hollering. They move through camp in hollow moonlight, sounding tougher than they are. "Step it up you dreamy

faggots! Brig Yapha's back from Manila, and he wants to see the boys of
Boxer Division grown into men by breakfast-time!"

The officers must mean Brig Yapha's breakfast and not theirs.
Efrem's unit wanders into the predawn wearing pajamas of various colors. They find the mess trailer dark, stoves cold, cooks asleep on tabletop bedrolls. Returning to the big tent they dress, grumbling among
crisscrossing flashlight beams. Efrem's boots are overlarge so he stuffs
rolled socks into the toes and tripleknots them. Before he's done Skinny
Vincent stumbles in, stinking awful, shouting big news. "It's not just
Brig Yapha!" he yells, breathless. "They have *the man* coming to see us—
they have Charlie Fuentes!"

Soldiers look up from what they're doing to stare gape-mouthed
at Skinny. Charlie Fuentes? Hero of the Ocampo Justice films? Biggest action star in the republic? "Yeah, right," someone grumbles, "quit
dreaming." And the tent gets noisy as men suggest different ways for
Skinny to fuck himself.

"No dream," Skinny insists, "and no lie. Honest to God!" He shakes a
little, and goes pale. He's either excited, or still very sick.

"How do you know?" Efrem asks, not looking up from his bootlaces.

"I heard it. Overheard it, firsthand," Skinny says. "I'm up at the
officer's latrine and first lieutenant's flexing in the stall right next to
me. Second lieutenant runs up and says he's got a radio call from Brig
Yapha. First lieutenant says bring the radio here because I can't quit
now and won't be done soon. Second lieutanant does but it won't
fit under the stall door, so he just high-ups the volume. They shout
all about it. Brig Yapha says we have guests coming for inspection.
A bunch of reporters, and Charlie-fucking-Fuentes! He says it twice—
loud."

The tent quiets down. They all come from different islands but not
a one of them has ever missed an Ocampo Justice film. Charlie Fuentes stars as Reynato Ocampo, the hardest cop in the country, maybe in
the whole damn world. The one and only Mr. Tough Knocks, the Dirty
Harry of the Wild Wild East, old Snaggletooth himself. They've all been
to movie houses to watch him stick up for the unstuckup for, fixing the

nation one dead criminal at a time. They've all seen him press Truth, his famous shitspilling pistol, into the foreheads of men who deserve it.

The silence stretches until it breaks into excited crosstalk, soldiers peppering Skinny with questions. Tell us what you heard again, not so fast this time. He's coming to inspection? Fuentes? The Ocampo Fuentes? Himself? This morning?

Efrem keeps his eyes on his laces, but they won't tie right. His fingers are shaking. He was nine when he saw his first Ocampo movie— first movie he ever saw. Back when his adoptive mother was still alive, back before he'd picked a side in the war, back before he'd switched sides. He'd been a little boy seated in the back near the projectionist. And Reynato Ocampo was the biggest man in the theater, so big they had to wheel the projector forward to squeeze him onto the screen, so bright they twice replaced the buzzing bulb that lit the film.

AN HOUR LATER the Boxer Boys stand stock still on a marching green south of camp. It's not a proper marching green. The Armed Forces of the Philippines have leased the land from a Davao-based sugar concern and it slopes irregularly to the east. Tenant farmers tend rice some kilometers down the way, paying the soldiers no mind. A lone carabao munches reeds in a fallow paddy. A boy walks the mounds between, followed by an underfed but energetic puppy. Beyond them all is a tree line of unclaimed, cowering jungle.

Efrem's in the front row, with soldiers spanning the green behind him and to either side. Hundreds of dirt-eaters, killer grunts, pride of the AFP. He looks sharper than usual this morning. Back straight, eyes forward, custom Tingin rifle shouldered. Beretta oiled and holstered snug. Dented helmet high. Boots tight as he can get them. The inspection's late, but when it comes he'll look his best.

Time passes. The sun wallows in low clouds over treetops. It's mid-April, still very much the dry season, but tell that to this drizzle starting up. Somewhere down the line a soldier sits and the officers give him twenty kilometers of marching with a pack full of ruined cinder blocks. They promise the same for the whole division if another knee grazes ground. The drizzle thickens to rain. Most of the soldiers prefer rainwater to sweat so they leave their plastic ponchos in their packs. They whisper freely under the patter. Skinny Vincent's story ricochets down the line. *Charlie Fuentes is coming.* The rumor makes it to the far end of the division and comes back an hour later as a rumor that the president's been overthrown. Some of the men who have family in Manila start to get upset. Officers calm them down by radioing Metro Command. The president is fine. She's breakfasting with Chinese businesspeople.

Another hour and the officers allow everybody to sit. Discouraged, they stretch their glutes and kick grass. Two soldiers in the back row loudly discuss what they'll do to Skinny Vincent if Charlie's a no-show. They settle on tying him to something with something and pissing on him. Gravely, they chug canteens.

"Not my fault," Skinny grumbles. "I just told you what I heard." He looks around for sympathy and gets none.

But Skinny has nothing to worry about. The jeeps are coming. As always, Efrem sees them before anyone else can. Three jeeps thread their way along a wooded road. He glimpses metal and rubber through distant rain-whipped foliage. The drivers wear humorless expressions. Brig. Gen. Antonio Yapha sits in the lead jeep, combing runny yolk out of his mustache. On Yapha's left is a short man in a modest workshirt, his chin patchy with salt-and-pepper stubble, gleaming orthodontic braces fencing in his ragged teeth. On Yapha's right is someone completely different—a tall man in a formal banana-fiber barong, smooth cheeks flush with health, hair slicked back into a wave like petrol on the ocean. Efrem nearly drops his custom Tingin rifle. Charlie Fuentes looks *exactly* like he does in the Ocampo movies.

The other soldiers know about Efrem's magic eyes, and when they see him staring—dilated pupils eclipsing his irises—they get excited. The officers make everybody stand and brush their trousers clean. Within a few minutes they all hear the puddle-splash and rumble of engines. The rain thins. Three jeeps emerge from the distant tree line and pass alongside the tenant farmers in their paddies. The boy with the puppy recognizes Charlie, and waves, and Charlie waves right back. The rain stops. The sun comes out like it's on a schedule. Skinny puffs up his chest and leers at the soldiers in the back row who are standing funny now because they really have to piss. The convoy breaks in front of the assembled division but the drivers keep their engines running. The second jeep back is filled with news people and they begin to dismount, fiddling with cameras and notebooks and battery-operated microphones. In the last jeep are men from the American-trained Light Reaction Battalion wearing ghillie suits of burlap and twigs that make them look like fuzzy, dirty animals. They jump out and secure the convoy by circling it and lying flat on their bellies, making themselves virtually indistinguishable from the mud and grass. This delights the newspeople, who stoop to take photographs.

But the men in the lead jeep take their time. Brig Yapha, looking fatter than before he left, hands a fresh cigar to Charlie and, oddly, to the short man as well. Charlie lights his with a wooden match and offers up the flame, but the short man declines and pockets his cigar. They dismount and approach the division. Yapha walks out ahead, puffing smokily, while the other two lag behind. They're an odd pair, but they look something like friends. Shorty's workshirt is only half tucked, and a tattered baseball cap shades his eyes. His hands are tiny, like a child's hands, and he's got a duckfooted walk, tennis shoes pointing opposite directions like they each want to go a different way. Efrem figures he's Charlie's bodyguard, given the pistol grip sprouting out the waistband of his jeans. Then he checks to see if his hero is also packing, hoping for a glance of Truth—that pistol so famous it gets second billing at the movies—but no such luck.

Heat follows the rain and wet soldiers steam like embers. They titter as Charlie approaches. The officers nearly forget to salute Brig Yapha as he rushes past, and he returns their gesture just as distractedly, with his cigar hand. Charlie reaches the far end of the line and begins the inspection, looking like Efrem's uncle when he'd shop for engine parts in the Davao port market. A much more glamorous version of Efrem's uncle. He moves among the men with generous grace, adjusting collars, tugging too-long hair and giving easy words to thrilled and terrified grunts. Efrem cranes his neck to watch. Then somebody hisses his name and his head snaps back. It's the brigadier general, moving up on him nose-to-nose, speaking, very strangely, in a whisper.

"Bakkar. I need your rounds, now."

"Sir?"

"Your rifle. Unload it."

Efrem hesitates only briefly before doing what he's told.

"The round in the chamber as well," Brig Yapha says, not looking him in the face. "And your spare magazine."

Efrem hands it all over without a word. Yapha stashes the ammunition in his deep vest pockets. "Now, you do whatever he tells you," he says, taking Efrem by the elbow. "But not a damn word."

And with that he leads Efrem down the line, right in the direction of Charlie Fuentes, Tough Knocks, Snaggletooth, the hero of his childhood.

THE FIRST TIME Efrem ever saw an Ocampo movie was the first time he left his tiny island home. They had no cinema, of course—no electricity, no roads. The only running water was a sulfur-tasting spring that bubbled below dry cliffs inland. But Efrem had an uncle, and his uncle had a boat. The *Hadji Himatayon* was big enough to sleep three adults, four if they were skinny, and whenever his uncle and cousins got the outboard working they'd disappear down south to Tubigan, around the far shores of Jolo, and due east along the southern coast of Mindanao. Stopping at every island along the way, they did unofficial mail rounds and traded what they could. At Davao City they'd unload pearls, deepwater fish and clamshells big enough to bathe children in. They'd buy plastic in the port market, scrap metal, tinned food, cane syrup and underpriced imported rice. Then it was home again, starving themselves to have some of it left when they got there.

When Efrem turned nine his arthritic mother gave him permission to go along. He still remembers how his older cousins, wise about the city, brought him to that outdoor movie house. The slick feeling of dropping two long-saved pesos into the palm of the shirtless usher. The wooden benches were full, so he sat cross-legged in the grassy aisle. His cousins explained what a double feature was. They pinned him when the projector sputtered up, alive, and his instinct said *run*. A man made of light stood before the crowd like a giant. It was Reynato Ocampo, played by a younger Charlie Fuentes, tall and dashing and mean as a motherfucker. For three hours he defended women on the screen and children in the audience from kidnapping kingpins. Efrem shielded his face from splinters as Old Snaggletooth kicked down a brothel door, Truth in hand, and gut-shot the fattest pimp so that his belly exploded into the hair of screaming topless go-go girls. He clapped and cheered at the finale when Reynato tied the kidnapper's head to rail tracks, extracting a confession just before a freight-and-passenger came roaring through his ear. Tough cop for a tough world.

As the brief credits rolled, as the crowd lingered in the bloody afterglow, the usher made his way up to the stage and reminded everybody to come back next month for the premiere of *Ocampo Justice XIII*: Reynato travels back in time to castrate Jap invaders!

"HELLO," CHARLIE SAYS, cracking a warm smile. "So, you're the one I've heard about?"

Efrem is unable to speak. But that's fine—he's not supposed to.

"This is him," Brig Yapha says. "He's our boy."

"Good to meet you, son," Charlie says. He offers his hand to shake. Efrem finds it surprisingly soft, and moist, melting pleasantly between his fingers. He tries to say "Hi" but it comes out as just a sigh. There's an empty canteen in his chest. His heart slows intolerably. His knees actually bounce together.

"Don't sweat it," the short, homely man says. "Charlie gets that look all the time. From ladies."

Everybody laughs at this and Efrem flushes at being so quickly embarrassed in front of his hero, but he doesn't dare snap back. The jokester, for his part, seems to realize he's riled. He stares at Efrem intensely, as though trying to read foreign words tattooed across his face.

"Well, let's go ahead and get this over with," Charlie says, turning to the idling caravan of jeeps.

Brig Yapha, still gripping Efrem's elbow, leads the way. They cross the stretch of empty grass and pass the officers without a word. A murmur goes up as the Boxer Boys notice Efrem among the important men, and it makes his bones tickle. "You're doing fine," Yapha whispers. "This won't take long." When they reach the caravan he sets Efrem loose, rummages through the lead jeep and produces an electric bullhorn. He throws his arm around Charlie's shoulders and turns to face the division. The few reporters jostle for space, framing their shots so as to include both speakers and crowd.

Yapha greets the assembled soldiers several times before realizing that he has to hold the switch down, but once he does, his "Good morning Boxer Boys!" echoes across the green. "I'll keep this short, especially because I know it's not me you're excited to hear from." He pauses to wink, though Efrem can't tell if it's at the cameras or at Charlie. "As you know, I spent the last week in Manila, educating the high-ups at Malacañang as to the excellent work you boys are doing. And the president herself wants you to know how very thankful she is for your bravery against the Moro insurgency. Fighting double fronts with the Abu Sayyaf and renegades from the MILF is no easy task, but your good work is essential to the health of our nation. In this light, her office deeply regrets to continue extended deployments for all—" here Brig Yapha is drowned out by boos and hissing from the crowd, and he makes no attempt to speak over them. The reporters turn their cameras and microphones on the Boxer Boys. The soldiers seem to notice this and, in a moment of spontaneous savvy, they play up their own displeasure. When the brigadier general continues, it's with a smile and a touch of mechanical levity. "But on to better news. You see, of course, that we have a very special guest with us here today. I'm honored to introduce Charlie Fuentes, though I suppose you all know him better for his role as the one and only *Reynato Ocampo*!"

Cheers shake the assembled division.

"Save it. Save it." He waves them down, good-naturedly. "Hey, now. Hey. Come on." Finally he just quits and hands the bullhorn off to

Charlie, who steps forward to redoubled cheering. Charlie shakes his head, grinning, like: What? All this? For me? Then, as the ruckus fades he does a sad double take, like: That's it? Done already? And the crowd goes wild again; laughing at themselves and at Charlie, delighted to participate so intimately in his joke.

Then, by degrees, they quiet down.

"Well, well, well, well, well," Charlie says, chuckling and easy. "I tell you . . . if our dear president could see how mean you boys look then there'd be none of this stupidity about extra months in the jungle."

He pauses briefly for some appreciative hollers. The short man, standing beside Efrem, gives a disgusted little snort. "That's a tough one," he whispers to Brig Yapha, who smiles and shrugs, just slightly.

"But for real," Charlie goes on, "no joke. One man to many. I want to say thanks. You know . . . one of the best things about deciding to run for the Senate, I mean, maybe *the only* good thing, has been that I get to travel all through these islands, meeting real men like you. Men who put everything on the line for the good of the country. And I tell you what, not everybody up in Manila takes you for granted. And I'm hoping that, come May 10, even fewer of them will."

Charlie goes on to say that he's come on the advice of his good friend, the brigadier general, to see the best that the AFP has to offer. He understands that the Boxer Boys are second to none in this fight, and he's asked one of them up here today to show these Manileño reporters what real soldiering looks like. "I think most of you probably know him. Your very own killer—*Efrem Khalid Bakkar.*" He pronounces the name so poorly that Efrem takes a minute to process it. When he does, he feels woozy with nerves.

Charlie stows the bullhorn and everybody turns to face Efrem. "Look at him," the short man says. "If he weren't such a darkie, he'd be white as a ghost."

"So," Charlie says, ignoring his companion. "Tell us a little something about your wonder boy, General."

Brig Yapha claps a hand on Efrem's shoulder, cheating him out toward the cameras. "Bakkar here is our undisputed best," he says.

"A graduate of the Scout Ranger School, he's a tactical sniper with the highest number of confirmed kills in Boxer Division history. And, while I haven't crosschecked this with AFP records, I wouldn't be surprised if he has the highest tally of anyone, in any branch of our armed forces, ever."

Charlie lets out a long, appreciative whistle, and the short man's creepily intense stare grows more creepy, and more intense. Efrem feels like he really needs to sit down.

"And what's he going to show us?" Charlie asks.

"Well," Yapha says, "as he's a sniper, it's probably best if he gives us a little shooting demonstration. We have some targets up, and I think you'll all enjoy watching him pick them off."

His hand tightens on Efrem's shoulder and together they turn to look into the far clearing. Sure enough, sometime during the brief speech one of the LRB soldiers had quit his chameleonic guard and set targets along the green at increasing distances, from 800 meters to about 1,800. More than just the traditionally crude wooden silhouettes, these targets are pasted over with the likenesses of regional and international terrorists—Kumander Robot, Abu Bakar Bashir, and old Osama himself.

"No point keeping us in suspense," Yapha says, taking a step back. Charlie and the reporters step back as well. The short man stays where he is.

Everybody waits. Efrem looks at the distant targets. He fingers the safety catch on his empty Tingin rifle. He levels the empty rifle at the targets, and then lowers it again. What on earth do they want from him? Finally, Yapha comes to the rescue.

"What's the matter, soldier?"

"I can't," Efrem says, his voice cracking like it's old. Or very new.

"The hell you can't," Yapha says. "I've seen you hit harder than that, plenty. No need to be shy, son."

"I'm not . . ." he waits. "I can't. I can't because my rifle's empty."

Some of the reporters gasp a little, and Charlie looks down at the ground like he's really sad. Efrem feels like he could die.

"Jesus," Yapha says, turning to Charlie. "I'm sorry about this, I should have—"

"Fuck no," Charlie says. "This isn't your fault, Tony. You were *just* up there. It's not your job to beg for their help." He turns, speaking now to the reporters. "Forgive the language, but it's shit like this that drives me crazy. I hate being reminded so often why I, *an actor*, have to run for office when our country's in the state it's in. To come down here, and see arguably our best soldier standing around with an empty weapon, utterly helpless . . . it just makes me so angry I can hardly put words together. It seems that under this administration, the only soldiers who get any kind of support are the Americans. While our own troops are underprepared and underequipped. I mean, do you see the state of his gear?" Without looking at Efrem, he points back at him. At his dented helmet. At his oversized hand-me-down boots. He goes on a little while longer, but Efrem can hardly hear it for the blood filling his ears. He has never been so humiliated in his life.

But he keeps quiet, like Yapha told him, and the ridicule doesn't last much longer. Charlie Fuentes finishes up with the reporters and then shakes hands all around. Some of them return to their jeep while others head down toward the division to get some stock footage. Charlie and Yapha start to wander off as well, when the short man pipes up.

"These games are fine and good," he says. "But *I'd* like to see what he can do."

THE EXPRESSION ON CHARLIE'S FACE IS STARTLING. He seems almost afraid of this small, insignificant person. "Now's not really the best—"

"Fuck that," the short man interrupts, plucking Efrem's magazine right out of Yapha's vest pocket. "You got your little scene. And I already wasted a whole day on this. You owe me."

He crosses to Efrem, snatches the custom Tingin out of his hands and drives the loaded magazine into the assembly. "So," he says. "Khalid Bakkar? Does that name mean that you're as Moro as you look?"

"I'm sorry, sir?" Ashamed as he is, it's all he can do to look this ugly little man in the face.

"Where do you come from?"

"Western Mindanao. A little isla—"

"Of course you do. You're a regular Mohammed."

Efrem's back tightens.

"And what kind of rounds does your service weapon fire?"

"Fifty-caliber BMGs, sir."

"Fifty cal? Shit, with a fifty cal, even I could hit those targets." He gestures vaguely at the plywood and paper terrorists dotting the field.

"If you say so, sir." Efrem speaks through clenched teeth.

"Easy, son." Yapha says.

"No worries." The short man grins. "I'm fine with lip, long as it backs itself up." He looks down at Efrem's Tingin, running his fingers from stock to barrel. "No scope?"

"The field issue comes with one. I shoot better without it."

The short man moves up on him, so close that the bill of his cap grazes Efrem's forehead. "Well shit, Mohammed, now it just sounds like you're bragging."

"It's better if you don't call me that, sir." Efrem says.

That's too much for Brig Yapha, who puts himself between them. "Button up," he hisses, glancing back at the reporters. "You have any idea that's *the* Reynato Ocampo you're talking to?"

Efrem blinks. He looks from Yapha, to Charlie, to the short man. Are they having another joke on him? The short man laughs and rubs a hand against his stubbly chin, making a sound like sand underfoot.

"What," he says, "you think they straight-up invented that shit? Mohammed . . . don't tell me. I mean, movie people get paid to lie, but could some Manila hack have dreamed *me* up?" He steps back so he and Charlie are side by side. "I give you this, they found an actor who looked plenty like the real thing, but you really think this pretty boy earned the street name Snaggletooth?" The short man—*Reynato*—bares his twisted metallic smile. Beside him, Charlie grins, sheepishly, perfectly.

For a moment Efrem feels disoriented. To him—to *most* of the Boxer Boys—Charlie Fuentes and the supercop Reynato Ocampo were always the same person. And to see them now, standing side by side, gives him a feeling like seasickness. But the moment passes, and just like that Efrem's lifelong esteem for Charlie Fuentes withers. Charlie is nothing to him. Charlie is worse than nothing. Charlie is a pretender— just one among a long line of false prophets. Nothing but a soft-ass Manileño who more than likely kisses boys. Reynato is the real thing.

"I'm sorry. I didn't know."

"I forgive you, Mohammed," Reynato says. "Now let's just forget those silly targets—that's baby games. If you're anywhere as special as you look, you should be able to hit something a little more challenging." He gazes out at the clearing. Brig Yapha has a pair of field glasses strapped to his belt, and Reynato snatches them, saying "thanks darling" as he does so. He scans the rice paddies by the tree line where the tenant farmers are still working and the water buffalo is still munching reeds and the underfed puppy is still running about madly. "You see that carabao?" he says.

Efrem can see sweat beading the animal's nose. He can count the flies perched on its horns and distinguish individual sun-bleached hairs on its flanks. "Yes," he says.

"How far away would you say that carabao is?"

"Twenty-seven, twenty-eight hundred meters."

"Ahh, I'll find something else."

"I can hit that, sir," Efrem says. "No problem."

Still staring through the glasses, Reynato smiles. "Well now, Mohammed, I'm not up on my caliber stats, but I think the maximum effective range for the BMG is just about two thousand."

"I can do it," Efrem says.

"Please . . ." Charlie stares at both of them, distressed. His cigar is almost burned down, and he hasn't puffed it in a long while. "Could you at least wait until the crew splits? I mean, we just made such a big deal about how the kid had no bullets."

"You mean *you* did." Reynato lowers the glasses. "I'll wait five. After that, I need to see some shooting."

Charlie must know Reynato is for real, because he doesn't waste any time. He rushes back down to the assembled soldiers and henpecks the camerapeople into joining the other reporters in the jeep. The vehicle isn't halfway down the green before Reynato gives Efrem the order to fire. He hits the animal mid-rump, and it lurches forward like a wasp-stung child, thrashing through the mud. Then, with a sigh and a faint shudder, it sits down.

"What about a moving target?" Reynato asks, not missing a beat. "Can you hit a runner at that distance?"

Efrem shifts his weight. He doesn't want to appear cocky, but he also doesn't want to lie. "At any distance," he says.

Reynato glances at Charlie and Brig Yapha. "Christ. I got the chills. I love a showoff. So . . ." turning back to Efrem, "I guess that dog would be no problem?"

Efrem sights his Tingin. The boy and his puppy have left the paddies and are running along the jungle's edge, almost four kilometers away by now. For anyone else it's a nightmare shot—the dog sprinting full tilt, stopping short, now a jump, now a double-back—but for Efrem it's an easy one. He could have hit this at twelve, maybe thirteen. The trick is to ignore the dog. Don't even look at her. Instead, find that perfect nest of air—the place where she isn't yet but will be. She helps it all along by running, rushing to the time and place. Efrem sights a hollow between the calling child's arms. One count, two counts, and he shoots. The puppy runs. She leaps, as though catching a ball. The round strikes her mid-trunk, and she all but evaporates, misting the boy and the trees around the boy. It seems to be some moments before he realizes what's happened.

"That's impossible," Brig Yapha says, taking the field glasses back from Reynato and gazing down at the distant, bloodsoaked child. Charlie looks as well, though not for long.

"It's cold, and it's twisted," Reynato says. "But clearly, it's been done, so it isn't impossible." He takes the cigar out of his pocket, plants it between his teeth but does not light it. "You don't even know, do you, Tony? What you've got on your hands here isn't just skill. This boy's a *bruho.*"

Everybody is silent. Finally Charlie says: "You mean . . . like the others you got? One of them?"

"No doubt," Reynato says. "Talent just oozes out of him. Caught my eye all the way from the jeep. It's kind of sad, when you think about it. You've been sitting on this resource for years, Tony."

"He never told me he could do that," Brig Yapha says, still not back to breathing normal.

"No surprise," Renato says. "In my experience, few bruhos go around advertising." He turns back to Efrem and the proud smile on his face enters the running for the highest point in the young soldier's life. "So, Mohammed, are you exaggerating when you say *any distance*, all icy like that?"

Efrem shakes his head.

"Well then, humor us just one more time. I got word last night that the barangay sentinels in Davao City picked up a suspect in the Silivan rape case. Any chance you could hit him?"

"If you know his name," Efrem says. "And where he is."

Reynato hesitates, only briefly, and then leans in close, lips brushing Efrem's ear. He tells him the rapist's name and gives him directions to a jailhouse on the outskirts of the city, the way you'd give a friend directions to a restaurant you like. "So, Mohammed, just how magical are you?"

The men on Efrem's island agreed that he'd been sent by God—sent for a reason. The Holy Man, someone who knew a lot about God, said it first. Efrem would take the world apart, so they could build it better. The gift was nothing to be afraid of. The angel of death was still an angel.

Efrem's eyes widen as he raises his Tingin rifle over the puppy's distant corpse, over the dripping trees, taking a straight aim at the sun. His pupils dilate. Out past iris, past white, they spill like oil to the rim of his open lids. Through shimmering black eyes he sees holes in the clouds, birds weaving through them, seeds of a storm still two days off. He sees sunlight bending over endless banana and palm. He rides the bend like a swell of seawater. Shirtless men move like ants through fruit plantations. An old woman does laundry outside while a young one wrings a hen's neck. Policemen direct traffic at the outskirts of the city, their orange batons pointing the way. The roof of the jailhouse is missing tiles. The windows all face west. A big man sticks his bruised face against the bars. He smokes a cigarette and looks out at a pair of barn swallows flitting to and from a mud nest in the eaves above his cell. For a moment he and Efrem almost make eye contact.

Efrem squeezes off a single round. He watches the bullet as it speeds up and over the trees, down onto the plantation roads, between the legs of traffic police. Reynato reaches into his pocket and takes out a bright pink telephone. He flips it open, dials and speaks impatiently with the answerer. "I don't care how recently. Check him again. Right now, and take the phone with you. Doing what? Who gave him cigarettes?" Reynato holds the phone to his chest. "The prisoner is fine. He's smoking at the window."

"Give it a minute," Efrem says.

Reynato gives it two. He puts the phone on loudspeaker and holds it out for everyone to hear. There's a whole lot of nothing, and then finally a faint whine, followed by wet coughing, followed by one person screaming, followed by two people screaming, followed by between four and six people screaming. Frightened obscenities and orders to take cover. The guard informs them that the jailhouse is under attack. Someone's shot the prisoner's face off. The guard has found a place to hide under a desk. Could they please send help very, very quickly? Reynato hangs up on him. He bends over at the middle and braces his little hands on his knees. It seems that even he wasn't expecting this.

"You can do that whenever you want?"

"Every time I've tried," Efrem says. "Sometimes I have trouble finding the right person, but with a name and a place it's easy."

"Shit. Shit." Reynato looks sick, and giddy. "You should . . . you need to come with us. We need to talk." He straightens up shakily and takes Efrem's arm. "Tony, is it cool if your boy tags along for the afternoon?"

"Hey, whatever . . . it's your call, Renny." Yapha sounds woozy, like he just woke.

Reynato pulls Efrem to the lead jeep and stows him in the back like luggage. Brig Yapha and Charlie Fuentes follow. From the backseat, Reynato salutes the troops. "Wave goodbye," he says. "If you ever see those boys again, it won't be soon."

Efrem glances back at them. Skinny looks utterly confused, but he's got his arm up in a wave, his opposite hand supporting his elbow to keep it airborne. They hadn't been close. Efrem keeps his arms at his sides. The driver releases the emergency brake. The engine shouts, and they're rolling. Down the marching green, past the tenant farmers and their wounded carabao, out into the trees still wet with dog's blood, away from the Boxer Boys.

*Chapter 5*

## THREE STRAYS

Howard leaves the club an hour after it closes, and when he gets out to the lot all the waiting taxicabs have left. That's all right. It's a fine, unusually quiet night, and he'd like to walk some of this drunk off anyway. He crosses Roxas to the promenade and heads south, hardly stumbling. The bay crumbles gently on the seawall to his right. It isn't long before he hears a sound in the darkness; something like a cough behind him. He hears it again—a sick sound, followed by footsteps and heavy breathing. He turns and sees three stray dogs, slouched and stinking. They've been skulking around the club for a month now. He's complained to the owner, but has she done anything? No, she has not.

"Get!" Howard says, but the dogs don't get. One of them approaches with a floppy, careless step. It looks at him and lets out another cough that skids into a faint, trembling growl. With some difficulty, Howard gets down on one knee and pantomimes picking up a stone. His chauffeur at the hotel taught him how to do this—our strays know what it means to have rocks thrown at them, he explained. The strays pace and whine, but they don't scatter. Howard holds up his cupped, empty fist. He makes a throwing motion and the dogs flinch, but regroup. They glare, awash in bluish moonlight. "Go home!" he says. The words ring lame in the empty night.

The closest dog, its patchy hair yellow as hay, takes another step. Howard drops the fake stone act and starts searching for a real one. Hesitant to take his eyes off the dog, he quickly scans the chipped, honeycombed promenade. Nothing but paper and gum. He reaches into his pocket and pulls out his ratty old wallet, swollen with receipts. He chucks it at the dog, striking it on the nose. The animal yelps in surprise and all three scamper darkly back across Roxas, making an off-duty taxi brake hard. Howard chuckles, bracing his hands on the sidewalk as he recovers his wallet and tries to stand back up. It takes some time. He's a large man.

Howard keeps walking. The promenade is silent and empty, as it never is in the daytime, and that puts him in a sentimental state of mind. He thinks about the busy day that brought him here. Meetings from midmorning until evening and food at every meeting. At breakfast he discussed slab marble with lesbians from Bangkok. Then to the Mandarin for good sushi and a bad argument. Dinner in the car on the way to the airport to pick up some prospective investors fresh in from Sydney and full of energy. He got them drunk on Red Horse and took them to the club, where they had a fabulous half hour before vomiting and retreating to private rooms upstairs—lightweights all.

Howard looks up as he walks, feeling disconnected from his feet falling invisibly below him in that pleasant, drunk way. The smog is low tonight, and the moon is full and weird looking. He stops and rubs his eyes. Is it just his drying contact lenses? He looks again and sees that, no, it isn't—the moon has a ring around it. An unbroken halo of hazy light, about two thumb-to-forefinger lengths from the center as measured by his outstretched arm. The far ends of the ring are marked by a faint pair of flares, looking like lesser siblings to the nearly full moon. Howard knows what they are. He's always had a memory for scientific miscellany—especially something as beautiful as this. They're called moondogs, caused by ice or some such in the upper atmosphere, and God, aren't they something? The sight delights him. He wants to tell somebody about it. He wants to tell his son, Benny, about it. He's so, so glad that they're speaking again.

Howard opens his phone and scrolls through work contacts—a country in parentheses beside each name—to Benny's number. He pauses before pressing call to check his watch and do the math. Early Saturday morning here, late Friday afternoon afternoon in Virginia. Classes should be out at the school where Benny works. This thought makes Howard happy enough to notice his happiness and be doubly pleased.

The phone rings for some time, and the connection is lousy. He thinks he hears Benny pick up, but realizes after saying hello that it's just voicemail. He wonders if he needs to leave a message; something to justify the unexpected call. But no. They're talking again. They're now people who call each other. He doesn't have to justify anything.

Howard's knees begin to hurt under the strain of walking. He hasn't always been overweight, and the fat sits poorly on him. More apple than pear-shaped—his abdomen and gut bulge while his neck and legs are still a trim impersonation of good health. He used to tell his wife that he'd rather be big all over than look made-from-pieces like this. She said it was proof he wasn't meant to be a fatty. He'd lost friend-ships over less, but coming from her, even over a chilly phone line, it sounded light and forgiving. He's tried to call her, once or twice, since her funeral. Or at least come home late and caught himself calculating the time in Chicago to see if it would be okay to call. The lapses always please him. It's nice to imagine that she's only far away.

HIS HEAD A LITTLE CLEARER NOW, he decides to go only as far as Gil Puyat and then flag the next empty taxi that passes. He reaches the end of the promenade—the bay beyond this point reclaimed by artificial land with artificial buildings on it—and crosses Roxas again. About halfway across the wide boulevard he realizes that the three stray dogs have been matching his pace on the opposite side, and he turns back. The dogs come upon an upturned trashcan and circle it like a kill, nip-ping at one another's hindquarters. From the pried-open lid and strewn debris, Howard can tell that squatters have already been through it. There won't be any food. The strays realize this after some searching and then just stare dumbly at the can. They bark at it, and at each other. Their bodies tighten and expand—each animal pulsing.

He has no desire to get near them when they're worked up, and decides to wait for a taxi on this side. He sits on the crumbling curb. It's a whole process—lowering himself down. A stoplight above the dogs flashes red at irregular intervals. Power lines spanning the intersection buzz in the wet, sooty air. A jeepney—one of the stretch passenger jeeps decked out with flags and streamers and shining like pounded foil—speeds by with the crack of fuel cut with kerosene. It slows, but Howard waves it on. He sees a white taxi and tries to flag it but the driver ignores him, swerving slightly before making a hard left at the intersection. Howard waits.

The sound of his phone ringing makes him jump and he shifts his weight to get at his belt loop. He's disappointed to see that it's just Hon. "Hallo Howie!" Hon yells. "Getting off the horn with Jack, you got a sec for me?"

"It's late," Howard says, not liking the way his voice carries over the empty promenade. "Can this wait?"

"Yup," Hon says, sounding very cheerful. "But you're not asleep. I got a couple questions for you in your e-mail. You get them?"

"No." Howard speaks in a near whisper. "Haven't had a chance to read them, yet."

"Oh Howie . . . am I a cock blocker? Listen, just take a sec, there's plenty of you to go around. I got them all listed out for you, just put something together and send to me so I can have Jack stop calling. Don't CC him, though. He's a schmuck. I haven't been able to shit in peace since he got my digits!"

"It'll have to wait. I'm not at the hotel."

"Howard Bridgewater, you are a very wild man, and I admire you."

Another white taxi rolls past. It looks like it could even be the same one. Howard flags it and it slows but doesn't stop. He says "motherfucker" and then he says "not you" to Hon. "Fucking taxis in this city."

"Taxis? Where's your boy?"

"Sent him home. It's late."

"You do know it's his J-O-B, *job*, don't you?"

"Yeah, yeah." Howard looks down Roxas, toward Gil Puyat and sees the white taxi stopped at the curb some hundred yards down. After idling a few seconds it reverses toward him, slowly. He pushes himself up and waves at it. "Hey, I've got to go. I should be back at the hotel in twenty or thirty."

"Don't rush on my account, baby."

Howard hangs up. The taxi inches backward, reverse lights red as embers. It takes awhile and he begins walking to meet it halfway. He jumps right in so the driver won't have a chance to turn him down on account of the destination being too far, or off his route, or some other bullshit. The cab smells of orange peels and the seats are coated in plastic. "Makati Avenue, corner of Ayala," Howard announces.

They sit idle, the driver eyeing him in the rearview mirror. He's thin and has bags under his eyes. There's a small green Mary statuette on the dashboard, as well as a cluster of bright feathers from a parrot or something. The driver looks from Howard, to the street, to Howard again. An empty bus passes, the shirtless conductor leaning out a window like a silent banshee. Howard puts his fingers under the door handle. "Makati Ave, you know the way?" he asks in a polite voice.

The driver smiles, revealing a mouth full of nubby gray teeth. He switches the meter on with a skinny finger and bright red numbers spring up on the dash.

"Meter plus fifty, boss?"

"Meter plus a hundred if you get me home soon," Howard says. The bargaining puts him at ease.

"Very nice," the driver says. "Very nice of you." He smiles again and eases onto the accelerator. The taxi continues in reverse, back to the intersection with the dogs, and then turns left hard. The animals are startled and chase after, nipping at the air behind the tires. Howard watches them out the back window—watches the bay lights fall away and then disappear as they make another turn. This doesn't feel like the most direct way, but what the hell. Obscure shortcuts are a point of pride with these taxi drivers. And if he's trying to run up the meter— who cares? Howard can afford it.

Hon calls back a few blocks later, and they speak as the car weaves through side streets. Richard in London wants figures on materials and labor for the restaurant, and Hon can't talk him out of sending his own cocksucker architect down. "You back home yet?" he asks. "I need the kind of nasty message that only Howie can write."

"I'm not back yet, but I can see Makati up ahead," Howard says, lying just a bit. Makati is actually to his right, receding. This driver is pushing his luck.

"Are you all the way out in Ermita again?" Hon asks. "I told you not to take the Aussies to that place. It's not classy."

"The Aussies didn't mind," Howard says.

"Well shit. What am I supposed to say to Richard?"

Howard tells Hon to open up his e-mail. He dictates a nasty message.

"Fuck me. That's filthy," Hon says, delighted. "*Send!*"

"Can I go now?"

The taxi hits a speed bump too fast and Howard lurches forward and drops his phone. It lands on the floor mat, illuminating the bottom of the cab. Reaching down, he sees that the floor is blanketed with green feathers—the same feathers that decorate the dash. When he puts the phone back to his ear he finds that Hon has hung up.

"Easy buddy," Howard says to the driver, forcing a smile. "You'll get what's on the meter plus a hundred no problem. No need to rush so much."

The driver sniffs. He rubs his face with his wrist. They come to a red light and stop beside a little white cathedral in stucco Gothic style—*Iglesia Ni Kristo* written in grand yellow letters above the door. The light turns green, but the taxi does not move. The driver looks down each street, as though making up his mind, and then turns. Makati is ahead of them now, the skyline blurred by smog. He must have decided to stop jerking Howard around.

The road widens and it begins to drizzle. A cloth billboard advertising skin whitener whips and drips like a sail. The taxi driver tailgates a brightly decorated jeepney—the only other vehicle on the road. Even through the rain Howard can clearly read *Ethel, Gemini* and *Bless Our*

*Trip* hand-painted on the rear mudflaps. Then, just as they emerge from under a series of overpasses, just as Howard recognizes the pink obelisk of his hotel not two miles away, the driver turns onto a quiet residential side street.

"Enough," Howard says, his patience at its end. "Makati Ave is back that way. You want your hundred, or not?"

The driver ignores him. The rain thickens and the taxi slows. It shudders to a sudden halt beneath a broken streetlight. The driver stares at the wheel. He stomps on the clutch and shifts jerkily through each gear.

"You hear me?"

"Something's wrong," the driver says.

"Yeah? What?"

The driver gives a kind of shrug. "Broken," he says. He scratches his cheeks and upper lip. He looks out the windows. The rain sounds like stones on the dented taxi roof. The street is quiet and dark, little townhouses on each side sealed up like ship hulls against the ocean.

"It's not broken," Howard says, unable to believe he has to go through this bullshit again. He's been robbed twice this year already—three times if you count pickpockets. "Let's get this over with," he says. "How much do you want?"

The driver smiles sheepishly and says: "Wait. I fix it." Without another word he jumps out and hurries across the street. He pounds hard on a closed door, yelling something in Tagalog, getting soaked by the rain.

Howard looks out the back for signs of life, but everything is empty. He calls the police and tells them he's getting robbed. No, he hasn't been hurt. He doesn't think he will be. Where is he? In a taxi. Somewhere north of Makati—he can see the Shangri-La from here. The license plate? Hold on, he'll check.

Howard puts a foot out of the taxi, keeping an eye on the driver as he does so. The banged-upon door suddenly opens and light pours out from inside, illuminating a corridor of raindrops. A large, rectangular face juts out into the rain. The two men speak and look back at the taxi. The large man disappears and emerges seconds later with a length of PVC pipe in his hand. Nausea hits Howard hard. This is not a petty-theft situation. The depth to which he's misjudged it opens below him like a hole in the asphalt. He has just enough time to slip his foot back inside and lock all four doors before the driver and his enormous friend reach the cab. They try each of the handles, tugging hard and cursing. Howard realizes that the driver, in his haste, has left the keys in the ignition. He reaches and stretches, but it's no use. He's too big to slide up to the wheel; he'll never fit between the seats.

"They're going to kill me," Howard says to the dispatcher. "They're going to kill me."

"You'll have to stop shouting," the dispatcher says. "I can't understand you."

But it's not Howard that's shouting. It's the men outside the taxi. Saying: "Open the door or we open you!"

"I'm sorry sir," the dispatcher says, "will you please stay on the line, please?"

Howard does not stay on the line. He hangs up and begins scrolling through numbers again. Why are there so fucking many of them? Why save the numbers for *three* florists? Why not just pick his favorite florist—would that be so hard? Outside the big man kicks Howard's door and the taxi bobbles on its shocks. It gets hard for Howard to see because his contacts are hurting him and because he's crying a lot. His big, stupid fingers have trouble finding the buttons.

The large man kicks the cab again, and then whips the rear passenger window with the length of PVC pipe. Howard puts his free hand on his ear to block out the sound of cracking glass. Through his tears he finds Benny's number and calls again. It rings once, twice, how many times before he hears his son's recorded voice? "Sorry! I'm away right now. I'll do my best to hit you back!" The window shatters before the beep. Chips of glass and raindrops rush onto his lap. A big hand reaches in, opens the door from the inside and grabs the phone from him. The men pull Howard out into the street. He tries to land on his elbows so he won't cut his palms up on the glass. They whip the pipe along his back, and legs. He pushes himself up and the pipe catches his cheek, breaking skin and knocking the molars loose. "You don't need to," he tries to shout, his hands in the air to demonstrate how he's not fighting. "You don't need to." They hit his hands and the air around his hands. They hit him in the ribs and on his knees. They stop for moment and talk to each other—or rather the big one gets talked at by the little one. Howard closes his eyes and opens them. He feels rain, and glass, and everything falling.

*Chapter 6*

## THE INTERNATIONAL DATE LINE

There was something that Benicio had never told Alice about his mother. He'd shared it with no one, not even with Howard back when the two of them still spoke—not just regularly, but with warmth and eagerness. His mother was off. She thought she could see the future in her dreams. She believed it the same way that she believed that communion wine became the blood of Christ before passing through her lips, which is to say, with every ounce of her conviction. Benicio couldn't remember when she'd first told him about what she called her *gift*, but it must have been when he was very young because for the longest time he'd believed it, too. Maybe that was why he'd never told the story to Alice—or to his father, which was conceivable now that the two were speaking again, however tentatively—because there was no way of telling it without including the fact that until his middle teens he'd believed something so foolish. Something that belonged to comic books or the summer movies based on them. He'd believed in superpowers.

His mother insisted that her dreams weren't just symbolic premonitions open to interpretation—Benicio had since come to find that Catholics, and Latinas chief among them, were especially skilled at this kind of kitchen-table fortune-telling—but visions of real people in real places doing things that would come to pass days, months and even years after the night they first marched into her sleeping head. He remembered a sunless afternoon, his mother tearing plastic wrap and translucent skin from a store-bought chicken, telling him with a rapt expression the story of how she met Howard in a dream before meeting him in San José. "It was three years," she said. "Three years before I ever saw him, and I knew exactly what he would look like. I wasn't even properly sleeping. It happened during a nap." She dropped a handful of skin into the wastebasket and began to cut the bird in half with a knife from the drawer Benicio wasn't allowed to open, working the heels of her palms over the back of the blade, throwing her shoulders into the job. They were just back from Christmas with his aunts, and as usual she returned from Costa Rica firmly resolved to cook more often and to experiment less while doing so. Benicio, who had been watching from the doorway, pulled up a stool and put his elbows on the cool marble slab of their kitchen island.

"Mom," he said, trying to use his most reasonable and grown-up voice. "We're back home now. Can you please speak in English?"

His mother let out a grunt as the blade finally struck the plastic cutting board, the chicken halves jumping a bit as they separated. "You're making a joke?" she asked. "You're trying to be funny?" She aimed the knife, handle first, in his direction. "After the last two weeks you think you need *less* practice than you already get? Today, all day, English is worse than Chinese. I don't speak it."

His mother returned to the chicken, first snapping the thighs between her knuckles and then using a fillet knife to cut away the flesh and tendons holding them limply to the body. "I was napping," she continued after a time, "on the bus. It was a hot bus, a long trip into San José. Your abuela had bought me a lace blouse for my interview and I sat hunched over it, trying to keep it from wrinkling, making sure no dirt or cigarette ash could stain the collar. And I just fell asleep."

She dropped the chicken pieces, still bigger and with more bones than Benicio liked, into a deep saucepan and washed her hands with water so hot that it steamed. "Your father was alone, in a nice new suit." She dried her hands and smiled, briefly. "A gray one. He'd had a spill, and knocked over a tray of drinks at a restaurant. He was blushing awfully." She placed the cutting board in the sink and faced him, the shiny slab of marble between them. "It was a short, plain dream. The bus stopped and I woke up. But I knew it. I knew he was the one I was going to marry. I knew a lot of things. I knew about you before you were *here*," she placed a finger on her belly, "or even *here*," she placed another on her forehead. I knew that you'd come earlier than the doctors said, but that you'd be healthy. I knew you'd be a rubio at first, but that every year you'd look more and more like us. I even know . . ." she paused, looking sly and a bit playful, "what your daughters are going to look like."

Benicio wrinkled his nose. She'd teased him about this before. "No te creo."

"You do too," she said, shifting her weight in a way that seemed girlish. "You'll have two of them. The first won't be born until you start to turn gray here," she reached across the island and stroked the hair over his right ear, "and here," she ran her finger just above his cold-chapped upper lip. "Que te pasa, mi hijo?" she asked after a long pause. "Why would you wait so long? I would have loved to know my grandchildren."

It wasn't until after Benicio graduated high school that he accepted how full of crap his mother was. How could she possibly be able to see the future when she couldn't even see what was going on right in front of her—couldn't see, for example, that she was being humiliated by a cheating husband. And if she really could see the future, then why would she have stepped out into that crosswalk just as the girl behind the wheel of the oncoming sedan was about to have a convulsive seizure. Obviously she hadn't seen herself in dreams the way the paramedics had seen her, pinned between a bumper and a brick wall. Or the way Benicio had seen her when he was called in to identify the body, lying on a metal table with half of her face and all of her body draped in blue blankets that he was instructed not to move for his own sake. If she could see the future she would have scheduled the salon before grocery shopping and not after. She would have crossed a block up from where she did, or a block down, or five blocks down. She would have gotten a divorce and moved to another city, maybe even back to San José. He would have visited her twice a year and he would have begrudged her nothing.

BENICIO'S DREAMS, like his mother's, were the most typical sort of nonsense. Like the one about snow falling among palms and vines on Corregidor Island that he had for a second time as he dozed in a hard chair with torn and taped-over upholstery in the Osaka airport and that he forced out of his mind as soon as he awoke. His chair faced a big picture window that overlooked crisscrossing runways, and warm light poured through it from a sun that was still refusing to set after twenty long hours. Someone a few seats over from Benicio greeted him with an accented "good evening." He turned to see that it was an old man, slim and bald, draped in orange robes. A monk. Benicio ran a sleeve across his chin and returned the greeting. He checked his watch and saw that only ten minutes had passed since he'd decided to nap. Osaka was the last of his three layovers on the way to the Philippines, and though it was the shortest it certainly didn't feel that way.

His history of the Philippines lay open on his lap, but even though he was just a few chapters away from finishing—he'd left the Second World War behind and was now deep into the Marcos dictatorship— he was too exhausted to read. He shoved it into his bag and got up to stretch his stiff legs. He began a slow lap around the terminal. Even though the roaming charges were sure to be outrageous, he dialed Alice on his cell phone. She wasn't home, so he left her a message, keeping track of how many times he said: "I love you." He limited it to two.

She hadn't stayed over the night before he left. This by itself wasn't all that unusual, she tended to spend at least one night a week at her place, but still it caught him off guard. The evening seemed to go as well as any other, which is to say that they play fought just hard enough to keep themselves entertained without graduating to real fighting. Alice copied the details of his itinerary into a yellow steno pad and helped him pack, filling his suitcase with neatly folded clothes still warm from the dryer. Benicio tried his best to appear somber as they did this, but the truth was that he'd become more excited about his trip to the Philippines than he'd expected, or cared to admit to. It started on the afternoon they picked up his dive gear and had gained momentum since. Squeezing his regulator, fins and BCD into his mesh duffel bag brought back that comforting and almost forgotten smell of neoprene and salt, a stink that would stick to his skin and hair for days after returning from a dive trip with his father. They used to go out twice a year, once during summer holidays and again over Christmas, always returning to the same Costa Rican resort on the Gulf of Papagayo. For a long time Benicio had only allowed himself to remember what had happened on their last trip—the sight of his father naked, hunched over, bare brown feet sprouting out from between his thighs, their soles to the ceiling—but now, as he tried his best to roll up his wetsuit, fonder memories snuck past. Like the flutter that danced through his chest as he sat on the edge of the dive boat, mask on and mouthpiece in as he awaited the final OK sign from the dive master before rolling backward, fins over head, into the cold water. Or the sinking, nauseous satisfaction he would take in slow-motion underwater acrobatics, spinning upside-down with a single scissor kick, coasting low over the reef like a cargo plane over high trees. Since making his reservations he'd been reluctant to think of this trip as a vacation and wary about raising his expectations too high, but despite his best efforts both were starting to happen.

Alice cooked up a big pot of soup once they were done packing, putting in all the things that she said would spoil while he was away. They ate in the living room in front of a muted television. She was quiet, and he figured he'd better say something. "I'm going to be really careful. And I'll be back before you know it."

Alice nodded. "It's not like you're going to Iraq," she said. "Take it easy. Have fun. And try not to be a jerk." This stung him, and she noticed. "What I mean is, go easy on him. I don't know a lot about it, but I know your dad wants this trip to go well."

"So do I," he said.

"That's good. Because it's important for you. It's important to have some family in your life."

Benicio wondered for a moment if she was fishing for him to say something like: *You're all I need*. But then, thinking about it, he decided she wasn't. That's not at all what she wanted to hear. "It will go well," he said. "He and I both want it to."

When they were done Alice gave him an open kiss on the mouth, the kind that usually means there's more to come, and got up to find her keys. He walked her out to her pickup. He said the word *love* with gameless honesty and she said "me, too."

Benicio spent the rest of that evening pouring leftover soup down his garbage disposal and waterlogging his houseplants. He called his father's cell phone and then his hotel room phone but couldn't get through on either and didn't bother leaving messages. It was the second time he'd tried and failed to make contact since missing those two calls last week, but rather than worrying him, it was actually a relief. After all, the arrangements were set—he had tickets, a tourist visa, plenty of cash, hotel reservations in a room next to his father's—and beyond that there really wasn't anything to talk about. All that remained was to go.

AFRAID OF MISSING HIS CONNECTION, he decided to stay up and get some coffee. At the far end of the terminal he found one of those ubiquitous airport café-bars. There was a menu in English plastered to the wall, along with prices in yen. He stared at it for a while, trying to make the clumsy conversions.

"If you want it, just go ahead and buy it, but if I were you I wouldn't do the math." The man seated at the bar spoke in a brittle smoker's voice. Benicio recognized him as a fellow passenger on the flight over from LAX. "Knowing that my Budweiser cost eight bucks means I ain't enjoying it half as much as I could be." Benicio smiled vaguely, ordered a coffee and joined him at the bar, leaving an empty stool between them. For a while they sipped in silence.

"So what brings you to Japan?" the man asked.

"Nothing does," Benicio said, "I'm on my way to Manila."

"The Philippines? No shit. Me, too. We must be waiting for the same connection. The name's Doug." He offered his hand and Benicio shook it. Doug finished his beer and ordered another from the woman behind the counter. He scrutinized the silver can draped in red calligraphy with a kind of suspicion before opening it. "So what brings you to the warmer world, then?"

"My father lives there."

"That's not bad," Doug said. "Not a bad place for a grown man to live in." He squinted awkwardly—maybe he was trying to wink? Either way, it was creepy. "I've got family there, too. I've got a wife there."

Benicio nodded, looking into his coffee.

"Yep. She's staying in this little place called Tay-Gay-Tay, or something like that. Looks real nice . . . hang on, I got a picture right here." He reached into his shirt pocket and pulled out a folded postcard that he slid down the bar to Benicio. It was a familiar picture; he had almost the exact same shot on the front cover of his paperback history. The ridges of an enormous crater were visible around the edges of the postcard. They were high, and stony-green, with dense little bushels of fog collecting along them like droplets of water on the rim of a glass. Inside the massive crater was a lake, marked here and there by the irregular grid lines of fish nurseries. In the middle of the lake another crater sprouted up, smaller but steeper, and inside that was still another lake. The craters and lakes made up a series of rings, like a giant, irregular bull's-eye on the surface of the earth. The sun burned orange under clouds on the horizon, and as he examined the postcard Benicio wondered if it was rising or setting.

"Ain't that something?" Doug said. "Living right on a volcano. Living on the edge."

"It's beautiful." He returned the postcard. Doug folded it up again, careful not to make any new crease lines, and put it back into his pocket. They both stared out into the terminal. Drowsy families wandered, towing bags and children, parting for stewardesses in smart pastel uniforms who walked succinctly in stilettos. The Buddhist monk had moved to a nearby lounge and sat before a bubbling fish tank that he watched like a television. A Japanese voice erupted over the loud-speaker, announcing an arrival, a departure, or a delay. Outside the sun finally skidded on the horizon. Doug must have noticed Benicio staring.

"We ain't gonna catch it," he said, pointing out the window. "We've been racing after it all day, chasing it over the whole country, over the whole damned Pacific Ocean to the other side of the world." He tapped the bar with his finger to indicate which side of the world he meant. "But it's no use. Watch it now, getting away, while we pit stop here. It'll be night before we know it, and the moon'll be out, and you know what? We ain't gonna catch that either."

Doug got up from his stool and moved over to the empty one that Benicio had left between them. Benicio took a burning gulp of coffee, eager to finish. "Say, do you feel like you're missing something?" For an awful moment it seemed Doug would begin speaking about God. "Because you are," he said. "You've lost a day. A whole day, gone just like that." He snapped his fingers. "Like you jumped into the future and skipped yesterday. And I bet you didn't even notice. Don't worry, though, you'll get it back. If you go home."

"The date line."

His participation pleased Doug, who laughed a little too loudly. "Sorry," he said. "So little sleep has got me goofy. And I took these things, on account of I'm afraid to fly." He paused to rub his chin. "You ever been there before? The Philippines, I mean. Not the date line. Because, of course you've been there. We were there together, just a few hours ago, you and I."

"No. I've never been to the Philippines."

"Me neither. I'm excited."

"Oh, I thought you said that your wife . . ." he thought better of it and stopped there. Doug didn't turn away or look embarrassed. He patted Benicio on the shoulder and left his hand there.

"I know what you're thinking," he said. "Mail order, right? Well it ain't that way at all. We've been talking, more than six months now on the Internet and the telephone. I'm headed out there to pick her up, maybe stay a while myself. She says this Tay-Gay-Tay is a real outdoorsy kind of place; sounds right up my alley. Says her father is a councilman, whatever that means. I figure I'll stay there for a while, maybe a few months, and then we can come back to civilization. Now, I know what you must be thinking. I've seen that mail order shit all over the Internet, too. You can't hardly type in *Philippines* without that stuff coming up. But this is totally different. I guess you could call it carryout." Doug laughed. It sounded deep and clogged, like wool over an amplifier.

"I don't think that's funny," Benicio said.

"Well . . . hell, kid—"

"I'm not a kid." Benicio straightened up on his stool. This tipsy creep was like a worse version of his father. Talking back to him felt good.

"You're a kid to me." Doug leaned in, smelling of beer and whatever the seafood option had been on the way over. "You should learn to take jokes as they're given."

"Really? You're going to lecture me, Doug?"

Doug blinked, and got off his stool. The bartender stared at them. "Arguing in airports is a bad idea," he said. "Everybody's touchy." He put more money down on the bar, even though he'd already paid, and left. Moments later a woman announced their boarding in halting English. Benicio grabbed his bag and rushed to follow.

AFTER HIS MOTHER had been taken away in a refrigerated van, he'd returned to the hospital to meet the person who'd killed her. It was a girl, just nineteen years old and a freshman at the University of Chicago. She'd come out of the accident with nothing more than a few scratches but shortly after being admitted she was diagnosed with viral meningitis. That's what had caused the seizure, which caused her to lose control of her car, which caused Benicio's mother to be plucked from the crosswalk and crushed against the red brick of a flower shop. The girl was inconsolable. She received treatment in a dark, quiet room that she filled up with sobbing as soon as Benicio entered and introduced himself. He visited twice—once two days after the accident and once again with Alice on his way to pick up his father from O'Hare. He wasn't able to get a word in either time. The doctors believed—and Benicio let them—that he was visiting to assure the girl that she was forgiven. That whatever the police might decide about suspended licenses, about liability, he didn't blame her for what had happened. But really he just wanted to ask a question. He wanted to know if his mother had looked. If she had seen it coming.

"I don't know," the girl insisted two months later. "My head was below the dash. Please, can you please stop calling me?"

The funeral was a big affair, and difficult to arrange. They delayed the event as long as possible to allow his three aunts and their children to fly in from Costa Rica, and in that time word of his mother's death spread through a tremendous group of friends that Benicio had never known she had. The church service was filled with Latinas in heavy coats, a few of them Costa Riqueñas and the rest Dominicanas and Puerto Riqueñas. They got along with his aunts and cousins at once, exchanging tears and smeared eyeliner as they hugged cheek-to-cheek. Benicio tried his best to greet them all as they entered the church, but he was overcome with a sudden and intense self-consciousness about his accent and pronunciation, and so limited what he said to "Gracias por venir," and "Dios te bendiga." When the service started he took his place between his father and Alice, and though he wasn't but one pew away from his mother's family and friends he felt oddly distanced from them—as though he'd come to a big country wedding only to discover that he was the only guest sitting on the deserted groom's side.

Benicio's father blubbered throughout the service, and when he reached down for his hand, Benicio let him take it. "I'm sorry," his father said. It came out as breathy and loud, but he seemed to think he was whispering. "Benny, I'm so sorry."

"Please," Benicio said. "Please, don't call me that."

His father's hand loosened but Benicio held on to it. They were quiet for a while.

"I'm going to forgive you," Benicio said. A tremble ran from Howard's fingers into his. "I haven't yet. But I will."

IT WAS DARK BY THE TIME Benicio landed in Manila, got through customs and exited the airport. Sliding glass doors opened out under an ugly concrete overhang, and as soon as he stepped through he could feel hot moisture in the air. People crowded all around, pressing themselves against metal barriers and gazing hopefully into the cavernous airport behind him. They looked like families, mostly—young women with infants in their arms and children hanging on the hems of their skirts. They reached out to wave, call and touch. A Filipino man who left the airport at the same time as him ran up to the barrier and was swallowed by arms. A uniformed woman on Benicio's side of the barrier came up to him and asked if he needed a taxi. Benicio blinked. "Do you need a taxi?" she asked, slower this time. Her English took him by surprise.

"No," he said. His father had warned against the airport taxis and promised to pick him up. Benicio wandered beyond the barrier and into the crowd, a little overwhelmed by the voices, the faces, the smells, the heat. He searched out his father in the crowd and didn't find him. He waited. He set his suitcase against one of the concrete columns, sat on it, and waited more. Doug emerged from the airport, so sleepy he looked strung out, and was set upon by a pretty, middle-aged woman and her family. There were hugs and handshakes all around. They'd taken the bus there, she explained, but if he was tired they could squeeze into a taxi. No, Doug said, the bus sounded great.

After a little over an hour of waiting, Benicio returned to the airport. He exchanged money at an unreasonable rate, called his father's room and got no answer. He called the front desk, and forty hot minutes later a hotel car arrived to pick him up. The driver was young and wore black slacks, a white button-down shirt and a red bowtie. He held a sign high above his head that read: *Mr. Bridgewater*. Benicio brusquely handed over his suitcase and didn't help as the young driver struggled to get it into the trunk. He boarded the white sedan and slammed the door behind him, regretting the petulant display almost immediately.

The car was cool, almost cold on the inside and smelled strongly of citrus. The driver got in and glanced at him in the rearview before releasing the hand brake and crawling down the airport ramp onto a four-lane road that ran alongside a wide storm drain. Benicio saw buildings in the smoggy distance, a few massive clusters to the north and west. The road ahead was packed with the red brake lights of trucks, air-conditioned taxicabs and loudly painted jeepneys that overmatched the descriptions from the book his father had sent. Motorcycles sputtered past, weaving through the traffic. Everything that moved spat out velvety black smoke.

The driver was quiet up front. Benicio unbuckled his seatbelt and scooched up, casually. "I'm sorry," he said. "I was rude to you back there. I didn't mean to be."

"You were not rude," the driver said. They knew it was a lie, but it relaxed them both. Benicio leaned back in his seat and the driver grinned. "Is this your first time in the Philippines, sir?" he asked.

"Yes," he said. "But my father lives here."

"That's good," the driver said. "Where does he stay?"

Benicio hesitated for a moment, watching as they passed the golden arches of a McDonald's. "At the Shangri-La."

"Ah-ha." The driver sounded pleased with himself. "Is your father's name Howard, sir?"

Benicio looked up at him in the rearview. "Yes, it is."

"I recognized your name," he said, "but I'm not sure . . . maybe Bridgewater very common in the States? Also, you don't look very much . . ." he trailed off. "I mean, your father is very . . ." he stopped completely.

"Pale."

"Yes," the driver said with audible relief. "And you're darker. You look almost like a Pinoy. You know that word? Pinoy, that means Filipino. That's good, because we Filipinos are very good-looking." The driver chuckled. They arrived at an intersection clogged with trucks and jeepneys and he kept talking as he drove up with two wheels on the sidewalk, pulled around the stopped vehicles and cut in front of three lanes of traffic to make a left turn. Benicio gripped the leather handhold above his window. "I know your father for almost two years, ever since I'm working at the Shangri-La. Sometimes, if I'm lucky, I'm his driver. He's a very nice man." The driver turned completely around and extended his hand. "My name's Edilberto, but please you can call me Berto."

Benicio gave his hand a quick shake. "When was the last time you saw my father?" he asked.

Edilberto looked up at the roof of the car, as though he was thinking this over very hard. "I don't know. I drove for him maybe one week ago . . . a little more?"

"Do you know where he is now?"

"He's always traveling," Edilberto said. "I'm taking him to the airport, usually, or to some bars." This wasn't really an answer, but Benicio didn't push it. Things had been better since the funeral, but it was vintage fucking Dad to go on some last-minute trip the day Benicio arrived. "It's always tough for families," Edilberto said, as though reading his mind, poorly. "I travel a lot also. Not like you or your father, but . . . away. My family lives very far. It's hard for my wife and for my daughters."

The word *daughters* surprised Benicio. He must have at least three or four years on Edilberto, who'd apparently gone from boy right to family man. Benicio felt self-consciously young by comparison. "Where do they live?" he asked.

"In Cebu. Cebu City, it's on an island to the south. Capital of Cebu province. That's also a very big city."

"As big as Manila?"

"No city's as big as Manila, sir." Edilberto smiled and adjusted his rearview mirror to get a better look into the backseat. They pulled up onto an overpass and soared above small concrete houses and palms. From this vantage Benicio saw people on the steps of huddled dwellings, ramshackle satellite dishes hanging off of corrugated roofs, and flashing neon signs above open doorways. They descended onto a road with no real lane markings that ran parallel to elevated light-rail tracks. A blue train passed them, lit from the inside and packed to bursting. Up ahead was a skyline that Benicio recognized from pictures his father had sent. "Is that Makati?" he asked, gesturing toward the brightness ahead.

"Yes, sir. And that one," Edilberto pointed to a pink building near the edge of the cluster, "is the Shangri-La." Benicio looked at the building and imagined his father as a speck in one of its many distant lighted windows. "Makati's a good place. If you like some nice restaurants and bars, they're all close by. You just let me know, I can show you the bars. You like karaoke?"

"I thought that was a Japanese thing?"

Edilberto contorted his face into a comic look of disapproval. "Japanese are very bad singers. But Filipinos have beautiful voices. Me especially."

Benicio laughed at this and Edilberto grinned again. Entering Makati gave him the impression of entering deep woods out of a grassland. They turned onto a wide avenue lined with magnificent trees with lights slung about their trunks. Well-dressed mannequins gazed out from expensive-looking storefronts. The towering, grayish-pink Shangri-La hotel loomed just ahead, and as they pulled up to the entrance two armed guards approached and greeted Edilberto with cool nods. One of them walked all around the car shining a mirror-on-wheels at its underbelly while the other inspected the trunk and under the hood. When the guards were done they each gave a thumbs-up and waved the car through. Edilberto drove on, stopping finally at the enormous glass doors of the hotel. Benicio took out his wallet, unsure about the difference between a polite tip and overkill.

"Thank you, Edilberto," he said, erring on the side of overkill.

"Please sir, just Berto." He unbuckled his seatbelt and turned around, accepting the wadded bills without looking at them, and deftly shaking Benicio's now empty hand. "It's very good to meet you, sir. Just let me know if you want me to take you someplace. Sometimes guests want to go to the pearl market, or to lunch at Tagaytay. Maybe they want to know where to meet nice friends, or where to have a party." He paused and stared at Benicio for a moment before continuing. "Just ask for Berto, sir, and if it's my shift then I'm very happy."

Before Benicio had a chance to respond a bellboy opened his door and welcomed him to the Shangri-La Makati. He insisted on wheeling Benicio's suitcase and escorted him past more guards with sniffing dogs, their noses pressing against luggage and legs, and into the cool air of the hotel. The lobby was immense and almost indescribably opulent. Above him was an open mezzanine, from which he could hear clanging glasses and flatware, as well as a piano and a woman's voice singing softly. Twin curved and carpeted staircases led down from the mezzanine and met at opposite ends of a huge round rug, in the middle of which sat a marble vase big as a Jacuzzi and overflowing with vegetation. Beyond the principal lobby was a second, much larger chamber decked out with green couches, tables and potted plants and filled with nicely dressed men and women. The far wall of the chamber was all made of glass and looked out on the hotel gardens. A small man-made stream ran outside among a cluster of reddish boulders and beautiful plants that looked both wild and arranged. Footlights hidden in the pebbles and grass illuminated everything, dimly.

"Welcome to the Shangri-La Makati." The concierge at the front desk repeated the greeting. She had a British accent and never broke eye contact or stopped clicking away at her computer while she spoke to Benicio. She told him that his father had reserved a single room adjacent to his own suite with a connecting door, and put up a slim, flat hand when Benicio slid his MasterCard across the desk. "It's already taken care of, sir. Your father asked that the bill be added to his own."

"I insist," Benicio said. The concierge hesitated only briefly before accepting the card from him. "My father didn't meet me at the airport like we'd planned," he added. "I think he may have forgotten to tell me about a last-minute trip. Did he leave any forwarding details?"

She continued clicking away at the computer, glanced for a moment at the screen and told Benicio politely that they didn't have anything. "Your father's suite is reserved through next January, but it's not at all irregular for him to leave it empty due to unexpected travel. Just in case, we'll slide a note under his door tonight. If you still have trouble reaching him just contact our business center and they'll put you in touch with your father's company." Benicio thanked her and collected his key-card. "Your father is one of our very special guests," she went on. "You'll find everyone here very eager to accommodate you."

He wished her a good evening and followed the bellboy to a bank of elevators beneath the mezzanine stairs. Up in his room, the full weight of his exhaustion hit him. He'd planned to take a shower before sleeping, but there was nothing doing. The room was cool and the bed soft, and he fell into it with his clothes on. Just as he was about to drift off, he remembered something Doug had said in the Osaka airport. He pushed himself back up and stumbled over to the window, pulling the curtain back and gazing out at the night sky. He was looking for the moon, but Doug was right, he'd already missed it.

*Chapter 7*

## SAMPAGUITA

Monique was the last to leave the office on Friday afternoon. She turned off lights, spun combination locks on filing cabinets and retrieved her cell phone from a heavy metal safe by the door. She was about to set the alarm when she noticed that she'd left something on her desk—an envelope with the words: *From the other man in your life,* scrawled across the front in red marker. How careless of her. Marines roved the offices at night, and any of them could have seen it! The envelope had arrived that afternoon and contained a flyer picturing a pair of illustrated dancers waltzing over a hardwood floor. *The Shangri-La Hotel Presents: Summer Ballroom Nights.* Both cartoon dancers were faceless, like mannequins in an upscale boutique. The self-described "other man in her life" had embellished the pictures, penciling his likeness over the man, and filling out the breasts and butt of the woman. He'd added the words *me* and *you* beneath their feet. On the back were several partially erased attempted haikus, and one that had been filled in with pen:

*Slick shoes, shiny floor.*
*Let's forget for a night that*
*this will not end well.*

The envelope was for official embassy interoffice memos, and she had no idea how he'd gotten hold of it. He was Filipino—a person of some importance to city politics, which was a professional reason to keep their relationship quiet on top of all the personal ones.

Monique folded the envelope twice, shoved it into the bottom of her purse and finished locking up. Joseph had come to the embassy that afternoon to pick up traveler's checks at the cashier and work out at the gym, and they planned to catch the late shuttle to Makati together. His spirits had risen as the countdown to home-leave entered single digits, and he'd suggested a date night. She'd said yes on impulse—she always said yes when he wanted to do things, which was infrequently—but regretted it now. Despite running late, she didn't rush. Her wedge heels echoed in the empty annex halls. She stopped to check her reflection in the one-way glass on the guard booth. Her new sandstone mock-neck dress had wilted in the afternoon heat, and the lilac jersey top underneath was dark at the collar with sweat. The catalogue had promised every-weather-ease. That was disappointing.

Outside the sun fell fast into the bay, sending streaks of color through the trees and across pastel towers along the boulevard. Drivers from the motor pool chatted beside the evening shuttles, all lined up in the roundabout with windows down. At the edge of the compound, out past the giant mechanical gates, some thirty protesters in surgical masks raised a racket. While never uncommon, the looming national elections had made this a daily occurrence. The protesters chanted the usual: "Go Home, Joe!" A refrain that'd freaked Joseph out until she explained that, in the Philippines, *Joe* was a standard soft slur for all Americans. Like Yankee, or Gringo.

The protesters shook rain-spotted signs at Monique as she crossed from the annex to the Chancery. She was normally good at ignoring them—she liked to think that their chants of "go home" weren't really meant for her, because in her own roundabout way she'd thought of the Philippines as home—but today something caught her eye that made her stop. Something blue, about the size of a softball, flew through the gate and splashed against the base of a tree ahead. She recognized the smell—they were throwing water-balloons filled with pig's blood again. Monique approached the bars even though she knew she shouldn't. She saw a grinning boy no older than Shawn holding up an illustration of presidents Bush and Arroyo kissing sloppily atop a pile of brown stick-figure corpses. His free hand cupped another balloon and her stomach turned at the thought of how warm it must feel in his palm. She shouted at him in Tagalog. "What's the matter with you? You can't throw things in here. It's serious trouble if they catch you!"

The boy shrank but everyone around him boiled. They beat their signs against the gates and shouted at Monique to go home. To go back where she was came from. That she wasn't welcome here. "Bunch of idiots," she said, in English now. "Do what you want, but get the kid away from the gate."

Her mood worsened, Monique continued to the shaded chancery steps. Joseph met her with a hug and what he must have thought was an indulgent smile. "You have to fight with everybody?"

"Not everybody," she said into his shoulder. She had to admit, he felt good. His long body, still damp from the workout, was lean and toned. He was coming up on fifty-five, so it wasn't just about pride anymore. The age gap between them—Monique was only thirty-six—was almost as hard to see now as when they'd first met, she an undergraduate and he a teaching assistant who talked and gesticulated like a genius. Joseph was still as trim as he'd been then, maybe a little more so. On nights when his insomnia was especially bad he'd do an extra hour on the cross-country ski machine in the den, sweating into threadbare briefs, listening to a book on tape, sometimes arguing with the recorded speaker.

Monique and Joseph boarded the lead shuttle. Jeff, the security officer, sat in the front passenger seat but other than that it was empty. The evening caravan rolled out, pulling onto the boulevard and through the throng of protesters. The boy hurled his balloon, but it bounced off the windshield and splashed on the curb. Moments later he was plucked roughly out of the crowd by a Filipino in fatigues. She'd warned them. "Well look at that," Jeff said, waving at the protesters like they were old friends. He fist-pumped the air. He raised the roof. "You go, girls! That'll get things done!"

Joseph inspected their signs and sighed in commiseration. "I suppose you can't blame them."

Jeff raised his hand in the front seat. "I can. I can blame them." He treated arguments as games. To Joseph, they were matters of survival. He looked to Monique for support, but she pretended not to see. She didn't want to look at the protesters either, and instead stared at her cell phone, painstakingly typing out a text message. *Are you back yet? I miss you.*

His response came quick—she doubted even Leila could compose a text that fast. *Back & lonely. Can I c u 2nite?*

She tilted the phone slightly so that the screen faced the window. *Tonight is bad. Dinner with my husband.*

He wrote back: *Where at? Ill met U. We can tell him 2gethr.*

*Don't ever joke about that.*

*Sorry. Caried away. Miss you a lot.* There was a pause before the next message came in. *He kno vac8on off?*

*Not yet*, she texted. Then, as always, she deleted all his messages. She also shut the phone off, just in case he got cute and tried to call at dinner. Joseph was staring by now, and she grunted: "It never ends," replacing the phone in her purse.

"It will soon." He cupped her cheek in his hand. "Just a few days, now."

Traffic was heavy as usual and the drivers passed time by chuckling to one another over the CB. They used callsigns like Iceman and Rocket and discussed weekend plans. One of them observed that Monique was looking very fine today and another argued the she didn't look so fine as she did yesterday. The first driver called the second driver dickless and said he wouldn't know what to do with her in a dark room. Tagalog fluency was rare among the American staff, and Monique often thought of how surprised they'd be if she chimed in. But the pleasure of revealing herself would be short-lived, while the pleasure of going undiscovered was deep and lasting.

They drove south on Roxas, leaving the seaside promenade behind for grassy plains of reclaimed land. Palm trees dotted the median, draped here and there with sooty yellow flags commemorating the death anniversary of the oppositionist, Ninoy Aquino. By August they'd be replaced with new, cleaner flags, and Aquino would be another year dead. Shirtless men lay on their backs in slim shadows cast by the narrow trees. Their bare feet, a shade lighter than their dark shins, jutted out a few inches over the curb. Motorcycles passed by close, and Monique winced.

The shuttle came to a stoplight and Jeff turned to face the backseat. "So! Saw that cake in your office today. Your crew give the bossman a good sendoff?"

Monique bit her bottom lip and shook her head slightly. Joseph, who'd been gazing out the window, perked up. "Chuck's gone? I didn't know he was taking home-leave at the same time as us."

"He's not." Jeff paused. "They sent him to Kabul." He turned back to Monique. "You feel ready for the next few weeks?"

"We can't wait," Joseph said. "We're heading out next Friday. Are you going anywhere interesting this summer, Jeffrey?"

Jeff looked from Monique to Joseph to Monique. "No. I'll be here. Our office is plenty busy with all the new folks coming in." His eyes went hard and he turned around in the front seat.

"That's a shame . . ." Joseph trailed off, staring at the back of Jeff's head. He turned to Monique, who met his gaze. Their silence was broken by a tapping sound; a little girl knuckling the windows. She looked a few years younger than Leila had been when they adopted her, but who knew. With lousy nutrition she could have been older. The girl held up a tattered string of sampaguita flowers. Joseph lowered his power window and told Monique to ask how much they cost.

"Don't do that," Jeff said from up front. He leaned over the driver and began to roll Joseph's window back up from the master control on the captain's chair. Joseph held his button down and the window stalemated halfway. He fumbled in his pockets for money. He passed a badly ripped twenty-peso note to the girl in exchange for the sampaguitas. The flowers fell apart when he laid them on his lap. He released the button and his window shot closed. The girl stayed where she was and kept tapping on the glass, now begging without pretense. She was joined by other girls. And boys. And men. All squatters living in the median. The light changed but the shuttle couldn't move because it was surrounded. Women leaned across the hood hawking washcloths. Their hands left smudges on the metal and glass.

"You see that?" Jeff snarled. "Real smart. Real safe."

The driver shouted at the squatters and leaned on his horn. He put the shuttle in reverse, pulled around them and grazed one with the sideview mirror hard enough to bend it. Monique watched out back as they scampered to the median. The woman they'd struck gave chase for a few paces, shouting angrily but still trying to make a sale.

"No need for all that," Joseph said, not daring to look up at the front seat.

"No, there wasn't. Not till you opened your window."

Jeff was quiet the rest of the trip. He disembarked at Magallanes with cool nods for them both. "Why do you always have to do stuff like that?" Monique asked as soon as the armored door slid shut.

"Do not speak to me in absolutes. I do not always do anything."

"That woman could have been hurt."

"I didn't accelerate. I didn't hit her. All I did was buy flowers from a little girl. And thanks, by the way, for backing me up."

"That's not my job, Joe."

"Actually, yes, it is."

The driver continued northeast, reporting about their bickering in a bemused voice over the CB. He let them out at Greenbelt—a multistory outdoor mall at the heart of Makati with air-conditioning so strong you could feel it a block away. Joseph hated what it *represented*. Monique hated that it was nothing like the home she remembered and had hoped for. But it was close, convenient, and the only place they could ever settle on.

MONIQUE'S CHILDHOOD HOME felt to her now like a different country. Subic Bay was leafy, clean and open. Her father had been stationed there when she was born. He still liked to joke raspily over the telephone that she'd been only minutes away from a Pinoy passport—her mother's water broke a month early on a hike up nearby Pinatubo. The delivery wasn't till later that evening, but the way he told it you'd think Monique popped out the moment his speeding jeep crossed the first MP checkpoint.

For most of the 1970s her family bounced around between Pacific bases—Monique still kept report cards from Guam and Hawaii in her scrapbook. She celebrated her first, seventh, tenth, and eleventh birthdays at Subic. On the last tour, the one she remembered best, they were assigned to a freestanding house some hundred yards down from the married officers quarters. It had a flagstone path lined with pink lava rocks and a back porch that opened out to sagging, vine-heavy woods. They shared a cleaning woman—or more of a girl, actually—with the family next door, and for reasons inexplicable to Monique, memories of this long-lost person held an intensity that nostalgia failed to account for. On some lucky afternoons, when her mother was away at the officers club or shopping at the PX, the cleaning woman would lead Monique on walks through the woods out back. Together they mapped out trees where flying foxes slept in the daytime, and discovered the little corner of All Hands Beach where hawksbill turtles laid their eggs. The cleaning woman threw stones at a troop of roadside macaques that kept getting too close. She taught Monique to coax spiders from their holes with balls of wax. Once, when the woman was away, Monique got bit by one of those spiders. She sat in the front yard bawling until her father came out and crushed it with his naked fingers. "Just like Peter Parker," he said. "You're a little hero now."

Greenbelt had nothing in common with that squat little house. The streams were artificial, the palms were potted, and guards flanked the flagstone paths leading in and out. There was a long line at the checkpoint that night. Men were frisked; women had their handbags searched. One of the guards noticed Monique and Joseph at the back of the line and tried to wave them through, but Joseph insisted on waiting like everybody else. They continued up a narrow neon alleyway and came to the door of their favorite restaurant—the only Italian place they'd found that didn't overcook or oversweeten. They took a table on the second-floor terrace overlooking the main courtyard. Monique ordered a light beer. Joseph leafed through the menu for minutes. He asked the waiter if they had mango juice. He asked if it was fresh or from concentrate. He asked if the mango smoothie was blended with milk, ice cream or yogurt. He asked if it was low-fat yogurt. He ordered a calamansi soda.

When the waiter left Joseph announced that he wasn't fighting anymore.

"You don't get to end it by yourself," Monique said.

"I did not say I was ending it. I just said I was done. You can keep fighting all you want." He turned and stared deliberately over the balcony. The courtyard below wasn't too crowded yet, though some of the first transvestite hookers already haunted the perimeter. Fountains gurgled and Chinese lanterns swayed from drooping palms. A restaurant band did a sound-check on a little stage, counting down into microphones, adjusting Panama hats and tuning acoustic guitars. Joseph tapped his fingers to the non-beat on the terrace railing.

Drinks arrived and Joseph raised his to make a toast. "To the great escape," he said, clinking his glass against Monique's beer.

"Uh-huh," she said. "I get it. It's so incredibly terrible here."

"Is that what I said?"

"You remember who they were escaping from in that movie? Nazis."

"I see. Are you going to be like this all evening?"

She chewed her lip and watched him sip his soda. She knew she was being awful, and wanted to be even worse. "You know, if you just came in with me, if you stuck with it for a week, your time here might feel less like torture. The construction job in the annex is a big deal, and Jeff needs all the trailing spouses he can get. He's got more than enough work to keep you busy. You don't even have to think of it as a job—it'd just be a way to fill up the day."

"Sweetheart." Joseph put his palms together and rested his nose on his middle fingers. Like prayer, but condescending. "You lay off the kids when they try something once. Please, could you extend me the same courtesy?"

To be fair, he had tried. He applied for his security clearance even before they packed out. He got his Interim Secret clearance pretty quick—prior drug use and a failed marriage, but no financial debts or questionable publications—and he spent a full month as an escort. He led Filipino cleaning crews through controlled-access areas, making sure they didn't slip printouts into their watering cans, getting snubbed by officers when he tried to make small talk. He was no star among his colleagues back at American University, but the step down still humiliated him.

"It even *sounds* demeaning." Joseph opened his palms and laid them flat. "Trailing spouse. Like toilet paper stuck on your shoe when you walk out of a public restroom. How embarrassing. Besides, Jeff is a Neanderthal."

The waiter returned to see if they were ready to order. Monique said something in Tagalog that made him leave the terrace.

"I can't go on vacation next week," she said.

Joseph stared at her.

"We're already understaffed, and with Chuck in Kabul I'm the only one left who can run American Citizen Services. I took over this afternoon. They need me here."

He opened his lips and sucked air through clenched teeth. "So, we have to postpone a little?"

"A lot. Chuck doesn't come back until September, and by then the kids are in school."

"Can someone else do it? We have been planning this for months."

"There's no one else. It's summer. Everyone's on their way out, and the replacements haven't arrived yet. I don't have a choice. And besides that, it's a big move for me. It's a lot of responsibility. You should be happy for me."

"Happy for you?" He sounded the words out. He put his calamansi soda to his lips and set it down again. Was he shaking? Was he tearing up? "No. No. In the shuttle—Jeff already knew about this, didn't he? Your whole office knows about this. And you have got me packing. I'm finding someone to look after the goddamn gecko and lovebird. I'm picking up traveler's checks." His voice rose with each sentence. People in the courtyard began to look up. "This is my vacation and I'm the last to find out? What the hell is the matter with you? How long have you known?"

"Just a week. I—"

"A week? *Seven times* you have gone to bed with me and failed to mention this? You have let me plan weekends with our friends. You have let me invite my sister down. I ask again: What is the matter with you?"

He'd never pushed back so hard on anything before, and it took Monique by surprise. But it didn't come out of his strength. It came out of his weakness. His total ineptness when caught anywhere other than Georgetown, or maybe Adams Morgan. He felt like a loser here, and for good reason.

When she didn't answer he just glared at her. "We are still going."

"Don't you tell me what I'm doing," she said.

"I'm not. *We* are going. Shawn and Leila and I."

"I told you I—" she caught herself. "What did you say?"

"It is just five weeks. We will be back before you know it."

She stared at him. She breathed out and it felt like her ribs were bending.

"The kids need a break."

She tried to contrive a laugh but instead just said "Ha" like it was a word. "Don't hide behind them. You need a break."

"I do. They do, too. And what would you know about it? You are at work when they come home from school. Shawn's friends drive him here. They follow him upstairs and he makes them sandwiches they don't eat. His voice changes around them. They call him . . . I don't like the nicknames they call him." For someone so precise, Joseph's vagueness was conspicuous. Again he was talking and not talking about the race thing. "Anyway, it is not good for him. It is not healthy. Not for Leila either. These rich kids treat them like pets."

"I can't be away from them that long." Monique almost blushed hearing how unconvincing she sounded.

"Then don't be. And don't pretend like it is not your choice."

Lantern light refracted in the corners of her eyes. She excused herself, went to the bathroom and stood in front of the mirror. She was exhilarated, overwhelmed and terrified of the joy creeping over her. Five weeks without feeling like shit in front of Shawn's locked room? Five weeks without tearing up at the thought of how lonely Leila was? Five weeks without making excuses to and for her insomniac husband? Five weeks alone, with him. Knowing it was a selfish, lousy thing to feel didn't make her feel it any less. This couldn't have gone better if she'd planned it.

She bumped into Joseph on her way out of the bathroom, catching him walking out on her. They faced off, awkwardly. She put a hand on his chest. "You can go if you want to. You should."

"I am not asking for permission. I don't need it."

"You have it."

"Well, I don't need it." He seemed ready to storm off, but lingered a moment longer. "Tell me there is nothing else going on here. Nothing funny."

She stared at him, and he repeated himself. That was it. It was out there. "There is nothing funny going on here," she said, almost believing her own shocked voice. "I resent the implication." And the funny thing was, she *did* resent it. She sensed that, on a visceral level, being wrongly accused would feel very much the same as this.

"Fine," Joseph said, glancing down at his feet. "Good. Sorry."

And with that he left the restaurant. Monique returned to the table and watched him exit through the courtyard below. Two hookers followed but gave up after a few paces. The lead singer got up on stage and said, "Hi, my name is Erwin," and the early diners said, "Hi, Erwin." Erwin tapped his microphone twice, making a static sound like distant explosions. The band burst into song.

 *Chapter 8*

## TASK FORCE KA-POW

Efrem Khalid Bakkar knows his life just changed forever. He's in a fast-moving jeep with the brigadier general of Southern Command, the biggest movie star in the republic, and the real-life supercop those movies are based on. Reynato, grinning wide, hasn't said anything since they left the marching green. No one has—they speed quietly through a tunnel of palm and bamboo. Efrem stares out back. He watches the Boxer Boys break formation, lean against one another, share hand-rolled cigarettes. He sees each of their faces through the impossibly woven jungle. It wasn't hard to leave them, but still, he's a little sad.

The jeep bounces on the rough dirt track. They pass the semi-paved plantation road leading to the city, but don't take it, pushing further into the overgrown dark. Reynato stays quiet, his breath heavy and slow, his loose smile giving him an open kind of look. Finally Efrem works up the courage to speak.

"Where are we going, sir?"

"My questions come first," Reynato says.

Efrem waits, but Reynato just keeps staring. It lasts minutes. They rumble silently past the mud lane leading to the airfield, past the last access road for the Bukidnon-Davao highway, without slowing. The forest thickens into a quiet blur of ferns slapping at the jeep. Reynato moves the unlit cigar from one corner of his mouth to the other. He sucks and puffs.

"So . . . there's got to be a limit," he says.

"I'm sorry, sir?"

"No sirs. That rapist you just killed . . . or suspected rapist, rather. Innocent until proven, right?" Reynato winks. "He couldn't have been closer than thirty kilometers away. Not to mention all the trees, hills, buildings, people and God-knows what else filling up the line that runs between you and him. So there's no way a shot out of your gun lands anywhere near him. Bullets don't go that far."

Efrem thinks for a moment, trying to find an answer that doesn't sound boastful. He can't. "Mine do."

Renato nods, like he's thinking about this really hard. "Sure, hey . . . that much is clear. But, then, what the hell? Does that mean the rule's flat-out broke? I mean, can you shoot someone in Zamboanga City from here? In Cebu? Can you bag me a jeepney driver in Manila?"

Now it's Efrem's turn to pause, and think. "I don't know. I can shoot as far as I can see."

"Well, can you see Manila?"

"I never tried."

"Never tried?" Reynato sucks his unlit cigar again and clenches his teeth, as though savoring smoke. "Where's your curiosity?"

"I wouldn't know what to look for," Efrem says.

"Problem solved; look for my wife. A name helps, right? She's Lorna Ocampo. We live at . . ." Reynato glances at his watch, "no . . . she'll be out now. Every week she does this damned expensive brunch with girl-friends at the Shangri-La hotel, corner of Makati Ave and Ayala. Should be there now. She'll be the chubby one at the table, but don't judge me for it. Lorna used to turn heads. Tell me what she looks like now."

Efrem grips the seat cushion to steady himself and faces the leaf mosaic above. His eyes open to shimmering black. There are so many shorelines between him and Lorna Ocampo, hundreds of islands with beaches and cliffs. Boats trace white as they motor through straits and into shallow green bays. Freighters hardly move. Efrem sees a long beach—a big island where the land rises up into mountains. A wet checkerboard of rice paddies. The concentric rings of a lake-filled volcano. Beyond is smog like morning mist and the peeking heads of towers. The Shangri-La is pinkish. Six women sit around plates of fruit. Lorna's plate is nearly empty. Efrem describes her hair in a high bee-hive, the string of black pearls around her neck. He lists the colors sewn into her blouse, and reads out some of the letters engraved onto her wedding band.

Reynato pats him once on the cheek and leaves his hand there. He can't whistle but he makes a blowing sound that resembles whistling. "So, if you wanted to, you could shoot that far?"

Efrem nods, rocking his face into Reynato's sweaty palm. "Can I ask you a question now, sir?"

"I said no sirs. You can ask me whatever you want."

"Do you have Truth with you?" He means, of course, the famous pistol from the Ocampo Justice movies. When he was a boy his prize possession was a knockoff plastic replica of that larger-than-life Colt, stolen off a market stall run by half-blind Chinese. "Can I see it?"

There is subdued laughter from Charlie and Brig Yapha up front. "Truth? Mohammed . . . you should know better. I wouldn't be caught dead with that queen pistol they got Charlie using in the movies." Rey-nato lifts his shirt and pulls the handgun from his pant waist—a Glock, dull and wordless. "This is my gun. It's no specialer than I am. So: very."

Efrem eyes the piece. Truth was a sixshooter, single-action army, name inlaid in gold along the cylinder, big enough to bludgeon, barrel long enough to parry and thrust in a swordfight, if you ever got into one, which Reynato did, in *Ocampo Justice XIII*, which he won, handily. But this gun is as regular as it gets, not even custom like Efrem's Tingin. He tries to keep the disappointment out of his voice. "Does this one have a name?"

"Sure does. Call it Glock."

Brig Yapha and Charlie laugh some more, and Efrem looks away, feeling foolish.

AROUND MIDDAY THEY STOP at a cleared hill overlooking a banana grove. Succulent leaves and trunks extend below like chop on a small green sea. A stream runs some hundred meters north, and on its bank sits a large but only partially constructed house. Smoke rises from a tin chimney on the east wing, and Efrem sees food being prepared through an open kitchen window. The brigadier general and Charlie dismount, looking old as they rub their backs and knees. Reynato leaps out, opens the door for Efrem and helps him down, as though he needs help down. "You hungry?" he asks, not pausing for an answer. "I'm starving! Down we go."

The four descend the shallow, sunny crest, following a narrow path into a forest of banana trees laden with harvest-ready fruit. Charlie plucks one from a low-hanging bushel and eats loudly. It seems that Efrem's unexpected presence and the magically outsized murder he's just witnessed have left the actor-turned-politician a little off-balance, but nonetheless he tries to play the happy, confident host. The Fuentes family has owned this land since Spanish times, he says. They maintain the road and lease out water rights from their stream. His cousin started to build this house under pretense of supervising the harvest, but he almost never comes down and when he does it's to hunt hornbills and macaques with shotguns or to impress his eco-cred on touristic white girlfriends.

The house looms large as they emerge from the trees. Smoke coils in still air above the chimney, hardly rising. They hear water rush over stones out back, the musical sound of pots and voices from the kitchen. The building isn't near finished; unused hardwood beams protrude from half-frames, looking like ship-ribs from some wreck dashed into the jungle by a tidal wave. Those parts that are complete are the sole survivors of calamity—not first progress. Charlie tosses his peel into a waste bin by the front door, sinking a swish. "Here we are," he says. "You're welcome . . . all of you."

Efrem steps toward the house but stops in his tracks. Something is wrong. He turns and sees them. Three men hide among the overgrown banana, staring at him. Reynato must know they're there as well, because he smiles and presses a finger to his lips. He shapes his hand into a pistol and points it at the trees. Pulling his thumb back like a steel hammer, he fires and mimes recoil. "Ka-Pow," he whispers.

A maid with straight hair and a light blue uniform comes to the door. She's seventeen maybe, no older. Charlie asks if lunch is ready and she nods, stepping aside and inviting them in with skinny arm and open palm. Charlie and Brig Yapha enter, brushing her as they pass. Reynato lingers on the lawn with Efrem, looking amused. The spies in the trees don't know they've been discovered. One sits among rotting leaves, cradling a bushel of green bananas in his arms. He slices the fruits lengthwise with a kitchen knife and eats them, peels and all. Another, barefoot and nude save for a pair of tattered basketball shorts, stands slim against a trunk. The third, looking gnarled and old, squats behind a log. Life in the jungle, life in the army, have made Efrem suspicious of those who would watch him. He raises his custom Tingin.

"Easy, Mohammed," Reynato says, putting his hand over the muzzle. "They won't give you any trouble. At least not the shooting kind of trouble." He turns back to the trees and yells, his voice rebounding and doubling against the shallow hill. "Fuckers! Lunch!"

Echo and return. Silence. Heavy leaves rustle and three men step out onto the grass before them. "Isn't that nice?" Reynato says.

The man in the middle still cradles his bushel of fruit. Knife dangling at his side, he speaks with a full mouth: "What's that?"

"His name is Efrem," Reynato says. The man cocks his head, evidently favoring a good ear. Reynato repeats himself. "He's my new friend. Maybe yours too, Lorenzo."

"Yeah? I got too many already." The man, Lorenzo, pauses to chew. "Is he what I think he is?"

Reynato does not answer, but he smiles.

"I figured. He looks weird like that. So, what's he *do*?"

"He kills people."

Lorenzo swallows and smiles right back, his teeth pulpy. "We all do that."

"Well, he does it better," Reynato says. He turns to Efrem. "Treat these boys with care, Mohammed. They may someday be like family. This idiot ruining his appetite is Lorenzo Sayoc. The handsome one," he points at the man with gnarled and twisted skin, "is Racha Casuco.

And finally we have sweet, simple Elvis Buwan. They leave a little to be desired, as family goes. But I promise you've got more in common with them than any fucking soldier boy. They're all bruhos, like you. And like me."

He claps once and rubs his hands together. "Let's eat."

LUNCH AT THE UNFINISHED FUENTES house is a big affair. Efrem walks through the kitchen into an open dining area where the maid sets food out on a long table made of varnished Philippine mahogany and flanked by benches of the same wood. Brig Yapha and Charlie, already seated, seem to have been in the middle of a hushed conversation, but they clam up as everybody enters. Charlie, a little startled by the appearance of Reynato's bruhos, signals to the maid to grab some extra plates. She adds them to the tabletop already covered with ceramic platters and stewpots, all set under the crossing breezes of electric fans to keep away flies. A big bowl of shredded purple banana flower fried with bits of pork fat, a crispy duck baked to near-blackness and served on layers of foil, beef-shank bulalo with chopped ampalaya and carrots sitting in a vat of oily broth, a whole braised grouper covered in diced garlic. There's rice of course, heaped and steaming in a plastic tub beside a bowl of sliced calamansi, soy sauce and a bottle of peppered coconut vinegar. Under the table is a cooler of beer, and a pilsner is set behind every plate, shortnecks and caps glistening with icy sweat.

At the sight of mismatched china and clean silverware, Efrem hesitates. He's used to field-issue crockery, eating on the ground by the mess trailer. He'd rather go hungry than take a seat not meant for him. Lorenzo pushes past, discarding his bananas to get a spot near the bulalo. Racha sits as well, eyeing the maid's threadbare dress. Elvis and Reynato join them. Efrem hovers.

Lorenzo breaks his staring contest with the food to glance at Efrem. "Ain't he even housetrained?"

"Never mind him." Reynato gestures to an open spot with his spoon. "Sit." Efrem leans his Tingin carefully against the wall and sits. Brig Yapha and Charlie bow their heads in prayer, but everyone else reaches out hungrily for scoops of rice and duck. Reynato gets the bony grouper head. Lorenzo comes away with the best piece of beef shank and goes right for the marrow. Charlie lets them fill their plates with his food before serving himself. He eats like a bird, chattering about the upcoming election—just twenty days away now—more than he chews. He's nervous about how he did today, and not shy about showing it, which lowers him even further in Efrem's esteem. His campaign manager's in the hospital, will be for a while yet, and this is his first trip solo. No talking points. No prepared remarks. Everything on-the-fly. He really hopes he didn't screw up.

"Fuck your nerves," Yapha says. "You're a natural. Did you even *see* the kids today. Swooning like girls at a concert."

They keep at it, and the pace of their talk makes Efrem's eyes unfocus. The discussion is difficult to follow. What they're saying, even who's saying what—it all pushes past faster than he can unjumble it. Yapha bemoans that he's not yet a full general and Charlie says forget it, quit, run with me. Don't laugh! Better than a soldier's pay, am I right? Second District, Davao del Sur, is coming open. Castillo's got nut cancer and his son's in New York learning how to be a better fag. You'll be a shoo-in, come up to Manila and give me some help against those fucking cha-cha crybabies. Brig Yapha shyly sucks shank. They'll never elect a Pangasinense down here, let alone a Yapha. Don't be so sure. They know you well enough and they won't care. What you need to do is start a fight. Get your name in the papers followed by a list of dead Abu Sayyaf terrorists. Who doesn't like a hero? I don't, Reynato says, picking his braces with a grouper bone. Don't you even! I'm not even going to start with you. Charlie grins a soft, cowardly grin. You and your tired excuses. You squanderer of big-ass chances. National hero, tough on crime, connections at the top and at the bottom. The *very* bottom . . . and the very top. No telling how far a *shred* of ambition could take you. Mayor of Manila? Or elected to the Senate, with me, assuming I get there? Goddamnit, Renny, the way your rep cleans up at the box office . . . you'd be a fucking force at the ballot box. I mean, running on your name, how could you lose? Reynato belches and sort of karate-chops the air. No doubt, he says. But haven't you beat me to it? Seems to me that you're already running on my name. And I guess there's only room for one Reynato Ocampo, real or fake, in voters' heads. But more power to you. Power, and luck.

Reynato reaches across the table and uses the edge of his spoon to cleave off a brittle duck leg. He pauses to chew, crunching charred fat and bone.

EFREM IS HUNGRY BUT EATS LITTLE. Queasily he turns down blood-dripping shank and pork-spoiled banana flower. He lets Lorenzo have his unopened beer and scans the table for a water jug. He swallows what he can, pushes his plate away and watches the three bruhos. Lorenzo eats with abandon, emptying his plate as fast as he fills it. He's dressed oddly. On his head is a wide-brimmed straw hat; the kind mothers make for daughters old enough to bend daylight on the rice paddies. Around his shoulders is a plastic rain poncho, clasped below his chin with a copper button. Open and flowing, it dances in the fan draft like a transparent cape.

Elvis is coated in thin filth, his hair a net for twigs and rainwater. He drinks more than he eats, looking just as vacant at the table as he did among the trees. It's not just an expression—his face is smooth, empty, featureless. Efrem can't place his age. He could be a tired thirty or a tight-skinned sixty.

But Racha, the man with the gnarled hide, is the most interesting. Efrem realizes that Racha's whole body is covered in scars. He's given and received pain enough times to know what mutilation looks like, the different marks left by different attacks. Just by looking at Racha's exposed forearms, neck and face, he can tell that he's been shot, stabbed, burned, bitten, whipped, strangled, stung by jellyfish, beaten with a manual can-opener and possibly scalped. Among those dark inches he can't find a scrap of healthy skin—Racha is all made of scar tissue. And what's more amazing than the scars is the fact that he survived long enough to collect them all.

Lunch concludes with plates of leche flan and small cups of civet coffee. Reynato sighs contentedly and leans back against the wall, look-ing across the table at Brig Yapha, and at Charlie. "Well," he says, "that was a treat. I hate to sour the afterglow by talking business."

Yapha puts on a quizzical expression. "You have business? What business do you have?"

"Cute." Reynato places his cigar back in the corner of his mouth. Still he does not light it. "What do you want for him?"

Brig Yapha and Charlie Fuentes exchange looks. "Well," Charlie says, all soft and friendly, "Tony and I were talking about that a little, before lunch. And you know, it's a hard, a tough loss for the Division, right? Because Efrem *is* his best, and—"

"Motherfucker, you didn't even know *what he was* till I told you."

"True enough," Brig Yapha says. "But the boy's still mine. He gets no transfer, no discharge without my say-so."

"Not that we'd keep him from you," Charlie rushes to add. "But, it's just, there's a whole lot of ways you could be helpful in the coming weeks. I mean, today was *great*—don't get me wrong . . . but, you know, it would also be cool if you stood out front a bit more. Gave a few nice words to the reporters. Amoroso's hammering my ass on law-and-order. Maybe you could say a little something at Director Babayon's next press conference. Maybe you could get some of the officers to come out for me. I mean, they worship the ground you walk on, Renny."

"Ah-ha." Reynato sits forward and places his elbows on the table. He puts his chin in his hands like a girl looking at her date, but his expres-sion is sour. "So, let me get this straight—for years you make yourself famous, and rich, pretending to be me. Then you turn that fame and money into a run for the Senate. You put my name on your campaign posters, fucking act like me while you're on stage. And now I'm sup-posed to go out and stump with you?"

"Hey . . ." Charlie sounds, and looks, genuinely hurt. "That's not fair. You've seen some scratch from those movies, too. I didn't write your contract. Hell, if you'd have shown it to me back then, *I'd* have told you to get a lawyer."

"And you?" Reynato turns on Brig Yapha. "What's in this for the not-quite general?"

"Don't get short, Renny," Yapha says. "What you saw back there wasn't just political stagecraft. My men are hurting—for ammunition, rations, body armor and some damn downtime. I need all the friends in Manila I can get, and Charlie promises to be one. Besides," he glances now at the bruhos from the trees, "it's more than a fair trade. Efrem would be the perfect addition to your wily crew."

The table goes quiet for a long while. Reynato stirs his coffee, spoon hammering the insides of the cup. Elvis, Lorenzo, and Racha all lean forward like birds over a kill. Finally Efrem breaks the silence with his first utterance since entering Fuentes's house. "Sorry, but what's happening? Where am I going?"

Everybody laughs. "Shit," Reynato says, downing the last of his coffee. "Sorry about that, Mohammed. Don't mean to treat you like a barter chip—I won't even take you if you don't want to come. You see, the boys and I, we run this little task force."

"Overmodest," Charlie protests, clearly thrilled by the diffused tension. "There's nothing little about it, Efrem. We're talking *presidential directive*. We're talking a four-time cover story in the *Bulletin*. Reynato here runs the finest police crew in—"

"Not strictly police," Reynato cuts him off. "Our shop gets funded by the National Bureau of Investigation, and we operate across jurisdictions. We specialize in kidnapping cases and the prosecution of outstanding warrants . . . basically we go in for high value arrests when the local cops can't close the deal. Some newsboy called us *Task Force Ka-Pow* a while back, which has kind of stuck. But I'll give you fair warning, Efrem, if you join up you'll be dealing with some real rough folks. From Chinese guns in shabu labs, to armored car hijackers with hand grenades, these boys do not play nice. My crew," he gestures to Lorenzo, Racha and Elvis, "are stretched thin as we get. Poor Racha got shot in the foot just last week."

Racha nods solemnly.

"So it's no dream job," Reynato says. "But our pay is a step up, I can promise that. And you'll likely get more chances to fight. You like that, don't you? How could you not, a man with your record?" He smiles. His gums are bleeding. "If you didn't enjoy pulling the trigger the ninth time, then you wouldn't have pulled it the tenth. So . . . would you want in on this dangerous silliness? Should I buy you an early discharge by signing my time away to these two slick motherfuckers?"

There's no choice here at all. Efrem enjoyed his years in the army, sure, but this is Reynato Ocampo. This is his chance to be the hero that his mother, that his whole island expected him to be—a chance to stick up for the unstuckup for. He can almost hear a pulsing beat coming in through the windows, the Ocampo Justice theme song filling the plantation the way it filled the outdoor movie house. Yes, he says, or maybe he just thinks it, because everybody keeps staring at him. "Yes," he tries again, his voice thick and gurgly.

"Well all right," Reynato says. "I'll probably regret this, knowing how hard these jerks will squeeze the lemon." Reynato puts an arm over Efrem's shoulder and chuckles. His breath is rot. "You all can fax me his discharge paperwork, and I'll have my girl back in Manila get him into our system. Now, if you don't mind, I think I need to get him oriented. Especially if you all plan to bring me on tour." Together he and Efrem walk out to the yard. Racha, Lorenzo and Elvis follow close behind.

Outside it's brilliant bright, and everybody must wear sunglasses. Task Force Ka-Pow moves back into the banana trees, up toward the road and the waiting jeep. Efrem feels himself pushed forward by a sea-swell. He can't grab onto anything, not a branch or vine, because it's all moving with him.

*Chapter 9*

## HOWARD'S ROOM

It's crazy-making how heavy this motherfucker is. Ignacio takes his legs and Littleboy his shoulders, but they only make it a few steps before the American slips fatly, wetly, out of their grip. Littleboy takes his legs and

Ignacio his shoulders. Not much better—they get to the curb and again he defeats them with dead heft. This is bad. Late as it is, it's still Manila. Any minute now a car, a jeepney, a motor-trike or night-roving squatter will be along. Early risers will hit the pavement as insomniacs stumble home. Someone is sure to hear this commotion in the steamy, after-rain quiet. Someone is sure to notice what they're doing. God, what *on earth* are they doing?

After a few tries it's clear they'll never get him up the concrete steps and through the front door without more help. Ignacio goes inside to wake his wife. Waking his wife is hard. She's crashing after a five-day tweak, courtesy of the rough shabu that Ignacio manufactures in his bathroom and sells to some of his regular taxi customers. Like all of Ignacio's schemes—the short-lived rental store for pirated movies, the cockfight training academy opened in the wake of Kelog's retirement— this one is small scale; successful mostly in maintaining their private stock. Always enough meth on hand to chase the dragon, should they care to. And they care to often. Ignacio is chasing the dragon right now. He's on three days running without sleep.

Finally he rouses her and drags her outside. To his surprise she takes the sight of the American, facedown and bleeding from his head and fingers, in stride. She only asks once what Ignacio is doing, and accepts his hollered response that he has no fucking idea without comment or critique. Together the three of them hoist the fat man up the steps and through the front door, which Ignacio closes and locks behind. Then they pause, catch their breath, and look at one another as though for answers. Kelog, roused by the commotion, hops atop the unconscious man and pecks at the blood spots speckling his shirt.

"Is he dead?" she finally asks.

"Of course he's not!" Ignacio pauses to check. And there it is—the tiny, regular spasm of a pulse. "Of course he's not."

She is clearly pleased by the news. "Well, where's he going to stay?"

"He can have my room," Littleboy says. "I can take the couch, no problem."

"Guys." Ignacio removes Kelog from the American's chest. "He's not a fucking houseguest."

"Ah-ha," his wife says, breathing evenly. "All right then, what is he? Who is he?"

A good question. Ignacio goes through the fat man's pockets and finds a ratty wallet, swollen and old. An expired driver's license inside identifies him as Howard Bridgewater, from Illinois. Ignacio had been confident he was from the States when he barked obscenely into his cell phone back in the taxi, but now there is no question: the man lying on his living room floor is American. Why does this thought thrill him so? Why, he wonders, does it terrify him so?

Ignacio's wife takes the wallet and inspects it carefully, leafing through the contents with her fingertips as though turning the pages of an old book. "No money," she says. There is nothing accusatory in her tone. She's just voicing an observation.

"Of course there's money." Ignacio snatches the wallet back and upends it on the floor. But she's right—nothing in there but faded paper and some generic-brand condoms. "He's got to have money. He was going to the Shangri-La. And he promised to pay me meter plus a hundred."

"Maybe he was going to rob you," she says, smiling a smile that makes her look old. Then her smile fades. "I don't see why you had to hurt him that badly. He can't have run away."

"Someone like him doesn't have to run." Ignacio leans over the unconscious American—over *Howard*—to search him. With Littleboy's help he tips him over to get at his back pockets, finding a key-card for the hotel as well as another wallet. This second one is new and cheap, containing nothing but two crisp hundred-peso notes. Junk change considering the risk Ignacio has taken, but it's promising—obviously a decoy for pickpockets. Which means there must be a real stash some-where else.

They find it in his socks and shoes. Twenty-thousand pesos, rumpled and stinking and wet from the rain. Not bad at all. Ignacio keeps searching while his wife and Littleboy lay the notes out to dry them. He unzips Howard's pants, hoping for one of those gut-hugging money-belts popular with tourists. But all he finds is a naked abdomen rubbed bare of body hair and rutted with stretch marks like the weathered slope of a mud hill. He zips Howard's fly back up and buttons his pants. Of all the things he's done tonight this is the only one that makes him squirm, just a little, with self-reproach.

"Do you want to bring him somewhere?" his wife asks. "We could leave him close to a hospital."

Ignacio shakes his head. He doesn't know what he wants to do, but he knows he isn't done with Howard yet. "You were right," he says. "We should put him in Littleboy's room."

"I'll make the bed," she says, nodding. Littleboy stands to help.

"Don't," Ignacio says. "Move it. The bed . . . everything. Let's get it all out of there."

And so they do. Still sore from dragging Howard inside, the three of them empty Littleboy's bedroom, moving the well-kept secondhand bed frame, the rattan hutch and electric fan like roomies helping a departing friend. They even take his Ocampo Justice posters off the walls, hanging them instead in the living room beside Ignacio's extensive collection— relics from his short-lived video rental place. Charlie Fuentes looks right at home beside Tim Roth and Kiefer Sutherland. Now that Littleboy's room is totally bare it becomes Howard's room. They drag him inside and close the door. Then they mill about, quietly. What do you do with your morning when you've already done this?

"I'm going to bed," Ignacio says. Then, to his wife: "You coming?"

"No," she says. "You know how it is."

He does know how it is. He pulled her out of a crash, and now that she's awake it'll be a few hours before she gets that urge to tweak again. She'll have some early breakfast, maybe watch some television. Ignacio, for his part, is ready for a crash of his own. He's ready for the clear head that he knows will follow sleep, and holy shit, he feels like he could sleep for hours, if not days. He goes into the master bedroom and curls into the still warm hollow his wife left in the mattress. Out in the living room she and Littleboy turn on the television, filling their home with the booming lullaby of international news. Ignacio is out in seconds.

And he dreams. A wonderful dream wherein he, Charlie Fuentes,

Roth and Sutherland rob a bank. They shoot up the place. They torture the safe combination out of the manager's throat. And they get away with millions.

TWO DAYS LATER, a Monday, Ignacio and Littleboy head to the Shangri-La hotel. Ignacio's plans at this point are still murky. Part One is find Howard Bridgewater's room. Part Two is steal whatever they discover in there—presumably luggage, jewelry and a shit-ton of cash. Part Three is yet to be determined, though Ignacio has vaguely considered a ransom note of some kind. Or a false suicide note. Or a fire. He's still in the brainstorming stage, really.

But even before Part One, at *Part Zero*, he and Littleboy run into complications. Ignacio had hoped to arrive in the morning, before the commotion of checkout and the attendant bustle of housekeeping. But he hadn't reckoned on how much the already-terrible Manila traffic would be worsened by the elections. He hadn't, in fact, even remembered that today was Election Day. But there it is; a big-ass rally right in the middle of EDSA, with Charlie Fuentes appearing in person to get out the vote. Littleboy asks if they can stay and watch and Ignacio says no. But it makes no difference. They idle in the gridlock for over an hour, catching most of the speech, Littleboy clapping and cheering out the passenger window.

It gets no easier when they finally arrive at the Shangri-La. Guards at the giant glass entryway take time patting them down and staring into their faces. They are allowed inside but aren't in the lobby—and Christ, *what a lobby*—for a full minute before a prim little concierge sets on them. "What do you want?" she asks, wasting no time on hospitality, or English.

"We are guests from—"

"What room?" she asks, a hand already on each of their arms, already walking them back to the giant glass doors.

"Room 506," Ignacio says, setting his heels but unable to resist the pull of her hard, tiny fingers.

"There is no room 506," the concierge says.

"I bet you there is," Ignacio says.

"Fine," she says, "there is. But it isn't yours." They have reached the glass doors now. Not wanting to make a scene, Ignacio frees himself from her grip and exits on his own steam. But the concierge follows. "These two," she says, talking now to the guards. "*No. No.* They are *not* allowed." The guards look at their shoes, ashamed. And Ignacio and Littleboy retreat to a Starbucks across the street, drinking frothy iced drinks for hours as they wait for a shift change.

THEY TRY AGAIN in the afternoon. Through the glass doors, past the new guards—staring, patting, cupping just as suspiciously—and into the shiny lobby. There's the bank of elevators just ahead and Ignacio goes for it at a jog-walk with Littleboy stumbling gape-mouthed behind. "Iggy," he says, "Iggy, are you *seeing* this?"

At the elevators Ignacio presses the button, hard. He and Littleboy wait. He presses the button again. And again.

"What do you want?" He turns and sees another concierge, this one just as prim, just as little, just as beautiful and cold. But now he's ready for her.

"Driver, ma'am," he answers, in broken taxicab English. "Boss stays here," he points above, vaguely. "Sends text he needs me." Then, remembering Littleboy: "Us."

"What room?"

"Room 506," Ignacio says. He has to restrain his smile. He feels that by repeating this arbitrary number he is somehow sticking it to them. And he is.

The concierge sighs—a light, scolding sigh—and tells them to next time use the service entrance. Then she takes a card from her uniform pocket and inserts it into a slot above the elevator button. The doors open promptly. Ignacio and Littleboy step inside and wave thanks to the concierge. The doors close, and now Ignacio restrains nothing. He smiles and he laughs and he gives her the finger. Littleboy does as well. And they remain like that, flicking off their reflections in the shiny doors as they are ferried upward to the fifth floor of the Shangri-La.

THEY DON'T GET OFF when the elevator stops, though Littleboy tries, saying: "But, 506?" when Ignacio pulls him back. Together they wait for the doors to close again. Then Ignacio removes Howard Bridge-water's key-card from his wallet. He's noticed a slot above the polished regiment of numbered buttons—a slot much like the one in the lobby below. Could it really be this easy? Howard's key-card fits in perfectly and gives Ignacio the appealing sensation of sliding a hot knife through brass. He removes it and one of the buttons lights up, as though pressed. Jackpot, he thinks.

The hallway on Howard's floor is quiet and empty, save an unmanned housekeeping trolley decked with towels and sheets and rich person freebies. The dark heavy doors are all closed, some with do-not-disturb signs lynched from their handles, others glowering over the remnants of room service, or newspapers in plastic sacks. Ignacio and Littleboy walk the length of the hallway twice, looking for some clue. Or at least Ignacio is looking for a clue. But Littleboy gets distracted by the papers. The front page bears an airbrushed cover photo of Charlie Fuentes under the headline: *On Election Day, Senate Braces for Dose of Justice.* That smarmy jackass has been on the cover of everything this month.

Littleboy stops by one of the closed doors, plucks up the paper and tears open the plastic sack. "Don't do that," Ignacio says. "Someone's going to notice."

"But, there's plenty," Littleboy says, gesturing down the hall. And he's right, there are plenty. Every third door has a special May 10 Election Edition of the *Bulletin* sitting before it. And Ignacio guesses that the other doors only lack newspapers because the guests inside have already claimed them. The guests inside . . .

Holy Christ. God is clearly, *clearly* on their side. Ignacio races back to the far end of the hall where he sees a door that has not one, but three newspapers lying before it. Monday May 10, Sunday May 9— bearing a cover story about some headless body found in Iraq—and Saturday May 8—the Presidential Palace promising honesty at the

polls. When had they taken Howard again? Sometime on Saturday, but
before dawn. Before the early edition, for sure. He jabs the key into the
door and a little green light blinks welcomingly. The locking mecha-
nism makes a futuristic unlocking sound. And as easily as that, all of
Howard Bridgewater's wealth and power are rendered open and available to Ignacio.

BUT NOW WHAT TO DO? Ignacio and Littleboy stand dumbstruck in
Howard's Bridgewater's room—or rather in his *rooms*. He expected
the suite to be nicer than his home, sure, but not bigger. Ignacio kicks
off his shoes and walks through the rooms one by one. Bedroom,
kitchenette, study, bathroom. Carpet on his toes, cool tile on his toes,
carpet again, tile again. He ends his circuit in the study, where a neat
stack of important-looking papers sits atop a table. Putting on an air of
informed purpose, Ignacio plants himself in one of several office-style
swivel chairs and begins leafing through the papers. He'd noticed a wet
bar off the kitchen, and he tells Littleboy to make him a drink.

Littleboy returns with a brimming tumbler—he's poured the scotch
as though it's juice—as well as a plastic tray of bluefin sushi from the
fridge. It's a few days old, but smells all right, and the scotch helps burn
away the after-tang. And it feels good, doesn't it? Sitting here in Howard's room. Drinking Howard's scotch and eating his sushi. Snooping
through what are no doubt very important business documents.

Ignacio allows himself to laugh a little. He feels so good he gets up
and, sloshing tumbler in hand, turns on the stereo, scanning stations
until he comes to "Bakit Papa?" by the SexBomb Girls and blasting it.
Because why not? The empty, pristine suite confirms that fatty is a
bachelor. A bachelor who hasn't been missed—not yet at least. They
have *plenty* of time to figure out what to do. Time to compose the perfect ransom letter. Time to take this suite apart panel by panel searching for cash and whatever else. Feeling confident, feeling downright
kingly, Ignacio swings open the balcony door and steps out into the
heat. All of Makati cowers at his feet—all the shops and towers and
banner-waving election marchers. All the Americans and Chinese and

rich-ass high-nosed Forbes Park coños. Ignacio lifts his ridiculously overfull tumbler to them, as though to toast, and gulps down as much of the expensive scotch as he can bear.

Then there's a loud knock on the door that straight up ruins his mood.

IGNACIO SETS HIS TUMBLER down and turns, looking back into the suite. Littleboy is in the study, facing the front door, frozen. And again the knocking—three hard raps, loud enough that they can hear it over the radio. Is it one of Howard's friends? Or maybe just housekeeping? A huge problem, either way. Littleboy makes for the door and Ignacio is suddenly, horribly certain that the simpleton is going to answer it. He's going to swing it wide and expose them. Ignacio knows he should chase after, but his lungs and legs have turned to mud. He briefly contemplates leaping off the balcony.

But instead of answering the door—Ignacio should have more faith in his brother, he's not that stupid—Littleboy just presses his face to the peephole. He looks through for a long while. Then there's another knock and he jerks backward, as though someone has struck his face. He turns to Ignacio. Are those tears in his eyes? Is he crying? No—*weeping*! Silently bawling. He waves Ignacio over, pointing at the peephole. Slowly Ignacio exits the balcony and puts his eye up to the minuscule little window.

There's a policeman out there.

An officer. Ignacio recognizes the classic light blue shirt and dark blue pants, the badge-blazed beret leaning off the side of his meanly shorn skull. He's out there, holding up a piece of paper, double and triple checking the number in his notes with the number on the door. "Hello," he calls. "Mr. Howard Bridgewater?"

Littleboy must be having trouble hearing, because he turns off the radio and leans his ear into the door. The policeman notices this and pauses, as though expecting some answer. Ignacio, now crying silently as well, slaps Littleboy on the forehead. His brother *is* stupid. It was wrong to have faith in him.

"Can you hear me, sir?" The officer's expression is put out, but his voice exceedingly polite. "I am here to follow up regarding your emergency call on the morning of the eighth." Another pause. "Mr. Bridgewater?"

He jiggles the handle.

Ignacio is in a flat panic. He knows that if he answers the door, that's it. They're done. And not just in the short term—they're finished *for life*. But if he fails to answer it, the officer will get worried. And he'll return with one of the steely concierges and a master key, which would be even worse. There's only one way for Ignacio to evade this fate. He closes his eyes and concentrates. He conjures, from memories of his DVD collection, the perfect American accent. Like Mel Gibson, from *Ransom*. Though, come to think of it, he's Australian. Maybe Tim Roth? But no . . . he's British, isn't he? Fuckitall. Here goes.

"What do you want?" Ignacio groans, all twang and marmalade.

A silence. Then: "Hello, sir? Mr. Bridgewater?"

"What do you want?" Ignacio repeats. "I was sleeping."

"I . . . you made an emergency call, sir? Some days ago?"

"And?"

More silence. "Are you all right? Did you want to file a report?"

"No. I mean, I'm fine. No report."

The officer takes a breath and briefly holds it. He looks back down at his notes, and then at the door again. Ignacio wonders if his shape is somehow visible through the tiny fish-eye glass. If the officer has some sense of him and his duplicity. "Sir," he asks, "are you sure there is no prob—"

"Go away," Ignacio says. "I need to sleep."

And, after a small pause, the officer does go away. He walks back down the quiet hallway. And distantly they hear the pleasant chime of the arriving elevator. He is gone.

IT'S HARD TO BE TOO ELATED. The foolishness of this visit to the Shangri-La springs up about Ignacio like a brushfire. What the hell was he thinking? He's seen enough movies to know that the story he's in—the story he's willingly hopped aboard—never ends well. Sooner or later the hostage gets away. Sooner or later Gibson or Fuentes or Sutherland gets the better of you. They tap your telephone. They put snipers on the roof. They hide paint bombs in the ransom money. Eventually they find you and hit you in the face, really hard. Eventually, reluctantly, they shoot and kill you. And the audience cheers, and you, in death, are humiliated.

Ignacio gazes about the suite, horrified by his own carelessness. He can only imagine his fingerprints—his bare *footprints* for God's sake!—spattered about the room like flecks of fallen snow. His spit on that leftover sushi. His dandruff flaked over Howard's documents. Moving slowly, as though to avoid further disturbing the very air of the suite, he puts his shoes back on. He closes the sliding glass door to the balcony. He and Littleboy slip out of Howard's room, hanging a Do-Not-Disturb sign on the handle as they depart.

They ride the elevator back down in something of a haze. Charlie Fuentes's get-out-the-vote rally has turned down Ayala Avenue, and they can hear the whistles and drums and chanting as they return to the lobby. None of the concierges hassle them as they cross the shining expanse of polished marble. In fact, other than the raucous sounds from outside, the vaulted space has turned quiet and still. Ignacio notices that everybody—the guests, the staff—is at the far end of the lobby, huddling in a couch-strewn grove of mustard-yellow columns. There are flat-screen televisions mounted to some of the columns. Everybody is watching them.

At first he thinks it's just election news, but as Ignacio passes he hears the word *kidnapped*. He stops for a moment to listen.

"Please can we go?" Littleboy asks.

"Hush. Just a second."

The report is about that headless body discovered in Iraq over the weekend. It turns out that it was the body of an American who was working in Baghdad. His kidnappers have released a video today. A video of the beheading. The American squats in an orange jumpsuit with a line of black-clad masked men behind him. Reading in Arabic.

Chanting in Arabic. Hollering in Arabic. The video cuts out and the news anchor explains why.

"Please, can we go, please?"

Littleboy tugs at Ignacio's arm, but he won't budge. His gaze has drifted from the television to the audience. To the suited, jeweled businesspeople looking up at the screen. Every one of them—the pale blondes and brunettes and redheads—is transfixed. And they are terrified. More terrified, Ignacio realizes, than even he is. More terrified than he could ever be. And this heartens him tremendously.

*Chapter 10*

## DANCER AND THE GREEN DRESS

Even though he was exhausted, Benicio slept poorly. He woke intermittently to kick off his travel clothes, drink all the bottled juice in his minibar, and have a long pee. He had the dream again—the one about snow falling in the jungle—but this time it was different. His father was there, standing on a path beneath a forest of palms, watching as the flakes floated down through the frond canopy. Snow covered the way forward and it covered the way back. His father took up a handful and it scattered from his grip like down in the wind. But the wind was just the air-conditioning. Benicio was in his room, awake, facing a picture window set before his bed like a hospital television. The sun was just above the horizon, burning.

He lingered under the warm blankets for a moment, getting his bearings. It was Friday morning, just after dawn. His suite, filled as it was with orange light, was beautiful. In fact, it was beyond expectation. The front door opened up to a carpeted sitting area that was larger than his living room back home, and unapologetically decadent. Long red couches and armchairs were arranged around a crystal-topped coffee table, upon which sat a varnished wooden bowl brimming with fruits that—aside from a banana and a Fuji apple as big as a grapefruit— he couldn't identify. Atop the fruits sat a single white and burgundy orchid, cut high and jagged at the stem but still looking fresh and alive. The orchid was one of perhaps fifty placed about the room with no apparent thought to diluting the effect—they sat in a soap dish by the sink, sprouted from a delicately arranged pot of smooth stones and moss on his bedside stand and filled two vases flanking the front door. All were bright and odorless. All nodded at him gently on the conditioned breeze.

The first thing he did was set his laptop on the crystal table. He logged on to the hotel WiFi and sent an e-mail to Alice letting her know that he'd gotten in fine, leaving out how his father had flaked and not shown at the airport. He figured it was too early to knock on the adjoining door to Howard's suite, so he switched on the TV and scanned channels. He flipped past news in Arabic and Chinese, past two Koreans fighting with brooms before a live audience, past Englishmen arguing about Iraq before finally stopping at a soap opera in Tagalog. He left the program on as he showered, brushed his teeth and dressed. He'd never heard the language before, but there was something familiar about it—sounds and phrases that could have escaped his mother's mouth. These were bisected by the occasional English word: a hard *Tuesday*, or a lilting *Bas-ket-ball*.

It was still barely light out by the time he'd dressed. In fact, it seemed darker. Benicio stared out the large window, watching the sun. It wasn't rising from the distant bay, but sinking into it. He checked his bedside clock and saw a tiny *pm* beside the time. Whether because of exhaustion or jetlag, he'd gone and slept through his whole first day in the Philippines. And if that wasn't annoying enough, there hadn't been so much as a fucking peep out of his father all day. Not a phone call, not a knock on the door, not even a note saying: *Welcome. Glad you're here. Thanks for coming.*

Benicio banged on his father's door, hard. There was no answer. He tried the handle, and found it unlocked. "Dad," he called as he pushed the door open. Still no answer. "Howard," he called louder, adding three hard raps on the now fully open door. Nothing. The curtains were drawn and Howard's suite was dark. A faint acrid smell hung in the air, and as Benicio's eyes adjusted he saw that the bed was made, and empty. "That's fine," he said out loud. "If that's how you want it, fine."

Benicio shut the adjoining door. Then he opened it again. That acrid smell troubled him. He took a step into the suite and found that it wasn't so faint at all. It was an unmistakable stink, like unclean dive gear that's been left to sit in the sun. He walked further into the room and experienced one of those morbid fantasies that has a whole life-cycle in three or four seconds—his father was dead, he was in here rotting, Benicio was about to discover the body, he'd have to bury it, he wouldn't have any parents, everybody would feel sorry for him. Get ahold of yourself, what an awful thing to think, who the hell cares if anybody is sorry for you, anyway? And besides, this is silly. A body would smell worse than this.

He groped along the dark wall and found a light switch. He flipped it on and stood there for a moment, shocked. His father's suite made his own gilded room look like the servant's quarters. It was the size of a large apartment, complete with a living room, bedroom, study, kitchenette and a tremendous balcony. The rooms were immaculately clean, save a round table in the study that the maids seemed to have gone to pains to avoid. It was strewn with papers that they must have assumed—perhaps correctly—were important. Benicio leafed through them, overturning some tented documents to reveal the source of the stink: a takeout tray of half eaten sushi that was yellow-green and festering. Once uncovered, the fish stank twice over. He had to hold the tray far away from his averted face as he dumped its contents into the toilet.

Even with the fish flushed, the suite still smelled like rot. Benicio opened the front door and jammed the deadbolt through the frame to keep it from snapping shut again. Then he opened the balcony doors, hoping that some cross breeze would help clean out the smell. There were two little chairs on the balcony and Benicio sat in one of them to wait while the air changed. A tumbler half filled with rainwater sat at the base of a chair leg and he picked it up. He imagined his father drinking from it—imagined him sitting in this same chair, looking out at the same view. He swirled the rainwater around in the tumbler and then poured it over the railing. The water fell, breaking into a thousand droplets that seemed to catch in the air, and float.

Where was his father, anyway? Benicio went back inside and listened to his messages. The first was from Hon, Howard's partner. It started cordially but dissolved into: "Howie, you fucking asshole. I can't believe you're going to pull this shit on me again." Other messages, all from people Benicio didn't know, had a similar tenor—angry but unsurprised. Howard had clearly let them down before. In a way, that was reassuring.

He let the messages play as he poked around the suite. Damn, it was big—how much must his father be paying? It had a walk-in closet for God's sake. Benicio stood in the closet, fingering expensive-looking suit jackets on wooden hangers. Shoeboxes lined the walls, as well as some packages wrapped in brown shipping paper with customs forms pasted on them. They seemed familiar, and when Benicio knelt down for a closer look he realized, with a kind of chill, that they were all the packages Howard had sent him in the years before his mother died. Packages he'd returned without opening. Atop each was an unsealed, unaddressed envelope containing a letter. Benicio read some of them. They were to him. Each letter started out the same. *Dear Benny, When I got this package back in the mail, it made me feel* . . . some variation of bad/sad/unhappy. But despite purporting to be about feelings, the letters were all formal and obligatory, probably the product of some exercise Howard's therapist had prescribed. Only the last one actually sounded like him. *Dear Benny*, it read, *Quit being an asshole. Grow up.*

Benicio didn't regret sending them back, but it was hard not to feel guilty when he saw them piled up like that, all at once. He began to wonder if the events of the last few days—not hearing from his father before leaving, not being met at the airport, not even being contacted on his first day here—were some kind of revenge on Howard's part.

Maybe he was finally getting even for all that silence. Could he really
be that petty? Yes, Benicio thought. Probably.

The messages were still playing when he returned to the bedroom,
and he shut the machine off. He closed the balcony and turned to the
front door, where he was startled to see a head peeking inside. It was an
older Filipino, his hair slick as a Broadway greaser's, his cheeks rouged.
"Hello," he said in a warm, high voice. He checked the number on the
door and looked back at Benicio. "Am I at the right room?" he asked.

Benicio stared at him. "That depends. Who are you looking for?"

"Howard. Is he here?"

"This is his room, but he's not here."

"He's not?" the man repeated, sounding overly surprised and sad,
as though Howard's not being here was a moderate crisis. He pushed
the door all the way open and stepped into the room. He was dressed
in a formal, long-sleeved barong, and smelled strongly of sherry. "But
he promised," he said. "He promised to celebrate with me tonight."

"Howard promises a lot of things," Benicio said. Then, feeling like
he was pushing the sullen thing a little far, he added: "Is there anything
you want me to tell him?"

"No, I don't think so," the older man said, glum now. He walked into
the room and sat in the armchair beside the bed. This made Benicio a
little uncomfortable. "I guess he'll call me when he gets back. Are you
going to tell me where he is?"

"I don't know where he is," Benicio said.

"Come on," the man waved at the air as though shooing flies, "don't
give me that." He crossed one leg over the other and pressed himself
into the chair. "You're new, aren't you? I know he told you not to give
out his number, but we're buddies, he and I. You won't get into trouble,
I promise." He paused to stare ingratiatingly, his eyes foggy.

"I don't work for him. I'm his son."

The man kept staring. After a few seconds' delay his countenance
changed and he shot to his feet. "Fuck me, how did I not see that?
You've got his, you know, his face." He gestured vaguely at his own face.
"I'm glad to meet you. It's Benny, right?"

"Benicio," he said. They shook hands.

"I'm Charlie. Your dad talks about you every chance he gets. It's really, really great you came." He sounded surprisingly sincere. "If I'd have known you were here already I'd have sent a bottle up. Say, did you get in early or something?"

"No. I got in when we'd planned."

There was another pause. Then Charlie smiled and clapped Benicio's shoulder, hard. "Hey, don't sweat it. He's pulled that number on all of us. Sometimes a man just needs to check out. In the meantime, why don't you come down with me? Like I said, I've got this celebration going tonight, and a bunch of your dad's buddies will be out." Benicio started to decline, but Charlie spoke over him. "Don't even try it. You can't pretend you have other plans. And besides, you're family to a man I consider family, which makes us closer than you think we are." Charlie kept smiling as he said this. He was somewhat creepy, and old, and drunk, but his warmth was undeniable and oddly genuine. And he was apparently a part of Howard's life here, which made him innately fascinating.

"If you're sure you don't mind," Benicio said.

"That's the spirit." Charlie threw an arm over his shoulder and began to lead him out of the suite. "Just give me an hour," he said. "If it's no fun after that, you can do your own thing. You won't hurt my feelings. I promise."

TOGETHER THEY TOOK THE ELEVATOR down to the mezzanine, which was busier than it had been the night before. As soon as Benicio emerged he felt conspicuous and underdressed. Guests lined the railings overlooking the grand lobby, drinking from snifters and flutes. Most of them were Filipino—men in formal white and ivory barongs, like Charlie, and women wearing dramatically shoulder-padded evening gowns—but there were also plenty of foreigners in the mix. From what he could catch of their conversations, nearly everybody spoke English. Charlie walked quickly through the throng, exchanging a few hellos, and turned at a large set of doors opening onto what seemed like an echo chamber filled with live music. A cloth banner hanging above the doors read: *The Shangri-La Presents: Summer Ballroom Nights.* Benicio followed Charlie inside.

Like everything else, the ballroom was enormous. In the middle was a hardwood floor where tipsy men and women hopped, shouted and spun. Ladies with eyeshadow invading their foreheads tore at the uniformed shoulders of young dance instructors while the men who could have been their husbands watched from banquet tables set along the perimeter. Couples on the floor twirled away, their arms tightening like strands of rope before collapsing back into embraces. At the far end of the ballroom was a little stage holding up a piano and a quintet of musicians. They wore nostalgic pinstripes and banded hats. Glasses of brandy sat atop stools beside their instruments and the musicians sipped while playing.

A bar sat against the opposite wall, and Charlie led them toward it. A young Filipino seated alone at the bar saw them coming, and waved. Even from a distance, Benicio noticed the bandages covering about half of his face. He wore a Western-style light gray suit and an elaborate looking brace was affixed to his left knee, atop his trousers. Charlie must have noticed him staring. "Better if you don't ask him about those," he said. "Your father asked him, and he kind of blew up. I think he's still sore about it."

They joined him at the bar, Charlie sitting to his right and Benicio sitting beside Charlie. The young man turned back around on his stool and stared intensely at a muted television mounted above the bar. "You almost missed it," he said, pointing up at the screen with the tip of a lighted cigarette. Benicio looked up and saw that the TV was tuned to the local news. A grave anchor spoke from behind a composite wood desk while some numbers and crude graphics scrolled in the background.

"That garbage bores me," Charlie said, waving him off. "Hey, look what I found!" He smacked Benicio's upper back, winding him a little. "Can you guess who this is?" He leaned back on the stool, to give his friend a view.

The young man looked at Benicio, and Benicio looked at the young man. The right side of his face was a patchwork of white and ivory. Gauze and medical tape covered part of his forehead, his jaw and most of his cheek, leaving a hole that was too small for his bloodshot right eye. The dressings looked fresh and clean, but the skin beneath was purple. The left side of his face, the one farthest from Benicio, was unblemished and handsome. He seemed a very odd friend for his father to have.

"I've got it," the young man said. "He's a foreigner. It's his first time here. He's come to go scuba diving."

"Quit teasing," Charlie said.

"Actually, he's right," Benicio said, a little intrigued, if not charmed.

The young man winked, or seemed to—it was hard to tell through his bandages—and tapped two fingers on his forehead. "You see that?" he said. "Powers."

"Yes, fine," Charlie said, "but in addition to those things, he's also Howie's kid."

"Is he now?" The young man leaned toward Benicio, as though to inspect him. "I'll be damned. You look just like your pictures. Older, though. Is it Benny?"

"Benicio," Charlie said. "He prefers Benicio."

"Benicio?" The young man looked amused. "Well, that explains the pretty cappuccino complexion he's got going." He patted down his shirtfront and produced a clip of business cards on rigid ivory stock. He carefully removed one and handed it over. Beneath a golden filigree it read: *Robert Danilo Cerrano, Atty and Political Consultant.* Under that was a second name. *Bobby Dancer.* "I prefer Bobby," he said. "So, your dad talks about you all the time. Why are we only meeting you now?"

"Because we don't have much of a relationship," Benicio said. His frankness put them both on their heels and, to soften it, he added: "Not for a while, anyway. We're working back up to it."

"Well, that's good," Charlie said in his oddly high voice. "That's good."

They were all quiet for a moment. Charlie motioned to the bar-

tender and ordered something in Tagalog. The bartender set three tumblers before them, added ice to each tumbler and poured in a measure
of fuming blue liquid. The drinks looked like Windex on the rocks.

Charlie didn't touch his. Neither did Bobby. Benicio followed their
lead.

"Have you seen Renny yet?" Charlie asked, looking back at the
crowd of dancers like a fidgety kid. "He said he might be here tonight."

"Saw him on the floor with some blondie about an hour ago," Bobby
said. "I don't know where he is now."

"Damn." Charlie picked his glass up and set it down again. "I'm
going to go find him. It's not a celebration without Renny there, right?"
He got off his stool and looked back at Benicio. "And don't you disappear anywhere, either. Don't get shy on us. You're Howie's kid, after all.
Shyness isn't in your blood! Anyway, I'll be back before the ice melts,
with Renny, and then we'll really get this started."

With that he disappeared into the crowd, leaving an open stool
between them. Bobby turned back up to the television, ignoring the
dancers jittering and jumping behind them, singularly focused on the
quiet little screen. The numbers kept scrolling along, and he put a hand
on his forehead. Smoke trickled up between his fingers, through his
spiked hair. He brought his cigarette back to his lips and blew a long
plume up at the TV. Then, whatever he must have been waiting for
happened. The shot switched to a cartoon map of the Philippines, and
one of the islands changed color. Bobby struck the bar top, hard, and
mumbled: "Son of a fuck." It was a happy exclamation.

"Good news?" Benicio asked.

"It's looking that way," Bobby said. He put his cigarette out, lit a
new one and turned back to Benicio. "Hey, I'm sorry about this," he said.
"Charlie hates to be alone. He can get a little pushy. Don't feel like you
need to stay."

He'd already considered excusing himself, but his curiosity was
piqued. He couldn't, for the life of him, picture his father sharing a
drink or even a conversation with this guy. "I'd like to stay," he said.

"Well, I'm glad." Bobby smiled, making his bandages pucker and pinch. "You'll be glad, too. We're fun." He picked up his glass and held it out, as though to make a toast. "Mabuhay," he said. "You saw that sign at the airport? Mabuhay means welcome."

Benicio lifted his own glass, eyeing the liquid a little suspiciously.

"Oh, it's terrible," Bobby assured him, but he said it as though terrible wasn't so terrible. "Lambanog. Coconut moonshine, flavored with bubblegum. Don't smile at me like that. You think I'm joking?"

Bobby clinked his glass and sipped. Benicio tasted the lambanog and found it so overwhelmingly foul and sweet that he couldn't help but make a face. But Bobby was right. It was kind of fun, how bad it was.

"So how did you know I was a scuba diver?" he asked as he set his glass down and pushed it away, slightly.

"That was simple," Bobby said, spreading his palms in a way that seemed to indicate he was going to start showing off. "There's only so many reasons people like you, foreigners I mean, come to the Philippines. You're not wide-eyed enough to be Peace Corps. You could be a Habitater, I suppose, but your hair doesn't shout *cause* to me. You're in good enough shape, but the granola backpack crowd doesn't wear khaki. Neither do young businessmen, who should, no offense, be trying a bit harder to impress. Mormons wear plenty of khaki, but they also wear black ties, bicycle helmets and fuck-face haircuts. You're not horrible looking, so I guess you don't have trouble getting laid . . . do you?" He paused, clearly expecting an answer.

"No trouble," Benicio said, restraining a half smile. While Bobby spoke he couldn't help but imagine the circumstances of his accident. He'd probably crashed a jet ski or something frivolous like that.

"That's good," Bobby said, "you'll live longer." He extinguished his cigarette and lit a new one. "So, if it wasn't sportsmanship, liberal guilt, romantic self-discovery, missionary work or the missionary position that brought you here, then I thought it had to be diving. I'm a diver, too. Or at least . . ." he flicked his knee brace with a fingernail and it made a pinging sound, "I used to be. You've come to a good place for it. A good—"

Just then something happened on the television that made
Bobby quit his speech. The shot changed and his head whipped back
up at it. "Ay nako," he said, "fuck, where's the sound?" He grabbed a
rubber-tipped cane that had been propped against his stool and used it
to stab at the volume button. The newscaster's voice grew and people
along the bar who'd been tapping their fingers to the music turned to
give them dirty looks. The screen went blue and then a single number
came up, followed by the headshot of a man in his early sixties. It was
a picture of Charlie, so doctored that it looked like an artist's rendition.
Bobby let out something between a laugh and a yelp. He struck the bar
hard with his fist, flipping his ashtray and sending butts flying. "Shit,
sorry," he said, shoulders dipping like scolded kid. He picked up a napkin and started wiping at the mess until the bartender came over and
cleaned it with two strokes. He gave Bobby a fresh ashtray and put the
television back on mute.

"What's Charlie doing on TV?" Benicio asked.

"You don't know? Oh, well, I guess . . . yeah, the whole not-talking
thing. Well, Ben, you've landed right at the climax of our election
season. Votes were cast on Monday, and they've been counting all week
since. First results are coming in tonight. Looks like good old Charlie
Fuentes has been elected to his first term in the Philippine Senate."

Benicio was lost for words. He looked back out at the dance floor
where he saw Charlie, the new senator, his father's buddy, glad-handing
the crowd. "That's what he's celebrating tonight?"

"Just tonight if I'm lucky," Bobby said. "But he's probably going to
want to party all week."

"But, he didn't even know if he'd won."

Bobby waved him off. "How big he'd win was the only real question, and the news there looks good. Those jerks in Malacañang will be
sweating in their sheets tonight. Malacañang—that's like our version of
the White House. Similar to your White House, it's full of jerks." Bobby
chuckled.

"But . . . Charlie didn't even want to watch this. How could he have
been so sure?"

"He was sure because I told him to be sure. And I was sure because I managed his campaign, and I'm good at what I do, and I saw it coming."

"Oh," Benicio paused. Now he was the one back on his heels. "Wow."

"Thanks, but there's not so much *wow* about it. It wasn't as big as an American campaign, but we do our best, God bless us." Bobby lit another cigarette and smoked it the way people in movies smoke cigarettes in bed after sex—languidly and happily. "Charlie has some money. A lot of money. So that helps. And he's a movie star. That helps even more. I mean, with his filmography, winning was pretty much a foregone conclusion. The voters know his name. They come out for all the speeches and parades. His movies are big with the jeepney set—all bang-bang and save the girl. Or girls. Or orphans. And this one time, an endangered eagle. He always plays a poor cop who doesn't take prisoners. The Ocampo Justice series. Heard of them? Just think of Schwarzenegger or Reagan, but with less experience. And I'll tell you, they eat it up. Charlie comes on stage, and they're playing his theme music, and he has this replica six-shooter holstered to his belt . . . it's a show! He's not your average baby kisser."

It was hard not to get caught up in Bobby's energy, and though he'd hardly touched his lambanog, Benicio felt a little tipsy. He felt as though his life—or at least his night—had become as opulent as the ballroom itself; filled with light and crystal and music and melodrama. It was exciting.

"I'm going to text him the good news," Bobby said, removing a cell phone from his jacket pocket. "You should know that he'll probably want to go someplace more booze-oriented than this. You can still bail out if you need to."

"No," Benicio said, "I'd love to come along."

THEY FINISHED THEIR LAMBANOGS while they waited for Charlie to finish schmoozing. Benicio got cozy on his stool and watched as a song ended, giving dancing guests an opportunity to sit and the sitting guests an opportunity to get up and dance. The instructors all stayed standing. As a new song began a woman in the crowd caught his attention and held it. A Filipina in a green dress stood near the edge of the dance floor, tapping lightly on shoulders as she tried to get by. She had black hair and skin a shade darker than most other women in the room. Her dress shimmered a bit as she turned, clinging loosely to her body and to the full swell of her small breasts. He watched her as she went, taken. Not just taken—turned on. She was heading for the bar.

The woman slid into the open space between him and Bobby. She leaned across the bar, trying to get the bartender's attention. The back of her dress was open and Benicio watched her muscles and shoulder blades move beneath the surface of her skin. Green fabric hung low around her hips—so low that he guessed she must be using some kind of tape to make sure the top of her ass stayed hidden—and then met again in a metal clasp at the back of her neck. The bartender came down to their end and her dress moved as she leaned farther forward to order a gin. He asked for her key and she patted down the sides of the dress, as though there were pockets there, and told him a room number.

"I'm sorry, I can't charge to a room without a key. You have cash?"

The woman snapped at him in Tagalog and to Benicio's surprise the bartender, who'd been so patient with Bobby, snapped right back at her. She sighed with theatrical exasperation and looked as though she were about to storm off. It could have been the lambanog, or the bright, buzzing feeling that his father's friends had given him, but Benicio felt something misguided rising inside him. He reached into his pocket, took hold of his key card, and paid for her drink. "She strikes again," Bobby said, with surprising humorlessness.

The woman in the green dress didn't look at either of them—she just watched as ice tumbled into her glass. When the bartender handed over the gin, she turned to Benicio.

"Thanks," she said a little flatly. "I didn't mean to interrupt you." He couldn't tell if she was slurring, or if it was just her English.

"Then you shouldn't have," Bobby said. He avoided looking at her with the kind of practiced disdain that older siblings have for younger ones. They must have known each other.

Benicio, for his part, did not avoid looking at her. She stood so close that her breath cooled his cheeks. Her face had an odd, beautiful economy to it. Her lips, painted chrome red and slightly pursed, the rouge on her cheeks, her plucked eyebrows, the single strand of black hair tumbling down and dividing her expression into unequal halves; they were all collected with a loose precision. Every part of her seemed to fit together like shaved bits of colored glass with no spaces in between and no overlap. She was stunning.

"Who is your friend, and why is he looking at me like this?" she asked. "Do I know him?"

"Don't you have somewhere to be?" Bobby asked.

"I'm busy for the next . . ." she held her naked wrist up to her face for a while and stared at it. "I'll be done soon. Will you still be here, new friend?"

"No," Benicio said, gripping his empty glass like an actor grips a prop. "I won't."

She shrugged, took her gin in hand and made her way back through the crowd. It wasn't an effortless or graceful exit. She took her time, sidestepping the jostling shoulders, trying her best not to spill the gin. Benicio couldn't look away. He saw her sit at a far banquet table next to an older white man who wore a dark turtleneck against the air-conditioning. He leaned in when she arrived, took the gin from her, and gave her a kiss on the cheek that wasn't fatherly. He was drunk, but not sloppy drunk.

"What's your budget?" Bobby asked.

"What do you mean?"

"Well, money can't buy you love, but it can buy you loving. She's not the most expensive, but she won't be cheap. At least not in this economy. You're interested?"

Benicio looked back at him. "I couldn't be less," he said.

BUT THAT WAS A LIE. As Charlie returned to announce, very sadly, that Renny would not be joining them, as he led them out of the hotel, as they caught a taxi in the hot, dark night, Benicio kept thinking of the woman in the green dress. He felt foolish about the drink thing, but not so foolish that he wasn't still, twenty minutes after the fact, deeply turned on. She reminded him, vividly, of the first woman he'd ever loved. Or at least, the first woman he ever consistently fantasized about—his Costa Rican dive instructor. He remembered watching her pull her wetsuit off under the rush of an outdoor showerhead more clearly than he remembered any of the dives themselves. She was from the Gulf of Papagayo and taught the introductory courses at one of the resorts his father helped manage. At fifteen he'd been just old enough to get an adult certification, and for the next three years fantasies about fucking his instructor in the tank room beside the deep but narrow training pool became an important part of every orgasm he had—including those he arrived at with a high school girlfriend whom he no longer spoke to. The instructor was, in retrospect, not amazing looking—certainly nothing close to the woman in the green dress. She was taller than Benicio by a few inches, she had a broad back, a mannish jaw and thick thighs. She seemed perpetually short of breath and her bust heaved even when she was relaxed. But in her one-piece bathing suit and cutoff denim shorts she was, to teenage Benicio, beyond desirable.

His father noticed him staring during their first classroom session and said: "I don't blame you. She's a hottie. You should stay after. Chat her up or something."

"I can't talk to her," he'd said, shocked. Because she was, after all, an adult. And he was a kid. And she was Costa Rican. And he was pretend Costa Rican. They were hardly the same species.

"You can do whatever you want," his father said. "I tell you what, before our next class I'll put a good word in for you."

And he did.

*Chapter 11*

## EFREM'S CURSE

Efrem Khalid Bakkar remembers it all. He remembers drifting. An unpainted badjao boat. Running aground on the island that would become home. It was a bad tide, overhigh, stranding parrotfish and jellies on the doorsteps of thatched huts. The waves carried his boat up past the tree line and left it near the center of the village; a new house sprung up overnight. Efrem remembers noontime, villagers returning from their dry cliffs to account for washed-out gardens and drowned hens. From his hiding place he watched them circle the boat, listened to them wonder aloud how long the dead aboard had been that way. The old woman who would be his mother was first to climb in. "No rice or fish," she said, "maybe they starved." A still older man, he would be Uncle, shook his head and fingered little round holes in the knotted decking.

"Not starvation," he said. "Army."

Everybody nodded. Their village lay some miles due north of Tubigan, itself north of Jolo in the Sulu Archipelago. The short year since martial law had brought gunboats to this place, wakes crisscrossing like chicken wire on the strait. Manileño soldiers inspected cargo and crew. Nervous at the prospect of actually discovering Moro fighters, they were known to shoot out of panic.

Nothing to be done.

The villagers uncircled and saw to their houses, mending pressed bamboo with palm twine. It wasn't until dusk, when they pulled the dead badjao from their boat so as to better salvage the wood and nails, that they discovered Efrem under burlap in the stern. He screamed and so did they. The old woman, new mother, jumped aboard and took him up. She laid him on a cot above her still-wet floor and fed him starfish.

Talk of curses started that night, before moonrise. The villagers didn't know he spoke their language and mingled just beyond the walls of his new mother's home. Boy from a deadboat was no good luck, they agreed. Lying there for weeks while the sun turned his people into leather, eating God-knows-what. *No good luck at all.* His new mother and uncle talked it over while he feigned sleep, and they agreed with the frightened neighbors. Efrem—the intended name of a neverborn that his adoptive mother carried for eight or nine months as many years ago, a hand-me-down name that replaced his old but not forgotten one—was cursed.

Days later, when he grew stronger and chased after children old enough to be playmates, they said the same thing. They called him deadluck and threw razor-clams at him, defending their tidepool kingdom. "Your new mother's so old she's burned up down there," they jeered. "And your uncle's the worst fisherman in three provinces. Risking us all because they've got nothing to lose." Efrem answered with shells of his own, sending even the oldest boys home with bleeding heads. His mother promised theirs that Efrem would be beat for it. But she didn't have the heart, and his uncle didn't dare.

TODAY EFREM SITS IN A JEEP as it makes slow progress from the Fuentes family plantation to Davao City. It is thirty-one years since he ran aground north of Tubigan to be adopted by the old, childless woman. In that time the dictator has been exiled, has died, and has had his family's request that he be buried in the heroes' cemetery declined. The war in the south is mostly on hold and Western Mindanao has autonomy. Though no longer master soldier-killer among rebels, nor master rebel-killer among soldiers, Efrem is still cursed. He's felt alone in this until today. But Reynato, steering with one hand and sucking his unlit cigar, explains that they're all freaks—all *bruhos*. Every member of Task Force Ka-Pow has some kind of magic.

"This motherfucker is the worst," Reynato says, jabbing a thumb at shirtless, rainwater dappled Elvis. "His trick'll make you shit, when you see it. He's a mountain boy of Baguio, the real outdoorsy kind with not a little Ifugao in his blood. He's loyal as a dog, and smart as one too. Probably because he *is* a dog. Turns himself into one just like you or I might snap our fingers." Reynato snaps his fingers to demonstrate how quick it is, and easy. "It's a deep act. Elvis can do almost anything you like providing he's seen one before. A bird. A centipede. Took him to the Manila zoo month before last just so he could learn giraffe and emu." Reynato twists around and seems annoyed by the dumb, blank way Efrem stares at him. "Come on Elvis, show Mohammed I'm no liar. Shock us with exotic."

Elvis smiles. His orderly white teeth part to reveal the healthy pink insides of his mouth. A long and pointed tongue emerges and goes rigid in what looks like a taunt. A bulge appears in Elvis's throat and it moves up like backward gulping. A spider, big as a mango seed, climbs out of Elvis's mouth and marches down his whitening tongue. Reaching the end, it dangles from the tip by a thread of spit-dripping silk, lowering itself down to where Elvis's lap should be but isn't, because there is no Elvis, just a spider, big as a mango seed, sitting alone on the vast empty rear passenger seat.

If the men in the jeep appreciate the trick, they don't let on. Lorenzo crosses his arms over his chest and puffs air out of his cheeks, mustache aflutter. Reynato, hardly watching the road, moves right along with the magical introductions. He grabs the gnarled forearm of the scar-covered man in the front seat. "Racha's act isn't so fancy, but it's just as useful. This poor son of a bitch has the *worst* luck in the world, and the very *best* luck in the world, all at once. He's our one and only shit magnet, and believe me, before too long you'll learn to love him the way I do. As members of Ka-Pow we get some doom thrown our way. I promise you right now that one of us will get hurt. Lucky for us, that person is always Racha. He's been shot more times than I've been laid—burned up, sliced, dragged on a rope behind horses and Toyotas. So much that he doesn't have an inch of baby-skin left—even his belly looks like ballsack. Racha will protect you whether he likes it or not, all the badness meant for you will land on him. And, worst of all, he always lives through it."

His eyes on Efrem as they are, Reynato doesn't see the knee-deep pothole ahead. They take it hard and Racha, unbelted, pitches face-first into the windshield. A trickle of purple blood unfolds, rolling thick down the bridge of his nose. He checks himself in the side mirror and wipes the blood off in a business-as-usual sort of way.

"What about me?" Lorenzo is reticent in the backseat, arms still tight across his chest, good ear cheated toward Reynato.

"Saving least for last," Reynato says, his smile not bereft of affection, but not full of it either. "If you've ever seen the act of a cheese-ass stage-magician, you've already got a fair idea of Lorenzo's sorry talents. He's a treasure at parties. I'm talking the full package—balloons in animal shapes, white rabbits, sawing a full-grown woman in half and putting her back together again. He can untie tricky knots, make fizzy water come out of flowers and even pluck coins out of a birthday-boy's ear. I know it sounds impossible, and call me a liar if you must, but it's God's honest truth. The man's an asset, I tell you."

Lorenzo assumes a shocked, offended, put out expression. "Ha ha ha," he says. "You don't *ever* tell it right." Turning to Efrem: "I'll show you myself." He uncrosses his arms and makes a show of demonstrating, with pinched fingers, that there's nothing up his nonexistent sleeves. Then he reaches into the folds of his transparent rain poncho and produces a tattered deck of cards. "Pick one," he says, fanning the deck.

Efrem picks a card. The designs on the back are floral; intricate blue and white, like the inlay accompanying Arabic verse in the mosque his uncle used to take him to. The card is a king of hearts. Lorenzo snatches it and returns it to the deck. He shuffles in a vigorous, complicated way that makes the cards travel up and down his forearm, then along his shoulders and finally back into his left hand. He removes his straw cap, dumps the cards inside, shakes them about and plucks one out. Efrem stares blankly at the king of hearts.

Reynato laughs from the driver's seat. "What did I tell you? Damn near indispensable. Can you imagine this boy in a gunfight?"

His chuckling cuts short when a bird strikes the base of the windshield, slides up its length and topples dead into the open-backed jeep. Lorenzo picks up the bird—a warbler just passing through—and opens its thin beak with his fingernails. He squeezes the bird and a playing card, rolled tight as a cigarette, pops wetly out of its gullet. He hands the card to Efrem, who unrolls it. It's the king of hearts—but now the illustrated king is Efrem's own spitting image, leering up at him like a shadow self.

"Now you're just showing off," Reynato says, sounding proud.

Efrem looks from the card to Lorenzo. "How did you do that?"

"Shit, don't Moros do birthdays? If I say how, it'll ruin—"

"No . . . that's not . . ." Efrem glances up at Racha, still bleeding lightly, at Elvis, who is no longer a spider, and asks the same question he's never been able to answer of himself. "How are you this way?"

"How did we get our magic, you mean?" Lorenzo asks, not relinquishing the spotlight. "That's easy, I got mine from the *people*. From the People Power Revolution. I'm a child of EDSA, born in the last hour before Dictator Marcos left our soil aboard a GI-Joe helio. Mom, a lefty, left my sisters at home for a February march; never mind she was nine months full of me. She stacked sandbags, laid down flat in front of tanks and led seven million with her rendition of "Bayan Ko." I was born to the sound of cheering, the sound of Cardinal Sin on Radio Veritas, the sound confetti makes in your hair." He puts on a contemplative look, sort of sad-happy. "The way I see it, People Power has a special kind of meaning for me. Can't help but think I represent—"

"Don't listen to his bullshit," Reynato interrupts. "He's teasing you, Mohammed. People Power has nothing to do with it. You want the truth?" He pauses to glance back through the rearview. "We are the way we are on account of gamma rays. The ones we all got exposed to in space. Out on the *Balut Thirteen*, first Pinoys to land on the moon. Maybe you saw us up there, with those eyes of yours. Planted flags all over that motherfucker."

The bruhos of Task Force Ka-Pow bray wildly, and they roll on. The road turns to asphalt. Trees thin. They hit light traffic and Reynato switches on a siren to get by.

THAT EVENING THEY ARRIVE at what Reynato calls a safehouse, but it isn't a house at all, it's a suite in the luxurious Secret Valley Hotel in Davao City. Lorenzo and Racha claim beds first, leaving Efrem to drop his bedroll on the floor. Still full from lunch, he follows his new friends downstairs and across the street to a dingy grill operated by a pink, peeling Australian. A thick waitress takes their order and returns Lorenzo's sex-eyes. After they eat, Ka-Pow orchestrates a party that they are the life of. Reynato sings with the house band on stage while Elvis commandeers the drums. Efrem accepts a single mug of warm beer—his first—but stops drinking when he discovers a raw pork cutlet floating near the bottom. He rushes to the bathroom with a finger down his throat. Lorenzo blames the bartender for the prank, so Efrem puts the bartender on the floor. The police are called and Reynato talks them down, autographing their billy clubs with a fancy pen that has glitter in the ink. They return to the Secret Valley an hour before dawn, where they're told by sleepy telephone voices that the kitchen is closed, and there will be no room service. Lorenzo, a man of solutions, produces a white rabbit and a brace of Mindanao doves from his straw hat. Racha butchers them in the bathtub, Elvis roasts them over sinkfire, and they all have something to eat come breakfast time.

By midmorning the air is heavy with promise, and the day begins much like Efrem's beloved Ocampo Justice movies. Reynato summons Task Force Ka-Pow to the roof of the hotel where, free from prying eyes and perked ears, he goes over the finer points of their upcoming sting. They've come to Davao City to arrest a pair of bald and toothless shabu dealers—brothers, twins. The two run a low-profile operation, just a handful of corpses to their credit, if you don't count the junkies in unmarked graves throughout the province, mangled from the inside out by the twins' rotgut shabu. They also spread their earnings generously enough that the local police, the barangay sentinels, even would-be rivals have allowed them to operate with impunity.

"This ends today," Reynato says, in an inspiring tone of voice. But no sooner has he spoken than his cell phone hollers madly. Charlie Fuentes requests his presence at a rally by the port, and tomorrow, at a town hall meeting all the way out in Zamboanga. He did *promise*, after all. Reynato hangs up, looking dour. "This ends shortly," he says. Lorenzo and Racha and Elvis cheer. The bender is reinstated.

For days on end Efrem lingers in the plush safehouse while his fellow bruhos, unsupervised by Reynato, stretch long nights of boozing into mornings spent retching up their sins out the open hotel window. They bring home girls, and whores, and new friends who invariably become enemies by dawn and find themselves on the losing ends of elaborate fistfights. Lorenzo orders meals on rolling trays and sends them hurtling downstairs when the food is unsatisfactory or too meager. Elvis watches dirty videos on a VCR annexed from the front desk and twice defended from terrorized bellhops charged with recovering it. Racha, bleary with drink, stares into the bathroom mirror for hours, sometimes shouting in fright and anger, other times exclaiming, "It really isn't *that* bad."

Efrem doesn't participate in this fun—as they describe it. He spends his days seated at the foot of Racha's unmade bed, casting his long gaze out the open window. Though Reynato left him with no explicit orders, he keeps watch on the shabu dealers, emptying bottles of eyedrops into his hardening pupils, hoping to see something that will be of use when the time finally comes to arrest them. Elvis and Racha let him be, avoiding him almost instinctively. But Lorenzo mocks him, drunk or sober. "How did we ever manage a stakeout before we got this magic Muslim?" he asks no one in particular. "You guys remember all those hours with binoculars? Always having to hole up close by to the baddies, usually a shit nest with no air-con? Like the fucking *dark ages*! I bet you know all about the dark ages, don't you, Mohammed? Growing up in some Basilan backwater, and all."

Efrem ignores Lorenzo as best he can, concentrating on the task at hand. He spies on the distant dealers, reporting the domestic minutia of their lives into a little tape recorder. They have a cat that is well cared for. They are loving gardeners. They enjoy sugary drinks. In the afternoons they take naps on either side of a girl bound at the wrists and ankles with synthetic rope.

IT'S A FULL WEEK before the aggravating routine ends. Reynato returns from the campaign trail, appearing in the doorway of their safe-house suite with to-go coffees and a bottle of aspirin. Efrem has already taken up his watchful perch at the foot of the unmade bed, and Reynato looks at him with such pride and approval that Efrem feels as though his full lungs have crystallized. He helps Reynato apply heavy makeup and a fake beard, and then watches as he heads across town to meet the dealers. In a sting one week delayed, Reynato begs the twins to sell him millions of pesos worth of their finest shabu. Efrem presses his back against Racha's bed and shoulders his Tingin, just in case the meeting goes awry. Racha, draped across a stack of dingy pillows, pays Efrem no mind. He whittles foot-calluses with a penknife, collecting the skin in a neat pile on the nightstand. Neither of them speak.

The discussion between Reynato and the dealers gets animated and Efrem wishes, as he often does, that he could read lips. One of the dealers gets up, walks around the table and sits down again. The other does the same. Reynato writes a number onto a little slip of paper and places it on the table. The dealers write another, much higher number. Reynato writes a number in between. They look at it for a long time. Slowly, as though stretching, Reynato puts a hand behind his back. He flashes Efrem, seven kilometers distant, a thumbs-up.

"Something just happened," Efrem says.

"What?" Racha does not look up from his calluses.

"I think Reynato just made a deal."

"Fuck, it's about time!" Lorenzo's voice booms from the bathroom. The door opens and he emerges in a thick cloud of steam, naked save a towel wrapped around his head like a turban. He takes no fewer than three hot showers daily and enjoys letting his naked body drip dry in the cool suite air. "I'm about ready to bust these fuckers, right Mohammed? I mean, a man as good as me can sit on an ass as good as mine for only so long."

Lorenzo saunters over to a table by the open window where the coffees have been left steaming and begins eating the sugar packets and drinking the little plastic cups of creamer. "Be real nice to have the twins wrapped up by lunchtime," he says, flicking each tiny piece of garbage down to the street below, the window a frame for his wet nudity. Spreading his legs and squaring his shoulders, Lorenzo jukes his hips so that his hanging genitals pendulate. They break Efrem's gaze and he loses his view of Reynato and the dealers. "Jesus, Mohammed, quit looking at my balls."

The phone rings. Lorenzo plucks a butt from the ashtray, lights it and sucks burning filter. He glances back at Efrem and despite a look that says: *Reconsider,* he continues. "They tell you about telephones on your island, Mohammed? If you pick it up, you'll hear a man in there. Or, sometimes, a lady. Now *that's* magic."

Efrem stands. The phone lets out a broken gurgle as he pulls it, handset and all, from the wall. One hit to the back of the head cracks the phone and floors Lorenzo. Then two slaps with the receiver across his upturned face make his lips and chin split like the seat of a fat man's pants.

Lorenzo looks even more naked when Efrem whips the coiled towel off his head and drags him across the suite. He tosses him out into the hall, closes the door and slides the deadbolt home. Racha, done filleting his feet, closes his penknife. Efrem can't read his expression through the scar tissue. A lady guest shouts from the hallway and Lorenzo jostles the doorknob frantically. A playing card shoots under the door and slides to Efrem's feet. It's the jack of spades, giving him the finger.

Another telephone rings, this time Racha's cell. "Yes, boss," he says, "I know. Sorry. Your boy . . . Efrem broke it." Racha looks at his watch, which got fused to the skin of his wrist some years back when he was left hogtied in a burning jeepney. "How long? The one by the bus station? All right."

He hangs up.

"All right?" Efrem asks.

"Renny got his deal," he says. "Wants us at the market in an hour. Also says you have to pay for the phone." Racha crosses to the window and leans out. He looks down a few floors to where Elvis has made a nest of twigs and dried palm overlooking the suite of young honeymooners. "I see you there!" he calls. "Yes, you. Come up here."

As soon as Racha makes space at the window a fat black hornbill flies straight in and performs a rough skid landing at the foot of the bed. The bird rights itself and cocks its head, looking around as though remembering past lives. Its feathers stand on end. A modest explosion plasters the walls and carpet with greasy down. Elvis stands at the center of the mess, all basketball shorts and rainwater. Efrem is still unaccustomed to this.

Racha glances at Efrem before unbolting the door. Lorenzo tumbles in with an empty ice bucket over his crotch and an inside-joke smirk on his dripping face.

"Fuck you buddy," he says, "you got me good." Efrem tenses as Lorenzo drops the ice bucket and claps him on the arm. "Won't be so easy next time. I've got eyes in the back of my head." Racha and Elvis chuckle, but Efrem is sure to walk behind Lorenzo on their way to the elevators so he can check.

NOT LONG AGO he would have sneered at a claim like this—seen it for the empty boast it was. But in the short time since joining up with Task Force Ka-Pow his world has gone topsy, and now anything seems possible. He'd always imagined his curse to be unique—kept those bugged-out wandering eyeballs a secret from his few friends among the Boxer Boys. The curse had, after all, rendered him a freak back home, in the village north of Tubigan. Someone to be feared and avoided. And everybody did. Everybody except for the Holy Man.

Like Efrem, the Holy Man was not born on their island. He arrived during a hard dry season, when the whole jungle inland seemed to yellow and shrug. Efrem was eleven and the island had changed in the short years since he'd run ashore on the deadboat. The fishing lanes had filled with trawlers, their synthetic nets brimming. Village fishermen, freedivers with rubber-sling hand spears, paddled their bangkas far beyond the breakers and still came home with too little. Some took up with the trawlers as deckhands. Others worked construction on islands big enough to build things on, or tapped rubber on Basilan plantations. Children on the island saw this rot as proof positive that Efrem was deadluck. But they never said so to his face, and scattered when he approached, arms cradling their heads.

The Holy Man received an equally cool reception—the villagers deciding early on that he was crazy. His hopeless motorboat leaked and he arrived all dressed from head to toe in silly white robes. One of his arms was missing at the elbow, and he wore a thick beard that cascaded down to where his navel probably was. He kept his little round sunglasses on even after sunset and spent his first evening on the island shambling from hut to hut so he could mumble thickly accented greetings to the men, and boys. He pitched a heavy tent on a small strip of level sand below the huts. Suspicious villagers watched him wrangling the poles with his one arm, not bothering to tell him that by midnight he'd have cold tidewater as a blanket.

They warmed to him in the weeks that followed, but not because he acted any less insane. He gave money away. Just like that—a stack of coins or some folded, rotting bills passed to anyone who asked for them. All he demanded in return was that you listen to his ramblings; stories of made-up countries and their made-up wars. He'd raise his nub high into the air and tell the children about how *Communists* shot his arm clean off. Communists were enemies of God and he had fought them among the dusty mountains of his imaginary homeland. God, according to the Holy Man, had a lot of enemies. And so, therefore, did the Holy Man. For God's enemies were his, just as God's friends were his friends. "Of course, you're all God's friends," he said. "And I'm happy about that." Not all of the villagers were won over, and those who were took time. But everyone became attached enough to the crazy stranger that they didn't ask questions when he suddenly broke camp and hid in the bamboo for days. They even lied to the Manileño soldiers that came looking for him, saying they'd seen nothing of a foreign fugitive.

Efrem avoided the Holy Man as he did everyone else. He spent his days atop the seaside cliffs, seated in a favorite little hollow overlooking the cove and huts below. By that time he'd already been to Davao City with his uncle, and from this perch he had an easy view out across the archipelago, beyond faraway Zamboanga City, past the cloud-speckled crater-peak of Mount Apo, out to the very dock in Davao where they'd tied off. His pupils, dilated to near hemorrhage, retraced the back-alley route his cousins once led him on to find the outdoor cinema. On some lucky afternoons he'd discover a new Ocampo movie showing—Charlie Fuentes in the title role, unloading his trusty six-shooter, Truth, into some liar. Efrem would watch as long as he could, struggling not to blink. He didn't want to miss a thing.

But on the hot afternoon that the Holy Man followed him up the cliffs there was no movie showing in Davao City, and so Efrem sat alone, throwing rocks at crabs. He unearthed a small chip of granite, picked out a dusky little target on the beach below and let the granite fly. It arced high, peaked, and fell. It landed square on the crab's back, throwing up a mess of yellow legs and eggs.

"A hit!" Efrem jumped at the voice behind him, a new stone already clenched in his little fist. "You are lucky boy," the Holy Man said, kicking off his sandals and taking a seat beside Efrem on the rotting log. He ran his hand over the hard soil, fingers closing on a jagged bit of quartz. "My turn," he said. "What do I aim for?"

Efrem stared at him. He pointed at a nearby branch.

"You are gaming on me? I mean challenge!" The Holy Man scanned the beach. "There," he said. "Empty oil drum, down by the huts. You think my stone goes inside?" He paused and Efrem did not answer—he was unaccustomed to being spoken to. "You are skeptical? I will reform you!" He stood, pulled his arm back and threw. The stone landed a few meters in front of the drum, skipped across the ground and banged loudly against the base. "Close!" He shot his one fist into the air, a smile parting his beard. "Your turn. In the drum."

Efrem threw his stone and it disappeared clean through the mouth of the drum. The Holy Man slapped his knee over and over like clapping. He handed Efrem another stone and told him to do it again. He cheered the second time, but not the third. Or the fourth.

"How are you doing that?" He sounded almost angry.

Efrem didn't know.

"Can you throw farther?"

Efrem didn't know.

The Holy Man stood and walked about. He found another stone, handed it to Efrem and pointed to a coconut at the far end of the beach. Efrem threw and it shattered wetly into shards of husk. The Holy Man pointed back into the woods where a spotted gecko nodded its head on a tree trunk. Efrem threw. The gecko was a smear of blood on pale bark. The Holy Man sat down and stood up again. He didn't say anything for a long time. Finally he handed Efrem one last stone and pointed at a pair of shearwaters circling above the cove.

"Which one?"

The Holy Man struggled to make words. "Whichever you like."

Efrem considered which bird he should kill. He took his time because he liked the way the Holy Man was staring at him—with admiration. With a father's love. Finally he threw. One of the birds—the darker, the drabber, the one that had not flown as high—stopped flapping as though caught suddenly between an invisible thumb and forefinger. It fell into blue waves. The Holy Man let out something between a laugh and a shout. Tears trickled out from under his dark, round lenses.

"How long have you been this way?" he asked.

Efrem didn't know.

"That's all right," the Holy Man said. "That's fine." He patted the back of Efrem's neck and returned down the cliff. He paused for a moment, on the beach, to poke at the dead crab. Then he walked to Efrem's mother's hut. She was atop the roof, mending thatching and did not seem surprised to see him. They had a short conversation.

AS MUCH AS EFREM GREW to love the Holy Man, he loves Reynato Ocampo more. He rushes to the Davao market and meets the hero of his childhood on the roof of a Christian butcher's shop. Reynato leans against the back of a billboard to stay hidden from the market below, eyeing Efrem bemusedly. "Describe yourself to me," he says. Efrem stares dumbly, sure that he's misheard the question. "Imagine I can't see so well," Reynato says, "and tell me what you look like."

So Efrem describes himself. He's squat, and dark. His chin is narrow, his forehead broad. His black hair is short, but in the week since he's left the Boxer Boys it's grown past regulation. Reynato listens thoughtfully and then waves him off, as though everything he's just said is nonsense.

"That's not what you look like at all," he says. "Not to me, anyway. When I look at you I see eyes as big as windows. So big, so clear that I feel like I could step through and walk around inside your head. And you've got this glow, like smoke. You stand out to me," Reynato says. "That's how I picked you out of those army boys."

He pauses to suck his unlit cigar. He adjusts his fake beard and checks his reflection in an oversized pair of aviator sunglasses. "I stand out to me, too," he says, a little sadly. "I don't look anything like my wife describes. I don't see myself the way she does, or the way you do, I'm sure. But that's my gift. I see bruhos like us for what we really are. I see special talents. I've got them, and so have the boys, and so have you. In this way, we're family."

Hearing this, Efrem swells. Families are loved, and needed, and to be loved and needed by Reynato Ocampo brings him to a point past joy. Reynato puffs his cigar smokelessly, and Efrem offers him some matches. Reynato accepts them with nodded thanks and tosses them off the roof.

They are silent. He pockets his cigar and checks his watch. To the south, beyond the skyline, heat-lightning blossoms. "Best leave your safety catch off," Reynato says. He pats Efrem's shoulder warmly. "You remember what to do?"

"Yes sir."

"Enough with the sirs, I'm begging you. Now, if you see anything fishy?"

"I'll call Racha."

"And if anyone tries anything?"

"They get two in the face."

"Or one. No need to show off. Just make them stop whatever they're doing is the point. And remember, I can't stress this enough, you save me first. Got it?" Reynato speaks slowly. "Me first. Others after." He stands, lifts his stained shirt, pulls out his pistol and sets it down next to Efrem. "If anything goes wrong, if anything happens to me out there, I want you to have Glock."

Efrem looks down at it. It isn't Truth from the movies, but it's still Renny-O's one and only piece. He's almost afraid to touch it.

"If anything . . . oh my, this is hard to say. If I die, then I want you to take this to my family in Manila. I want you to stand in our living room. I want you to put it in your mouth and pull the trigger because you fucking let something happen to me." Reynato winks and swings himself over a utility ladder at the back of the building. Just before his head disappears he stops and looks at Efrem. "Me first."

Efrem tucks in his elbows and crawls to the edge of the warm tar roof. He lines up his custom Tingin, the barrel just coming out over the torn green awning of the butcher's shop. It's just like so many mornings of his youth, lying among fallen trees, the Holy Man whispering in his ear, aiming at unwary soldiers wearing the same uniform he'd one day look taller in.

The busy market below is a dense collection of open-air stalls in a wide courtyard, surrounded on all sides by an arcade of permanent shops. The butcher's is on the south end of the arcade and from his vantage on the roof Efrem can take clean shots at everything. He lays still, pupils dilating to accommodate the sea of details. Women spread tarps to shade their vegetables and sell grain from open burlap sacks. They stack boxes of sugary cereal like bricks and swat children away from buckets of hard and soft candy. Music pours from portable radios and clusters of men read newspapers and roll cigarettes. A single voice emerges above the scattered rhythms, mottled with static—a recorded call to prayer. People roll out mats and bring their foreheads to the earth. Others, rosaries dangling under their loose cotton shirts, stay standing.

Reynato paces back and forth near the north end of the courtyard holding a hard briefcase filled with a few big bills and a whole lot of magazine clippings. The dealers are nowhere to be seen and his impatience is no act. Lorenzo wanders between stalls at the east end of the market. He's supposed to be keeping an eye out for trouble but has become distracted at a fruit stand, haggling with an ancient woman over a big stinking durian. They reach a price and he counts out coins, producing them one at a time from his deaf ear. Racha is at a shop window in the northwest corner of the arcade, pretending to browse a collection of pirated DVDs. A big black mangy dog pads back and forth, circling Reynato a few times before turning to look up at Efrem's hiding place. It moves so natural that he wonders if Elvis isn't really a dog pretending to be human instead of the other way around.

They arrive. The bald dealers look like tourists in their lycra pants and Hawaiian shirts, and each pulls a little suitcase packed with shabu. They find Reynato right away and keep their distance as they speak. They eye his briefcase, talking to each other more than to him. Reynato reaches out to take one of the shabu-filled suitcases but they hold tight, pushing his hand away. Efrem scans the rest of the market. Lorenzo munches his durian, dropping chunks of spiky rind into the dirt and watching from a safe distance. Racha is alert as well, already fingering the cherry stock of the snubnosed revolver in his pocket. The mangy dog sits behind the dealers, sniffing their cases and pant legs. They don't seem to notice.

Something isn't right. Just behind Reynato is a fresh fish stall attended to by three young fishmen. Their table is covered with fat tanigue and spotted lapu lapu that shine on a thin bed of melting ice. The fishmen clutch slim fillet knives, but as Efrem watches he realizes that they aren't scraping off scales or chopping away fins or really doing anything. When a woman comes to buy a fish they hand it to her clumsily, gripping the slippery head without hooking fingers into gills. They don't look at Reynato but they don't look anywhere else either. Their expressions are blank, their attention forcedly unspecific. Efrem flips open his phone and dials Racha.

"Go to the stall behind Reynato and buy a fish," he says.

"You're hungry?"

"The vendors aren't vendors."

"You'll pay me back?"

Efrem hangs up and sights his Tingin. Racha moves quickly, both

hands in his pockets. Lorenzo sees him, drops his durian and heads
in the same direction. Racha arrives at the fish stall and gestures with
his nose and chin to what he wants. The young fishmen don't move,
shocked like actors who've forgotten their lines. They turn and see
Lorenzo closing in from the other direction. Efrem takes a breath and
lets it out slow to keep his muzzle steady.

The fishmen move first. One stands and sinks his fillet knife up
to the hilt into Racha's chest. Racha steps back like a drunk, gawking
at the handle sprouting from his ribs. Then he takes the snubnosed
revolver from his pocket and makes a mess of the north slope of first
fishman's face. Second fishman pulls a pistol from a gapemouth grouper and aims it at Reynato. Efrem puts a hole in the back of his head big
enough to hide things in. The sight of dead friends makes third fishman panic. He recovers the scale-speckled pistol from where it fell and
turns on Lorenzo, who approaches jauntily. Third fishman fires. There
is no bang. A festive flag on a miniature pole sprouts from the barrel; a
red *Ka-Pow!* on spotless canary yellow. Third fishman stares at the gun,
confused and betrayed and somehow a little delighted. He tosses the
toy and stabs at Lorenzo's chest with his fillet knife. The blade bends,
floppy as gag-shop rubber. He doesn't even put up a fight when Lorenzo
relieves him of the limp knife. Lorenzo flicks his wrist and the blade
straightens. He sheaths it between third fishman's collarbone and top
rib. He takes it out and puts it in again. He takes it out and puts it in
again. He takes it out. Third fishman lowers himself to his knees, gulping air. Lorenzo puts it in again. Third fishman dies.

The bald dealers, who until this moment have been doppelgang-
ers, have opposite reactions. One drops his suitcase and springs for the
nearest exit while the other stays, fumbling with a gun in his too-tight
lycra pants. Efrem is about to put one through the fumbler's mouth
when Reynato clocks him with his clipping-filled briefcase. Efrem
pivots, hoping to hobble the fleeing dealer, but sees he's already been
tripped up at the heels by the black dog, jaws closing on his chubby
neck. The crowd has been screaming since Racha's first shot, taking
cover under nearby stalls and inside arcade shops, but Efrem only hears
them now.

He hurries down the ladder at the back of the butcher shop, his smoking Tingin still in hand. He rushes to Reynato who, blood-freckled, is trying to calm the hysterical crowd by holding his badge up in the air. "I could kiss you," Reynato says. "Would you like that?"

Efrem doesn't answer, and Reynato plants one on his cheek. He looks down at the unconscious dealer and grins wide. "I'd hoped for more arrests," he says, "but your philosophy suits me fine. Better safe than sorry, especially when it's dear me on the line." He turns to Elvis, who's an upright man again and rubbing blood off his chin. "That's disgusting," he says. Elvis gives a little shrug, and Reynato hands him a plastic zip-tie. "Get that on the live one before he wakes up."

Racha crawls toward them, reaching for Reynato's feet.

"Are you going to be a baby," Reynato asks, "or can you walk to the hospital?"

Racha stands. He falls.

"Baby it is. Help him up, Lorenzo. And find us a taxi."

Elvis and Lorenzo set about their tasks. Efrem, still light-headed from the affection Reynato's shown him, asks how he can help. "You just keep being super," Reynato says, taking his cigar out of his pocket and planting it back between his teeth. He throws his arm around Efrem's shoulder and keeps it there. Sunshine pours down on them, and up in the baby-blue sky they can see a crescent moon. It looks pale, like it always does in the daytime.

*Chapter 12*

## AFTER BILIBID

"Good evening, ma'am," Amartina said as Monique came inside and dropped her purse by the door. A whole year now and still no Tagalog.

"Magandang gabi." Monique stood on one leg to pull off her pumps. She smelled pork in the oven. Fluorescent light spilled out the kitchen into the dark, empty den. A kettle whistled and oil hissed in a saucepan. "I said no need for dinner tonight. I'm not eating."

"It's no problem, ma'am," Amartina said, already returning to the kitchen.

Monique followed her and sat at the breakfast table. Even with Joe and the kids gone a week, Amartina still prepared enough for four. She poured green tea into a coffee mug emblazoned with a bearcat—mascot for Shawn and Leila's new school—and set it, along with a bowl of sugar, on the table. Monique sipped. It had been a long, tough day. Actually, more like a long, tough week—no day stood out as most or least aggravating. It was as though all the crazies, the trusty regulars, had received the memo that Chuck would be out of the country, gotten together and decided to run amok. Monique went on no fewer than four prison visits a day, fishing lambanog-stinking retirees out of various barangay drunk tanks, telephoning strangers in the States to let them know that some unheard-from relative was being held for disorderly conduct, taking meetings with weepy young men in ties who were charged with bribing government officials because they hadn't bribed the right ones. She'd never been so happy to have a weekend. Especially this weekend. She had plans.

"So," Monique looked up from her tea, trying not to appear too eager, "you're still going home tonight?" Amartina usually left the city on Saturday mornings to spend a day and a night with her family in Cavite, but Monique was trying to get her to take full weekends while Joseph and the kids were away.

"You do not need me?" she spoke into a pot of boiled potatoes, mashing them with one hand and drizzling in whole milk with the other.

"I don't. You can go. You should."

"Yes, ma'am." Her wrist tipped a little too far and an extra cup or so of milk tumbled into the potatoes. She frowned and turned the gas burner on to simmer them down and thicken them up.

"Is that yes-yes or yes-no? Because I really don't need you."

Amartina looked up from her pot and said yes ma'am again.

Out in the den the telephone rang, which got Shawn's gecko chirping and Leila's lovebird hollering. Monique looked at her watch and figured that Joseph must have just finished his morning run. He'd been cold before leaving—downright nasty when she brought him and the kids to the airport. But since then his fury was annotated with remorse. She found his apologies difficult to listen to. After all, she'd let him go without a fight and was using these five weeks to enjoy her affair for what it was. Five weeks should be enough to get it out of her system for good.

Monique let the phone ring. The gecko and lovebird went on for a few minutes after it stopped.

"Dinner's ready, ma'am." Amartina turned from the stove, drying her hands on a rag. "You would like to eat now?"

"No, thank you. Just leave it and I'll help myself later." Monique noticed Amartina was staring at her. "It's late. If you go soon you can still catch the cheap bus."

"So sorry, ma'am, but you have something . . ." Amartina reached out and then stopped herself. "Better you take off your jacket, ma'am."

Monique traced Amartina's gaze to the shoulderpad of her double-breasted cobalt jacket. There was something there. Bird shit? No. A glob of translucent phlegm, just inches from her neck and collarbone. It was dry, frozen mid-drip as it had oozed down her top lapel. It must have been there for a while. Monique's muscles tightened as she stood and pulled the jacket off. Her arms were so rigid she half expected to tear the rayon fabric. Amartina helped, coming around behind her, snatching the jacket away.

"I'll wash it now, ma'am." She disappeared though the narrow door to her bedroom, which was also the laundry room.

Monique felt nausea trickle up from her stomach. "No," she called after. "Thank you. No. Just leave it soaking and I'll deal with it tomorrow." She followed Amartina to the laundry/bedroom. "You should be with your family."

"It's no trouble ma'am." She'd already filled a plastic basin with water and suds. She dropped the jacket in the basin.

"Yes it is." Monique took the basin from Amartina and carried it out through the kitchen, past the den, into the master bedroom. "I can clean this," she called back. "You should go home. Go home, please. I'll see you on Sunday night."

SHE WASN'T SURE exactly when it happened, but she could guess. She'd ended her day in a holding room at Bilibid; always the worst prison to visit. An American, not two full days into his visa, had been accused of rape. His name was Doug and he looked at her the way a kid who's screwed-up looks at his mother. He explained that it was a misunderstanding. The girl was his fiancée. Her father had walked in on them having sex and she'd just started screaming. Monique asked Doug if the police or guards had mistreated him and wrote down most of his long answer. She handed over a laminated list of local attorneys and offered to contact his family if he signed a release form. He declined, which was fine with her. She had plenty to do already.

She didn't think it was Doug's phlegm, but plenty other new inmates had hooted and howled when they saw her, many of them red-eyed, still rolling on shabu. A boy with an old man's face came right up against the bars and grabbed at her. Another gurgled "I love you" in English while sitting on the toilet, tugging himself, never mind men napping on adjacent bunks. Monique imagined him flicking a palm-full of semen as she passed. She imagined the boy sucking mucus threads out of his sinuses. She imagined whatever-it-was dripping down her jacket as she rode home. Crusting over. She carted the basin into the master bath, hung her open mouth over the sink and was almost sick.

She laid towels all around the edge of the basin so soapy water wouldn't get on the floor. She rolled up her blouse sleeves, got on her knees and held her jacket down below the surface as though drowning it. Her fingers grazed the phlegm, now loose and slick. She stood, unbuttoned her blouse and added it to the basin. She added her patent belt, her narrow slacks and seamless camisole. Naked, she returned to the entryway and grabbed the purse she'd brought to work that day. She emptied the contents out on her bed before dropping it into the basin as well. She got in the shower. She left the lights off and curtain open.

She soaped, rinsed and soaped again. When she was done she stood there, dripping dry.

The phone rang again and the animals sang accompaniment. Monique walked into the den, leaving a trail of wet footprints behind. Caller ID said it was *him*, but she would have picked up even if it was Joseph. Or the ambassador with some last-minute tasking. Or a wrong number.

"Hey." His voice was coarse, soft, and so familiar. "What are you wearing?"

"Now is not the time."

He normally didn't pick up on tone, but that night he got the picture. "Are you all right? Would you rather skip tonight?"

"No." She paced with the cordless, stepping on her own wet prints. "I haven't seen you in forever. And I got the maid to go home early. I thought when we're done, we could come back here."

"That sounds great . . . but only if you want. We'll do whatever you want."

"We'll come back here, then," she said. She hung up and changed into a burgundy gown that she hadn't worn since the Marine Ball and hastily blow-dried her hair—at the beginning of the week she'd actually thought she'd have time and energy enough to get it done at the Peninsula. She fed crickets to the gecko and grapes to the lovebird. She sat in the den and waited.

He was only a little late, a pleasant surprise. She didn't even answer his buzz at the intercom, she just rushed out to the elevator. Avoiding the lobby with its helpful, perky staff, she turned down the concrete loading ramp to the side exit—the same one she took on weekday mornings to board the armored embassy shuttle. Reynato waited in the gloom outside, one hand on the roof of his beat-up old Honda, another deep in his pants pocket. He wore a summer suit without a tie and had some kind of product combed into his gray-black hair. The air-conditioning in his sedan had been busted for months, and his forehead and cheeks glistened with sweat.

"My love." He kissed her neck, her jaw line, her ear. "My love."

She slid her hands under his suit jacket, along the damp fabric of his button-down shirt. He smelled sweet, and good. He felt soft, and good. She could already feel herself relaxing. "You don't love me."

"I know," Reynato toyed with a lock of her still-damp hair. "But I like you plenty. And I feel like I could love you. With time." He pat-slapped her behind. "I missed the hell out of you."

"I missed you, too." She negotiated her way around the sedan, glancing nervously at the tower of lit and unlit windows above. "How's your friend?"

"My who, now?" He got inside and leaned over to open the front passenger door for her—the outside handle stuck.

"Your friend." She got in and buckled up. "The one in the hospital in Davao."

"Oh him! He's fine. Misdiagnosed. No problem at all." Reynato smiled and had a brief fistfight with the gearshift. "In fact, there are no problems anywhere right now. It's rare. Like an eclipse." He got the sedan into second, pulled out of the parking lot and turned down McKinley Road with a jolt.

They were headed to ballroom night at the Shangri-La. It was sure to be packed with expats and local bureaucrats, likely a few people they each knew, but it was also the only public place they could be seen together without arousing suspicion. After all, they each had their own reasons to go. And it was natural to bump into people at Shangri-La functions. That's how they'd first met—at a cocktail hour on the mezzanine, hosted jointly by the legal attaché and the director of the National Bureau of Investigation. The first impression hadn't been great. Reynato watched Monique from across the room, sucking an unlit cigar that waiters kept trying to take from him. It got obvious. Joseph sulked. Jeff offered to go over and say something. She said no and stared right back at the pudgy, graying stranger. Over the course of the night she watched him drain enough tumblers to put a fat man in the hospital, but by last call he could still walk a straight line. He came right up to her and leaned in, showing off clean metal braces that made his mouth—just his mouth—look young. "Describe yourself," he said.

"Do what?"

"Describe yourself to me. I can't see so well."

Monique answered in Tagalog, hoping to catch him off balance. She said she was five foot five. She said her brown hair was dyed blond and cut shorter than usual this year, that she weighed a hundred and forty pounds, that her dress was black and her measurements were so-and-so. She wasn't a knockout, but she was out of his league. And besides that, she was married. "You want me to describe you, now?" she asked. "It'll be easy."

"No point." He waived a small hand in the air. "You got *you* wrong. That's not what you look like at all." Then came some nonsense about her being the tallest woman in the room and not wearing any shoes. Her feet were part of the floor and went all the way down into it, like tree roots into the ground. She had a glow. An aura. A how-do-you-call-it. He was obviously drunker than he looked. Monique left him where he stood and she and Joe returned home. That night, after sex, he asked what she'd said to him. She answered honestly, and he got mad, called her a flirt, and slept in the den, like an infant.

Reynato telephoned the next morning. Monique asked how he got her number and her name. "I really, really wanted to talk to you," he said. That's all he said.

THERE WAS NO VALET PARKING, but that didn't stop Reynato from leaving his Honda at the security checkpoint and tossing the guards his keys. He braced his foot on the front tire and tugged hard to open Monique's door. They walked up to the hotel, through the tremendous glass doors and into the Shangri-La. The lobby was packed. People in barongs and business suits mingled by the staircases and lined the mezzanine railing with drinks in hand. Two or three of the Filipinos recognized Reynato and pointed him out to others who pointed him out to more others. He waved as they ascended the stairs, stopping once to sign an autograph and again to be photographed with someone's wife. They asked him what he thought Charlie Fuentes's chances were, and he answered that Charlie Fuentes was a great friend and a good man.

Monique started to wonder if coming here wasn't a bad idea—if it wasn't begging to be caught. After all, she was with a man who still sent flowers to her apartment and love notes to her office. If he pulled just one cutesy stunt here, that was it.

Thankfully, Reynato seemed as eager to ditch these people as she was, hurrying them both into the ballroom. He strode right to the floor, ignoring Monique's protest that she'd rather watch first, not even waiting for a new song to begin. She quickly set her arms like she remembered—she and Joe took a three-week course in the lead-up to their wedding—but before she got her feet right Reynato started moving. Using their outstretched arms and clasped hands as a wedge, he cut through the crowd to an open area by the low stage. The steps were familiar enough—Monique stared down, watching her toes trace box corners on the parquet—but everything else felt awkward. She bumped hard into an older woman and got a dirty, mascara-faced glare.

"You're all right," Reynato said, leaning in close, awash in his particular fruity smell, more perfume than cologne. "But you're drifting left."

She glanced up from her feet and they stopped doing what she wanted. Reynato's hand went firm on her back as he moved her out of a passing couple's way. "I was just trying to follow the line of dance."

"Ah," he grinned, almost apologetically. "No such thing here. Manila dancing is like Manila driving. If you see space, take it. If there's no space, make it. Also some of our dances are different. Your hustle is our swing. Your swing is our boogie."

Monique didn't know hustle, swing or boogie. The song ended and when a new one began Reynato came around behind her. He took her hands in his and stepped on the shadows of her feet. "Lindy hop," he whispered, as though lindy hop meant something.

"You're a cheater. You said you didn't dance."

"I said I didn't dance well. I don't. You dance terribly."

"Ha." She let go his hand and discreetly pinched his outer thigh, hard. She focused on the floor below. When he started moving, she did too.

MONIQUE FELT CONSPICUOUS after four dances with the same partner, so she mixed it up. She did a few turns with a tuxedoed Korean and then waltzed with a bespectacled economist from the AmCham who kept saying: "It's all right," even though she didn't exactly know what she was doing wrong. She watched Reynato over the shoulders of her other partners, looking solid and confident and charming. He was still going strong when she called it quits and grabbed a stool at the bar. His latest partner, a skinny-armed girl in a sparkly prom-style dress, seemed very taken with him. Reynato visited Monique between dances to dab his forehead on a cocktail napkin, down one of the two Southern Comforts she'd ordered and announce that the Argentine Tango could kiss his saggy ass. His new partner waited, awkwardly patient in the middle of the floor. She reminded Monique of Leila, which was odd because Leila was younger and not as conventionally beautiful. Still, she imagined Leila in that silly dress, standing alone, just waiting. She pictured Leila with that hopeful, rejected expression. It got so that she couldn't look at the girl anymore.

The next time Reynato came to the bar she said she wanted to go.

"Your wish, my love."

"You don't love me, remember?"

"I do, actually," he said. "Between then and now, I started." He stared at her. He clearly wanted to kiss her. She wanted him to. But thank God he didn't. He just squeezed her hand, and they both made for the exit.

They were almost to the double doors when Charlie Fuentes—she recognized him from billboards splattered above Roxas, from his televised campaign speeches, from the absurd little dance he'd done during the candidate debates—tackled Reynato in an enthused hug. Monique kept walking, her ears and cheeks turning red as a drunk's. Everybody knew Charlie, or knew of him. He was even on the embassy guest list for the July Fourth barbecue.

She walked a safe distance away and listened. "Son of a whore. Look at you, you son of a whore," Charlie quit hugging and began shaking Reynato's hand. "What, you don't answer my calls? You must have heard the good news. It's not a victory party without you!"

"It's not a victory without me." Reynato's irritation seemed lost on his tipsy friend, who beamed warmly. "No parties tonight. I'm on my way out."

"Aww, hell, don't tell me. You're probably going to some super-secret-stakeout, am I right? Look at this man," Charlie paused to lean back and give him an exaggerated eyeballing. "Renny *never* stops working. I guess if I'm a dud as senator then I can at least count on you to generate enough good material for another few Ocampo flicks." Charlie wouldn't let go his hand. People at a nearby banquet table noticed the pair and began snapping photos of them.

"I'll do my best," Reynato said, his expression pained.

"No, but honestly, for real . . ." Charlie leaned in. He must have thought he was lowering his voice, but it remained the same volume and just got huskier. "I couldn't have done this without you. I mean that. One of these days I've got to invite you and Lorna over for—"

"We'll do it. I know. Dinner or something." Reynato pulled his hand free and made for the doors. Charlie followed, chatting him up, causing a stir. Monique rushed to the mezzanine, down the curved stair and out into the hot, sooty evening. Reynato caught up some minutes later, grinning bitterly.

"You should've stayed. I'd have introduced you to the republic's least promising new senator."

"This isn't a joke," she snapped. "We could have gotten caught."

Reynato's wry, oddly cavalier smile slackened. "I know," he said. "I'm sorry. I joke about lots of things that aren't jokes." He came in for a kiss and she pushed him away. "No one can see us here," he protested.

"Not until we get home," she said, the sound of her blood still filling her ears.

He'd never been to her place before. He didn't ask for the tour. They started undressing in the entryway and were naked by the time they got to the master bedroom. Sex was usually a rush deal. They did it in hotel suites, friends' apartments and once in Reynato's office. Now the whole night hung over them.

"Something's wrong," he said, "and it's not whiskey-dick."

"I'm sorry." Monique covered herself with the blanket and he uncovered her. "Can we not do it here? I mean in this room."

"Of course." Reynato hopped out of bed and followed her back into the den. He walked with his gut stuck out, his hands on his lower back, his long skinny penis pointing the way like a ridiculous divining rod. Uncomfortable as she was, Monique had to laugh a little, which is what she knew he wanted. He swung his hips to point at the open door to Shawn's room, where the gecko had begun chirping again, demanding more crickets.

"My son. Too creepy."

He spun again and pointed to Amartina's quarters.

"That's the maid's room."

"Hot. Do you fit into her outfits?"

"No. But they're not sexy, anyway."

"They would be on you." He negotiated her onto the couch facing the television. Monique was afraid of getting sweat—or something worse—on the leather, but she figured things were already awkward enough and went with it. Reynato had lied about the whiskey-dick, and it took him a while to finish. From where she lay, with her head on the armrest, Monique could see right into Shawn's room. The gecko pressed up against the glass, all eyeballs and throat. Somehow seeing the animal thrilled her with remorse so strong it approached grief. That was her son's pet. Never mind he only bought it because he was angry with her—he loved it. And that was his room. And this was the den where he and Leila sat sullenly and argued over television channels. This was the couch that Joseph slept on when he was angry, or desperately tired, or both. And here she was with Reynato, a nice enough guy but also a creep in a lot of ways, humiliating them all in absentia. She was cheating on everybody. And as awful as she felt, she didn't think she could stop.

Then the building moved. Reynato gripped the leather and let out a shout—not the good kind. The terrarium toppled from its stand and crashed to the floor. The door to Shawn's room slammed closed. Books leapt off shelves and Joseph's big eighties-era speakers face-planted like drunks. It wasn't a big earthquake, but they always feel worse in high-rises. For people on the topmost floors it's like being perched atop a palm in a whipping storm. Reynato held on to her tight and shouted, "That's enough. Whatever it is you're doing, stop."

*Chapter 13*

## THE SQUARE WINDOW

Howard wakes to the sound of a rooster crowing. It's dark. Not
night-dark, but blind-person dark. The floor below him is cool, and slick.
He thinks he should try to sit up. He sits up. That was easy, he thinks,
determined to be an optimist about this. I'm not bound, or gagged. I
have strength enough to move. And my sitting-up parts still work. So
far, so good.

Sitting in the dark, Howard takes stock of how badly he's been hurt.
The news here is less good. His fingers are in terrible shape; all but
the thumb on his left hand are swollen and can hardly bend. There's a
menacing numbness floating beneath his right kneecap that, in a pinch,
turns into an unforgettable shooting pain when he tries to move. He
runs his hands over his lap, grazing glass chips and feathers soft as ash,
and then touches his shirtfront, rigid with rivulets of dried blood. He
can only imagine what his face looks like. He hesitates for a moment
and then puts his good thumb on the tip of his nose. It's still in the
right place, at least. He moves his thumb down to trace the lines of his
cheekbones and chin, his lips and eyebrows. It's a slow process. There
are ridges where there shouldn't be, some open cuts cresting bruises.
The gash in his cheek is still oozing freely, and the molars beneath it
are loose. Howard works his tongue over them and rocks them in their
sockets, the way he used to do as a boy, with baby teeth. Not good, all
in all. But not the end of the world.

After feeling his body out, Howard feels out the space. He reaches
in front and finds nothing but air. He reaches behind and his tender
hands strike a wall. Sliding on his butt, he backs into it and runs his
palms over the baked oatmeal texture of cinder block. No paint, no
molding, no outlets or fixtures. Just the blocks, placed irregularly, and
some nubbins of overflowed mortar like welling puss. It's an amateur
job, for sure. Howard has contempt for amateurs.

The rooster has been crowing this whole time, and it rises to crescendo now. It sounds close, but muffled, as though the wall extends between them. A sudden blade of light, nearly a yard long, opens up opposite Howard's feet—the sliver of space under a closed door. "Fuck off!" someone yells. It's the taxi driver. "Fuck off, fuck off, fuck off. How many times do I have to tell you? It is too *goddamn* early!"

The light goes out and a door slams somewhere. The rooster clucks a bit, as though grumbling, and is quiet. The sound of the taxi driver's voice spooks Howard a little, but also fills him with anger. He reaches instinctively for his belt loop. But of course his cell phone isn't there. His pockets are empty, and they've taken his shoes and the cash inside his shoes. But it's all right. It'll be all right. You were stupid last night, he tells himself, but not completely stupid. You called the police. You gave them your name. They'll check in with your hotel. They'll contact your phone provider and do that satellite thing you've seen on TV. They'll find your phone. And they'll find you. And you'll be fine.

He says this out loud, quietly. I'm going to be fine. It's not the end of the world. He also says: These idiots are in big, big trouble. When I get out of this it won't be fine for them. It will be the end of the world.

SOME TIME LATER, he can't tell how long or if he's slept, the sun creeps in through a square window set just below the ceiling. The window is tiny, maybe nothing more than a placeholder for an eventual condenser or vent, but it lets in enough light for Howard to get a sense of the room. It's about the size of his bathroom at the Shangri-La and is bare save the tiniest scraps of tape where something had, until recently, been pasted to the wall. Half the floor is tiled with glossy blue ceramic while the other half remains covered in a crumbling mosaic of vinyl-asbestos. There's one door, and it is new and sits on heavy brass hinges. The room has the look of an unfinished home improvement job. It also looks fuzzy, and oddly lopsided. It's not just shoddy workmanship. The floor inclines dizzyingly and the walls all limbo back. Howard realizes that one of his contact lenses is missing—it must have been knocked out when they dragged him to the street and beat him. The remaining lens hurts and gives him a squinting headache. It's been in almost a day too long. He considers popping it into his mouth to give his eye a rest, but that'd invite an infection for sure. And he isn't ready to give up seeing, just yet.

THE POLICE ARE COMING. The police are coming. He repeats this, under his breath, to pass some time. Sometimes he varies it. The police have come. The police are here. The police are beating those idiots senseless. The quiet chanting dries his mouth out, and reminds him that he's very thirsty. He thinks about calling for water, but doesn't. It's up to the idiots to make the first move.

The light ages. Clouds roll in to soften it. No one comes inside Howard's little room all day. The rooster crows, occasionally, and somebody on the other side of the door watches television at high volume. Sounds from the outside world flit in through the square window. Water dripping from gutters. Car horns, urgent and close. Howard imagines that, were he on his toes, he could look out there and get his bearings. He braces himself on the floor and pushes up gingerly. A vague tickle strokes the inside of his right knee. Something clicks lamely, like a misaligned cog. Howard loses his balance and falls back on his butt, breathing hard. He can hear footsteps outside the window. There are fading voices. What was it he'd read in the *Bulletin* last week? Something like eleven out of every ten Manileños have cell phones—or, there are eleven cell phones for every ten Manileños? Something like that.

He tries again, pushing up with his good leg and arms. He stands. The pain is intense, but subsides as he leans into the wall. He hops to the base of the window, reaches up and finds that he can pass his hand through—there's no glass or screen at all. Bracing his swollen fingers on the base, he jumps and gets a brief glance outside. The news is good. The news is fucking excellent. He can see Makati out there. He can see the Shangri-La. The idiots must be keeping him in their house—the same place the taxi driver stopped at the night before.

Hoping to get a better look, Howard squats and jumps again, but this time he fouls the landing. His knee crumbles under him. An agonized, percussive cry springs out of his chest. There's very shortly a commotion in the other room. Something large is pushed or pulled across the floor, and the door opens. The slim taxi driver steps inside, framed in fresh, expensive wood. He's quiet for a moment, twitching, looking almost confused.

"Be careful," he finally says with an air of vague threat. "You don't want to hurt yourself." He pauses, significantly.

Even with his brain still ringing with pain, Howard takes the chance to peer past the taxi driver, into the adjacent room. He sees the scuffed back of a loveseat and a patio table with plastic chairs. The far wall is virtually plastered over with movie posters—mostly for Tarantino and Ocampo Justice films, and the sight of his pal Charlie Fuentes staring at him heroically is a jarring one. A television sits against the wall, partially covering Ocampo's *Stick Up for the Unstuckup For* motto. It's tuned to the international news. Two young women, one of them in a lovely neckerchief, discuss bombings at police recruitment centers in Iraq.

"I have money," Howard says, still not making eye contact with the taxi driver, hoping he looks submissive. "Plenty. Cash. A lot more than what you found in my shoes. More than you could spend in a year, even if you spent it stupidly. More than you need."

The taxi driver squats down on his haunches and clasps his hands together. Behind him the news changes to international weather. "What do you know about what I need?"

"Nothing. I don't know anything about what you need," Howard says. He pauses. An expert at the weather desk discusses the minor earthquakes in Taiwan and Mexico. There have been disturbances all along the ring of fire and she expects more to come. Someone else at the weather desk points out that this isn't really weather related, is it? They both laugh about this.

"So tell me then," Howard says. "Tell me what you need."

The taxi driver shifts on his haunches. "What's wrong with your voice? You sick or something?"

Howard shakes his head. "Just thirsty."

The taxi driver looks about the little room. Then he disappears, leaving the door open. This jars Howard. He contemplates breaking for it. But he doesn't know where the front door is, and with this knee any mad dash will be short. New experts come on the news, listing precautions one should take against the bird flu. Everybody should have canned goods and bottled water on hand. You should be able, if necessary, to be indoors for a very long time. Duct tape is an incredible, versatile tool, they say. Buy some.

The taxi driver returns with a plastic bowl filled to the brim with water. "Thank you," Howard says, and drinks. "Thanks."

The taxi driver takes the bowl back from him.

"Let's talk about this," Howard says. "Let's talk about what you need, and how I can give it to you. There's no reason this has to be hard."

The taxi driver slaps him across the face with the empty plastic bowl. It hardly hurts, but Howard cups his cheek and squints so that his eyes water. He looks at the floor like he's cowering. It's important that this turd feel powerful.

The taxi driver leaves the room and closes the door. The floor vibrates as he slides a makeshift barricade—it must be the loveseat—back into place. Outside the sky clears a little and the room brightens. Light comes through the square window and dances about on the walls of Howard's small cell. For a brief moment a sagging palm frond breaks the light into thin shadows that resemble prison bars. Then, with a gust, they look like feathered wings. Then they settle, and just look like a palm frond.

THE NEXT TIME HE WAKES, it's night. The air is cool. The window is a narrow box for the moon. Howard breathes slowly, his body sore as he changes positions on the hard floor. He turns to the door and sees that it's cracked open. There's a woman there, staring at him. He closes his bad eye and tries to get a better look at her. She's young, and her black hair is streaked with peroxide-blond highlights. She slides a cardboard tray toward him—his refilled water bowl and a dish of boiled rice.

The television is off and Howard recognizes a familiar sound coming from the adjacent room. His cell phone is ringing. That's wonderful. The fact that it's still on and that it's so near means the police will definitely be able to do the satellite thing he's seen on TV. They've had time enough to double-check with the hotel and learn he never made it back. They could be here as early as tonight. The particular quality of the ring raises Howard's spirits even more. He's set a different tone for each of his favorite contacts. This is Benny's ring. Benny is calling him. The ringing stops and starts again after a few seconds. Still Benny.

Howard looks past the woman, into the room beyond. The taxi driver and his big friend—the one who beat Howard with the PVC pipe—sit at the plastic patio table. They stare down at Howard's ringing phone, which sits in the middle of the table. They look perplexed, as though agonizing over what to do. There's also someone new, someone weird-looking beside them. It takes Howard a moment to process the fact that it's a green rooster, smoking a cigarette. The rooster stares intensely at the air. It jukes its head to ash the cigarette. Then it crows, erupting with smoke like a science-fair volcano.

"Ignacio!" the woman calls. "Littleboy! He's awake."

The taxi driver, Ignacio, looks up. "Goddamnit woman," he hollers. "Weren't you paying attention to our briefing? I said no names!"

Briefing? Howard laughs—he can't help it. Ignacio pushes past the woman and starts kicking at Howard gingerly. That makes him laugh even harder. He forces himself to stop, which is difficult and feels a little like choking, which happened to him once, at a wedding. He can't believe these morons—these wannabe badasses. They're clearly afraid of hurting him any more than they've already done, and rightly so. They're too frightened to just answer the phone and make demands, and too stupid to have smashed the phone in the first place.

"Listen," Howard says, blocking Ignacio's last kick with his elbows, panting like a man tickled. "Listen. This is silly. We both know you didn't really think this over. You're not prepared to do the whole ransom thing. That's fine. I've got enough cash in my hotel room for you to retire on. I'll tell you where it's all hidden. Be smart about this. There's no need to drag it out."

Ignacio leaves the room. He returns with a curved razor blade that Howard recognizes as a cockfighting spur.

"What's wrong with you? Why threaten me? You'll get what you want if you just—"

Ignacio braces Howard's head between his knees and slices his ear off with the spur. It takes a moment for the pain to register, because his ear couldn't have just been sliced off. It's *his ear*. Ignacio staunches the bleeding with a dishcloth and crams the cloth into Howard's mouth to stop him screaming. Because he's screaming now. Because his ear's been cut off.

Ignacio stays with him until he passes out.

MORNING AGAIN, AND THEN NIGHT. Ignacio and Littleboy seal up the square window with plywood and spackle. Hon calls, and then Benicio calls, and then the kidnappers place the phone beside Howard like a fellow captive and smash it to pieces under their heels. The woman comes inside and changes Howard's bandages, and it's only then that he realizes he was bandaged at all. She brings him a bucket to shit in and some toilet paper, but Howard doesn't need it, because the police will be here soon. The police are coming. The police are coming. The police are here. Any minute, now. Any day.

MORNING. NIGHT. REPEAT. Ignacio and Littleboy do not come in and they do not answer when Howard calls out to them. Roaches, attracted by Howard's gauze and uneaten dinners, crawl in through holes in the mortar. They flutter lightly over his fingers and run straight up the walls and he is wowed by their abilities. His cheeks become stubbly, and then velvety. His eye hurts more and more. He starts giving it little breaks by popping the lens into his mouth, but it always feels like a hot dime under his lid when he puts it back. Finally he gives up and deposits the lens in his water dish. He pushes the dish into the far corner of the room, peels off his filthy button-down and covers it. The woman believes him when he says she forgot his water, and brings him a new dish with his next meal.

Essentially blind now, Howard has time to think. He feels as though when he could almost see he was busy almost seeing, but now he's not busy with anything. He tries to account for the days that have passed and becomes certain that his son is in Manila by now. Benny's already so oversensitive—he'll be furious that Howard wasn't there to meet him. Then, when he finds out what really happened, he'll feel rotten about being furious. Howard will tell Benny not to sweat it, but Benny will still sweat it. He'll want to ask about Howard's missing ear, but it'll take years to work up the comfort and nerve. What happened when you were kidnapped? he'll finally say, and the word *kidnapped* will be foreign and harmless to him. Like a sparrow in the living room. Howard will laugh, and then he'll get serious, and somber, and put on a faraway look. Benny will admire him, and say he can't imagine what he went through. And he'll be right.

Howard stops saying: "The police are coming." He starts saying: "Where the fuck are the police?" Boy, have they ever dropped the fucking ball. Someone, somewhere, is going to be fired when Howard gets out of this. He's going to bankroll a study and discover what office or branch failed to file what, or call whom, and then find those people, and fucking ruin every one of them. You incompetent assholes. You sons of bitches.

It's not till the blurry shape of Ignacio comes into the room that Howard realizes he was saying these last things aloud. Yelling them.

"I'm sorry," Howard says, moving his hands up over his face.

Ignacio ignores him. His posture is somehow thoughtful. He calls Littleboy and tells him to go stand outside, below the sealed window. Then he tells Howard to repeat what he was just saying.

"You incompetent assholes?"

"Yeah, that. But say it how you said it. Yell it."

Howard yells: "You incompetent assholes!"

A moment later Littleboy comes back inside and Ignacio asks him if he heard it.

"I heard everything," Littleboy says. "Even the *talking*."

"I'm sorry," Howard says. "I won't yell any more."

"The hell you won't," Ignacio says. He disappears and returns carrying a boxy black blur. He sets it on the floor in front of Howard, who guesses from its shape that it's the television. Ignacio sits atop the set, panting, while Littleboy fiddles with the cords.

"I don't want you to turn this off," he says. "And it's my only set, so I don't want you to break it."

"I'll buy you a new TV," Howard sobs. "I'll buy you a plasma."

"Hush," Ignacio says. "Now, I'm going to turn this on. I'm serious about you breaking it. Whatever you do to this TV, I do to you. The screen is your face. The cords are your cock. Leave them alone."

With that Ignacio flips on the set and leaves, closing the door behind him. It's still tuned to the same international twenty-four-hour news network. The lady announcers are back, talking about a car bomb at an Iraqi market. Their voices are so loud that Howard could shout himself hoarse and still not be heard by anyone outside. The Nikkei and the Hang Seng are up. Moscow has a favorable jobs report. In Venezuela, protesters threw stones at the American Embassy. Somewhere in Africa, a woman is president. There are more cases of bird flu, in China. Let's not forget to be prepared, the bird flu expert says. Here is what you'll need to stock at home.

*Chapter 14*

## OTHER HOMES

Benicio, Charlie, and Bobby took a taxi to the bay. Traffic was terrible. Charlie went on and on about missing his own victory party and when the car slowed to a standstill he insisted that they get out and walk. That wasn't much faster, though, because of Bobby's limp, which was pronounced and awkward. It looked like something he was still getting used to.

After a few hot blocks they made it to the smoky cold breeze of a restaurant doorway. A dwarf standing at a shortened host's table greeted Charlie and Bobby by name, tucked some drink menus under one arm and led them through a packed chamber with a low ceiling. They passed a live band playing funk, every member a little person wrangling a full sized instrument, and as Benicio rubbernecked he nearly ran into a heavy tray of food that bobbed just above waist level. It was everyone, he realized. Everyone who worked there was a little person.

People called out to Charlie from a long, family-style table, and he joined them with some moderate drunken fanfare. Benicio was about to follow when Bobby took his elbow and whispered: "That's not for us." Actually, it was more of a shout, but with the music it sounded like a whisper. He led Benicio to an alcove against the back wall, where four people in their mid-twenties were squeezed around a tiny table. They all stood up to clap when they saw Bobby. One of them unfurled a long piece of brown paper that looked like it came from a bathroom dispenser and held it above his head—an improvised *Congratulations* banner. Another started up a chant of "Dan-Cer, Dan-Cer, Dan-Cer," that quickly devolved into "Pils-Ner, Pils-Ner, Pils-Ner," as he waved to their waiter for more beer. It was a louder reception than Charlie had received, and from a smaller crowd.

The host struggled to drag over two additional chairs, and Benicio and Bobby sat. Bobby's boisterous friends, two men and two women, didn't seem to notice that Benicio was there at first. They took turns clapping Bobby on the shoulder and pinching his unbandaged cheek with both hands. For a while only the words "congratulations," "victory," and "hot shit" were used. Then one of the women turned to Benicio with an electric suddenness and smiled, revealing a set of glow-in-the-dark teeth.

"Who's your friend?" she asked, her slur masked behind good posture.

"This is Benicio," Bobby said. "He's Howie's kid."

This elicited a round of incredulous laughter. Someone said, "Fuck you, he's not." Another asked, sarcastically, "Which one?" Bobby said something in Tagalog that shut them up, and then went around the table making introductions. The woman with the glowing teeth and pretty smile was Katrina. The man with the beard and loosened tie— the one who'd asked: *Which one?* and who came off as a schmuck—was Ping. And the other two, well, he wasn't sure he'd heard right. But their names sounded like Bong and Baby Cookie.

Katrina put a hand on his wrist. "And what do you do, Ben?" she asked.

"He's a talent scout," Bobby said. "They're filming another Vietnam War movie here come December. Benicio's out early to get a jump on casting rice farmers, basket weavers, people to run from napalm, and—"

"I'm in computers," Benicio cut in.

"Coding?" Ping asked, fingering the tip of his immaculate beard. His shirt was black and his tie was black. Benicio felt his lousy first impression confirmed.

"No. Systems. I run a network for a school."

"You should have stuck with my story," Bobby shouted across the table. "Katrina does outreach for the party, but she's like, really awful at it. She's actually an aspiring actress, and take it from me, the girl has no morals."

Katrina laughed a little too loud and cuffed Bobby hard on the shoulder. Then she put the tips of her fingers to her mouth and gasped. "I'm so sorry! I forgot."

"My shoulder's just fine," Bobby said.

The waiter returned and power-lifted a pair of ice buckets filled with brown bottles onto the table. Katrina pulled a dripping beer from the ice and gave it to Benicio. Still a little buzzed, he protested that he wasn't usually a drinker.

"Tonight isn't usual," Bobby said. "You should try one. It's better than the lambanog, I promise."

"Wait, you mean you've never tried San Mig?" Katrina's mouth hung open and she tapped herself rapidly between her collarbones, as though to calm sudden palpitations. "My God, you're not even *here* yet!

You haven't arrived. You're still in the airport waiting for your bags to spin out of that spinner." She pushed the beer closer and watched until he took his first sip and gave her an it's-good smile. He didn't even have to fake it.

For a while Benicio just listened as Bobby's tipsy friends laughed, drank and chain-smoked. They all spoke at the same time, talking over and under one another, weaving a conversation below the strum and boom of the band. Benicio guessed they were discussing the election, and though all the particulars and many acronyms—Ping, it seemed, spoke exclusively in letter combinations—might as well have been in another language, their excitement was difficult to not get caught up in. Occasionally Bobby leaned in to offer some explanation.

"OJS—that's not an agency or anything. That's the Ocampo Justice Series."

"I remember, you said Charlie used to be an actor?"

"Still is. He's got a movie coming out this Christmas, and he's cast in another that starts filming in August. Katrina's been hounding me to get her a part ever since I started working for him."

"How long is that?"

"Few months. Charlie's been entertaining the public for twenty years, but this is his first time serving them. The party assigned me to his race once he signed up on our ticket."

"Ah." Benicio took a long swig of beer and joined Bobby's friends in ordering more when the waiter trotted past. "So he wasn't your choice?"

"He would have been," Bobby said. "I'm good at my job, so I can usually have my pick. If I didn't want to work for Charlie I could have had someone else. There were a few others," he paused, "who wanted me. But I wanted Charlie."

Benicio glanced over at the big table, where Charlie was standing up, drinking from a yard of beer. A woman on his arm took time with a stopwatch. "So . . . he's never done anything like this before?" He saw the bandage on the side of Bobby's face rise just a little bit, as though somewhere under all that gauze he was cocking an eyebrow. "Sorry," he said, "I don't mean—"

"No," Bobby said, "you do. But it's fair. To tell you the truth," he leaned in very close so that only Benicio could hear him, "I'm used to getting that expression. The intellectuals in this city have nothing but skepticism for Charlie Fuentes. And I'll be honest—he's got no real experience. None. I've got more. *You've* probably got more. I can't even stretch and say he has relevant experience. And I don't know if he'll be a great senator, or even a good one. Good may be too much to hope for. But I know one thing for sure. He'll be better, which is better than worse. I don't kid myself—I know why he won. Big-town actor who plays a small-town cop, sticking up for the unstuckup for. People voted for a character they saw in the movies. But Charlie Fuentes is a mostly honest person with a good heart. That makes him an improvement on those same intellectuals who've been fucking us sideways for years now."

As Bobby spoke Benicio felt a swell of admiration. He began to have thoughts that only came when he'd been drinking—that Bobby was really real and that he, in contrast, was not very real at all. And with that feeling came the too-familiar urge to overcorrect. "That's pretty good," he said. "You've practiced it a few times?"

"Fuck you very much." Bobby leaned back in his chair with a pot-belly smile. "When did it start to show? Was it the good heart line?" He took a drink, beating the beer about his cheeks before swallowing. "I've been working on that damn line. It's just too fucking true to be good."

Four rounds later Katrina turned to Benicio and started saying "karaoke" over and over. She shook him lightly by the shoulders, as though he didn't understand, but needed to. They split the tab five ways and then, on their way out, Benicio and Ping swung by the men's room. There was a line, so they waited together in awkward silence. From where they stood they could see Charlie's table. One of the dwarf waiters had been lifted onto the tabletop, where he kicked and spun in a stubby impersonation of Riverdance. Everybody at the table howled. Benicio chuckled, and rolled his eyes.

"What?" Ping asked.

Benicio shrugged, and gestured to the dwarf on the table. "That."

"What about that?"

"Well . . . come on. I mean, this was fun and all, but that's pretty skeezy, isn't it? I mean, this whole place is exploitive. It's like a carnival from the fifties."

"Ah-ha," Ping said, again stroking his well-groomed beard. "Hey, do me a favor. Check out the picture on the men's room door."

Benicio leaned out of line to get a better look at the door. On the ladies' room there was a generic photo of a model, all cleavage and eyeballs, in a cheap wooden frame. On the men's room there was another framed photo of a shirtless teenager on a beach. Benicio recognized the photo. It was a photo of him. His wetsuit was on up to his waist and he was posing beside his assembled dive gear. His torso was leaner and tanner than it would ever be again, and he was mugging goofily for the camera.

"Daddy owns this place," Ping said. "Does that make daddy exploitive and skeezy, too?"

"Yeah," he said, looking right back at Ping. "It does."

OUTSIDE IT HAD SOMEHOW gotten hotter. A few car alarms were going off, and someone announced that there'd been a tremor, but Benicio hadn't felt anything. Katrina grabbed his wrist and they ran— what she did was more of a skip, actually—through three lanes of sluggish traffic. They waited on the sunburned grassy median for Bobby, Ping and the others to catch up before running through another three. Benicio lost track of how long they walked, but he was dripping with sweat by the time they finally entered a little karaoke club with purple light and synthesized music.

Katrina headed to the front to wait her turn at the microphone while the rest of them tumbled into soft chairs like melting ice. Bobby's friends ordered drinks, but only so they wouldn't be hassled about taking up a table, and continued discussing politics with hot, drunk enthusiasm. Ping sat beside Benicio and stared at him like there was something on his mind. Benicio's hackles were still up from seeing his picture on the men's room door, and he stared right back, inviting him to spill.

"Where did you say you came from, again?" Ping finally asked.

"I didn't. My family lives in Chicago." Even as he said this he realized it wasn't true anymore. His mother was dead, and his father essentially lived here. "I flew out of a place called Virginia."

"Where in Virginia?"

"Around the middle. It's a smallish town in the mountains."

"Ah-ha." Ping nodded for a long while, staring at Benicio, eyes fixed in his moving head. "Assume, for a moment, that I can understand an answer slightly more complex than that."

Benicio shifted in his chair, aware that Bobby and Baby Cookie were listening in. "Charlottesville."

"So, you're a Wahoo?" Ping asked. Wahoo was slang for the collar-popping students at the University of Virginia, among whom Benicio had felt comfortable but never completely at home.

"You know UVA?" he asked, unable to hide his surprise.

"Bobby and I were roommates at Georgetown. Sometimes in the fall we'd rent a car and drive down to watch you guys lose football games."

"Small world."

"Actually, it's pretty big." Ping took a tiny swig of his beer. "So, are you as red as your state? Are you a Balikatan man?"

"A what? I don't speak—"

"It's the name of a military operation in the south," Bobby said, looking wary.

"It's the name of your military operation," Ping said, directing the *your* and a rigid index finger square at Benicio's chest. "It's been in all the newspapers for a long, long, long time."

"Well, I just got here," Benicio said. "And I haven't read any newspapers, yet."

"They don't tell you about it back home?" There was surprise in Ping's expression, but none of it in his voice. "They don't tell you that your army has troops fighting in our country? Against our constitution. You didn't know that? Our constitution says no armed foreign troops, but you are here, and you are foreign, and you are armed."

"I'm not anywhere," Benicio said.

"Cop-out!" Baby Cookie singsonged from across the table.

"That's right," Ping said. "Everybody's somewhere. Everybody's either active or complicit. Are you going to tell me that you only use that harsh judgment on daddy?"

Benicio leaned closer to him, trying his best to steady his voice. "If you're trying to pick a fight, you'll get one."

"Oh, that's classic." Ping was uncowed. "That's your answer to everything, isn't it? You sure know how to be nasty, don't you? Tell us, nasty—why, after so many years, have you finally decided to grace your father with a visit? What caused this sudden generosity of spirit?"

"Guys," Bobby interrupted, "enough. It's a happy night, and you're all officially in violation of the no-assholes policy I've just instituted."

"We're not being assholes," Ping said. "We're talking about them. There's a difference. And don't pretend you don't feel the same way."

"You don't know what I feel," Bobby said. "So don't try to guess."

This caused an awkward silence to descend on the table. When Ping started talking again it was, ostensibly, just about politics. Benicio went to the bathroom to wash his face and cool off, but when he got back they were still at it. Bobby's friends hopped between topics like reliable stones in a frequently crossed stream. Iraq. Trade and unfair trade and downright evil trade. Global warming and the poisoning of the world. Iraq. All those crazy whack-jobs with wide brimmed hats who need gun racks to hold all their guns because they have so many guns. Iraq. Benicio didn't even try to participate. He sensed with a kind of articulate drunk certainty that they wouldn't have let him share in the warmth of a common opinion even if he had one and wanted to. Instead he watched the stage, where Katrina was in an open-mouth kiss with the microphone, mangling something from Paul Simon—*diamonds on the shoals of her choose.* She paused to wink at him, as if to say: I may be hamming it up now, but it's a choice. I can also be very serious. Looking at her, he felt angry and drunk and a little turned on. He decided it was time to go.

"Off so soon?" Ping said as Benicio got up, even though it wasn't soon—he'd been out and drinking for hours. "I guess it's easier not to listen, right? I mean we've hardly touched the good stuff. Guantánamo and—"

He fell into shocked silence as Benicio reached over and fished the pack of cigarettes out of the pocket of his black dress shirt. He opened the pack and turned it upside-down, sending the cigarettes rolling across the table, some tumbling down to the dirty floor and others way-laid in pools of condensation around the bases of warming San Miguels. "Anyone have a pen?" Benicio asked. Bobby handed him a ballpoint and he wrote, *Suggestion Box, USA*, on the front of the now-empty pack.

He held it up so Ping could read it. "Tell you what," he said. "Just write down everything I miss. Put it all on little strips of paper, and put the paper in the box. Then, when I go back home, I can share your thoughts with everyone. I'll go door to fucking door."

Bobby, and even Baby Cookie laughed at this. Ping looked from Benicio, to the floor, to Benicio. "What's wrong with you?" he asked. "Those were my cigs."

"I'm sorry about this," Benicio said to Bobby. "Thanks for inviting me out."

Ping stood and took him roughly by the collar. "Those were my cigs," he said.

"Let go of me."

Ping let loose a string of Tagalog words that Benicio couldn't under-stand, punctuated by a spit-flecked and familiar "Puta!" He brought his open palm to Benicio's cheek—not quite a slap, more like a loose, soggy pat. It could almost have been friendly, had they been friends. But it was all the provocation, all the excuse he needed.

His fist came out quick, catching Ping right in the nose. Ping didn't fall or let go of his shirt, but after Benicio punched him a second time he did both. Everybody was looking at them now. Bobby stood and started to walk Benicio to the door at a fast limp. Bong and Baby Cookie held Ping's arms to keep him from coming after. It was hot outside the karaoke club. The night was bright, smudged and stumbling.

THE NEXT MORNING BENICIO woke sprawled on a wicker couch with a blanket wrapped around his legs. He was in a sitting room with white tile floors, lying beneath the lazy swing of a ceiling fan. The room was spotlessly clean and filled with inward-facing chairs. Beside the wicker couch was a coffee table that was bare save a shallow bowl filled with ice cubes. The space would have felt sterile if not for the bright doggy chew-toys scattered across the floor—rubber squeakers in the shapes of hotdogs, chicken drumsticks and cats—and the crooked tilt of three landscape paintings on the wall. Benicio tried to sit up, realizing as he did how dizzy and nauseous he still felt. His whole body was slick with sweat, and the only place that felt dry was the inside of his mouth.

An older man entered the room and even though Benicio was fully dressed he pulled the blanket up to his chest. The man wore a robe and had a newspaper tucked under his arm. He acknowledged Benicio with a small nod and then turned to the wall, grumbling a bit as he straightened each of the paintings. The man said something loud in Tagalog and Benicio heard Bobby answer from somewhere behind him. The man wrinkled his nose and left.

"My father," Bobby said, coming around the couch and taking a seat in a chair across from Benicio. His bandages looked slightly moist, and wilted, and he shuffled slowly without his cane. "It's polite here to stand when an older man enters the room," he said, leaning in and lowering his voice.

Benicio held his breath as he sat up. "I didn't know," he said.

"Why would you have?" They looked at each other for a while, the fan clicking away above. The night before Bobby had insisted he come back to his family's home in Dasmariñas. Benicio regretted it now, wishing he'd stepped out of the cab at the first red light or bottleneck and found one of his own. He could have pointed the driver to the hulking pink hotel on the dark horizon and avoided this awkwardness.

"Hey . . ." he ran his throbbing hand though his hair. "I was a jerk last night."

Bobby just looked at him for a while. "Yeah, but they were jerks first. Ping especially. Believe me, if you'd said anything about his family he'd have reacted worse."

"Well, I'm really sorry."

"I know. You told me in the taxi. And while I was opening up the gate. And while I looked through the closet for a blanket. You're even better at staying on message than Charlie is." He grinned and drummed his hands on his thighs.

"Is Ping all right?"

"Yes, believe it or not he's alive. The doctors say it was a close one, but he'll pull through, thank Jesus." The beat on Bobby's thighs quickened and he slapped Benicio's knee a few times like a high-hat. "Lighten up."

"I don't feel light."

"Well, you're just a short taxi ride from your hotel. It's early yet. You can go back, sleep for a few hours, and wake up with the whole day ahead of you. Any plans?"

"Not really. My father should be in by now. So we'll probably just be visiting."

"And if he's not?"

Benicio paused, thinking this possibility over. "I guess I've kind of wanted to see what Corregidor really looks like," he said.

Bobby shrugged. "You could," he said. "The tours are a little hammy, but it's not a bad trip. Or, if you want, you could come south with us. Katrina and I are going to take a break from Charlie's parties and do a little diving. Well, she is, at least. It'll be an overnighter, but we'd have you back by lunchtime on Sunday. And you don't have to worry—we're not inviting any of the jerks. Well, actually, we're inviting one. But that jerk is you."

"Thanks," he said, "but I don't think so. My father will be in, I'm sure." He reached down for his shoes at the foot of the couch and pulled them on. They felt stiff and too small, like they would after a long flight. "What kind of dogs do you have?" he asked, gesturing to the toys scattered across the floor.

"No kind," Bobby said. His smile slackened almost imperceptibly. "They used to be Labradors."

Benicio focused on tying his shoes. As he finished he heard a kind of singing drifting through the hallway. They were joined by a stocky woman in an apron. She hummed loudly to herself and went straight for the paintings on the wall. She turned each one about fifteen degrees crooked.

"My mother," Bobby said.

Benicio shot to his feet a little too fast and said "Good morning," very loud. The woman spun and said something in Tagalog.

"English, mother," Bobby said. His mother turned to him and said more things that Benicio couldn't understand. "Yes," Bobby said, "I feel much better. Mother, speak in English please."

She started in Tagalog again but changed midstream. "I can have the girls make some eggs, or toast, and we have juice or coffee, or they could fry sausages—"

"Any breakfast?" Bobby cut in.

"Nothing, thank you. I think I should get going."

"You're sure?" Bobby's mother came over and took Benicio's bruised hand between her chubby palms. "We can't ask you to stay? Bobby, ask him to stay."

"He has to leave, mother," Bobby said. Then his tone changed a bit and he went on in Tagalog.

"English, Robert," she said, holding hard onto Benicio's hand and looking up at him. "Oh dear. You know it shouldn't be long now at all." She leaned in and almost whispered. "Those bandages will be off before you know it."

"Thank you mother," Bobby said, moving in to gently pry her hands off of Benicio. "He's got to go."

Bobby walked him through the house and out to a walled-in, lush garden. A guard in a blue uniform opened the gate for them and they waited in silence for an empty taxi to roll by. Benicio examined the garden out of the corner of his eye while they waited. A sprinkler spun between piles of mowed grass. A big tree in the corner wept yellow flowers onto the roofs of two freshly painted doghouses. Bobby caught him staring, and he looked away.

"So, why the crooked paintings?" Benicio asked.

Bobby searched the road for empty cabs. "She does it so that devils can't sit on the frames. If the frames are crooked, the devils slide off." He demonstrated by holding his left forearm out and walking the fingers of his right hand up and down it. He dipped the forearm down sharply and his walking hand fell.

Benicio took a moment to mull this over. "The devil?"

"Not *the devil*, as in the one and only, but devils. That's not even a very good word for them, but it's one you'd understand."

"Ah." Minutes passed without a taxi. "You know . . ." he trailed off, his voice hoarse. "My mother used to have this thing. She used to say that she could tell the future. Said she could see it in her dreams."

"Really," Bobby looked from the street back to Benicio. "Could she?"

WHEN BENICIO GOT BACK to the hotel, he realized that his father was finally home. Music thrummed dully through the adjoining door to Howard's suite, and when he opened it he saw that the bed was slept in and some of the lights were on. He stepped inside, expecting to find Howard hunched over papers in his study. But the first thing he noticed was a dress. A green dress, crumpled at the foot of the bed. There were high heel shoes beside it, but no business loafers or slacks. Not a shred of men's clothing anywhere, in fact.

The sound of a high-pressure shower spattered and hissed behind the music, and thin wisps of steam emanated from the open bathroom door. Benicio approached the door and saw, through the bathroom mirror, a lithe shape blurred behind the translucent shower curtain. He returned to the bedroom and switched the music off. A moment later, the shower switched off as well.

"It's about damn time," the woman called from inside the bathroom. "I'm getting sick of this—I waited up for hours last night."

Benicio didn't say anything. He sat on the edge of the bed, and then stood again. From the bathroom came the downy, frictive sound of a towel on skin.

"Quit fuming," she said after a moment of silence. "I didn't touch anything, you big baby. But next time, I will. Next time you're not here when you're supposed to be, I'll rob you blind." She laughed at this. A moment later she emerged from the bathroom, wearing a towel around her bust. She was, indeed, the woman from the night before. Water still beaded her dark shoulders, making her skin look sequined. Her fingers rested as lightly on the doorframe as the towel rested on her.

"Howard's not here," he said.

She was startled to see him there, but not as startled as he felt she should be. "Who are you?" she asked without so much as shifting her weight.

"I'm his son," Benicio said. He watched her collarbones rise and fall as she breathed. "What's your name?" he asked.

"Solita." She let go the doorframe and took a step toward him. "When does Howard come back?"

"I don't know. When he does I'll tell him you were here."

Solita took another step toward him. Her wet feet left prints on the carpet. "I know you," she said.

"No, you don't. You haven't met me. I'd like you to leave now, please."

"Last night," she said, "you were with Bobby. You bought me a drink." Then, without the kind of announcement that he felt himself entitled to, Solita lowered the towel down below her waist. Her skin was the same color all over and smooth save a long scar below her belly button and a little tattoo that sat low on her right hip. It was a black sun, dipping below the nubby towel like a horizon.

She reached out for his hand and placed it on one of her small breasts, his palm first grazing her dark nipple and then pressing hard against it. He was used to girls with heft—even Alice had a soft weight in his hands. Solita's breast felt firmer, like a muscle after stretching. He forced his hand back to his side and she laughed at him. "You want me to stay," she said.

"I don't."

She grabbed hold of the khaki just beneath his belt buckle. "You're a liar."

He stepped back. "Get out of here, please."

Solita's face stayed soft but her top lip curled just a bit. She dropped the towel completely and stepped back into her crumpled green dress. "Howard didn't say his son was a faggot."

"That's fine." He took her by the wrist and started to walk her to the door. Her pace quickened, so much so that it felt for a moment like he . was holding her back.

"Fuck you," she said as he pushed her out of the room. He closed the door on her and locked it. He left his father's suite, closed the adjoining door to his own and locked that as well.

FINDING A WOMAN in his father's room was no surprise. This was the second time it had happened. The first was on the last day of the father and son dive trip they'd taken five years back, a trip to celebrate his graduation and impending move to college in Virginia. Benicio was supposed to be out all day on a resort boat in the Murcielagos, but the corroded purge valve on his regulator got jammed and the boat crew had been unable to fix it or swap it for a spare. So they headed back a few hours early.

Benicio didn't knock—why should he have?—before returning to the room he shared with his father. His first thought upon opening the door was that he'd walked in on strangers. The two twin beds had been pushed together to make a king-size with a crack in it. On his knees on the left bed was a nude man draped in fat like fabric. A woman was in front of him, halfway between kneeling and lying on her belly. Her knees made deep indentations in the mattress, her backside bucking up against his looming weight. Both of them looked up at Benicio as soon as he opened the door and surprisingly enough he recognized the woman first. It was the dive instructor with the mannish jaw—the woman he'd been flirting with and dreaming about fucking on the concrete floor of the tank room for years, since he'd first seen her bend over the velcro and hoses of a BCD. The woman with whom his father had promised to put in a good word. Benicio stared the fat man in the face but still didn't recognize him until he started vomiting out apologies. Howard was actually talking to him while naked and still inside the sweating, broad-backed dive instructor. Benicio walked out of the room and left the door wide open behind him. After a few minutes his father came chasing after him in a white bathrobe that didn't fit well enough to close properly. Howard wasn't hard to outrun.

And, God, how Benicio had made him suffer for it.

*Chapter 15*

**BRUHA**

The first thing Monique heard when she woke was something in the kitchen. Amartina was in there making usual morning sounds. Running water. Opening and closing squeaky drawers. Clanging cast-iron crockery. But aside from the sounds, everything else was unusual. Monique wasn't in her bed. She was naked on the leather couch in the den. Reynato slept on the floor just below her, a blanket coiled around his gut, covering little. Monique's memory of the night before returned like a houseguest—the earthquake, the sex, the conversation she'd had with Amartina; telling her, very clearly, to go home. But Amartina wasn't home, with her family, in Cavite. She was in the kitchen.

Monique slid off the couch and rushed into the master bedroom. The tremor had tipped her dresser over, trapping her clothes. The basin her jacket had been soaking in—along with everything else she'd worn to work the day before—was overturned. Spent suds covered the bathroom tile, snaked out to the bedroom, and seeped into hardwood. Monique edged along the mess, grabbed a robe from the towel rack and put it on.

Reynato was still asleep when she passed him on her way to the kitchen. She glanced back and saw that while the couch obstructed his body, his bare feet jutted out conspicuously. There was a chance Amartina hadn't seen them, but if she'd taken even a few steps into the den she'd surely have noticed his shins, his knees, his thighs, his balls. And beyond that, she'd likely heard them the night before. Yelping in fear at the tremor. Fucking a second time on the carpet and a third back on the couch. They'd even had a midnight heart-to-heart in the kitchen, not six feet from Amartina's closed door, about what they thought was really wrong with their respective spouses. Joseph was petrified of not being impressive. Lorna, Reynato's wife, was scared of looking like a phony among the "real" society women. This was a disaster.

The kitchen was a disaster, too. Dishes lay broken on the floor and the cupboards had disgorged cookware onto countertops. The spice rack had fallen from its nail perch, glass jars shattering where they landed. Amartina didn't turn when Monique entered, but she must have sensed her. She walked barefoot through the mess, smashing ruined plates into a garbage pail and slamming cupboard doors, grumbling as she did so—a performance for Monique's benefit. So much for feeling her out.

"I told you to go home last night."

Amartina turned and faced her. The tear streaks down her cheeks made Monique incredibly uncomfortable. "It's all a mess."

"What?"

Amartina looked around the kitchen. She held the garbage pail in one hand and a chipped drinking glass in the other, and shook them as though explaining to a simpleton. "Look at this," she said, marching out of the kitchen, pail and glass still in hand.

Monique followed, repeating, "I asked you to go home" a little lamely. Amartina opened the door to Leila's room and stepped aside so Monique could see. The flat-screen computer monitor was wedged between the desk and the wall, and the lovebird's cage had toppled over. The miniature wrought-iron door was open and the cage was empty.

"Gone. I don't know where." Amartina turned, walked through the den, right past Reynato, and into Shawn's room. Monique raced after. Her son's room was almost as clean as usual, but the terrarium had toppled off the bed-stand and broken into a few large pieces. The heat lamp seared a neat rectangular burn into the carpet. The gecko was nowhere to be seen and feed-crickets hopped everywhere. "Gone. You made a big mess," she said, as though she blamed Monique not just for the nude man in the den, but for the earthquake itself: for shattered belongings and escaped pets.

Monique's cheeks filled with hot blood. What an incredible pain in the ass this woman was. Why couldn't she have just listened? Why spout reflexive, meaningless yeses? The maid's quarters were tiny, the bed narrow as an ironing board, and still she'd insisted on staying when Monique had asked her—*told her!*—not to. Now the only choices left were bad ones. Monique could threaten her and spend the next year worrying she'd spill, or fire her and feel guilty for maybe much longer than that.

Out in the den Reynato stirred. He got up and wrapped the blanket around his waist. His eyebrows, his mustache, even the silver hair ringing his nipples was wild and matted. He forced a smile and said, "Magandang umaga."

Amartina spun on him. "I don't care who you are," she said in sudden Tagalog, "you don't open your mouth to me." She got in his face, garbage pail raised as though she meant to use it as a weapon. She called him filth. She called him cheat. She called him parasite and devil. Reynato took the pail from her and set it down on the floor, but other than that he averted his eyes and accepted the assault.

"No. No. No," Monique said, her whole body burning under the horrible awkwardness of it—she used to speak that way to the cat, before it died. "You don't talk to anyone like that when you're in my house." She grabbed Amartina's knobby elbow but Amartina pulled away, spinning on her heels, slapping Monique clean across the face. For a moment they could have been each other's reflections—shocked and still.

"That's enough," Reynato said, in English.

Amartina blinked first, charging into her quarters off the kitchen. She emerged seconds later with an already packed bag, more bloated than usual for a weekend at home. "Shame on you," she said without looking back at them. "I cannot work here anymore." She fumbled with the deadbolt. She went out into the landing and rang for the elevator. A sound like a bicycle bell announced its slow approach. "I won't be back on Monday," she called, the steel gone from her voice. She sounded stressed, and distracted, and only slightly less determined.

MONIQUE SAT ON THE COUCH, staring dumbly at Joseph's overturned speakers, catching her breath even though she hadn't lost it. Reynato dropped his blanket and joined her. He began to have trouble restraining his giggles.

"This is funny to you?"

"Certainly not." He pursed his lips and made a show of stopping.

One of the escaped pets—or maybe both of them—twittered in the hall. Reynato smoothed out his mustache and looked about the wrecked apartment like an appraising buyer. "She's right about one thing, though. You really made a mess."

Monique let out a laugh-grunt and put her head in his lap. He ran his small fingers through her hair.

"Anything like this ever happen before?" he asked.

"You mean did I ever screw up this badly before? Did I ever get caught cheating? Did I ever ruin my marriage?"

His fingers stopped and started again. He worked his thumbs behind her ears, soothingly. "This is a featherweight screwup. Totally fixable. What I meant was: Did you ever make weird shit happen before?" He pointed an accusing finger at the overturned speakers.

"Ha. You're blaming me for that?"

"Should I?" Reynato glanced about the room again. "I think your maid does. Caviteños can be superstitious. I'm pretty superstitious myself." He quit stroking her hair and placed his hand on her chest, as though to keep her from sitting up. "Could be she thinks the Duwendes saw us last night, and got pissed. You know what Duwendes are?"

Monique nodded. The cleaning woman in Subic had told her all about those sometimes troublesome, sometimes lucky little goblins. An especially mean one supposedly lived in the eaves above their single-family house. The cleaning woman was terrified of him.

"Those little fuckers hold a grudge. You're getting off easy if they quit after breaking your shit. When I was young my mother sat on a Duwende and to get even they ganged up and pushed her down the stairs. She was on crutches for months and never sat down again without saying: *Lookout, here I come, get off my chair, please.*" He stared down at her, sunlight glinting in his braces and eyes. "Or, it could be she thinks you're a bruha. Shaking the place up with some black magic. Look at you, bruha. Making earthquakes when you get off."

Monique sat up. "I don't care what she thinks. I care what she says and doesn't say. What if she calls Joseph?"

Reynato was quiet for a moment before speaking. "Again, this is a small-scale problem. Just call him first and say you canned her. You caught her stealing, or something. Then, on the off chance she says anything, he'll chalk it up to disgruntled."

"I'm not going to lie about her."

"You lie about me all the time. Listen, if you're feeling guilty about it, *I* could offer her a job. I'll add a grand a week to whatever you were paying. Everybody wins."

"What about your wife?"

He laughed—a big, round sound. "If my wife believed the help I'd have been divorced years ago."

REYNATO HAD A BUSY DAY AHEAD, but he stayed to help Monique clean. They swept broken glass and repotted overturned plants by the window. He righted Leila's computer and got the Internet working again. Monique chased the lovebird and the gecko, trying to trap them under a plastic colander, without any luck. Reynato offered to bring his cat over—he had this incredibly obedient, incredibly smart black cat. But the kids would have been devastated if anything happened to the pets. Sooner or later they'd get tired, and Monique would catch them.

They cleaned Shawn's room last. Reynato crawled around on all fours, catching feed-crickets in unbroken spice jars. Monique vacuumed mulch and wood-chips out of the burned carpet. Just being in there made her feel like some kind of intruder. Joseph thought it essential that the children's rooms be a "private space" and Shawn defended his as though life and honor depended on it. Only Amartina was allowed in to get laundry, make the bed and feed the gecko when Shawn let it starve.

Reynato chased a cricket under the bed and stayed there for a moment, his butt and legs protruding. When he spoke his voice had a muffled, echoing quality. "Do you want bad news you can ignore or bad news you should probably know about?"

Monique shut the vacuum off. "I want both."

"All right. Well, the bad news you can ignore is that I've found your son's porn stash. Hardcore but not scary-freaky. And . . . how to put this delicately . . . well used."

"What's the other bad news?"

Reynato's legs twisted as he shimmied out from under the bed. He stood, his left hand cupping something translucent—a zip-lock baggie. Inside was a stubby little glass pipe, a plastic lighter and a tiny smattering of gray-green pot. Monique felt punched in her abdomen. "Hey," he said, "hey, no need to get so upset."

She snatched the bag from him and sat on Shawn's perfectly made bed. "I'm going to murder him."

"This is nothing." He sat beside her and rubbed a hand up and down her back. "There's hardly an hour's worth of fun in here. And the pipe looks new, no resin burns and no ash. Either he cleans it like a pro or he's only used it a handful of times."

"He's thirteen."

"That's young. But I've seen younger do worse."

If only Joseph were here, she thought. He'd feel so fucking vindicated. She unzipped the baggie and took the pipe out, turning it over in her hands. Reynato took it from her. He put all the pot into the bowl and it was hardly half full. He lit it, puffed and coughed.

"Oh my. Can't get this just anywhere." He offered her the pipe.

"I could lose my clearance for that."

"You could lose your clearance for a lot of things. Many of which are things you've done. With me. In that room and in others." He offered again. The pungent, familiar smell ringed their bodies. She shook her head. "Suit yourself."

Reynato puffed and coughed. He scrutinized a framed photograph of Shawn hanging lopsided on the wall. He scrutinized Monique.

"He must take after his father."

"Not after Joseph. Shawn and Leila are adopted."

"Oh. But . . . you've had at least one of your own." She looked at him and he put both palms in the air, contrite. "Hey, I'm no stalker. Bea, my daughter, was a breech birth. I know what the scar looks like."

"We had a son, named Walter. He died."

"I'm sorry."

"It was a long time ago. He was gone before we knew him."

They were quiet for a while, but Reynato kept rubbing her back, hitting the pipe occasionally. The smell reminded her of dates with Joe that ended with a joint in his overpriced Georgetown studio. He used to wear a full beard, and the scent would linger about his face until the next morning. Reynato finished the bowl. He put it back in the baggie, which melted around the hot glass pipe, and placed the plasticky mess on the end table. The lovebird hopped past the open door, retreating through the den, doing its best to fly with clipped wings. The gecko chased after, chirping. Music began to play. A synthetic beat, cymbals, and a voice singing Tagalog a few octaves deeper than it should. "Villie Manilie," Reynato said. "My daughter loves them."

The music was coming from Shawn's closet. Monique opened it and jumped a little—one of his hanging shirts trembled as though dancing. She reached into the pocket and pulled out a vibrating, singing mobile phone that she'd never seen before. It was thinner than a candy bar and had a silver trim that made it look swanky and mean. She waited for it to quiet down before flipping it open. A picture of a girl in a too-tight sweater greeted her; the same girl who'd invited Shawn to the prom and financed his ear piercing. There were seven missed calls, all from her, and the inbox was full of bubbly texts addressed to *Shugs*.

Monique tossed the phone to Reynato, who held it up to the light and whistled like he was impressed. "That girl must have given it to him," she said, chewing her bottom lip. She looked around her son's room, so much emptier and cleaner than his room in Washington had been. The desk, the walls, the closet; all orderly and spotless. Even the shirt she still held with one hand was ironed, fashionable and new—so new she didn't recognize it. She slid the shirt down the bar and went through Shawn's other hanging clothes, the way she used to before they had a maid, before it was an unforgivable intrusion. She couldn't remember buying most of these clothes, and she felt a little sick as she realized that maybe she hadn't. Everything she didn't recognize she pulled off the bar, tore from its plastic hanger, and piled on the floor. Wrinkled pants four sizes too big, scuzzy metallic button-downs, and jackets that he'd never need in a country like this. She added white sneakers that looked like they'd never been worn, as well as a basketball and pump that she found, overtaken suddenly by a nervous dawning, in the back of the closet. She went back to the desk and pulled the drawer out, emptying its contents on the bed. There were cuff links in there, an empty leather wallet, two pairs of oversized sunglasses and a blinged-out necklace with links cut to look like dollar signs—Joseph would have had a field day with this. Monique put both hands under Shawn's mattress and told Reynato to move his butt. He got up and helped her flip the mattress, sending it crashing against the far wall. She had to sit then to control her breathing. Three ziplock baggies lay on the box spring, each filled with a fistful of twisted leaves and seeds. So much for hardly ever smoking it.

Monique watched Reynato open her son's phone. He hit redial and switched it to loudspeaker, holding the phone out in the space between them. Ringing filled the room, followed by a tinny, lilting voice. "Hey Shugs, I've been trying to call you all week! Where you been?"

"Shawn isn't here," Monique said. "Who is this?"

There was a long pause. "Who's this?"

"This is Monique Thomas. Shawn's mother. Did you give my son this phone? Are you selling him drugs?"

The girl huffed impatiently and Monique imagined overlong bangs skipping in the plume of her breath. "I'm not selling anything."

"I said a month ago that you weren't to bother him again."

"Which would mean something if you were my mother. I'm not bothering anyone."

"You're bothering me." She took the phone from Reynato and held it tight. "My son's thirteen. I don't know or care why you can't find a boy your own age, but you're crossing a major line here." She took a breath, trying to find the tamest version of the threats inside her. "Put your father on the phone."

"Step off, cunt." The girl hung up.

"Snap," Reynato said. "This girl. This girl is asking for it. Doesn't know who she's messing with."

Monique dropped the cell phone, still open, on the floor. In the den she found the school directory and dialed the girl's home number.

A maid picked up after a few rings but before Monique could say anything she heard the girl's voice as well on another line. "It's all right Lucy," she said. "It's for me." The maid apologized, called the teenager ma'am and hung up.

"Your father," Monique said. "Now."

"What's wrong with you lady? Why do you have to be such a bitch?"

"Listen to me. Just because your parents let you act like trash doesn't mean everyone else will. My son is not in the Philippines for your entertainment. You're never to speak to him again, and I'll be seeing the police about the drugs you've given him."

"Get a life, bitch. Everyone we know will say I didn't give him shit, just a phone and some clothes. He's embarrassed to wear the kiddy shit you still buy." The girl hung up. Monique let the round hum of the dial tone fill her head. She called three more times but the line was busy. Then, as calmly as she could, she went into the bedroom and took one of Joseph's old sports bags from the closet. She opened the locked drawer, fished out the diamond earring she'd confiscated that spring and dropped it into the empty sports bag. She brought the bag into Shawn's room and filled it with the clothes she'd piled on the floor. Reynato helped, stuffing in the bling chain, the cuff links, the cell phone, the glass pipe and swollen baggies. The school directory said that the girl lived in Dasmariñas Village, a gated community not three miles from Fort Bonifacio. Reynato offered to drive. Minutes later Monique stood outside a strange house on Calamansi Street, Reynato waiting in his Honda across the road, in case she needed him.

The maid answered Monique's knock at the gate and told her "for a while," which meant wait. She heard an argument moving through the house and out into the yard, alternating between some kind of Chinese and Tagalog, but not enough of the latter for her to make it out. It was the girl's voice, for sure, and an older man who must have been her father. They spoke for nearly a minute on the other side of the door before the father opened it, looking more conciliatory than Monique expected. He wore a business shirt and slacks, his tie draped loose around his shoulders, reading glasses on the bridge of his nose. The girl stood with her arms crossed tight over her chest, white high-heel shoes puncturing the grassy yard.

"I understand that you called earlier," the father said. "Unfortunately I wasn't home. I'm sorry you went through all the trouble of coming here. Something like this is better discussed over the telephone."

"It wasn't any trouble," Monique said, pleased to be so in control of her voice, "and I'm sorry if I'm disturbing you. I just wanted to return these things." She hoisted the swollen sports bag through the open gate and spilled the contents out on the flagstones. The basketball rolled over wet grass to rest at the girl's feet. Two of the plastic baggies protruded from the top of the pile. "These are gifts that your daughter has given my son. They look expensive, and he can't accept them. You should also know that she's been giving him drugs."

The girl whipped a few consonants at her father's back and he smiled, sadly. He plucked up one of the plastic baggies. "You're mistaken. Your son got this elsewhere. It's a problem, among some of the Western students."

"She's lying to you."

The father's smile grew sadder—he looked absolutely grief-stricken. "This is very unfortunate. I will have to call the police if you don't take this off my property and leave right away."

"That's great, in fact, I've already brought them." She turned back to Reynato, whom she only now noticed was giving the old man and his daughter a slim middle-finger. "If you'd like I can call him over."

"Bitch, you are in-fucking-sane," the girl shouted over her father's shoulder. "Just because the ugly little horndog you call your son is a stoner, it's not my fault." Monique turned to look at her. "Yeah, he told me," she said. "And now that I see you, it's no surprise either. That shit is *obvious*."

The father began closing the gate but Monique put her fingers on the frame to stop him. "This," he said, pointing to her fingers, "is trespassing." He slid the metal gate so that it rested lightly on her knuckles without pushing on them. "I'm calling the police," he said. "I'm calling them now."

Monique let go of the frame and the gate slammed shut. On the other side she heard the father speaking Tagalog into his telephone—the skinny shit really was calling the police. She stood there dumbly as he described her to the dispatcher. Then he threw the baggies of pot over the wall and out to the sidewalk. One of them struck her in the shoulder. No. No. Shawn was her son. She wouldn't let that spoiled bitch do this to her son.

Monique collected the baggies from the sidewalk and threw them back over the wall.

"This is very silly," the father shouted, exasperated now. He threw the baggies over again, as well as the basketball and a bunch of shirts. They came over fast—his daughter must have helped. "The police are coming. The police have been called."

She didn't notice Reynato until he stood right beside her, bracing a galvanized garbage can on his shoulder. "I'm old," he grunted. "Help." Monique took hold of half the can and together they hurled it over the wall, a tongue of garbage licking out as it flew. The father shrieked and Monique imagined the can crashing wetly on his landscaping. Reynato hurled the gifts back over, getting a shirt and one of the baggies as far as the terra-cotta roof. He retreated to his Honda and lightly rammed the front gate, shattering a headlight and denting the wrought-iron. The father was out and out screaming now. Monique dove into the car. After wrestling with the gearshift, Reynato peeled out. Monique laughed so hard she cried. Or vice versa.

"Thank you," she managed. "That was great."

"Those rich shits got off easy," Reynato said. "You should've *earth-quaked* them."

"Ha." She wiped her cheeks with the back of her hand. "Imagine if I really could. That awful girl deserves it."

"Yes, she does. And yes, you can." He winked and it made half of his face look older. "You should have." He pulled down Calamansi and out onto Palm Avenue. A patrol car stopped them but after just a few words the grinning officers left them alone. No one bothered them as they exited the gated village.

"But that would make me a pretty bad bruha, wouldn't it?" Monique said.

"It would make you the kind of bruha you already are. It would make you like all other bruhas. Beautiful. Powerful. Scary. And bad."

*Chapter 16*

## DIVE

The first thing Benicio did after Solita left was call Bobby and ask if it wasn't too late to get in on that dive trip. He was eager to get away, not just from the hotel, but from the whole city. And besides, Bobby knew Solita, and he knew Howard, and he could maybe shed some light on how long their fucked-up arrangement had been going on. Since the funeral? Since before the funeral? Since Howard's first trip to the country, nearly thirteen years ago now?

Bobby picked up after just one ring. "Almost too late," he said, "but not quite." Benicio was pleased to hear how pleased he sounded. Bobby was already on the road and had to swing through Alabang to pick up Katrina, but they agreed to meet halfway, at Josephine's restaurant in Tagaytay. As soon as they hung up Benicio dialed the front desk and booked Edilberto for the day. Then he wrote a note to his father on a clean sheet of hotel stationery and slid it under the adjoining door. Just four words long, it read: *Met her. Done waiting.*

The trip out to Tagaytay took no time at all. Berto was an even greater maniac on the country roads than he was inside Manila—lead-footing the open stretches and braking hard at every turn, unable to maintain a constant speed without the orienting crush of traffic—and he got them there a good half hour before the scheduled meeting. Josephine's restaurant was large and open on the inside, with floors of glazed granite and tables cut from dark wood. It was arranged more like a theater than a restaurant, the seating area divided into three steps that all faced the same set of floor-to-ceiling windows. Benicio's travel guide mentioned this place. On a normal day the windows held a picture-perfect view of Taal volcano, but all he could see today was milky white. Clouds pressed against every square inch of glass, so thick that Josephine's may as well have been adrift in the sky.

It was late for lunch but many tables were still full—packed with mothers ladling stew from steaming pots and pudgy boys in wooden booster-chairs drinking from green coconuts with twisty straws. Benicio sat at a table near the glass, ordered a San Miguel, and waited. He thought about going back outside to ask Edilberto to join him but decided against it—not sure what the etiquette was for drivers on the clock—and instead leafed through a menu to look busy and less alone. On the last page was an illustrated picture of the view he should have been enjoying—concentric craters and lakes, a young volcano inside of an older one.

"Boy, you've got some bad timing." Benicio felt a hand on his shoulder, fingers grazing his neck. He turned to see Katrina standing over him. "Taal's on break now," she said. "I think the next show starts tomorrow morning."

"Hi there." Benicio stood. She turned down his awkward handshake for a quick, awkward hug.

"Bobby's out parking the car," she said. "He'll be with us in a minute."

"Does he need any help?"

"Probably. He won't take any, though. Especially from you." They sat and Katrina put both her elbows on the table and rested her chin on her palms. "So," she said, "Bobby filled me in on the way here. I guess there was a bit of draaama," she stretched the word in an attempted drawl, "last night? It's a little embarrassing to admit, but I don't really remember . . . well, any of it. That's embarrassing isn't it?" She paused. "And you know, I just wanted to say sorry. I mean, I don't think I was, but just in case I was, you know, one of the chief offenders."

"You weren't. It was mostly my fault."

"That's what I suspected." Her grin was oddly manic. "I mean, not about you, but about me. Because, normally, I'm pretty nice. But you never know. That's an expectation I've been known to defy, from time to time. When drinking. And hey," she gestured down to his still mostly full San Miguel, "I guess the night can't have been a total bust. You converted, all the same."

Bobby Dancer entered the restaurant some minutes later. He must have changed his bandages since that morning, because these were crisp and dry. In addition to layers of gauze he wore an airy cotton shirt and a pair of denim jeans—one of those expensive acid-wash brands that come pre-faded, pre-torn and pre-mended. Bobby waved at them and made his way over. He took the stairs slowly; his feet turned sideways like a mountain climber, one hand gripping the railing and the other balled tight around the head of his cane. Benicio rose to go to him but Katrina grabbed his forearm and pinned it to the table with surprising force.

"Well," Bobby said when he finally reached them, "it's good to see you." He pulled a chair back, lowered himself into it like an old man, and leaned his cane against the table. "I was worried that we wouldn't get the chance to make second impressions on each other, considering the first one." He reached across the table and shook Benicio's hand. "I spoke to Ping. He sends his apologies and would also like me to tell you that you hit like a baby."

"Don't tease!" Katrina said, taking Benicio's wrist in a way that made him a little uneasy and also pleased him. "Given the choice between someone with no practice hitting faces and someone who is really good at hitting faces, I'd rather know, or get to know, the first person. The one with no practice." She flagged down a passing waitress, pointed at Benicio's bottle, and stuck two fingers in the air. "Come on, let's not talk about it anymore."

"Yes," Bobby said as he slowly unfolded his napkin and laid it over his lap, "let's not." The waitress arrived with two more beers and Bobby lifted his to make a toast. "To America," he said. "Let no one talk shit about her, lest they have their faces busted in by GI Ben."

Benicio raised his own bottle. Despite the fight last night, and despite the discovery this morning, he felt himself relaxing. It was somehow very easy to be in this place, with these people. "Except for you," he said as he clinked his bottle against Bobby's. "You can talk all the shit you want because you've had your face pre-busted."

Katrina coughed through an aborted swallow. Bobby lowered his San Miguel without drinking and looked at Benicio. "Well imagine that," he said. "Who would have thought that there was a sense of humor underneath all that khaki?"

BOBBY ORDERED FOR THE TABLE and they ate quickly. Benicio found the food—like the language—hauntingly familiar. The pork adobo wasn't totally unlike his mother's adobo, and there was some pickled fish with peppers that resembled the ceviche she'd stopped making by the time he got to high school. Bobby let him pick up the check without an argument and led them, slowly, out to the lot.

It had cooled outside, and a breeze spilled fog up from the basin of the crater and out over the road. Benicio retrieved his dive bag from the Shangri-La sedan and followed Bobby and Katrina to a big white Expedition that took up two handicapped spaces right in front of the restaurant. "Hey," Bobby said as he opened the back so Benicio could hoist his gear inside, "at least the parking's better lately." He shot Katrina a grim smile that she didn't return and then took his time getting into the high driver's seat. Benicio found space in the back between mesh bags overflowing with fins and wetsuits. He looked back as they pulled out of the lot, hoping to catch a glimpse of the volcano, or at least the inner rim of the crater. All he could see was a warm spot behind the clouds.

Their trip south brought them back along Taal's outer rim and then down through fields of pineapple and palm. After about an hour, once the ground evened out and everybody's ears popped, Bobby turned onto a dirt road cut jagged by tiny dry riverbeds. He winced as the Expedition bounced and jostled, but he didn't slow down. The brush thickened about the road; a mix of bamboo and tree trunks that looked like premature driftwood, broken here and there by hand-painted signs advertising dive hotels. "That's us," Bobby said through gritted teeth, pointing out the window to a piece of plywood reading: *Balayan Bay*

*Dive Club—Welcome Friends!—Management not responsible for vehicles parked overnight.* The lot was just a clearing of tire-flattened grass, and theirs was the only car.

They were still a few hundred feet above the water, and narrow concrete stairs snaked down a wooded slope to the beach below. Benicio looked down and saw the thatched roofs of whitewashed hotel bungalows—their backs to the dense hillside jungle and their doors opening upon the alternating indigo and turquoise of reef and sandy bottom. The deeper water was marked by the moving shadows of clouds, vast smudges that could just as well be the backs of great things that traveled beneath the surface.

"I'll go first and get someone to help us with the bags," Katrina announced. Bobby, who'd just managed to lower himself from the driver's seat and was dabbing sweat from the exposed parts of his face, watched as she took the stairs two and three at a time.

"You'll be all right to get down?" Benicio asked.

"Just fine," Bobby said without looking at him. "I'll take it slow." Behind them a skinny goat emerged from the grass and blinked at the tracks left by the Expedition. Bobby made a puckered kissing sound like you might to a dog, and the goat swished its tail but didn't look at him. He took out a cigarette, lit it and blew a plume of smoke at the animal. "It's just going to be you and Katrina today," he said. "On the dive, I mean."

"I figured as much."

Bobby shook his pack of cigarettes in Benicio's direction and pocketed it when the offer was refused. "Normally I'd be going, too . . ." he sounded almost apologetic. "We got certified together a few years back and we try to go whenever we get the chance. I made this reservation about two months ago . . . I thought, hey, if Charlie wins then this trip'll be a damn good way to celebrate. If he loses, it'll be a chance to get wet, get drunk and get the fuck over it. A man needs a break either way, right? But lately I've been less," he stabbed his cane into the long blades of yellowing grass, "graceful. Katrina wanted to cancel at first." Bobby took a long drag and held it inside. "It's good you came."

"You had an accident," Benicio said. It sounded more like a procla-
mation than the question he intended it to be.

"You could call it that. I sure as hell didn't do it on purpose." He
reached down, plucked up a handful of grass and held it out to the goat
in offering, making that same kissing sound. The goat eyed him with its
horizontal cat pupils and shuffled backward. "I'm sorry about Katrina,"
Bobby said, his tone suddenly much lighter. "She's not bothering you,
is she?"

"What do you mean?" Benicio asked.

"She comes on strong. The flirting thing can be a bit much."

Benicio nodded slowly for a while. "She's really nice," he said. He
wanted to be polite, but clear. "She's not my type."

Bobby turned to him, the ember of his cigarette a slow pulse. "No?"
The word came out as smoke. It floated between them, changed shape a
few times, and disappeared. Benicio returned his gaze, wondering how
best to bring up the Solita thing. But Katrina was back before he could
say anything. Two shirtless boys trailed behind her and they exchanged
big grins at the sight of Benicio. "You see that?" Bobby asked. "They like
you, too."

"Who likes who?" Katrina asked, still panting a bit from her jog
back up the stairs.

"Nobody," Bobby said. "Nobody likes anybody else. Except for me. I
like everybody else. I'm loving."

"You are." Katrina gave Bobby a very light pinch on the tip of his
nose. "I could eat you up and shit out puppies." She opened the hatch-
back trunk and handed off dive gear to the shirtless boys, each of whom
donned mesh duffel bags like backpacks, hand straps slung over their
shoulders. "You mind checking us all in?" she asked. "If Ben and I get
going now we can probably still fit two dives in before it gets dark."

"Go ahead." Bobby dropped his cigarette in the grass and extinguished it with the rubber tip of his cane. "I'll see you when you surface."

Katrina took Benicio's hand and, together with the shirtless boys,
they headed down toward the beach.

BENICIO'S FIRST DIVE, the one with his father in Costa Rica, had not gone well at all. Not for either of them. Within the first minute he'd almost ruptured a lung and by the end of the dive his father had managed to get thoroughly drugged on the nitrogen in his tank. As Benicio thought about it now, he blamed those early mistakes on his hard-on for the Costa Riqueña dive instructor. Days earlier, when she'd lined them up beside the training pool to go through each and every piece of gear, all he'd learned was that it was nearly impossible to hide an erection in a wetsuit.

The instructor started slow. "This is a mask," she said. "It goes on your face." She put it on to demonstrate. She stripped down to a modest one-piece bathing suit—a few sizes too small for her slightly chubby frame—and began donning the rest of the dive gear, taking time to explain the uses of each device. By the time she got to: "This is the first stage regulator," all Benicio saw was a mess of metal bulbs and hoses that blocked his view of the gully that ran between her tits. "It connects directly to your tank and sends air to the mouthpiece, your pressure gages, your octopus and into your buoyancy control device, which we'll get to in a minute. The mouthpiece goes in your mouth." Again, she demonstrated. "Da thick ith doo juth breathe noomal." Her breasts moved when she laughed, which sounded a little like panic through the mess of rubber and plastic. When she pulled the mouthpiece out she looked grave and serious. "Whatever you do, do not, not ever, hold your breath. That's what your instincts will say, but your instincts are wrong."

But sure enough, after doing a backward roll into the cold water on his first checkout dive, Benicio did what came natural. He held his breath. It wasn't until his depth gauge read *25 feet* that he realized what he was doing. Claustrophobia and panic set in quick. He took a single gulp of air through his mouthpiece and began to kick wildly for the surface, his eyes shut tight and tearing. A pain rose inside his chest—only later would he understand that it was the air expanding in his lungs, looking for a place to go. Something grabbed his ankle and when he opened his eyes and looked down he saw the dive instructor staring up at him with an expression of forced calm. She held him tight with one hand to keep him from ascending further. With the other she removed the regulator from her mouth. A steady stream of small bubbles poured out of her puckered lips and she pointed to them. "Respira," she mouthed. "Breathe out." Benicio exhaled and felt his insides scraped as air rushed out of his deflating chest. Then he took a single breath in. Out again. In again. Slowly, and not without embarrassment, he let her pull him back down to the sandy bottom where the other students were arranged in a clumsy, swaying semicircle.

The rest of the dive passed uneventfully for Benicio—he even redeemed himself a bit by being the first to be able to take his mask off, put it back on and fill it with air from his purged mouthpiece—but just before it was time to surface his father fell into his own trouble. They were drifting over a ledge of coral when his father, who'd loaded his weight belt to make up for the natural buoyancy of fat, began sinking much faster than he should have. He didn't seem to notice at first, and even when he looked up and saw that the other members of the group had become vague silhouettes above, he didn't try to swim back to them. In fact, to Benicio's horror, he did the opposite. He started swimming down, kicking with a wild determination. Benicio made to follow him but the dive instructor gave him a very unambiguous hand signal indicating that he should wait with the other students. She disappeared into the haze below and returned some minutes later towing Howard behind her like a small parade float. Benicio pressed himself to his father's mask and saw behind it two eyes that rolled about euphorically. His father pulled his mouthpiece out and let it float freely until the instructor put it back in. Once they surfaced she explained that he'd gotten himself stoned—that was her word, not Benicio's—on the nitrogen in his tank by descending too quickly and too deeply. She also told them, in private back at the resort, that they both had to take all of the classroom sessions over again before she would let them back in the open water.

• • •

BUT THAT WAS A LONG TIME AGO. Benicio was a much better diver now, and despite his lack of practice, the excursion with Katrina went well. They stayed shallow, hit swift but manageable current and flirted casually on their decompression stop. It was twilight when they got back to the hotel. They rinsed their gear in barrels of brackish water and left it drying on bamboo racks. Benicio was urgently hungry—diving, he remembered now, always did that; whatever you felt, you felt more after diving; whatever you needed, you needed more—so he and Katrina put their day clothes on over their swimsuits and headed straight to dinner. They walked down the narrow beach to the two-story main building of the Balayan Bay Dive Club. White-washed and thatched like all the bungalows, it housed an open-air restaurant on the lower level and an observation deck that supported a slow cascade of purple bougainvillea on the upper. Bobby was already there when they arrived, helping himself to the small buffet. "Fuck," he said, his plate wobbling slightly. "I've ordered beers. Catch up."

The meal was awkward. Bobby was already very drunk, and he got drunker at a pace that neither of them cared to match. He toasted to them both, first individually and then as a pair. He toasted to the shirt-less boys who came by to light beachside torches anchored deep in the rocky sand. He toasted to Charlie Fuentes, and to his alter ego, the real Ocampo. And he toasted Howard, "Wherever he might be." Torchlight flickered wickedly over his divided face. One of the boys returned to the table to say that, while they did have more beer to offer, it was all warm. Katrina suggested this was a sign that Bobby should go to bed.

"Nonsense," he said, waving her off. "This is a problem that I have a solution for. I am a man of solutions. I am a solver." He brought his empty beer to his lips and then, remembering it was empty, set it back on the table. "In my room. In my duffel bag which is in my room . . ." he paused. "I have a fifth of rye."

"I think you've had enough," Katrina said.

"You, my love, should talk." He got up and left the restaurant, walking across the sand toward the guest bungalows. After getting about twenty yards away he stopped and pitched forward a bit, nearly stumbling. They all seemed to realize at the same moment that he didn't have his cane.

"I'm not bringing it to you," she called, her voice carrying over broken shells. "If you're going to use it to get more booze, I'm not helping."

"Do I need help? I do not. I have the reflexes of a dancer," Bobby shouted. "Onward." But he didn't go on, or come back. He stood for a long time in that spot. Then he sat and faced the water.

"He's stubborn," Katrina said in a low voice. "He'll stay there until he falls asleep, likely." Then she put her fingers around Benicio's wrist, as she had been doing since the night before, when they'd met in his father's restaurant. Could it really have been just the night before? "I'm going down to the water," she said. "You should come with me."

Benicio couldn't escape the feeling that he'd already lost. Even if he didn't do it, he really, really wanted to. "I think I'll keep an eye on Bobby," he managed. Katrina lingered at the table for a moment, still holding his wrist. Then she let it go and walked down to the shore, in the opposite direction that Bobby had gone. Benicio watched her fade to nothing in the torchlight. He picked up Bobby's cane and went to sit beside him in the coarse sand.

"Hey," Bobby said, "you want the key to my room?" He jingled it in the dark space between them. "The fifth is almost full."

"I'm not getting it," Benicio said. "You shouldn't, either."

"I shouldn't," Bobby agreed. "I should not." He took his cane and worked it into the sand. A little mound rose above it, like the mounds of earth above Bugs Bunny when he tunnels somewhere. Benicio heard a noise behind them and turned. The shirtless boys were back there, watching from amid the palm trunks that caught the last traces of torchlight like a sieve. They stared back at him fearlessly, delightedly, before returning to the main bungalow at a fast walk.

Benicio turned back around and found Bobby's face and mouth closer than they should have been. There was weight on his chest and dry, soft gauze against his cheek. He made sure not to push him away too hard, for fear of hurting him.

"I'm sorry," Benicio said.

"What for?" Bobby rubbed the back of his hand over his lower lip. There was spit and sand on it.

"I didn't mean to . . . I didn't know."

"You didn't?" He pulled a cigarette from the pack in his pocket and struggled to light it. "Man. Maybe I should get new business cards." The flame finally caught and he sucked in deep. "Or like, a custom shirt or something like that."

"No," Benicio said. "I mean I didn't know you were serious about me."

"Who's serious?" Bobby looked at him. "So . . . is it the bandages?"

"I'm not gay."

Bobby laughed, but he'd been dragging on his cigarette, so he also coughed a lot. "Then what the fuck are you doing with a pretty, strange boy like myself, on a pretty, strange beach? Why did you even come with us today? Don't—do not tell me it's for Katrina. Because that shit is a game."

"I wanted to ask you about the woman in the green dress. The one in the ballroom. I wanted to ask how long my father's been with her." *With* sounded like the wrong word, but he couldn't bring himself to say *fucking.*

Bobby looked at him. "Oh Benny." He sounded disappointed. "Sneaky and dishonest is much worse than careless and deluded. It's not any of your business."

"It's as much mine as it is yours. It's more mine than it is yours."

"This is a conversation you should be having with Howard."

"He's not around to have it with."

Bobby lay back in the sand, filling the empty sky above him with smoke. "Since as long as I've known him," he said. "Going on three years."

"Is it a relationship?"

"If you're asking if he pays, then yes. He pays."

Benicio sat there for a moment. He felt more deflated than angry. It was no huge shock that his father, even as he tried to fix their relationship, kept on doing the same thing that broke it. He was a cheat before his mother died and that made him still a cheat now that she was gone.

Benicio stood. "What's this about a game?" he asked. "What do you mean about Katrina?"

Bobby flicked his cigarette straight up in the air and it landed a few feet downwind. "The bubbly bimbo thing is an act," he said, "which I guess you would have noticed if you ever did more than just glance at her. She's out for revenge. She had a thing for this boy, a while back. And I had a thing *with* him. Twice. She got mad. You were in her cross-hairs as soon as she saw I liked you." Bobby laughed and then, noticing his expression, said, "Oh, woe is you."

Benicio left him where he lay. He headed down to the water, shat-tering what could have been perfect little shells under his dive booties. It struck him that Bobby and Katrina were just like his dad. They were all frivolous, irresponsible rich people playing screwed-up games. He again wondered about Bobby's injuries. He imagined him crashing a borrowed car, or sleeping with the son of hardcore Catholics just to prove he could, and then having to reckon with a beefy uncle. Up ahead small waves crushed and sucked. His ankles went cold as he strode into the gentle surf.

Katrina was some yards out, standing in water up to her thighs. Odd lights swirled about her. Tiny, blue-green dots flicked atop the low waves, glowing in a thick band where they washed up along shore.

"Benny." It was Katrina's voice but it wasn't her name to call him. "Are you seeing this?" She splashed the water a little and that agitated the lights, sent them sparkling. "Plankton! It washes up sometimes on this beach. Not all the time, though. We're lucky."

Benicio waded out to her. His mother had described a scene very much like this a few months before she died. It was Thanksgiving. He'd come home from Virginia, and Howard had come home from the Philippines. As always, Benicio hardly spoke to him. But this time his mother wouldn't have it. She cornered him in the kitchen and said, "Sinvergüenza. Are you a man or are you a child? Whatever you're mad about, get over it."

"Whatever *I'm* mad about?" he asked. "You should be just as angry. It's you he cheats on, not me."

And then his mother slapped him. She slapped him so hard he

almost lost his balance and fell to the kitchen linoleum like a decked welterweight. "What the hell do you know about it?" she asked, hardly trying to keep her voice from carrying to the dining room, where his father sat alone at the table. "You're a little saint, aren't you? Well, I know for a fact that you'll do the same thing. You'll be on some beach, with some skinny muñeca's tongue in your mouth while Alice is asleep, thinking that you're nothing but good to her. It'll happen, that's a promise."

But it hadn't happened. It wouldn't. His mother's dreams were bullshit. She didn't know what she was talking about. Benicio told Katrina good night. He told her to stop playing games with him. He told her that her friend was on the beach and needed to be helped to his room.

Chapter 17

## PIE AND PIRATES

Efrem Khalid Bakkar watches doctors hem and haw over the best way to save Racha Casuco's life. He sits, transfixed, on an elevated observation deck. Racha lies beyond the aquarium-style glass, skimming the surface of dying, submerging—now for a minute, now for two—and surfacing. No one on Task Force Ka-Pow seems to be concerned. Lorenzo stalks the hospital in search of a cafeteria. Reynato is outdoors, fielding questions from concerned reporters. Shirtless Elvis sits in an adjacent folding chair, nose in a glossy American magazine, bare feet propped against the glass, ignoring the butchering and mending below.

A full hour gone by and the doctors are still unable to get the fish-man's blade out of Racha's chest. They yank at the handle, working the steel about his insides, unable to loose it. They bring in specialists, and strong young interns, and a priest, who sits on a stool in the corner, horrified. "Does it usually last this long?" Efrem asks.

"Depends," Elvis says, still examining the best and worst dressed of Santa Barbara. "Sometimes Racha gets off easy. Door slams on his finger, sprains his ankle—something like that. We once arrested a whole cell of New People's Army in Quezon, and all Racha had to show for it was a splinter in his ass cheek. But sometimes it's pretty bad. This one's bad, but not the worst." Elvis looks up from his magazine. "Last year I was picking shrapnel out of the poor kid's ear. Good old Racha. Get him bloody, but you won't get him down."

Cheering erupts below. One of the interns has managed to work the blade out. Surgeons descend upon the open wound with needles and thread. To Efrem they look like the old men back home, squatting beneath gum trees, all mending different pieces of the same big net.

Elvis turns to pictures of frail women carrying dogs. "I'll tell you something," he says, "I wouldn't ever trade what he does for what I do. Always getting hurt and never dying? *No thanks.* Not for me. I'd rather be a dog, full time. A mosquito, even."

Efrem says nothing. He watches machines pump blood and air in and out of Racha. One of them begins a beeping protest and a jagged line goes flat. He's dead again. Doctors quit sewing and defibrillate. The priest in the corner stands, ready to do his part. Still, Elvis seems unconcerned.

"You a religious man?" he asks, glancing down briefly at the robed father.

"My family was," Efrem says. "They thought God gave me these." He makes a backward peace sign and puts a finger under each magic eye.

Elvis leans back, propping his feet higher on the glass. "They sound like my family," he says. "My dad and brothers all went to seminary in Vigan. Tried to send me also . . . a few times. They never did figure out how I kept getting away. I could do a great impression of our dog, Biag. Dad once went out looking for me with *me* leading the way, hot on my own scent. He stopped every few minutes to hold my paws and pray. He was crazy for that shit."

Elvis pauses for a while, smiling. This is the most ever said in Efrem's company. "Are you crazy for it?" he asks.

"I pray."

"You think someone's listening?"

"I wouldn't if I didn't."

Below them Racha breathes again, and the agitated machines calm down. Nurses dismiss the priest while surgeons backtrack to tighten the wet seam holding Racha closed. The door to the observation deck opens and Reynato strides in, sucking his soggy cigar, fanning himself with his cap. Lorenzo enters a moment later, riding a decked-out dessert trolley like a go-cart. He parks beside Efrem and, to his surprise, offers him a slice of buko pie. Efrem accepts. It's delicious.

The doctors complete their final stitch and a happy commotion grows in the theater below. Everybody shakes hands, posing beside Racha's bloodied form as a nurse takes pictures with her telephone. The head surgeon looks up at the observation window and flashes a big bloody thumbs-up. Stripping off his gloves and mask, he joins them in the cool air behind the glass. He tries and fails to look somber, pacing and twitching like a meth-addled junkie. "I once had a patient," he says, "stabbed deep through the chest. He lived only because of the slimmest—*the stupidest*—luck. The knife navigated the maze of his guts perfectly, damaging nothing. Let me be clear," he says, "your friend is *not* this patient. It's no less crazy, but your friend is the opposite. The blade has done minor damage to virtually every organ in Racha's body. Pierced skin, cracked ribs, hewn heart valve, nicked lungs, skewered liver, grazed stomach lining, whittled esophagus and—at the point where it came to a denting stop—a fractured upper vertebrae. It took an effort from every department in this hospital, but we're confident he'll survive. He has a long and extremely painful recovery ahead."

"I'm sure you're right about the painful part," Reynato says. He approaches the viewing glass and knocks hard. "Racha! Quick-quick this time. That cocksucker Fuentes needs my ass in Manila by Friday. I already got flights, and so help me, if I get charged a rebooking fee on account of you being a sulky baby I'll take the difference out of your paycheck!"

Racha is unresponsive below. Reynato looks at where the viewing glass meets the wall to gauge its thickness. He turns back to the head surgeon. "Can he hear me down there?" he asks. "I think I'd better go to him."

The surgeon takes Reynato by the wrist. "Sir! Mr. Ocampo . . . I don't think you understand. He'll need months of bed rest. He'll need supervised rehabilitation. Traveling this week isn't just unhealthy, it's impossible. And besides, you can't go down there. There's no smoking in the operating rooms."

Reynato plucks the cigar from his teeth and taps it with his pinky, as though ashing. "You see smoke?" he asks. He frees himself politely from the surgeon's grip and leads Ka-Pow below to collect their friend.

HE'S RIGHT, OF COURSE. Racha recovers in three days, but in that time he travels through more pain than Efrem thinks it possible to emerge whole from. Wide awake the whole time, he shivers and calls for blankets even with the air-conditioning off, mosquitoes buzzing joyfully though open windows. He picks his stitches, sweats blood, bleeds sweat, and loses his screaming voice before running out of things to scream about. Efrem and Elvis tend to him as best they can, which mostly means hitting rewind, play, and sometimes slow-motion on pornos in the VCR. "You see what I mean?" Elvis asks, patting Racha's hacking torso. "This boy came up short in the bruho department. This isn't the kind of power you wear a costume for."

By Friday Racha looks about as healed as he's ever going to get, and that afternoon Task Force Ka-Pow boards a flight bound for the capital. They land shortly before dark, Manila stretching all around like a high, dry reef. Immediately upon deplaning Reynato is swallowed by a modest bevy of reporters and Ocampo enthusiasts, but once they discover that Charlie Fuentes isn't with him their excitement flags, and they disperse. Apparently the real Ocampo interests them far less than the false one. Efrem, for his life, can't imagine why. Neither, it seems, can Reynato, who looks hurt as the cameramen pack their gear and grumble about an evening wasted.

Though Efrem doesn't remember anyone having suitcases when they left Davao, they each grab one from the baggage carousel before squeezing into a taxicab—Reynato up front and the four bruhos crammed impossibly into the back. Thankfully the ride to Reynato's home is brief. He lives in Magallanes Village, a gated community nestled grimly between EDSA and the South Superhighway. As they pass through the guarded checkpoint Reynato explains that this neighborhood isn't so swanky as Dasmariñas, where Charlie Fuentes lives, but to Efrem it looks swanky as hell. He's dumbstruck by Reynato's house—three stories of plaster, wood and limestone tile, all walled in by a concrete bulwark topped with mortar and shards of Tanduay bottles. Beyond the wrought-iron gate is a front yard overgrown with lush calamansi trees, bisected by winding flagstones that lead to great double-doors affixed with an antique Intramuros knocker. Out back there's a veritable papaya grove, a lawn cut neat as a putting green and a small swimming pool.

"That's movie cash for you," Lorenzo says, amused at Efrem's evident shock. "He still won't give us a taste of those royalty checks."

"That's because I don't get any," Reynato says from up front, still sore about the reporters' cold shoulders back on the tarmac. "I just know how to invest . . . and dabble." He winks bitterly into the rearview, opens the door and retrieves one of the suitcases from the trunk. Efrem opens his own door, set to get out as well. Reynato gives him a brief, quiet look; embarrassed for his sake. "I don't think so, Mohammed. I love you, and all. But mi casa, *mi casa.*"

He turns his back on the cab, fiddling with keys, working them into a series of iron locks. Lorenzo chuckles, not unkindly, as Efrem shuts his door. The taxi departs the gated village, continuing down EDSA, into the heat-pumped heart of downtown Makati.

THEY NEXT STOP among the dingily landscaped roots of an apartment high-rise. Lorenzo, Racha and Elvis pile out. Efrem remains in the taxi. Lorenzo raps on the glass and stares him in the face. "Come on, kid. We've had our differences, you and I, but I wouldn't do you like that. Follow me."

With that he breezily leads the others into the lobby, leaving Efrem to pay the fare. By the time he catches up they're already in the elevator, Elvis transformed into a svelte black cat, staring intensely at the lighted buttons like they're tiny yellow birds. To Efrem's continued amazement, the elevator stops at the penthouse, where the bruhos wander out into a tremendous flat, floored in marble of alternating white and black. He's never been inside—*never even seen*—a place like this. It's even more incredible to him than Reynato's massive house. As a bona-fide national hero, Reynato deserves to live like that. But they, surely, do not.

Racha, still weak from his ordeal, heads straight to bed and Elvis races down the hall, leaping up on the windowsill to gaze lustily at the lighted streets below. Lorenzo lingers with Efrem on the landing, regarding him bemusedly. "I know what you're thinking," he says. "You're thinking: No way these boys can afford this on police salaries. And there isn't anybody making movies about *them*. So they've got to have something on the side—some source of dirty money." Efrem nods, because yes, that's exactly what he's thinking. "Well, you're righter than you know." Wincing a bit, Lorenzo reaches into his ear and produces a filthy twenty-five sentimo coin—earwax coating the entire thing, some blood speckling the words *Bangko* and *Sentral*. "Took years," he says. "It's when I got impatient and upgraded to those fat five peso coins that my eardrum burst. But it was and continues to be worth it." He steps across the massive entryway, arms outstretched as though to hug his own home.

"So . . . I'm staying here?" Efrem can't quite wrap his mind around it.

Lorenzo doesn't turn around, but Efrem sees his reflection grin in the window. "You've got somewhere else to go?"

"No," he says, "I don't."

"Well then. You're welcome." Lorenzo crosses to the glass, gazing out at Makati. He strokes Elvis's neck lightly and Elvis, like a perfect alley cat, affects an unconvincing indifference. "Best make yourself at home, because Renny won't have much use for us until after this election. That slick fucker Fuentes means to squeeze him dry. He'll have him running all over the city, cashing in favors, rallying support, smiling like he means it. Because as of now, you're still on layaway. Renny's gotta *pay* for your ass."

Efrem joins Lorenzo at the window, gazing out at the night-drenched avenues and towers. Commuter helicopters drift and trawl through the smog, and the traffic below sparkles like phosphorescent plankton. His deep shame at being a source of aggravation for his life-long hero is counterbalanced by the exhilarating thought that Reynato deems him *worth it*. Lorenzo glances at him sidelong and misreads his expression as one of continued awe at the opulent bruho apartment.

"Who's your daddy?" he says.

"I don't know," Efrem responds, flatly, and without guile.

Lorenzo blinks at him for a moment. Then he laughs so hard that his forehead strikes the window and scares Elvis off the sill. The glass vibrates with the strike, and for a moment it looks as though the city itself is shaking.

AND SO, FOR TEN-ODD DAYS Ka-Pow lays dormant while their leader shills for the windbag would-be senator. Reynato doesn't show until the evening after the election, and he looks supremely put out, grumbling: "So help me, Mohammed, you better be worth this silly shit." He says it's time they got back to their true calling. He says the country needs Ka-Pow tonight. He says they'll be hunting pirates.

The target is a well-known smuggler of knockoff medications—sugar tablets sold throughout the provinces as cancer medicine, heart drugs, antibiotics, even boner-pills. The right size and color, packaged up in bottles looking just like the real thing. "But they're as good as rat poison to people who are sick," Reynato says. "He's moving a shipment from producers to a distribution warehouse tonight. They've already escaped three raids by the Manila Police, so the NBI has requested that we come in for the assist." Lorenzo gives an appreciative hoot at this, and Reynato grins. Everybody, it seems, is hurting for some action.

Ka-Pow collects just after sunset on the garbage-strewn banks of the Pasig River, some hundred meters upstream of the warehouse. They hide behind the hull of a rusted, mudsunk jeepney, awash in stinking steam rising off the green water. Efrem uses his fantastical peepers to gaze up the loading ramp, under the door and into every corner of the warehouse. Three men await the pirate—two playing Pusoy Dos in the back office, another sleeping on a chair just inside the loading dock.

"Three doesn't sound too bad," Racha says, furrowing his welted brow, maybe wondering how bad his injuries will be this time around. Efrem feels little sympathy for him. Knowing that only Racha will be hurt tonight is calming.

The moon intrudes on twilight, and stilted shanties on the opposite bank go dark, snuffing their electric and oil-fueled lamps. Finally a little truck turns a corner and wrecks the quiet with air-brakes. The loading dock opens and men inside wave the pirate up the ramp. A second engine in the warehouse barks and a small forklift emerges. The pirate opens his truck and loads boxes onto an empty palate. Efrem tenses. Reynato grabs him by the wrist.

"Easy, killer. You see any weapons inside?"

His eyes are all pupil. "One shotgun on a desk in the office," he says. "And the pirate has a Colt in his belt. That's it."

Silence. Warehouse tenders finish loading the pallet and the pirate follows them inside. "Elvis!" Reynato hisses. "You first. Get inside. You're on that shotgun."

Elvis stands, kicking mud off his toes. He performs the first half of a high jump and disappears. A bald starling fills his spot in the sky. Wings beating air like a swimmer, he flies clumsily over the riverbank and into an air vent on the warehouse roof. Efrem watches him negotiate the rafters, perching beside pigeons above the open cubicle office. Then, following Reynato, he creeps through syrupy garbage. Edging along the wall, they stop just short of the dock. Reynato takes Glock out of his belt. "Be loud," he says. "Scaring them is more than half of it." He breathes long and deep, cramming air, chambering a shout. When it comes it's big enough to wake shanties on the opposite bank. "Police!" Lorenzo, Racha and Efrem shout as well. Guns drawn, Ka-Pow pours in.

The pirate and three warehouse tenders stand wide-eyed about the forklift, loose fingers on celebratory San Mig shortnecks. One makes for the office but stops at the sight of shirtless Elvis in the doorway, shotgun leveled. Reynato chants orders. "Hands on heads. Knees on the ground. Hands on heads. Knees on the ground." He breaks rhythm to shoot out the forklift tires. The pirate and warehouse men let their beers shatter. They put hands on their heads. They put knees on the ground. They look at Efrem, horrified, and he imagines himself a man made of light. Tall as a palm tree. Towering over cheering children in the outdoor movie house.

Reynato orders Racha to cuff them and Racha knows it's time. His snubnosed pistol shakes as he edges toward the pirate. Snatching the Colt from the pirate's belt, he lets the magazine fall, ejects a round from the chamber and throws the empty piece to the other end of the warehouse. He cuffs the pirate. He cuffs two of the warehouse tenders and turns to the third, a chubby man in an informal, short-sleeved barong. He has a fountain pen behind his ear, and when Racha reaches for him he stabs it clean through Racha's palm, where it protrudes like a sixth finger. The snubnosed pistol falls and the two become a tangle of arms and cursing as they grab for it.

Efrem's silenced Tingin makes the sound of whipped air. His shot nicks the chubby man's earlobe and the tiny wound is enough to get him down and sobbing out of a scrunched-up face. Racha blinks at the pen half through his bleeding hand. He recovers his snubnosed and beats the chubby man's face with it. Reynato grabs his gnarled scruff like a puppy and pulls him back. "Easy!" he scolds. "Man needs a mouth to answer questions with." Racha goes easy. He handcuffs the man and gives him a final slap with his skewered palm.

What happens next is mostly a blur. It doesn't go by quick, but it doesn't go the way it should. Elvis discovers a pleatherbound briefcase full of pesos in the office. A quick count puts it over twenty million. Everybody goes silent. Reynato fans himself with a stack of bills. He talks to the pirate in his polite voice. He asks about suppliers and contacts. He asks why there's so much money. He asks about dates, weights and destinations. All he gets back is a mess of beer-thick spit on his shoes.

Lorenzo approaches, flamboyant, heel-toe. He does a little bow, a flourish and lays the pirate out on concrete. Then, from the folds of his clear plastic poncho he produces a singing handsaw. Warehouse men scream as Lorenzo halves the pirate just above the waist. It takes no time at all. Lower half kicking, upper half shouting a past-tense protest, just a finger of red space between. "You killed me," he shouts. "You killed me. I died."

Reynato encourages the upper half to get ahold of itself. "This isn't what you think," he says, "this is just an illusion. The fear you're feeling is real—the pain isn't. Pain never is. Just tell me what I want to know and we'll put you back together, good as new."

The pirate's upper half stares about, wildly. Surnames, nicknames, middlenames jumble in his mouth. Reynato pulls the fountain pen the rest of the way through Racha's palm and takes dictation on a thousand-peso bill. He fills both sides with tiny block lettering, gore blotting the ink. After that the halved pirate has trouble breathing enough air to make words. "That's enough," Reynato says. "Fix him." Lorenzo prances back over, hamming it up for the trembling warehouse men. He unclasps his poncho and lays it over the pirate. He pulls a string of multicolored kerchiefs from his straw hat and waves them about in the air. He taps once on the poncho, above the sawslice. "Pesto!" He pulls the poncho off with a flourish.

The pirate is still neatly divided. His lower half no longer kicks and his upper half just blinks. For the first time, Reynato looks concerned. "Enough goofing," he says, "the man did what I asked. Fix him."

Lorenzo repeats the routine with less flair. Now neither half moves at all. Blood snakes about the warehouse floor, seeking a drain to the Pasig. Lorenzo puts a finger on the tip of his chin and looks contemplative. He announces that the only kind of news he has is bad. He's never, come to think of it, tried this on a man. "Only ladies," he says. "Correction—only pretty ladies. It works on them, honest to God."

The weather outside gets bad and some garbage blows into the loading dock. Reynato uncuffs the pirate's upper half. He uncuffs the warehouse men. They look at one another, confused. He tells Lorenzo to try one more time and Lorenzo tries one more time. The pirate remains dead in two pieces. Reynato squats and massages his temples. One of the warehouse men messes his pants. Another prays in Latin. Reynato plucks a pack of cigarettes from the pirate's shirt pocket. He snaps the filter off of one, clusters it with three more in his fist and has Ka-Pow draw lots. Efrem loses the game, and he doesn't know what that means, at first.

CELEBRATION ON THE RIDE home starts out a little forced. Racha blinks at them through the hole in his palm, grinning because he considers this getting off easy. Lorenzo sings along to English tunes on the radio. He stomps to the beat, muddy feet on a bright blanket of spilled money. Back at the high-rise flat they pile into the kitchen for beers. Efrem washes his hands a long time and fills a glass with the tapwater that only he dares drink. He retires to his room, sits on the edge of his bedroll and listens to toasts and roughhousing down the hall.

Efrem wipes away the signs of his crying when he hears Reynato coming. He walks past the open door twice, cigar backward in his mouth, before looking in and saying: "There you are, Mohammed. We're missing you."

"I'll be right there," Efrem says. But what he wants to say is: *What I did tonight does not feel like sticking up for the unstuckup for.*

"Hey. Hey." Reynato sits beside him, taking his measure with a long, sympathetic stare. "I see the look behind that look. No need to fake happy, if it's fake. But I'll tell you what; I'm a little surprised at you, Mohammed. Not in a bad way. It's just . . ." Reynato puts a hand on Efrem's knee. "Given the time you spent killing rebels, given your tally . . . I guess I assumed this'd be business as usual for you. Hardly thought you could *feel* anything about it—figured if you let even a splinter of that in then you'd have hung yourself with your army belt years back. But you know, I'm kind of touched that I'm wrong. It's good to know this isn't easy for you. It shouldn't be."

Reynato's hand tightens, just slightly, on his knee. When it lifts Efrem sees a neat stack of thousand-peso notes. On top is the one with the pirate's network written all over it in blood and ink. Efrem wonders: *Will I be asked to execute these people, as well?* He wonders: *Will I do it, if I'm asked?*

"Get some rest," Reynato says. He squeezes Efrem's shoulder, and leaves. Efrem turns out the light and lays down on his bedroll. His room is fantastically large, but empty of furniture. With the bedroll unfurled in the middle of the floor, it feels just like camping. Just like when he was a boy.

 *Chapter 18*

## MEANWHILE, AT THE BLUE MOSQUE

Ignacio sits in the ablution room, negotiating Howard Bridgewater's sale to Joey, the Imam. He tries hard to keep his poker-face from crumbling into a big, stupid smile, but it isn't easy. Not since Kelog's heyday as a gamecock has his life ever vibrated with so much promise. The Imam goes into a huddle with the two young ballplayers and they whisper in a foreign language. Ignacio imagines they're discussing pricing, timing and delivery. He leans back on the edge of the concrete tub, confidence cutting a quick track through his belly like alcohol.

The Imam breaks the huddle and turns back to face him. "Please forgive me," he says. "I just want to be sure I'm not misunderstanding you . . . so, you have, in your personal custody, a kidnapped American businessperson?"

"That's right."

"And you want to *sell* this person to me?"

"To you, or to someone else. I have other prospects," Ignacio says. He runs his bare foot through the trough at the base of the concrete tub, so as to look relaxed. But he is not relaxed. No one has answered his coyly worded postings online, other than to ask if he's for real or to call him an idiot. He has no other prospects.

"Is the American nearby? Did you bring him with you?" one of the young ballplayers asks. The thinly veiled desperation in his voice is promising.

"Never mind where he is now," Ignacio says. "If we come to an arrangement then he'll be here. As soon as tonight."

The Imam sits beside Ignacio, leaving a half-space between them. "And how do I know you didn't just pickpocket a tourist? The license is even expired. You could have found it on the street."

Ignacio grins at this. He takes Howard's ear out of his pocket and holds it out so the Imam and ballplayers can see. It's become wrinkled, but hasn't completely dried, and it smells. "You think I found this on the street?"

"You've hurt him," the Imam says, his voice getting crumbly.

"Not hardly," Ignacio says. "This is nothing compared to the shit you people will pull. I saw that video on the news—that unlucky motherfucker in Iraq. Sick stuff, if you ask me . . ." Ignacio pulls a pack of cigarettes from his slacks. "Do you mind if I smoke?"

"Yes, I do," the Imam says.

Ignacio lights up anyway, because it's essential to never cede ground while negotiating.

The Imam watches him smoke and does nothing. "He needs to be healthy," he says, finally. "I need to know that he's alive and in no medical danger."

Ignacio's grin widens. He's made ready for this question and is therefore happy it's been asked. He takes out his cell phone, extends his arm, snaps a picture of his own smiling face and sends it to his wife. He hands the phone to the Imam, and in less than a minute a picture of Howard arrives in reply. His head is bandaged and the front page of the *Philippine Star* is pasted to his chest. Wednesday, May 12—today.

"Is that the kind of proof you're looking for?" Ignacio asks. It strikes him that he should do this for a living.

"Yes," the Imam says, looking down at the photo. "Just one more thing, before we can talk about money. We need to know that you are not a policeman. They've tried to entrap us before."

"Hey, that's fair," Ignacio says, his palms flat in concession. "That's a reasonable, smart request. Search away."

The two young men approach Ignacio and stand on either side of him. Everyone in the ablution room exchanges a glance and shares an awkward pause. This is something they've all seen on TV, but have never done before, and they're seized suddenly by stage fright. The young men reach down and tentatively pull his shirt up. They grope along his pant legs, down his thighs and calves. His shoes are still sitting by the entrance to the prayer room, but they inspect his bare feet anyway, because the feet are supposed to be inspected. Then they roughly grip his forearms and pin them to his sides.

"Easy, there," Ignacio says.

The Imam stands and removes his wire-frame glasses. He places them in his shirt pocket. He looks Ignacio in the face, sadly. The energy in the room has changed. "You are a bad person," he says. He sounds so let down. "You are a terrible person."

After saying this soft, damning thing, Joey, the prissy Manileño Imam, uses Ignacio's phone to call the local barangay sentinels. "I need you here now," he says. "I need the police, also."

Ignacio's worst nightmares are realized. It's a Moro double-cross! In a full-on panic, he bucks against the young men, tipping back into the concrete water tub with a splash, his cigarette fizzling. He kicks his bare feet at the Imam, shouting like a broken bellows, calling for his brother and his rooster to come and save him.

"He's a crazy person," the Imam says to the sentinels on the phone. "Come as fast as you can, please."

"No!" Ignacio yells. "No. *Not Iggy.* I won't go down that way!"

The young men let out odd, embarrassed chuckles and Ignacio, wet and slippery as he is, frees himself from their grasp. He almost makes it to the closed door when the Imam decks him with an elbow to the nose, breaking it. The young men dive down on him, bracing their knees on his lean torso. Ignacio calls again for Littleboy and Kelog, scenes from his certain capture fogging his eyes like cataracts. He sees himself beaten and carted away by sentinels, driven to a grassy field where the CIA wait like old trees. He sees himself traded in exchange for some coño visa violators. He sees blond Americans with nice smiles torturing him on the ride back to whatever boat they came from, hanging him out the open helicopter and telling the pilot to fly low so the palms will whip his face. He sees himself sleeping in a basin, brought to the edge of drowning so many times that he's started to believe he died the session prior. He sees himself really dying. And he can't believe it.

Then the door crashes open, spilling light into the ablution room and over the wrestling bodies. Ignacio looks up at a silhouette in the light. The Imam turns back and squints at the brightness, first white, then green. He doesn't know what hits him. In an instant he's on the floor, his arms over his face as he tries to protect himself from pecking, scratching, wing-beating Kelog.

Littleboy is next inside, filling up so much of the doorframe that the ablution room goes dark again. Two long steps bring him to Ignacio's side and he grabs each of the young men by their throats and hurls them into the tiled walls. Littleboy helps Ignacio up and points out, politely, that everything is going wrong.

Barefoot and soaking, Ignacio runs through the courtyard, out the mosque entrance and back down the Cavite alleyways. Littleboy follows, and then Kelog, flapping his wings madly. They regroup a few blocks away and do a fast-walk to the car, trying their best to look like normal people. The normal people they pass are unconvinced and stare at them.

Once in the car, Ignacio takes his shirt off and bunches it up under his bleeding nose. He calls his wife on Littleboy's phone.

"You need another picture?" she asks. "I'm about to give him his lunch."

"Throw the phone away," Ignacio says.

"What are you talking about? It's brand new."

"Throw it away. The police are going to get the other one, and it has your number in it."

"The who has what? Are you eating something? I can't understand a word you're saying."

Ignacio pulls the bunched shirt off of his busted nose and half-clotted blood tumbles down his lip. "Keep the damn phone then," he yells. "Just open it up and cut the Sim card in half. If anyone knocks, pretend you're not there. And gag Howard."

"I wish you wouldn't call him that," she says. "It's hard enough for me to do these things, but when you call him that—"

"You're killing me," Ignacio says. "You're ruining my life."

"What an awful thing to say."

Ignacio is quiet for a while. "You're right," he says. "I'm sorry. I love you. We won't be home for a few hours. I want to take the long way back, in case we're followed."

"Who would be following you?" she asks.

Ignacio hangs up. He looks out the window. Littleboy speeds to overtake a truck on the highway, signaling as he does so. Ignacio puts a hand on him and a hand on Kelog. "I love you, also," he says.

*Chapter 19*

## ARRIVAL

That night Benicio had the dream again. His father was on Corregidor Island, in a snowbound jungle. Fat flakes tumbled down through shivering vines, drifting about palm trunks rooted in the loamy soil. His father looked up at the sky and flakes settled on his face. He was not alone. A dark shape emerged from the trees and stood a few paces away. It was a dog, big as a small pony, dusted with snow.

The dog eyed Howard with ears back and tail swishing. It pawed the turf and whined. Howard began to walk away, but the dog followed, matching him step for step. Howard broke into a sprint, bounding into the brush, but the dog kept up at an easy canter. And in the dream, Benicio *was* Howard. He was fat, and almost blind, and bleeding heavily from his chest. He was terrified. And he was dying.

BENICIO WOKE WITH A START. It took him a few moments to remember where he was. The Philippines. A beach south of the city. A hard, uncomfortable cot, in a rented bungalow. He lay there for a moment, blinking at the ceiling. It was still dark outside, and geckos chattered in the trees above. An odd bird called from very close by. No, not a bird. A telephone.

Benicio got up and rushed out to the deck. His pants were slung over the sanded driftwood railing, still wet to the thighs from when he'd waded out to Katrina. He frisked the limp pockets for his phone, found it and flipped it open. "Hello," he said. "Dad. Can you hear me?"

"Benicio?" It wasn't his father. It was Alice. "Hello?"

"Alice. Hi." He sat down on the deck and scooted backward to rest his spine against the wall. "Sorry, I was sleeping." He pulled the phone away from his ear for a moment to check the time. "Is everything all right?"

"Of course. Everything's fine," she said. She was quiet for a while, and Benicio wondered if maybe she'd done the time zone math wrong. But no, of course she hadn't done it wrong.

"Why are you calling so late?" he asked.

"Oh," she paused. "I didn't think I'd get you."

"You didn't want to get me?" He gently banged the back of his sweaty head on the wall. He'd called, sent e-mails and texts, and this was the first he'd heard from her since arriving.

"No, I mean, I thought I'd just leave a voicemail. I wanted to give you and your dad some space. This trip is about you guys, after all."

"I don't think I want space," he said.

"Well, babe, I think you need it." She paused again and Benicio heard a clicking sound in the background. The turn signal on her truck. She was driving somewhere. "Anyway, I can't talk," she said. "The roaming charges are probably costing both of us a fortune. I just wanted to check-in."

"My dad's not here," Benicio said.

Alice was quiet for a moment. "What?"

"My father. He wasn't at the airport. And he's not at the hotel."

"What does that mean?"

"I don't know. It means that I'm here, and he's somewhere else."

"Are you worried?" she asked. Even over the poor connection, she must have heard his voice break. "Honey," she said, "don't be. Have you spoken to any—"

"I'm not," he cut in. His eyes had watered and he pinched them closed. He was embarrassed. "I'm with his friends now. They say he pulls this shit all the time. So no, I'm not worried. I'm angry."

"Well," she said, "try not to be angry, either."

"I'll try," he said. "I'm trying."

HE SLEPT FOR ANOTHER few hours after they hung up. Then, when the sun rose, he dressed in his still-wet clothes and shared a tense, silent breakfast with Katrina. Bobby was nowhere to be seen, at first. Then he appeared at the far end of the tide-stretched beach, presumably returning from an early-morning walk. Or maybe he'd been up all night, walking. Even as a distant silhouette his limp was pronounced. Benicio and Katrina watched from the restaurant as he approached, so slowly.

"He knew them," she said. Her voice had a faraway quality that sounded put-on. "He knew the people who did that to him."

Benicio turned to her. "What?"

"The people who hurt him," she said.

So. It was an attack. Bobby had been attacked. Benicio was startled—taken aback by the depth to which this news shook him.

"They used to work together," she said. "They all used to work for the senator."

"You mean, Charlie—"

"No." She glanced at him sidelong. She would have looked annoyed but for her eyes, which had gone wet and shifty. "Bobby left the senator to work on Charlie's campaign. And they, those fucking meatheads . . . they grabbed him. They grabbed him right off the street. Took him to an empty house and beat on him for hours. Bobby had his dogs with him—he'd been walking his dogs. They killed the dogs. They almost killed him."

She stopped and brought her napkin up to one of her eyes. Her napkin had ketchup on it. Silence settled over them. Benicio wondered what he should say. Or was it better to say nothing? There was nothing he could say, after all, that would make the story she'd just told suck less. And besides, he hardly knew Bobby. And this information about his injuries was unsolicited. Benicio even felt cornered by it, as though his previous assumption—that Bobby's injuries were the result of some frivolity of character—indicated a smallness on his part. A meagerness of spirit. And who knows. Maybe it did.

Bobby arrived some long minutes later, and Katrina greeted him with her usual airy vigor. Together they checked out of the hotel and headed up the long wooded stairway, back to his Expedition. The shirtless boys followed, carting dive gear on their backs, eagerly accepting stacks of coins when they reached the top and pantomiming oral sex—their tongues pressed to the insides of their cheeks, their fingers clasped around invisible pricks—when Bobby turned his back on them. "Bakla!" They shouted in unison as the Expedition drove off. Benicio made the not-too-wild guess that *bakla* meant *faggot*. But Bobby seemed nonplussed by it. He rolled down all the windows and put the radio on high.

BACK IN MANILA they exchanged cheery, forced goodbyes. Benicio returned to the cool air of the Shangri-La lobby with his dive bag hoisted on his shoulder. He stopped in at the reception before going upstairs, just on the off chance that his father might have left a message while he was gone. "No messages," the concierge said as she typed away at her little computer, "but someone has been waiting to see you all morning. If you just have a seat in the lounge," she pointed toward a grove of plush green armchairs at the far end of the lobby, "I'll contact them right away."

Benicio rushed to the lounge and dumped himself into a chair. "Hello first," he said, coaching himself. "Hello first. Hello first. Not: Nice of you to show up. Not: Where the fuck've you been? Not: They don't have phones in Singapore? Just hello. Hello, Dad. It's good to see you, you careless, fat, lying . . . Hello Dad. Just hello."

"Hi, Benny." The voice that came from behind him was not his father's voice.

He stood up and turned to face Solita. "Don't call me that," he said.

She didn't look anything like she did in the green dress—or in his father's shower. Her hair was up in a messy bun and she wore a pink T-shirt so tight that the stitching on her padded bra showed through in relief. Behind her stood a young boy, maybe about nine years old, clinging to the frayed hem of her miniskirt. "This is June," she said, grabbing the boy by the scruff of his neck and pushing him toward Benicio. "June, say hello to Kuya Benny."

The boy kept his eyes on the deep carpet as he shuffled toward Benicio. He took hold of Benicio's hand and without saying a word pressed his warm, slightly greasy forehead to the back of it. "Howard's," Solita said, gesturing to the boy with her lips and chin. "He's your brother."

Benicio snapped his hand away and the startled boy ran back behind Solita. "He isn't," he said.

"He is. He looks as much like Howard as you do. I think he looks more like Howard than you do."

Benicio's fingers trembled and he balled them into loose fists to keep it from showing. "You want money," he said. "You want cash, from me."

"No." Solita furrowed her brow and took a step toward him. The boy stayed where he was, one outstretched arm still clinging to the threads of her skirt. "Yes. But that does not make June less your brother."

"My father wouldn't do that."

"Your father did. Your father does. How else did I get into his room? We are regular."

"Stop talking." Benicio hadn't realized that he'd shouted until other people in the lounge started looking his way. "I don't mean he wouldn't be with you," he said, half-mastering his voice. "Because he would. But if he had a kid, if your kid was his kid . . ." he paused to get better control of himself. He didn't know how good the boy's English was and didn't want to say anything too devastating. Or rather, he was looking for a soft way to say a devastating thing. "If that boy was my father's, then you wouldn't have to do what you do. You wouldn't be you."

His vitriol took them both off guard and Solita seemed to lose her balance for a moment. She took another step forward and the boy lost hold of her skirt and stood frozen—stranded atop the plush carpet. "He gives me some extra," she said. "Not enough that I don't have to work. School, for June. Food, for June. Some books. He's late with the money."

"Then it's his business," Benicio said. "Whatever arrangement you have with my father, you'll have to sort out with him. He'll be back any day now. But I don't want to hear about it. I don't care." He turned his back on them, grabbed his dive bag and headed for the bank of elevators below the mezzanine stair, going just slow enough so he didn't feel like he was running. After a moment Solita collected her son—if it even was her son and not her baby brother, cousin or just some kid who lived on her street—and followed him. When Benicio stepped into an open elevator she jammed her elbow against the door to keep it from closing.

"He's a week late," she said. "They'll take June out of his class."

"Talk to Howard about it."

"Howard's not here." The elevator door bounced lightly off of Solita's elbow as it tried and failed to close. A pair of small speakers began releasing a pleasant chiming noise. Benicio felt trapped. Like there was no way today for him to act like, look like or feel like a good person.

"Please," he said. "Go away." He held down the close-door button. When Solita still wouldn't move her elbow he moved it for her—a measured shove just strong enough to send her a half step backward. The doors closed, and even through them he heard her shouting. First English and then Tagalog.

Once in his room he dropped his dive gear more roughly than he should have. There were three messages on his hotel room phone, but rather than anything from his father they were all just notifications from the front desk that a woman had arrived at the hotel and needed to speak with him, urgently. After listening to all three Benicio pulled the cord out of the wall and threw the phone, handset and all, across the room. When he heard hard, determined knocking on his door he felt about ready to explode.

"I don't know how to say it better," he almost screamed. "Leave me the fuck alone." He swung the door open, his fist tight around the handle.

"Mr. Bridgewater?" A white woman in business attire stood in his doorway. Benicio stared at her. He didn't know her, but he knew why she was here. She introduced herself as Monique Thomas and said something or other about American Citizen Services. Benicio said nothing at all. He imagined soldiers, on a doorstep, in America, in the forties. Their hats were in their hands. That's how real this was to him.

"Do you mind if I come in?" she asked. "I think it's better that we talk in private."

"He's dead, isn't he?" Benicio said. Hearing it in his own voice made it final, and then he was sure. "My father is dead."

BOOK TWO *Moondogs*

*Chapter 20*

## CONTACT PEOPLE

The Marine manning Post One seemed to know something was up. He slid an after-hours sign-in ledger under the bulletproof glass and opened the blast door leading into the chancery. "Am I the last one here?" Monique asked.

"Yes, ma'am." He had to lean down in his elevated booth to get his soft pink lips to a microphone. He couldn't have been more than six years older than Shawn. "They've been coming in for the past hour. Ambo's chopper touched down a few minutes ago." Well, that was just great. Monique rushed though the blast door.

A small crowd was gathered in the Country Team conference room upstairs. The ambassador sat at the end of a long Philippine-mahogany table, reading a stack of papers and looking incongruous in denim and plaid. Beside him was the deputy chief in a bowling league jersey, who'd be taking over next week as chargé d'affaires when the ambassador flew back to Texas to attend his own divorce proceedings. Tom, who was filling in for Joyce, represented Public Affairs. He chatted with Jeff and the new legal attaché, whose name Monique hadn't learned yet and who was still green from the food-poisoning he'd gotten on the flight over. They all looked at her as she sat, flushed and sweating. The ambassador's secretary passed out paper cups half-filled with cold coffee.

"Thanks for coming," the ambassador said. "It's late, so I'll get right to it. An American businessman named Howard Bridgewater has been kidnapped. The National Police don't have a timeline yet but they suspect it happened about a week ago, and the thinking is that he's still in Manila. No one has reported Mr. Bridgewater missing, and the police were only alerted to the kidnapping when an Imam from Cavite called in about some suspicious characters. They were purportedly hoping to sell an American hostage to the Abu Sayyaf."

Those last two words turned the air around the conference table to gelatin. The SuperFerry bombing in late February was still fresh in everybody's minds. Jeff, who'd been stationed in Manila long enough to remember the Sobero beheading, shifted in his chair. The new legal attaché excused himself to vomit in the adjoining washroom, but probably more because of the food poisoning than because he was overcome.

"Is the story public?" Tom, who was filling in for Joyce, asked.

"Not yet," the ambassador said, "but they want to include it in their weekly brief on Tuesday. It'll leak before then, of course. Let's do what we can to contact next of kin before that happens. Mona?" He looked at Monique and it took her a moment to look back. He slid a sheet of paper to her, which glided across the desk almost playfully, like a puck on an air-hockey table. It was a faxed copy of Howard Bridgewater's driver's license. "I know that's not much to go off of, but see if you can find a contact person for him. He may have registered with us when he arrived in country. If he's got a wife, we should let her know. If he's got an ex-wife, let's just skip it, am I right?" The ambassador laughed. "But no," he said, "this is nothing to joke about."

Monique left the fax on the table so it wouldn't shake in her hands. She stared into Howard's grainy, black-and-white face. He was a heavy man, not ugly but close to it, and just a few years younger than Joseph.

Big people never look good in little pictures, but his was especially bad. He filled the square frame, a bewildered, almost worried expression on his face, as though he'd known when they took his picture at the DMV that some day it'd be used as evidence. Staring down at the picture, Monique couldn't help but imagine him reading a long list of demands in a pixelated Internet video. A slogan-spattered drop cloth would hang inert behind his head. He'd be flanked by men in masks with rockets on their shoulders. She imagined newscasters explaining how they'd come to the decision to air—or not to air—the execution, imagined Howard's headshot transposed onto the upper right corner of her television, a death date accompanying the birth date, bracketing his life. As she looked down at the picture she longed for it to be nothing more than that; one of the dramatic evils gravely celebrated in the news. Of course she felt pity, tenderness, terror, but a louder part of her said: *No thanks*. I'm full right now. I have an affair to enjoy and then end. I have a marriage to rebuild, and children to rescue from themselves and from others. This kidnapped man doesn't belong anywhere near my life.

UNFORTUNATELY, IT WASN'T ALL that hard to find a contact person. When the meeting was over Monique unlocked her office in the annex and waded through smudgy registration files. After working her way back to February she gave up and started cold-calling luxury hotels— there were only so many, after all. She got lucky on her third try. Yes, Howard Bridgewater was a guest at the Shangri-La. Yes, they did have an emergency contact person on file. They could even do her one better; the contact person was in the Philippines and was also staying at the Shangri-La. Perfect. It was Howard's son. Even better. The concierge transferred her and she was so, so thankful that the kid didn't pick up. How the hell was she going to tell him anyway? She decided to write up a script when she got home and practice it before going to bed. Then, tomorrow morning, she'd give that boy the news.

It was past midnight when Monique left the annex, motion sensors brightening empty halls as she passed, tracing a trail of lights through the building that ended at the main exit. She signed out with the young

Marine at Post One and returned to the promenade. She walked south on Roxas, past the yachts waltzing darkly in their moorings. The moon was out, and though it was almost full it looked aloof; excluded and humiliated by the brighter skyline. There was a dark shape ahead; a car parked in the middle of the promenade. Reynato's car. They'd been out to dinner when the call came in, and he'd dropped her off a few blocks away so as not to be seen. He sat on the hood, elbows on his knees, chin propped on his little hands.

"You didn't need to wait for me," she said, so thankful that he had.

"Don't be silly," he said, hopping off the hood. He reached into the open passenger-side window and produced her purse, dangling from his rigid finger by a leather shoulder strap. "Besides, you forgot this."

"Thank you."

"Don't thank me." He kissed her lightly and handed over her phone, which was supposed to be in her purse. "Your husband has been trying to call," he said. "Don't look at me like that. I joke plenty, but I would never answer it. I was just trying to turn it on silent."

She looked at the screen and saw five missed calls from Joseph. He knew how late it was here. Something must be wrong. Monique took a few quick steps over to the seawall—for privacy—and called Joseph back.

"Are the kids all right?" she asked, stepping on his "hello."

"I'm sorry?"

"Joe? Can you hear me? Is everything okay?"

"What are you talking about? Everything's fine here."

Air rushed out of her lungs, pushing up words. "Shit, Joe. Why are you calling me in the middle of the night? You had me scared to death."

"What?" He always said "what" when he was hurt. Like he couldn't believe you'd hurt him. "I was calling to *check on you*. Jeffrey phoned a few hours ago and he told me what happened."

"Oh." She put a hand on the seawall, the concrete moist under her fingertips.

"I thought you would want to talk."

She did want to talk, but not now. And not over the telephone. And maybe not even to him, but admitting that felt lousy. "Thanks. Thank you."

"Listen . . ." he sighed. He must have been sitting, because she heard him stand. She imagined light coming through the windows, a closed book on the table beside their recliner. "I have been thinking about this. I have been giving this a lot of thought. And I want to say I'm sorry. I'm still angry, though, about the way you treated me. You should have told me, Monique." He paused, maybe giving her time to concede the point. "I don't regret leaving. But I didn't think about you, not as much as I should have, at least. I regret that. I know that being there is hard on you, too. I know it's not . . . really what you were expecting, I guess. I know how important it was for you to have that place feel like home. I'm sure my complaining all the time did not make it easier. And now I have left you there alone, with so much extra work . . . with this horrible thing to deal with."

"The thing wouldn't be less horrible if you were here. But thank you. And you're right not to feel bad about going. Leaving made sense, for you and for the kids."

"Of course it did." She heard the crumpling sound of leather as he sat again. Then the metal-spring creak of the leg rest extending. "So, would you like to talk about it? I cannot imagine how it feels to work on something like this."

"It doesn't feel like anything, yet. Oh—" she jumped a bit when Reynato touched her lower back. She hadn't noticed him join her at the seawall. His hard little fingers pushed up and down her spine like he was sewing crops. "I'm seeing the man's son tomorrow," she said. "I'm the one who has to tell him."

Reynato made a sound like "piff-piff" and she glanced at him, turning the phone into her chest. His fingers were pinched before his lips, puffing an invisible joint, reminding her about the pot they'd discovered in Shawn's room that morning. What the fuck—he was helping her parent now? She was working up to it.

Monique brought the phone back to her ear and came in on Joseph advising her how best to break it to the kid. "They should be the first words out of your mouth. You should be direct and honest. It isn't your job to console anybody. When my father—"

She cut him off by saying his name a bunch of times. Then, without letting him interrupt, she told him what she'd found in Shawn's room. The new clothes. The cell phone. The pipe and baggies swollen with pot. Joseph was quiet for a while.

"I'm going to murder him."

She laughed a little. "That's exactly what I said when I found it." Then she bit her lip, worried he might ask: *To whom?*

"How could I have missed the smell?" he asked. "We know that smell. And the clothes. How did I not notice new clothes?"

"Don't beat yourself up," she said. "You were surrounded by new everything."

"You, at least, had an excuse. You were so busy. I feel terrible, Monique."

"You have nothing to feel terrible about." Saying this threw her off balance. She'd been sure his first response would fall along the lines of I-told-you-so. But he was being generous and empathetic. And she was standing there with Reynato working his fingers up and down her spine, getting closer to her ass each time, leaving a just-touched chill over her skin. She felt good and rotten.

"It's late," she said. "I should go."

"You want input on his punishment?"

"Let him explain himself. Depending on how he does, nuke him."

"I thought I might go easy. He's had a tough year, too."

"This wasn't a recreational amount, Joe. It was a distribution, expelled from school, me losing my job kind of amount."

"Shit." He almost never swore. "I will talk to him."

They said good night and hung up. Reynato swallowed Monique in a hug, one hand still knuckling her backbone. He was shorter than her, so she had to bend down to put her face in the crook between his neck and shoulder. He smelled faintly of fireworks.

"It's the Bridgewater boy, isn't it? The one you're seeing tomorrow?"

"You know about this?" she asked.

"I do. News like that moves quick around the department, especially when the victim is the buddy of a newly minted senator. Even more especially when the victim is a white American . . ." Reynato trailed off, the corners of his lips twisting bitterly. "You tell that boy his father's going to be just fine."

She brought her face up from his neck.

"How can you be sure?"

"Because I know he's in trouble." He emphasized the word *I*. "Tell the kid that he can bank on it."

"I'm not making any promises," she said.

"Well, I am."

MONIQUE GOT ALMOST no rest that night. She wrote out a script of what she'd say and practiced it for hours. When she finally got to bed it was nearly impossible to sleep for those goddamn animals making so much noise. She woke once to find the lovebird perched on the footboard, singing at her, and again some time later to see the gecko walking along the ceiling directly above, green and peach-colored feathers jutting from its leathery mouth like fingers. She thought it was a nightmare until the next day around noon, when she woke to find a dusting of beautiful feathers on the hardwood, a severed foot, and a blood speck no bigger than a lentil. The gecko was still on the ceiling, digesting, but managed to escape when she went after it with a broom. Her loathing for the gecko tasted like a mouthful of batteries.

It was a Sunday, but Monique dressed as though heading to the office. She wore a long-sleeved bolero—her blazers all needed cleaning—over a conservative, border-print skirt and blouse. She applied heavy makeup to cover the rings under her eyes and then washed some of it off, not wanting to look too severe or plasticky. Howard Bridgewater's son wasn't in when she arrived at the Shangri-La, so she waited, returning to his room every half hour or so to knock on it, hard. When he finally answered it was with a raised voice and a clenched fist, his hair standing up on end, looking crazy.

Benicio Bridgewater took the news of his father's kidnapping better than she thought he would—better, even, than she thought he *should*. She'd expected some glazed shock, sure. The kind of disbelief that paralyzes you. The kind of disbelief she felt when doctors told her that her son had died. But this didn't seem like shock. Benicio Bridgewater sat on the edge of the bed and stared out at the hazy city. His eyes teared up a little and he wiped the tears away, as though embarrassed by them. Monique was embarrassed, too.

She talked through her script, which sounded so much lamer now. She gave him contact information and reading materials—a local crisis hotline, a support group for expats, a long privacy statement he'd have to read and sign before the embassy could say anything on his behalf. She promised to be available whenever he needed her, even though the thought of keeping that promise was unpleasant. She collected her things to go. "I can't imagine how awful this feels," she said, even though she was pretty sure she could. "And I know it's a lot to take in, all at once. But are you sure you don't have any questions?"

Benicio turned to her, as though realizing for the first time that she was still there. "I just have one," he said. "This is going to sound a little stupid. Does it ever snow in the Philippines? I mean . . . even if it's just a freak thing? Do you know if that ever happens?"

"No," she said, flatly. "There are some mountains in the north that are pretty high, but I don't even think it snows up there. That's it?"

He turned back to the window. "I've got lots of questions, but that's the only one for you."

So she closed the door and left him there. And on the way home, she cried.

*Chapter 21*

## GOOD STRANGE

Benicio saw the stuffy, overdressed embassy woman every day after that. On Wednesday they sat across from each other in a little sandwich shop just inside the security gates of Ninoy Aquino International Airport, quietly drinking too-sweet lattes from paper cups as they waited for Alice to deplane. He'd called to tell her the news a few hours after hearing it himself, waiting for daytime to move to her side of the world before picking up the phone. She'd been on her way to work and pulled off on the shoulder as soon as he said the word *kidnapped.* Hearing her cry made him cry a little bit. Later that night she called back to tell him that she had a ticket to Manila and was on her way up to D.C. to see if she couldn't get a rush visa from the Philippine Consulate.

There was a bit of commotion on the other side of the security barrier as two photographers changed out their wide-angle lenses for telephotos. A reporter with curled hair and a short skirt tried to position herself so that Benicio and Monique would appear in the background of her segment. Just as Monique warned, the kidnapping had made the front pages of the *Inquirer, Star* and *Manila Bulletin.* They'd been followed ever since. Jeff—a security officer from the embassy who spoke with a drawl so long that it trailed on the floor after him—did his best to make the reporters' jobs difficult. He leaned against the security barrier, screwing up their pictures. When the curly haired reporter began to tape her segment he took out his cell phone and launched into a boomingly animated conversation with his cable provider. She gave up and retreated a little ways down the terminal.

"It's good of your girlfriend to come," Monique said as she emptied yet another pack of no-calorie sweetener into her latte. "You've been together long?"

"A year. Not long." He stared at the table as he spoke.

"Well, don't let her go. It's a good thing to have someone who'll be there for you. Especially when there is this far."

He nodded slowly, still not looking at her. They only knew each other because of what had happened to Howard, and the mere sight of her shoulder-padded lilac jacket, her peach lipstick and clumped mascara, set his stomach churning. She seemed to recognize this, and if she took offense, she hid it.

"Are we going to be on time?" he asked. The police commander tasked with his father's case was supposed to brief them this afternoon.

Monique flipped her wrist so that her cuff fell below her watch. "We have a little over an hour. But don't worry. He'll wait." Across the terminal the heavy jetway doors swung open with a loud clack and travelers began pouring out looking exhausted and lost. Benicio stood, fingers drumming against the back of his chair, weight shifting as he watched for Alice's brown hair among the uniformly black and close-cropped. She was one of the last out, eyes red and watery, nothing but a bloated purse as her carryon. He rushed to meet her in the middle of the corridor, where they hugged tight, agitating the foot-traffic. Alice started to cry but stopped when she felt his whole body tighten. She kissed him.

"I'm sorry," he said.

"About what?" She gripped his shoulders and extended her arms; a kind of taking-you-in gesture that an older relative might do to a child that had grown since the last time they'd seen them. She looked exhausted and pink. For a quick moment she glanced at the cameras beyond the security conveyors, their flashbulbs reflecting in her blood-shot eyes. "About nothing. It's a stupid . . . it's a silly thing to say."

Monique and Jeff joined them. They escorted Alice on the fast track through customs and out under the ugly concrete overhang where Benicio had waited for his father not a full week ago. Edilberto was out there, holding a handmade sign above his head that read *Mrs. Bridgewater* even though Benicio had been very clear that they weren't married. Seeing the sign, Alice laughed a little. She loaded her bags into the Shangri-La car, but wouldn't get inside herself.

"Screw that," she said, "I'm going wherever you're going." She pulled a yellow steno pad from her purse that they used to keep atop his fridge at home. The front page reminded Benicio that he still needed cilantro, red onions and boullion cubes. "I came to be useful." She pivoted to face Monique and Jeff. "You two are coming with us? What are your names? Wait . . ." she fumbled in her purse for a ballpoint pen. "Could you spell that, please?"

ALICE SCRIBBLED NOTES as they boarded the embassy shuttle—a boxy minivan with tinted windows and doors so heavy they were hard to open. She and Benicio sat in the back. She left her seatbelt unbuckled and shot questions at the front seat, filling her yellow steno with the answers. *Jeffrey Tober, Regional Security Officer, ext. 4415. Big guy, southern, green polo. Monique Thomas, Acting Chief, American Citizen Services, ext. 5656. Acting? Remember to ask B. Bright suit. Bright makeup. Going to E-R-M-I-T-A station for briefing by R. Ocampo. New to case. Green polo knows him. Doesn't seem to like him.* Benicio unbuckled his own seatbelt so he could sit closer to her. "If you get too tired," he whispered, "just say the word." Alice didn't answer him, but she wrote *not tired* at the bottom of her notes. She tapped the words a few times with the tip of her pen before crossing the *not* out. She wrote, *least I can do*, underlining the first word twice and then circling it.

They arrived a few minutes late and hurried into the station lobby, nearly slipping, the floors covered in runoff from a dripping air conditioner. A uniformed receptionist behind a chin-high desk directed them to wait on a pair of wooden benches sitting beneath a big clock ticking twice a second to catch up with the right time. Benicio sat and took Alice's hand. Her notes lay ready atop her knees. He kissed her cheek and her ear. A few officers looked up from their desks and pointed. He did it again.

"Sorry I'm late," boomed a big voice behind them. A short Filipino stood in the station entrance wearing frayed jeans, a white T-shirt and a blue baseball cap. If not for the polished badge clipped to his belt he would have looked like just some dude who'd wandered in off the street. "The traffic in this city! A nightmare, am I right?" He smiled and showed off a set of orthodontic braces that looked out of place on someone already gracelessly pushing middle age. "The kind of nightmare you have every night. What's the word for that? Fuck. Recurring."

Monique got up from her bench and stepped forward to introduce herself. She seemed to wince as the man shook her hand, vigorously. "Tickled," he said. "Delighted. You're the son?"

She snapped her hand from his grip, and the force of it pulled him off balance and made him take a half step forward. His grin hardly slackened. "Jiff," he went on, gazing past her, "a pleasure, as it sometimes is, to see you. I'm guessing you're not the son, either?" Jeff stood as well and crossed his arms tight over his broad chest. "Well hell. It's too early for police work, but here goes . . ." he pointed a finger in the air and let its aim drift until it settled on Benicio. "Elimination is the process."

Benicio stood and spoke with a voice slightly deeper than usual. "Yes, I'm Howard Bridgewater's son."

"I'm glad to meet you, son." They shook hands and became enveloped in a sudden and very strange silence. The policeman's fingers went limp. He stared Benicio in the face and said nothing. "Sorry," he finally managed, dropping his hand back to his side. "You just look . . . let's say familiar. You look like some people I know. No matter." He wiped his fingers, which had been sweaty, on his jeans. "I'm Reynato Ocampo," he said. "I'm the guy who's going to save your father's life."

Monique gasped a little and Jeff uncrossed his arms. "Christ, Reynato, what's wrong with you? Why would you say that?"

He smiled a bit and raised his small palms in the air—a mock surrender. "Hey, you got me. Zealous, as charged. Sometimes I carry myself away. Let me put it like this—Mr. Howard Bridgewater is a valued resident of Metro Manila, and I've been directed to spare no expense in securing his safe recovery. I run an elite task force and the resolution of kidnapping cases is one of our most special specialties. My team and I, we are very good at our jobs. Forgive me if that sounds immodest, I'm just trying to be as accurate as possible—we are really *excellent* at them. And as of right now, getting your father back is our only job."

With that he turned abruptly, crossed the station lobby and disappeared through a saloon-style door. He clearly expected them to follow, and they rushed to do so. Benicio glanced at Alice's notes as they walked and saw that beside Ocampo's name she'd written nothing but a series of deeply inked exclamation points. "What do you think?" he asked.

"He's strange." She gestured to a group of officers and secretaries who'd stopped typing as Reynato passed and were peeping up from their desks as though desperate to watch him but afraid of being caught doing so. "But, good strange."

Benicio looked back at his father's self-anointed savior, thinking that Charlie Fuentes was an odd pick to play him in the movies. Reynato was duckfooted and had a bobbing, almost boyish stride. He walked not just like he owned the place, but like he'd thought it up. As though the entire collection of walls, ceiling tiles, telephones and the people who spoke on them were gathered there as a special treat for him. Something to play with. "I'm not so sure," Benicio said.

Reynato brought them to a conference room with maps pasted across the dusty glass walls and invited them all to take a chair. Once they were seated he paced around the table, asking questions as he went. When was the last time Benicio had spoken to his father? Did Benicio know of any enemies his father might have? Did Howard have any outstanding medical conditions like heart disease, high blood pressure, diabetes, peptic ulcers, acid reflux disease, schizophrenia, priapism, bipolar disorder, chronic cough, and if so was he taking any prescription medications to combat the ailment or ailments? How familiar was Howard with the city? With the country? Did Howard speak Tagalog? Did Howard speak Cebuano or Visayan? Did Howard speak Spanish? Did Howard speak anything other than English?

"Mr. Ocampo," Monique raised her voice over Reynato's questions. It looked like speaking to him made her nervous, but she went ahead anyway. "Benicio already gave a statement. If you need another we'll arrange it. But I thought our meeting today was for a progress update. At least that's how Director Babayon . . ." she lingered for a moment, "described it in his memo to our embassy."

Reynato quit circling the table and went to stand beside Monique's chair. He got down on one knee, moved his hand over the carpet and stood again. "Excuse me," he said as he extended his cupped hand toward her. "You dropped this name. Do you need it back?"

She glared at him. "If you're not taking this seriously, then I'll request that someone else brief us."

Reynato was quiet for a while, his hand still extended in mock offering. Then he gingerly pantomimed putting Director Babayon's name into his pocket. "Forgive me," he said, "but I take this very seriously. That's why I ask questions—things just don't seem real to me until I hear them for myself. But you're right. I'm sure you're all exhausted," he nodded toward Alice, "and very busy, besides." The room was quiet, and uncomfortable, and he seemed to revel in it for a moment before stabbing his pen at one of the maps of Luzon pasted to the glass wall. "This is the location of the Blue Mosque, some two hours south of Manila, in Cavite province. On the afternoon of Wednesday, May 12, a group of as-yet unidentified persons apparently entered this mosque and engaged the Imam in some discussion regarding Mr. Howard Bridgewater. Since then our detectives, myself among them, have thoroughly interrogated this Imam. Naturally we haven't ruled him out as a potential suspect, but as of now there's no credible evidence of his involvement. He's been very forthcoming, and I try to be open-minded about these things. We can't pigeonhole an entire people, after all. Frequency does not a rule make."

Reynato paused a moment, presumably to let them all consider his fair-mindedness, before drawing an *X* on the map at the location of the Blue Mosque. Then he traced a big uneven circle around the city limits of Metro Manila. "Based on materials recovered from the mosque we have good reason to believe that your father is still being held somewhere in Manila, though we're not sure he'll be here much longer. The Imam was a little vague on the suspects but we've gathered that there were likely three men. Two Filipinos, and some kind of foreigner with a high degree of martial arts training." He assumed a karate-chop stance to demonstrate. "We've had our best sketch artist working with the Imam for the past few days, but as of now we don't have a realistic likeness of this individual."

Alice looked up from her notes and blinked a few times, as though trying to clear her eyes of dust. "So, what do they want? I mean, they're not ransoming Benicio's dad, right?" She took a long breath. "Are they terrorists?"

"Not exactly." Reynato flashed his braces. "We don't believe they have any ideological or religious grudge against the United States. But they realize that there are plenty of people in the world, and plenty of people in this country, I'm sorry to say, that do. It's to those people that they would like to sell your father." He paused, only briefly, and the word *sell* filled the room. "The fact that a sight-unseen visit to a mosque was their first try is a good thing. It means that they're idiots. And they don't have leads."

"Have they hurt him?" Alice asked.

The fact that Reynato didn't answer right away was answer enough. His slick, too-cool-for-school persona dissolved and, for the first time since hearing the news, Benicio really started crying. He wasn't even embarrassed about it, he just cried. Because this was so fucking awful. Because somebody had hurt his father. They'd probably hurt him badly. And they would maybe kill him. And his father's best hope for being rescued was this guy, who, let's face it, was looking more and more like a maniac.

"He's not in immediate medical danger," Reynato said. "The kidnappers left a mobile phone at the mosque with a picture of Mr. Bridgewater on it—a proof of life for the Imam. The director told me not to use the word *torture*, but I know it when I see it." Now it was Alice who started crying. Benicio had moved on to nausea. "I know this is difficult to hear, but you should consider that mobile phone a little Finnish-made blessing. Not only does it leave us with a record of the kidnapper's contacts and call history, but with any luck we can use it to track down the vendor. If he keeps good receipts he'll have a record of who bought it."

Alice wiped her cheeks and wrote this all down in her pad. When Reynato finished talking she asked for a copy of the map he'd marked up. He peeled it right off the wall, rolled it up and handed it over. He shook hands with everybody and walked them to the station door. Outside it had begun to drizzle—a sunshower—and everything was incongruously beautiful. Reynato stood in the doorway, waving as they made for the shuttle, like a homeowner would with departing guests. Despite the rain, Benicio cracked his window open, sure that he'd be sick. Then, when he wasn't sick, he felt guilty. Like maybe he still wasn't sad enough. A good son, a son who loved his father unreservedly, would be vomiting his guts up right now.

IT WAS ALMOST DARK by the time he and Alice got to the Shangri-La. They ate a quick, quiet meal in the hotel restaurant and took the elevator up to his suite. Edilberto had left Alice's bag sitting at the foot of the bed and she squatted down to open it. "Where should I put these things?" she asked, holding up a stack of poorly folded blouses.

"Let me." He took the clothes from her and laid them in the dresser. She sat on the edge of the bed, watching as he slung pants and dresses over dark wooden hangers. He lined her toiletries up beneath the bathroom mirror. He placed her shoes beside the door.

They fucked. She initiated. It was filthy, and good, the way filthy sex is good. He thought about his dive instructor, and about Solita, a little bit. He wondered what Alice was thinking of, because she was going wild. Upon finishing they were rendered messy and embarrassed. The same thing had happened, he remembered, when his mother died. Sex was excellent after his mother was dead. Now, with his father kidnapped, sex was super-excellent. He was a lousy person.

Alice slept and Benicio took a shower. Steam filled the bathroom. It was velvety in his throat and lungs, and when he got out the towels were damp with it. Alice's toiletries sat where he'd lined them up below the big mirror. He began going through them. He unzipped little pouches, wheedling through face cream, generic painkillers, some cheapo perfumes and foundation a shade darker than she could pull off. It didn't take long to find—a blue envelope with slots for twenty-eight little pills, most of them custard-yellow but the last seven pure white. He popped each pill out of the packet and dropped them, one by one, into the toilet. Then, using a small pair of scissors, he cut the packet into tiny pieces and dropped those into the toilet as well. This wasn't

sabotage. It's not like he wanted children—God, he wanted the opposite of children. He just wanted—*needed*—some space to think. And
he couldn't find that space in the dirty routine they'd settled into; the
fucking, the rough play. It was getting corrosive and had to stop. It was
a way of moving farther apart, not closer together. And he didn't want
them to move apart. He was so afraid of moving apart that his fingers
shook as he flushed her birth control pills.

Back in the bedroom, Alice snored. It was totally dark outside and
the moon hung in the top corner of his picture window like the head
of a hammered nail. He stood naked in the middle of the room, his
body still steaming, his pores drinking the chill of the air-conditioning.
He lifted a corner of the heavy blankets and began to slide in. Then he
heard a noise, and stopped. Something—a door? a drawer?—opened
and slammed closed again. Footsteps smacked with the sound of sandal
flapping against heel, and a moment later came the bang of something
heavy dropped on something hard. The sounds were coming from his
father's suite. The police had been in there, of course, in the first days
after the news broke. But it was supposed to be empty now. Benicio
dressed as quickly as he could—no underwear or shoes, just the slacks
he'd worn to the meeting that day and an unbuttoned work shirt—and
slipped through the door to the adjoining suite.

It looked different than when he'd explored it nearly a week ago.
The mess of papers on the desk had been scattered across the study
floor, as far as the kitchenette and living area. His father's sport coats
and blazers—big billowing things that Benicio could have wrapped two
or three times around his own shoulders—lay with their pockets turned
out atop a kindling tent of wooden hangers on the bed. More noises
came from the walk-in closet. Solita was in there, squatting with her
back to him, turning his father's folded socks inside out. At least this
time she hadn't brought the kid.

"If you leave right now, I won't have you arrested," he said.

Solita jolted up and spun to face him. In one hand she held a purse
made of worn denim and in the other dangled a knot of socks. "Your
father owes me money," she said.

"If you have business with my father, come back when he's home."

"What if he's never home? What if he dies?" She saw the change in his face and switched tactics, quick. "June and I can't wait forever. I need the money for *him*. He needs a good doctor."

"Yeah? Tell me what he has and you can walk out with whatever you can carry."

"Cancer," she said without hesitating.

"What kind of cancer?"

"In his hands." She looked down at her own hands, and then back up at Benicio. She seemed to know the lie was spoiled. He left her in the closet and dialed the front desk on the bedside telephone. He gave them the suite number and said there was an intruder in his father's room, speaking loud enough for her to hear.

"I'm not a thief," she said as she emerged from the closet, heading to the front door at a fast walk.

"You're stealing," he said. "You're a thief." He caught her by one of the faded straps of her denim purse and she pivoted to punch him in the neck. He brought his forearm up, braced it against her collarbones and pinned her to the wall beside the door. She kept hitting him until he was able to pull the purse away, fling it to the opposite corner of the room and use his free hand to pin her wrist as well. He realized at that moment that he was on the verge of the kind of violence that would change the shape of his life. He was capable of it.

"He's not even your kid, is he?" Some of his spit spotted her forehead. "What is he, your little brother? And you're using him to steal from my dad when he's in trouble."

"Your little brother," she said. "Not mine." Her hips bucked against his and her knee struck out, but missed. The skin of her belly touched the skin of his. She anticipated the change in him, and pressed in close. He let her go.

"Leave now," he said.

"I need my purse."

He retrieved the purse from where he'd flung it, upended the contents on the floor and offered it to her.

"Some of that is mine."

"I'm supposed to believe you?"

Solita didn't move. Her eyes darted from him to the small pile of tissue paper, photographs and bright peso bills on the floor. They could both hear the elevator dinging in the hall outside. "I need to get home," she said. "First a bus, then a taxi."

He didn't realize that he wasn't breathing until his chest started to hurt. "That's fine," he said. "You can have it. What do I care?" He scooped everything back into the purse and handed it to her. The second she had it she rushed out the door.

A QUINTET OF SECURITY GUARDS arrived in short order and Benicio had to persuade them that he was unharmed. They checked every room in the suite and examined the electric lock with little penlights and dental mirrors. They reprogrammed the lock and issued him a new key. They knew who Solita was—described her as "Howard Bridgewater's usual friend." Benicio asked that she not be allowed back into the hotel. They said she never would be again. They said they were sorry she ever had been. They said good night, and they left.

*Chapter 22*

## THE VILLAINS' DAYS ARE NUMBERED

The incident at the Blue Mosque shakes Ignacio's confidence something awful. Then, when news of what he's done breaks across the country— across the *world*—he just about goes over the edge. He tweaks again, smoking rough crystals off of rutty takeout tinfoil—his first high since they kidnapped Howard. He paces the living room in his underwear, a frozen orange pressed against his busted nose, grating his addled teeth down to almost nothing. News reports boom through Howard's shuttered door, each more horrifying than the last. The Manila Police announce that they have a sketch of the kidnapper. The National Bureau of Investigation steps in to coordinate. The American Embassy offers logistical assistance and, in his hysteria, Ignacio imagines this to mean: *Commandos.* But worst of all is news that Reynato Ocampo has personally taken charge of the case. In typical fashion the supercop— upon whose life Littleboy's beloved Ocampo Justice films are based— stands before a fawning clutch of reporters and says: "The villains' days are numbered." Littleboy, failing at first to understand that *they* are the villains, becomes very excited. Then, when Ignacio explains things to him, he cries for a long, long time.

It's Wednesday, exactly a week after the fiasco, before Ignacio skews up the courage to leave the house. Even then it's under cover of an over-sized ball cap and a slathering of his wife's pale makeup. He drives the family taxi to the ritzy Glorietta shopping mall, seeking the anonymity of an Internet café. There's really only one thing he can do now. He's got to call it off. The plan to sell Howard to insurgent Moros is kaput, having been exposed to—and *ridiculed by*—the Pinoy punditocracy. He figures that his only way out of this mess is to ditch the evidence—all those coy, carefully worded, but still plenty incriminating posts he'd made on popular Moro blogs and websites. He's also got to think of something to do with Howard. And yes, *something* maybe means killing him. It's not that he wants to! Cutting Howard's ear off was one thing, but stabbing him in the throat until his heart stops would be something else entirely. Ignacio isn't sure he can do it.

But first things first. He parks in a covered garage and heads to the café with his eyes on the sidewalk, bearing nothing but the bill of his cap to the security cameras mounted in the palms above. It begins to rain, a steady sunshower. Ignacio's parents would have winced at the bad sign—a sunshower to them meant that Tikbalang, the horse people, were getting married. Which meant more horse people. And horse people were a problem, apparently. But all the sunshower does is help disguise Ignacio's nervous perspiration, and he's glad for it. He reaches the café and finds it full of uniformed children fresh out of school, all playing together on the local network, filling the room up with the sound of trash talk and artificial guns. Ignacio pays up front and settles before one of the few open machines. He glances about to see if anybody is looking. And *everybody* is looking—all the kids have turned away from their monitors to stare at him. Ignacio feels a tickle on his upper lip. It's not rainwater—his nose is bleeding again, specking the keyboard below. There is a collective: *Eww gross!* It's like he's in goddamn school again. Anything he says will egg them on, so he just grins at the room, blood dribbling thinly down both sides of his lips, down his cheeks and connecting at the point of his chin in goatee form. Eventually they turn away. Even the clerk up front looks spooked and stares deliberately down at his ledger.

Ignacio gets to work. The connection is agonizingly slow, but he's determined. He comes to his first posting, weeding through thickets of mockery before he can delete it. That becomes a pattern. On the Moro Islamic Liberation Front message boards they are calling him the stupidest man in the nation. On the Bangsamoro homepage they are calling him an idiot who deserves to be hit by a truck. A blogger from Mindanao has even gone about linking Ignacio's police sketch—a distressingly accurate likeness—to the discussion boards and forums. *He even looks like a genius,* written beneath in caustic italic. "Yeah, well fuck you, too," Ignacio responds, aloud. The child immediately beside him gets up to change computers. "I still think it was a good idea."

Then, about halfway through his work, Ignacio comes across a different reply. One that doesn't start with *Dummy* or *Moron* or *What is he thinking?* It's from someone with the username Khalid Bakkar, a slightly off-kilter crescent moon as his profile image. The message is just a number—a phone number!—followed by five short words. *If you're for real, call.*

Ignacio's throat catches. He knew it. He fucking *knew* it. All those politically correct jackasses on TV saying there was nothing to his strategy. All those self-righteous citified Moros saying it would never work. Ignacio gives a little hoot and jumps up from his chair, sending it crashing to the floor behind him. All the children look again, but he doesn't care. He borrows the clerk's pen and writes Khalid Bakkar's phone number on the dry, tucked hem of his shirt. Then he shuts the computer down and strides triumphantly out of the Internet café, out into the wedding of the horse people, out into the drizzle and dazzle.

*Chapter 23*

## EFREM'S FATHERS

Efrem Khalid Bakkar follows Ka-Pow up to the roof at midnight. From atop the apartment high-rise the city looks like nothing but tendrils of metal and light sprung from a void. The lit homes and offices float like satellites, drifting among sparkshower from welding torches, held by untethered workmen on steel, building more homes, and more offices. Elvis and Racha spread a drop cloth over the roof and lie on their backs to watch the moon reckon with this smoggy, starless world. Lorenzo gulps a two-liter with more rum in it than cola, passing it around like he's at a picnic. Reynato sucks his unlit cigar. Only Efrem is tense. It's been just over a week since the raid against the pirate. And now, as he clutches a list of the pirate's criminal network written in ink and Racha's blood on a thousand-peso bill, they expect him to finish the job.

"You know Efrem, this puts me in a holiday mood," Reynato says, his tone warm and easy. "This is just like New Year's in Manila. You have that problem down south? Up here it's the same story every damn year. A pretty little honor student, or a mother of six, killed while walking home from a party, their brain a landing strip for vertical gunfire. Struck down by a bullet just falling out of the damned sky like some kind of apocalyptic birdshit. Bullets belonging to one of ten thousand morons who prefer shooting the moon to fireworks. It never fails, and on January first every year I sit in my kitchen with the paper and just fucking *marvel* at it. I can't tell you how many times I've wished shit like that would happen to the people who actually deserve it. I mean, if this is going to be a country where it can rain bullets, and I mean really *rain* them, then shouldn't it at least be a country where they land right?"

"On with the show!" Lorenzo calls, spilling rum and cola as he shakes his bottle. Efrem crosses to the center of the roof, Tingin loose at his side, eyes turned up. Reynato follows and puts his soft, tiny palms on Efrem's shoulders.

"Don't let him rush you," he says. "You just take your time. I can see how a decision like this is tough, even for a man with your history. To be honest, I'd be turned off if you said yes right away. Stone-cold killers can't be trusted. I like a man who gives the rules some good consideration before he breaks them. And I know you expected things to go different when you joined up. The problem with the lies we're told is we start out wanting to believe them. Wanting to believe that the shabu dealer in Davao spent more than just a week in jail; that he isn't back home, one-man-banding his poorest lady customer as we speak. Wanting to believe that we could really arrest every man and woman on this list and that they wouldn't wind up snug between bribed judges and threatened prosecutors. Wanting to believe that our country would be better off spending millions of pesos just so some Manileños can wear suits for a few afternoons in a row. Wanting to believe the faith healers who tell us we're not so sick that we can't get better."

"Come on already," Lorenzo yells, cupping his hands around his mouth as though calling to people on the other side of a ravine. "Get to the shooting!"

Without turning around Reynato threatens to toss Lorenzo off the roof and see if he can't pull a parachute from that ear of his. "I can send them away," he says, all quiet, "if you'd rather do this alone."

Efrem shakes his head. "They won't be able to see anything, anyway." He hands the note to Reynato and asks him to read it aloud. Shouldering his Tingin, he aims straight up, eyes agape, pupils unhinged.

"You don't even know, do you? You don't even know how good you are," Reynato says. He steps back, puts on his reading glasses and holds the list up so it catches floodlight spilling off the adjacent scaffolding. He reads like a radio announcer. "Ting Dangwa!" Efrem exhales slowly and lets his gaze trickle upward. He floats, clutching sooty clouds for purchase, climbing to a spot from which to spy upon the marked men. It always takes longer if he doesn't know where to start, but the name is the important part. Manila glows in darkness below. Many Tings, doing Ting things, flicker among long gridlines of incandescent yellow. One twinkles brighter than the rest. Alone in his apartment, he reheats a steaming meal still frozen inside. He's naked save an undershirt, nose pressed against the microwave door to watch his dinner spin. Efrem picks out a little window in the hallway and shoots, his silenced Tingin making a puff-cheek sound. Ting passes by carrying his plate just in time to catch it in the neck. Reynato reads another name. "Melvin Alao . . ." sits in a girly bar on Roxas, getting a lap dance in the back room. A woman wearing nothing but sequins twists her shoulders, flips her hair and runs out the neon door when Melvin's face gets on hers. "Ed Recto and Joey Tanga . . ." both doze in the back of a jeepney traveling north on the superhighway. The kerosine engine is so loud that no one hears gasping replace their snores. "Angel Saya . . ." is farthest away. Efrem doesn't recognize the place, but it's daylight wherever she is. She walks along a leaky canal wearing a light jacket and hat decorated with plastic flowers. When she falls a blond man tries to help her up, as though all she's done is slip on a slick cobblestone.

The list is done. A breeze scores the roof and Reynato lets the scrawled-upon bill fly out of his hand and disappear over the edge. He's still close enough to touch Efrem, but doesn't. "I've got one last name for you," he says. "Howard Bridgewater." He puts a hand flat along Efrem's rifle-sight and pushes it down, breaking his aim. "You're not killing this one," he says. "I just want you to tell me if he's still breathing."

"Who is he?" Efrem asks.

"Howard's one lucky asshole, that's who he is," Reynato says. "He's American. One of Charlie Fuentes's buddies who had sense enough to donate a whole lot of scratch to the campaign. And those facts have earned him the right to some scary-ass guardian angels." Reynato cups his hands around the tip of his cigar, as if to block wind from fire that isn't there, and puffs. He waits patiently while Efrem stares. "See him yet?"

"I see him. He's hurt badly, but alive."

"Fine," Reynato says. "Super. I guess we're going to have to keep him that way." He shakes his head, as though amazed. "I help get the motherfucker elected and still he feels like he can call in favors. He swears this is the *last* one. Charlie wants us to rescue that clown."

THIS IS NOT THE FIRST TIME Efrem's used his ability to check in on people from afar. He'd been a frightened child; convinced his adoptive mother could fall ill at any moment. He used to cast long glances homeward, ready to sprint back if she stumbled in the rock garden or tumbled off the roof while mending thatching. He was beside himself when she let the Holy Man—self-appointed nurturer and interpreter of Efrem's curse—take him away to practice soldierkilling. They motored about in the Holy Man's low-lying boat for nearly a year, searching for and never finding a horizon beyond which Efrem couldn't see. He knocked whole flocks of pelagic birds out of the sky with lengths of dried coral. The Holy Man gave him an ancient Russian rifle and taught him to shoot pigs drinking at the distant sulfur spring. Together they peopled a deserted island with fake soldiers, placing coconut heads atop driftwood bodies, scattering the wooden mannequins in beach caves and beneath the root-canopy of a giant strangler fig. They motored some fifty kilometers away and Efrem decimated the imaginary battalion in a quarter of an hour.

Years later, after he'd graduated from wooden soldiers to real ones, Efrem still glanced homeward to check in on his mother. He lived among rebels, fellow apprentices of the Holy Man who made fertilizer bombs and dug tiger pits. From their hidden camp he watched, helpless, as his mother woke in moonlight and struggled to find a position she could breath in. He watched his uncle and cousins load her into their boat, the *Hadji Himatayon,* giving her sips of fresh water as they raced northeast to Zamboanga City. His uncle traded the unreliable outboard for a room near the hospital and sold the boat itself to pay the Manileño doctor's fee. Efrem was still watching when his family returned home by slow ferry a month later—his mother's symptoms diminished but not gone. No one aboard noticed the bomb hidden below a rice sack. It was a small charge, just strong enough to knock the knees off of an old man and punch a hole in the hull. His family survived the blast. They all escaped the sinking ferry. They swam for hours. Currents separated them, out of earshot, out of eyeshot. His cousins each drowned alone. His uncle drowned alone. His mother drowned in the arms of a stranger, held under by those arms till she screamed in a lungful of ocean. The stranger, a young rubber tapper, took her floating barrel for himself. He survived, washing ashore that afternoon and wandering about praising Jesus. He got a few hours' celebration in before falling stone dead on a dark street, nailed to the ground by fifteen shots out of the sky.

Efrem would have liked to return to his village north of Tubigan. He would have liked to bury his uncle's rubber-sling spear and his mother's trowel together in a shallow grave. He would have liked to set the hut she once lived in on fire. But he didn't want to raise suspicion. He wept when the Holy Man clutched him tight and told him that his family had been executed by soldiers in a gunboat—the story was true, after all. That's how his first parents had died. But his new family had been killed by rebels—killed by the Holy Man.

Two weeks later he took up with some passing badjao fishermen. He rode with them to Davao City, lied about his age to army recruiters and became a Boxer Boy.

EFREM SLEEPS SOON AFTER CONFIRMING that Howard Bridgewater is still alive. The next morning he wakes to the sound of unshod horse hoofs on tile floors. A taller, blacker, four-legged Elvis gallops up and down the hall. Lorenzo sits atop him, riding bareback, whooping as they wreck the dearly bought flat, the pair of them looking ridiculous and free. Reynato and Racha are in the kitchen, planning Howard's rescue over pancakes and coffee, gazing at his syrup-stained photograph. The kidnappers had posted poorly coded sale announcements on the Internet in the days before their failure at the Blue Mosque, and Reynato has contacted them under the guise of an interested southern buyer—someone who'd be happy to dress Howard in orange, lock him in a bamboo pig crate and make a home movie out of hacking through his neck with a bolo knife. Still bruised and gun-shy, the kidnappers insisted on meeting alone and in public. Reynato considers breaking out his bogus beard and brownface, but it strikes him as too risky. And besides, someone else in Ka-Pow already looks and sounds the part of a Moro terrorist. Efrem is the man for the job.

They meet that afternoon at an uptown cockfighting arena. Efrem approaches slowly, standing square in the entrance just as he's been told. Down in the pit a fight's about to start and the air shakes with shouted bets. Fists of folded bills wave like sea grass above four sets of wooden bleachers. Two men circle the arena, each holding a rooster high for the crowd's appraisal. People push past Efrem to get inside, cursing him for slowing traffic, but he stays put. Then, as betting winds down, someone grabs his wrist.

"Are you Khalid Bakkar?"

"I am," Efrem says.

The man—no shorter than him, but much smaller—smiles to reveal pointed gray teeth. "Good," he says. "Put your arms out."

Before Efrem can move he feels a pair of large, powerful hands come down on his shoulders from behind. He resists the instinct to throw them off, unsure if he even could. A big man with uneven hair spins him around and feels down his front. He jams his fingers into Efrem's pockets, runs them along the inside of his pant-waist and up and down his thighs. "Apologies," Ignacio says, tapping the tip of his swollen, crooked nose. "But our last buyer was not honest."

Efrem nods, praying the search doesn't stray to his head. Elvis, in the guise of a tarantula, hides out there under strands of his tussled hair. Reynato ordered him along—backup in case Efrem's a screwup and needs it.

Littleboy finishes frisking and announces that Efrem's clean. Eight legs drum his scalp in relief.

"That's a good start," Ignacio says, grabbing Efrem's elbow and leaning in close. "But don't be stupid. People know me here. If you start anything, the odds will be a lot worse than two against one."

Keeping hold of his elbow, Ignacio leads him toward the dirt arena, along a narrow aisle, to an open spot atop the bleachers. Efrem sits between them, unsure who is supposed to talk first. Down in the pit final bets are in and the crowd settles. The roosters glare at each other while the sentenciador inspects the razor sharp longspurs fastened to their feet. Cradling their cocks, the owners enter a rough chalk circle drawn around the arena's center. They bring the birds close, almost within pecking distance. This riles them. The owners step back, whisper encouragements and douse their beaks and combs with disinfectant to rile them even more. "You see the one on the right?" Ignacio asks, pointing. "The tan fringe? That one wins. He dies also, but he takes the match."

The sentenciador blows a whistle and owners drop their birds and back away fast. The gamecocks eye each other. They turn sideways, crabwalking, circling the patch of dirt that one of them will die in. The arena is filled with crowing from caged roosters, but the two in the pit are silent. The tan fringe freezes, neck-feathers erect in a mane of greasy, trembling barbs. He jumps and meets his opponent in midair— a jumble of thumping wings and skinny kicks. They fall and jump again. They fall and jump again. The bird on the left sits down in a pile of his own feathers. His head lolls and rests gently on the dirt. The rooster with the tan fringe limps over and pecks at his head, nipping away pieces of comb.

The sentenciador approaches and lifts each bird by their ruffed back-scruff. He holds them knee high and drops them. The rooster on the left tries to stand and can't. The sentenciador drops them again, and now the bird on the left does not move at all. The match is over, and the crowd erupts with cheers and groans as people collect and pay up. Owners retrieve the birds while the sentenciador sweeps away feathers and blood-whips with a dried palm frond. It looks as though Ignacio was right. Tan fringe's owner sits on the lowest bleacher, struggling to sew up his winning bird while it twitches in a way that implies last breaths.

Ignacio drums his knees. "It's easy to find a winner when you know what a winner looks like," he says. He stares at Efrem, or rather, a space several inches in front of Efrem. They're quiet for a long time. Elvis shifts uncomfortably on Efrem's scalp. Ignacio keeps drumming, moving up his thighs, up his belly, to his chest. Then he stops, all his energy, it seems, invested in staying still. "What?" he asks. "What? You're here to jerk me off?" He pantomimes jerking off.

Efrem says that is not why he is here.

"That's right, you're not," Ignacio says. "Now get your hands off me and listen. My terms are fair and easy. This is how much I want . . ." he hands Efrem a crumpled paper with a number written on it. Efrem glances down and nods. "That's in dollars, not pesos." Efrem nods again. Ignacio looks very surprised and then tries to hide that he's very surprised by drumming his knees again.

"Also, if we do this deal we do it *tomorrow*, no later. I'll only meet you outside the city, on Corregidor Island. You know that place? It's in the bay. You come with one other person, not more. You buy two roundtrip Sun Cruise tourist passes to the island. Me and my brother take our own boat there and land on the northwest side, past Battery Point, away from the ruins and the hotel. We trade on the beach. You give us your return tickets and we go home with all the tourists. You take our boat and the American and you go wherever the fuck you want."

Elvis strays down Efrem's temple and dips his spider head into his ear. Efrem repeats his whisper as though the words are his own. "That's a bad idea. Corregidor Island is full of foreign tourists. That's the worst place in the world if you get caught."

Ignacio smiles and quits drumming himself. He glances about. "No," he says, "it's the worst place in the world for a *Moro* like you to get caught. You try anything and I'll be star witness at your trial." His voice goes up an octave: "Oh, the terrorists were trying to kill our foreign guests! They shot that poor American. They desecrated the ruins. Their geopolitical vision would erase our history, depress our economy and embarrass our leaders! You got me, Moro?"

Efrem imagines killing this tiny man with the change in his pocket.

He could go to Howard Bridgewater right now and rescue him. But for all that's happened, he still trusts Reynato and Reynato wants it done this way. "I get you," he says.

"Good. I'll need some cash now, too. Like, an advance. I've got a little boat down by the harbor, but it needs gas. And I've got to rent a truck to move him through the city."

"Whatever you need," Efrem says.

Down in the pit another fight begins. Gamecocks paw the dirt and puff up large. They leap at each other just as they'd do on any farm; neither realizing that the longspurs on their feet mean higher stakes.

EFREM ONLY SAW THE HOLY MAN once after leaving home. It was in Davao City, in front of a shabby enlistment office abuzz with electric fans. Efrem had just come from the outdoor movie house, his resolve to sign up hardened by an afternoon watching Renny-O stick up for the unstuckup for, when he noticed the Holy Man lurking by garbage bins across the street. He was almost unrecognizable in torn slacks and a bright Lakers jersey that fell past his knees. His scalp and chin were bald and razor-burned. All he retained were his little round sunglasses and the lopsided look of an amputee.

As Efrem crossed the street the Holy Man busied himself picking through trash, not daring to look up. "This is humiliation!" he said, his voice trembling on the sharp edge of a whisper.

"You shouldn't be here," Efrem said, with real concern. "It's not safe."

"Not for you either." The Holy Man grabbed at his shirtfront. "This is mistaken," he hissed. "Come home with me."

Efrem shook his head.

"Apostasy! You betray your people!"

"My people are dead," Efrem said, his throat tight. "The people who became my people are dead, also. One of your bombs sank their ferry. I watched them drown."

The Holy Man let go his shirt and smoothed it out. "Efrem. Son." Tears rolled from behind his dark glasses in perfectly straight lines as though along tracks. "The ferry was an accident. We did not know they would be there . . . we *failed*. But I beg you not to do this. The army kills even Moros among their own ranks. Ask the twenty-eight Jabidah commandos, murdered by their officers. Wearing their uniform is no protection."

"I don't need protection," Efrem said.

The Holy Man's face loosened and went blank. The pistol in his hand, half concealed by garbage, was no surprise. Efrem had noticed it from across the street. "I cannot let you do this," he said, his tone resigned but still pitchy with fear. "My death will be a martyr's." He raised the pistol and in one move Efrem snatched it from his grip and tossed it skyward. It didn't land.

"You may be martyred," Efrem said, "but not by me." He turned and walked back across the street and into the recruiting office. Outside the Holy Man waited some moments for his pistol to fall back to earth before finally giving up and retreating down the street. In coming years Efrem would never regret letting him live. It pleased him to know that wherever the Holy Man was—the wreckage of a jungleside camp, picking garbage in Davao, riding through a dust storm to his made-up country—that he would forever be frozen in that aspect; neck craned and face up. Always afraid of the long fall. Always afraid of Efrem's vengeance coming down, plummeting out of the cloudless afternoon sky.

*Chapter 24*

## TAPSILOG

The next week was shit. Amartina returned on Monday morning, but only to demand that her résumé be passed along to incoming families—her threat to otherwise expose Monique's affair unspoken but implied. Less than an hour after that news of the kidnapping hit casual morning radio, the wire services, international cable—the works. Her telephone rang all day, harmonizing with other telephones in empty offices. She begged the consul general to pull some interviewers off the visa line to help her screen and answer calls. He responded with a curt e-mail. *You think you're overwhelmed? Welcome to my world.*

The calls didn't stop all week. They followed her home. Colleagues back at Main State arrived at their desks a little after dinnertime on Monique's end of the world, and they called her on the IVG line with taskings, action items and info requests. She spent most nights bleary-eyed in front of her laptop, trying to ignore the gecko—still swollen with the undigested lovebird—as it scampered across the ceiling and walls. She made the mistake of reading up on the Abu Sayyaf. She made the bigger mistake of watching one of their execution videos online. It left her with nightmares of Joseph and Shawn and Leila tied to palm trees, getting their heads hacked off with bolo knives.

It got so bad that Reynato couldn't hide his concern when he came over on Friday evening. He went straight to the dirty kitchen, washed out two mugs and put the kettle on. "Is there anything I can do?"

"Nothing more than you're already doing," she said, listlessly.

Reynato rooted about the pantry for tea bags. The kettle began to steam and he rushed to switch the burner off, knowing she preferred warm to hot. He steeped the tea, set the mugs on the table and pulled a chair out for her. He'd been like this all week.

They sat. "Still awful at the office?" he asked.

She nodded. The ambassador had called her a fuckup in front of the whole Country Team that afternoon. Later he apologized, in front of no one. He was just a little on edge, with this kidnapping business and the divorce and all. He was sure she understood. And she did.

"Hey." Reynato rapped his knuckles lightly on the table like he was knocking on a door. "You still with me?"

"What? Sorry. Yes." She sipped, the temperature on her lips just right. "Can we not talk about it?"

"Of course." He looked down into his mug. "You know what I think might help, though? If we got you out of this empty place." He gestured at the dark apartment looming around them. "Out of this dirty city. You could use some fresh air. You could use . . . what do you call it? A mini-break."

"That's the English. The English say mini-break."

"Same difference; you talk it, you are it."

"You speak English. What does that make you?" She couldn't help but smile, a little.

"Versatile. How long would it take you to pack an overnight bag?"

"It doesn't matter. I can't get away."

"Why not? Tomorrow's Saturday. And you've got e-mail on that phone of yours, it's not like you'll be out of touch. It's a whole new futuristic world we're living in."

"But . . ." she stammered. "Where would we even go? Do I need evening clothes, or walking shoes, or—"

"You need nothing." He took her hands in his. "You're what you need. And what I need." He hugged her, working his face into her neck. He smelled like fireworks and fruit.

"All right." She hugged him back. "Why not? Let's go."

MONIQUE THREW SOME SWEATS into one of Shawn's backpacks and followed Reynato down to his parked Honda. She didn't ask where they were going until they'd left Fort Bonifacio and turned onto EDSA. The answer cheered her more than she could have imagined. *Subic Bay.*

"I can't believe that in a whole year your husband never took you back."

"That's not fair," she protested. "I could have taken me back."

"Fine then. You're to blame. But it's a wrong I'm righting." Reynato smiled wide. He loved to see himself as a fixer.

Traffic was heavy in the city and didn't get any better when they hit the northern expressway. He stopped the car once to buy boxed juices and twice more so he could pee beside other people peeing beside the road. Monique didn't mind, consumed as she was by easy memories of life on the base—memories of home. She told him about their single-story house beside the officers' barracks, about the front walk lined with porous lava rocks. She told him about the cleaning woman and their trips to and from All Hands Beach. About flying foxes, macaques and turtle eggs. Reynato, normally so skeptical of easy senti-ment, went right ahead and indulged her nostalgia. He even coaxed her with questions when she started to flag. What kind of spider was it that bit you? Where was your mother when she went into labor? Have your parents ever been back? Why not?

Traffic got better when they turned onto the Subic-Tipo Expressway and passed an overturned cattle truck blocking the left lane. Plump animals spilled out the back like a litter of stillborn kittens. Butterflies alit on horns and upturned hoofs, supping blood with their delicate curved mouthparts. A lone survivor munched cud in the median, her eyes round and running. Reynato wouldn't look at her as they passed; he kept his eyes glued to oncoming billboards. Monique couldn't stop looking.

Mount Pinatubo emerged as a dark shape against dark clouds in the distance. It looked smaller than she remembered. It *was* smaller than she remembered—the eruption in 1991 knocked nearly a thousand feet off the peak. She'd watched the coverage from her hospital room, recov-ering from labor while Walter slowly died. Clark Air Base was evacuated right about when he went into the incubator. Nonessential personnel left Subic when they brought him up to the ICU. Monique remem-bered the ash plume, higher than anything she'd seen since, including 9/11. It was like black-and-white footage of atomic bomb blasts. She never told anyone that she *felt* Pinatubo erupting. Felt it in her chest. Like there was a string tied around her lungs, running down her leg, out her foot, through the floor, all the way down through the hot, dark planet; attached to the volcano at the other end. The string tugged her lungs when Pinatubo went off. She tugged back and Pinatubo went off harder. She kept all of this from Reynato as well, not wanting to be called a bruha again, even if he was joking.

"I wouldn't get your hopes up." His voice broke the quiet in the warm Honda. "The bay is different since they made it a free port. Could be your house is kaput by now. But who knows, your ya-ya might still be there." He meant the cleaning lady. "What's her name? We'll look her up."

"She wasn't my ya-ya. And I don't know her name."

He glanced at her, sidelong. "I thought you said you were close."

"We were, but I was little." Monique chewed her lip. "It was a long time ago. I hardly knew my parents' first names. I called her Tiya."

"Auntie? That's sweet. I'm sure all is forgiven."

"She has nothing to forgive me of."

"Sure now," Reynato said, and went quiet. Sweet as he was trying to be, she could tell something was grating on him. But she couldn't be bothered to push it, and they finished the drive in silence. The trees ahead became backlit by shimmering port lights. Passing the remains of an MP checkpoint, they rounded a bend and got their first good look at the old base. In a way it wasn't all that different; the runway down south, the beaches, the orderly rows of housing like suburban sprawl were all familiar. But Olongapo had surged—it glowed bright as any Manila neighborhood—and the low skyline was spiked irregularly with neon.

"I'm starving," Reynato announced, slowing so abruptly that Monique's seatbelt locked. "Sorry. Just remembered that there's a place here I love." He pulled off the main road, returning the horn-honks of the jeepney behind them, and stopped at a shabby food stand slouching between American franchise burger joints. Greasy smoke rose from a little tin kiosk, licking a plywood sign on the roof that read *Junior's Tapsihan*. Reynato ordered for them both: cured beef tapa, garlic rice and eggs over-easy, with bottles of banana ketchup and coconut vinegar for the table. The smell of the food redoubled Monique's nostalgia. Why on earth had she suffered through Amartina's faux-American cooking for a whole year when she could have been eating this? Joseph and the kids would have learned to love it.

They sat at one of several rotting picnic tables and ate. The other patrons watched Monique like she was a curious object. A man with horribly scarred arms stared with particular intensity, but turned away whenever she glanced back. Reynato ignored them all, speaking with his mouth full, some yolk clotting the stubble on his upper lip. "You should know that it's looking pretty good for this Bridgewater guy. It's confirmed, without a doubt, that he's alive. We've made contact with the kidnappers—"

Monique swallowed too fast and felt the brief vertigo of almost choking. "Can we talk about something else, please?"

"Hey, I know it's not your favorite subject. But the news is *good*. One of my best people met them today—and if I trust a life in anybody's hands, they're his. Folks on TV say this kidnapping is going to be a long, drawn-out ordeal. But no. I promise you it ends in days, not weeks or months."

"And how does it end?"

"Howard Bridgewater lives. Good guys go home happy. Bad guys don't go home at all."

"Good guys?" Monique grunted in a way that she hoped sounded good-natured. "You sound like my son."

"Your son's smarter than you give him credit for. And speaking of that—how's Howard's kid holding up?"

"I don't know. He doesn't talk to me much."

Reynato paused, as though he was giving Howard's kid serious thought. "He's lucky to have you."

"Lucky?" Monique put down her large, bent spoon. "How do you figure? I mean, what good am I, exactly? Acting chief of American Citizen Services," she sounded it out with revulsion. "Bullshit. I'm a *phony*! I do nothing all day but answer telephones. I carry tiny pieces of useless information from one person to another, and nothing I do makes that kid's life—or anybody's life, for that matter—any easier. And the few meaningful things I know—that the kidnappers are talking to police, for example—I can't share because I'm not supposed to know them. I'm just as useless as all the people sitting at home and watching this awfulness on the news. More so, in fact, because they can at least turn it off when they want to."

Reynato put his hand on hers. He still had egg on his lip. "You are not a phony."

She pulled away. Of course she was a phony—it was just another word for *liar*. And he knew that. Saccharin sweet wasn't in his usual repertoire. Nor was the quiet, supportive, steady behavior he'd practiced all week. He hadn't even pulled any cute shit at Benicio's briefing—he pretended not to know Monique from Eve.

"Why are you being so nice to me?" she asked. "I mean, why take me on a mini-break to Subic? Why feed me tapsilog? Why bring me ballroom dancing? Why help me confront the girl who sold my son drugs? What the hell are we even doing here?" She looked around at the outdoor seating and caught the man with scarred arms staring again.

Reynato shifted his weight and smiled cagily. "You fascinate me."

"What about me?"

"Your bruha powers, that's what."

"Be serious. Don't lie to me."

"Honest and serious are different. Which do you want?"

"Honest, then. Give me honest."

"Fine. It's your bruha powers." He dropped the evasive smile for a stone cold poker face and stared at her. "I've never met a bruha before, and believe me, I've been looking. I think this could be the start of something special."

Monique avoided his eyes and sighed like she was put out. "You're exhausting." She took another bite of tapsilog but the tangy, greasy beef was cold and had lost its charm. Reynato cleaned his plate, and hers, and said nothing more.

THEY GOT BACK ON THE ROAD, but instead of heading into the heart of the base they turned south, winding up the hills in the direction of Monique's childhood home on Cubi Point. They drove just a few minutes and stopped at a cluster of low concrete bungalows that looked like opaque little greenhouses. It was the old bachelor officers quarters, subdivided and converted into a sort of interstate-style motel. An old administration building served as a front desk and lobby, and it looked out onto the officers' pool that was dry and filled with brittle dead palm.

"It's no Shangri-La," Reynato said. "But I thought we'd get some proper sleep, and maybe tomorrow we'll see if we can find that house of yours. Does that sound all right?"

"It sounds great," she said, too tired to go on questioning his motives. Reynato got out and trotted across the gravel lot to check them in. Monique got out as well, leaned against the Honda and gazed out over Subic Bay. From this distance the beaches looked like slivers of granite between the black water and the incandescent buildings. Cars pulsed between the shipping warehouses, now converted to nightclubs or shopping arcades or some such. Clouds rolled thick, blotting out most of the stars and Pinatubo, which didn't bother her one bit.

Monique heard gravel crunching and turned, thinking Reynato had returned from the makeshift lobby. He had, but he wasn't alone. The man with the horribly scarred arms who'd sat across from them at *Junior's Tapsihan* stood beside him. Actually, slightly behind him. So close that they were touching. It took Monique a moment to process what she was seeing. Reynato's right arm was pinned behind his back. The scarred man held a stubby little penknife to his throat. He must have followed them. He must have caught Reynato as he exited the lobby.

"It's all right," Reynato cooed. "Don't panic."

Monique was panicking.

"I think he just wants the car," Reynato said, sounding less than calm himself. The man with the scarred arms nodded, exposing his face under his ball-cap as he did so. It wasn't just his arms—his whole face looked like hamburger. Monique edged back to the Honda, pulled the keys out of the ignition and threw them at Reynato's feet. The scarred man snorted and kicked them away.

"What's wrong with you?" she asked in Tagalog. "What do you want?"

The scarred man didn't answer. His penknife sank a quarter of an inch into Reynato's neck. Blood bubbled about the blade, trickling down his throat and disappearing below the fabric of his polo shirt. Monique remembered the nightmares she'd been having. Shawn and Joseph and

Leila tied to palm trees in the jungle. Bandits hacking them to death with bolo knives, holding their heads in the air and posing for a digital camera. Her chest began to shake with sobs—she couldn't help it. She felt pressure squeeze her lungs. Reynato's eyes widened. "You're almost there," he whispered. "Do it. You can do it. Do it."

"Wait," she managed. "I've got something . . ." She edged back to the Honda and retrieved her purse from the backseat. She unzipped it and inched toward Reynato and the scarred man.

"Do it," Reynato said. "Fucking *do it*. Bring the world down on him."

Monique held out the open purse and the scarred man peered inside, a little hesitantly. She pulled out some bright cash and dropped it on the gravel between them. The scarred man looked down, and when he looked back up she had her pepper spray in hand. There was no way to get just him. She pressed the plunger home and doused them both in poison mist. They howled, Reynato dropping to the ground and the scarred man staggering backward. Monique gave him a running kick to the crotch, and when he fell she sprayed him again, almost emptying the can into his eyes and mouth. She took the penknife from his limp fingers and stabbed the puny, one-inch blade into his arm. She saw Shawn and Joseph, bloodied, in her head. Her rage was uncontainable.

The scarred man ran for it and Monique chased after, punching him in the back of the head, tripping him up at the heels. Blind, he crashed into a parked car and then toppled into the empty officers' swimming pool. He scrambled out at the far end, disappearing into a bamboo thicket, howling as he went.

Monique rushed to the old administration building and told them to call the police. Then she helped Reynato into their room, locking the door, deadbolt and chain. He went into the tiny bathroom to wash out his eyes while she sat on the edge of the bed and tried to calm herself. For the longest time she was sure he was weeping. But when she went into the bathroom she realized he was laughing. Uncontrollably.

*Chapter 25*

## THE ONE WITH THE SUN ON HER

After chasing Solita out and getting her barred from the hotel, Benicio spent some time tidying up his father's ransacked suite. He began by collecting the papers she'd scattered across the floor and arranging them in vaguely relevant stacks on the table in the study. There were invoices, travel itineraries and printed e-mails—some achingly polite, others laced with profanity. There were also a few coffee-stained designers' sketches for a some-day dive resort that Howard must have been planning to build down south. In one of the sketches the resort was called *Benny's*. In another, *Paradise Rock*. He rolled the sketches together and placed them on the table as well.

The bedroom was a disaster, so he hit that next. He got the blazers and suit-jackets off the bed, turned their pockets back in and left them swaying quietly on wooden hangers in the closet. He picked socks up off the floor and folded them in pairs, turning one inside the other the way his mother used to. One of the socks had something hard inside the toe—a tightly folded wad of pesos that Solita must have missed. Benicio opened a dresser drawer to replace the socks, but after hovering over it for a full minute he found himself taking things out instead of putting them back in. He went through all the rolls of long black business socks that Solita hadn't got to. Most were empty but many contained dollars, euros, and brightly colored pesos; bank-fresh and of high denominations. Benicio pulled the whole drawer out and emptied it onto the bed. He did this with all the dresser drawers, as well as his father's nightstand and the storage cubbies in the closet. He went into the bathroom, where the sight of his father's dive gear hanging from a sturdy towel rack momentarily startled him. It reflected darkly in the medicine cabinet door like the ghost of a frogman. He opened the cabinet, scooped the contents into a billowing undershirt, and added that to the mess atop the bed.

His fingers shook a little as he set about unfolding, unwrapping and unscrewing Howard's things. He anticipated—even hungered for—a discovery that would shock him. Maybe a coke-dusted pocket mirror, a threatening letter from a missing person, some precious stones in a nondescript satchel or a ball gag. But all he found was money and a few nude photographs of Solita. He folded one of the photos three times over and placed it between Bobby's and Monique's business cards in his wallet. Then he laid out the cash in neat piles of like currencies. He counted it, and after converting those he was familiar with got a sum that was a little over $500,000. Christ. They were well off, he knew that, but half a million dollars? With no more security than a rubber band and a not-so-creative hiding place? Benicio counted a second time to make sure and then a third time to make sure of that. He did it a fourth time, and then a fifth.

HE AND ALICE spent the next two days at the embassy. On Thursday the Marine on duty granted them visitor's badges, and they passed hours in a tiny media center in the annex. They were idle, mostly. Alice read yellowing stacks of back-issue *Inquirers* and *Bulletins*—her notes beside her always—while Benicio pretended to do research about the Abu Sayyaf online. But he was really just thinking about Solita. Solita and June. Solita and June, and all that cash he'd found in his father's suite. The hours passed very slowly.

On Friday they met his father's business partner for lunch at a carpeted Chinese restaurant across the boulevard. No one ate much. Hon was already there when they arrived, and he shot up from his table. His face shone with the memory of blubbering, and when they hugged—Benicio tried for the handshake but Hon was intent on the hug—Benicio felt the unpleasant slickness of cooled tears on his cheek. Hon hugged Alice as well, and Benicio was reminded of Howard when they'd picked him up at O'Hare, before the funeral. Howard had hugged her just like that. He hadn't known who Alice was, but he knew she was with Benicio, and it was a sad time, so she got a hug, too.

Hon led them back to his table, where he'd been drinking ice water from a beer mug and eating a bowl of maraschino cherries. They sat.

Hon stared at Benicio for a long while. "You're different," he finally said. "In the last picture I saw, you looked very different. You looked so much younger." He ate a cherry. It seemed he was going to start crying again. "I'm so fucking sorry," he said, quavering. "I know I'm not, but I feel responsible."

"You shouldn't feel responsible," Alice said. She briefly touched his arm.

"I know. I'm not. But still. I should have said something. I should have checked in with other people when Howie was a no-show. I just figured he was with Charlie. I guess he figured that Howie was with me. And it's just like Howie, you know? When he wants something . . . he *wants* it. He needs a break—he goes. He takes it. He ignores your calls. How could I have known what happened?"

"You couldn't," Benicio said.

"I couldn't," Hon said. He smiled sadly, as though happy they three agreed on this. He ate another cherry. "I saw you today, late morning," he said. "If your dad could see it, he'd be really proud."

"Thanks," Benicio said, but he was pretty sure his father wouldn't be proud. That morning he'd given a brief statement; hemmed-in under a scrim of cameras and boom microphones, just a rickety composite podium between him and the pressing press. Monique had been confident it would get carried wide but even she seemed surprised as they watched Benicio on CNN International not ten minutes later on a television in her office. The shot changed to stock footage of a jungle clearing where Abu Sayyaf terrorists rested rifle butts on their hips and pumped rocket-propelled grenade launchers above their heads like little barbells, the audio from Benicio's statement still running as their mouths moved soundlessly. Then the picture of his father filled the screen—the one recovered from the kidnappers' cell phone. It was the first time Benicio had seen it, and it was terrible. The shot switched back to him as he concluded the statement and took questions. He looked much more composed on TV than he remembered feeling. Too composed, he thought.

Benicio got up from his chair across from Hon and moved to sit in the one beside him. "I have something I need to ask you," he said. The gesture, and the question, seemed to put Hon on guard. He straightened and rubbed his cheeks with his shirtsleeve. He reached for another cherry and, finding that they were all gone, just left his fingers in the syrup at the bottom of the bowl.

"You found out about her," Hon said. "I already know. Bobby told me how you cornered him last weekend. He shouldn't have said anything. She's none of his business."

Alice perked up and shifted in her chair. Benicio hoped she'd excuse herself, but she didn't. "That's not what I want to talk about," he said.

"Good," Hon said, "because she's none of my business, either."

"I know she's not. She's nobody's business but Howard's."

Hon nodded. His eyes had dried, but his cheeks were still wet, and fluorescent light shimmered off of them. "Well, what else can I tell you?" he asked.

Benicio leaned forward. "I want to know where Howard stands—money-wise. Why is there cash hidden all over his suite?"

Hon went from looking sad to just plain uncomfortable. He pulled his fingers from the cherry bowl and wiped them clean on a cocktail napkin. "Is this really the best time to be thinking bad thoughts about Howie?"

"I'm not thinking bad thoughts. But I want to know why he has eight thousand euros in his tissue box."

Again, Alice straightened. Her leg touched Benicio's under the table, but if it was a signal, he ignored it.

"You think Howie's not straight with you?" Hon asked.

"I know he's not straight with me. I'd like you to be." Benicio tried to scooch his chair a little closer to Hon, but because of the deep carpet all he did was rock forward and back. "Was my father . . . is he into something illegal?"

"Illegal?" Hon grimaced and snorted. "You need laws for illegal. That's *cash-on-hand*." He said it as a single word. "That's workable business work."

"It's a lot of cash on hand."

"We have a lot of business."

"How much? How much money has he hidden away?"

Hon's expression completely hardened. He finished his ice water and set the glass down roughly. "Your father, my friend, is in some big-time trouble. We don't know where he is. And all you want to know is how much money he has?"

"That's not all I want to know," Benicio said. "That's all that you can tell me."

Hon moved his tongue over his teeth. He pulled a little pencil out of his suit pocket—it looked like something a bookie would use, or a mini-golfer—and carefully etched a number on the syrup-smeared cocktail napkin. He slid the napkin across the table and snapped his hands back, like it was a dirty note passed in class. Alice made a show of not looking at it.

Benicio picked up the napkin and counted zeroes—five, six, seven of them—enough to render the preceding digit almost meaningless. Enough to make this situation with Solita and June a lot more complicated than it had been. Hon patted down his lapels and pants pockets in preparation to leave. "That's only more or less," he said. "Not counting his private investments or bonds, which I don't know about. Not our establishments either, which are all half-half, anyway. Howie's very liquid." He stood and looked down at them, quietly. It was plain that he wanted to say something else before leaving and was working out the wording. Finally he mumbled: "Maybe Howie doesn't deserve better than you. But I wish he had it."

"Hey," Alice said. "Hey. You're upset. But that's enough."

"That's right," Hon said, turning to her as though he could persuade her to switch sides. As though there were sides. "Yes. I'm upset. I shouldn't be the only one."

"You're not the only one," Benicio said.

"Well . . ." Hon's chin crinkled. Another tear jumped down his cheek. "Good, I guess." They were all quiet for a moment and then, without another word, Hon left. A busboy came by and cleared the mug and cherry bowl off the table. He must have been watching them, because he knew not to touch the napkin. Benicio folded it over a few times and put it into his pants pocket.

"I knew there was a woman," Alice said. "That's why you two didn't talk for so long, isn't it? You never said as much, but I knew it." She touched his leg under the table again. "What happened?"

"I caught him," Benicio said. "Not with this woman—she's a new one. But I caught him having sex with our dive instructor in Costa Rica. It was on my last trip, just before I moved down to school. It doesn't even sound so bad to me now. But it was different then. She was only a few years older than me, and I had a thing for her. It was silly—an infatuation. But I'd had it for years, and my dad knew. And all that time, he was fucking her. I was so humiliated. I was so goddamn angry."

"I would have cut his balls off," Alice said. Her frankness startled him.

"If you'd been me?"

"If I'd been your mother. Did she know about this dive-girl?"

"Your guess is as good as mine."

"It wouldn't be, if you'd told her," Alice said.

"Hey, I told her he was a cheat, but I didn't do specifics. If she wanted specifics, she could have found them out herself." He stood and noticed that the cherry syrup from the napkin had bled through the lining of his pants pocket. "I don't want to talk about this."

Alice stayed seated. "You know, just because something bad happened . . . I mean, what he did—what he was doing—it's still lousy. You can be mad at him and worried for him at the same time. It doesn't mean you love him less. Don't think that you have to choose." She slowly got up from her chair. "Have you met this other one? His new girl?" she asked.

"No," Benicio said. "I haven't. And I don't want to." He made for the exit, eager to put the scene with Hon behind him. Alice caught up and took his hand. They made it halfway across the boulevard before a waiter from the restaurant caught up with them. The cherries, the ice water, had to be paid for.

THE NEXT DAY WAS SATURDAY, but with nowhere else to go they returned to the embassy. Alice continued to plow through back-issue papers, expanding her search to include articles about the recent election, and Charlie Fuentes, and Howard's glittering circle of friends. Meanwhile Benicio dozed in front of the computer, still tired from a night spent chasing away that goddamn silly dream about Howard in the snow. By afternoon the annex was deserted, and they explored a little. They examined framed photos of long-dead soldiers at the VA. They stood behind bulletproof glass at the visa lines. They fucked in a restroom and called each other filthy names. One of the names he called her was "Solita." He couldn't get his father's woman, or June, or all that cash out of his head. He was still thinking about her when Edilberto came to pick them up in the evening.

They'd just gotten back to the Shangri-La when Benicio announced that he'd forgotten his wallet and cell phone with the Marine at Post One.

"No biggie," Alice said. "We'll go back."

"It's silly for us both to go," Benicio said. "Why don't Berto and I drop you off? It shouldn't take us more than an hour."

Alice was sleepy—still not over her jet lag—and she didn't put up a fight. She kissed him and got out of the car. Then, once they were safely out of sight, Benicio took his wallet out of his back pocket and set it in his lap. He unbuckled his seatbelt, leaned forward and told Edilberto that they weren't really going back to the embassy.

"Sir?"

"I want you to take me somewhere else."

"Where, sir?"

"I don't know where yet, but I think you know." He paused. "My father sometimes takes girls home with him, doesn't he?"

Edilberto sat motionless in the front, his eyes avoiding the rearview mirror. The jeepney ahead lurched forward, and when he didn't follow a motorized tricycle zipped into the void. "I'm sorry, sir, I don't really . . ." he paused and glanced back. His expression hardened. "It's not your business."

Benicio shifted in his seat. He didn't expect Edilberto to be forthcoming about his father's nightlife, but the direct rebuff was startling. "You're right," he said as he opened the wallet in his lap, pulled out four thousand-peso notes and dropped them into the front passenger seat. Two of the notes got caught in a gust from the air-conditioning vent and fluttered inelegantly into the crack between the seat and door. Benicio tried not to let it faze him. "I'm making it my business," he said.

Edilberto glanced at the bills riding shotgun and let out a sudden laugh. He mimicked Benicio, poorly: "I make it my business. You act like you're on TV." He retrieved the two bills from the seat and then unbuckled his seatbelt, leaned below the dash and rooted around for the other two that had blown to the floor. The traffic light ahead turned green but it made no difference because no one was going anywhere anyway. "Not many girls," he said, straightening back up. "One girl. Many times. Sometime she come to him, sometime I bring him to her. You want one for yourself? I know the best place. One on P. Burgos, up Makati Ave, by the old international school. Another in Ermita, along Roxas."

"I don't want to take any girl home."

"Some boy then? Some boys?" He grinned disconcertingly into the rearview. Benicio had felt ready for this conversation—it was supposed to be the easy part of the night. Edilberto was supposed to be polite and demure and do what he asked.

"No," Benicio said. "No. I just want you to take me to her. To my father's girl."

Edilberto turned fully around in the front seat and gaped at him.

"It's not for that," Benicio said. "But, I don't have to tell you what it's for. If you don't want to do it you can give me those bills back."

A fissure opened in the brake lights ahead and the windowless bus behind them honked like a foghorn. Edilberto spun back around and accelerated through the broken congestion, making a sharp right onto Roxas Boulevard. It was the same route they took to the embassy, but it looked different in the dark. Buildings he'd thought abandoned now burned with neon signage and light ropes slung like Spanish moss. Clubs poured music while cigarette vendors and idling taxicabs loitered out front. Edilberto maneuvered into the outer lane and stopped abruptly by a stretch of squat buildings that looked like houses made of nail polish and stucco. Their signs competed like saplings for altitude. "That one," Edilberto said, pointing to the banana-yellow and headband-pink building in the middle. "Your father's girl works in that one."

"Thanks," Benicio said. "I won't be long."

"Good, sir. And what about Alice, sir?"

Benicio's foot was already out the door, but he froze. "What about her?"

"Does she need me to take her someplace?"

"She's sleeping."

"I don't mind, I can bring her anyplace. When you finish, we can meet you. We can meet you right here. And afterward, I could take the two of you for dancing. I know the best place. All in Malate. All close by."

Taking his meaning, Benicio bristled. Just because he wanted to keep this trip—and the fact that his father might be letting his baby's mother work in a whorehouse—private, that didn't mean *he* had anything to be ashamed of. But then, even as he balked, he felt a grim awareness of his own hypocrisy. Because he was ashamed of plenty— the way he'd felt when he'd counted the zeros on Hon's used napkin, for example. And the hard longing he had to watch Solita step out of his father's shower again, glistening. So he opened his wallet back up and counted out four more thousand-peso bills. He didn't let go when Edilberto grabbed hold, and for a moment the bills went taut and threatened to rip between their pinched fingers. "It's a pretty good nice-guy act you've cultivated there, Berto."

"Acting?" His pained expression looked sincere. "No, sir. No act. I am a nice guy. I just follow your lead tonight. And please, sir, it's Edil-berto."

Benicio released the bills and Edilberto's hand jerked back. He got out, closed the door behind him and headed toward the club. Three middle-aged men who sat on the curb passing around a single unfil-tered cigarette got to their feet and rushed to intercept him. They called him "friend" and each pointed at a different brightly lit doorway. "All the best, all the best," one of the men chanted, taking Benicio's wrist and trying to lead him to a place called *The Coconut Grove.* "No charge, no door," another insisted, pointing at another: *Queen Bonobo's.* "Free first round and half-price lady drinks until midnight."

Benicio pivoted to twist free and shoved his hands deep into his pockets to keep from being grabbed at. He quickened his pace toward the middle doorway and was followed all the way by the men from the other clubs who urged him to reconsider. They didn't leave him alone until he was through the door, and even then they called after, each making offers that the other was quick to top.

Benicio had never been to a brothel before, but he imagined that this was what it should look like. A big room was filled with flimsy card tables and mismatched chairs where men, both foreigners and Filipinos, sat and sipped from brown short-neck bottles. They watched a two-foot-high stage set against the front wall where a girl with a face five years older than her body swayed in a way that wasn't quite dancing. She wore no tassels of any kind, no thong or even high heel shoes—she was nude save the film of alternating red and green light that made her look young, then sick, then young again. Along the back wall was a row of eight doorframes, each draped over with thick black cloth, and as Benicio stood there trying to decide what to do with himself he saw a white man with whiter hair disappear behind one of the curtains towing behind him a Filipina wearing boy-shorts, high glossy boots and a plastic cowboy hat.

A pudgy woman with short hair approached Benicio and flashed him a big smile that alternated yellow and gold. "Welcome," she said, leading him to an open table that was just about an arm's length from the naked dancer. "Something to drink for you?"

"No, thank you." Benicio had to shout to be heard over the music— Johnny Cash's "Ring of Fire" remixed over a synthetic house beat. "I'm looking for someone. Is Solita here?"

The woman didn't answer. She waddled back to a bar by the entrance, picked up a tin bucket filled with ice and three bottles of San Miguel and returned to Benicio's table. She set the bucket down, and placed one of the bottles in front of him. All of them were pre-opened.

"Nothing to drink for me, thank you."

"Compliment," the woman said, sliding back a chair so she could sit beside him. She grinned and gestured to the dancer on stage with her chin and lips. The girl must have noticed the attention because her legs sprang out as though they'd been electrified. She squatted, pouted, and did things that would have looked better were she clothed.

"Just Solita," Benicio said. "I'm just looking for Solita."

The pudgy woman stared at him. She cocked her head, as though tipping water from her ear.

"I met her here a month ago," he said. "She has a tattoo, of the sun, down here . . ." he pointed down at the inside of his own hip. "Does she still work here? She's the only one I'm interested in."

"I have," she said, her face lighting up. "Very special, and with a tattoo. I have for you." She got up and trotted over to the other side of the room, drawing a set of black curtains back and disappearing through them. The girl on the stage didn't look disappointed or relieved that she hadn't been chosen. She went back to flailing limply, her eyes on the chipped and shellacked wood beneath her bare feet.

The lady proprietor returned with her arm around the waist of a Filipina with dyed cherry-syrup hair and puffy nipples. She brought her right to Benicio's table, spun her around and lifted up the hem of her Catholic schoolgirl plaid to show him Bugs Bunny munching a carrot on her left ass cheek. "Very special," the woman repeated, peering around from behind the girl's torso.

"No, you don't understand, it's supposed to be a sun."

"*No son.*" The woman wrinkled her nose at him and spun the girl back around so that he could see the front of her. She patted a flat hand on the girl's flat belly. "No children. Just new this month. Very special."

"She's not who I want," Benicio said, his revulsion—in himself and in everything—rising. "I'm sorry."

The woman shrugged and released the cherry redhead. She sat back down again and placed her hands flat on the table with a determined look that said: We're going to work this out, you and I. "What did you say was her name?"

"Solita. So-Lee-Ta? Something like that."

She shook her head slowly. "I don't have. I have Soo. I have Linda."

Then, with a jolt, Benicio remembered that he'd taken one of his father's pictures of her and folded it up in his wallet—a proof and reminder of his own muddy intentions. He pulled it out, keeping the wallet below the table, and slid the picture over to the pudgy woman.

"Solita?" She smiled again, her gold crowns catching in the strobe. "She said her name was Solita?"

"I don't care about her name. Is she here?"

The woman nodded. "She's busy now."

Benicio imagined busy meant: *With a customer*, and the thought of his father in this place made him want to catch the first flight home. "I'll pay double if I can see her now," he said.

"I don't interrupt," the woman said. "You can wait."

"Triple, then. I only want to talk to her. And I won't be long."

The woman stood and disappeared again behind the far curtain. She emerged a moment later towing Solita—or the woman he knew as Solita—by the elbow. Her outfit was so clichéd it was embarrassing; panties, thigh-highs and a cheapo corset. As soon as she saw Benicio she set her weight on her heels and extended two middle fingers in his direction. She and the pudgy woman exchanged words. Solita kept her eyes on the floor as they spoke, but didn't budge an inch as the woman tugged on her elbow and shoulder.

"My girls have a choice," the woman said as she returned to the table. "She says no." Two men from behind the bar had accompanied her, their arms crossed over their too-tight shirts. "I'm sorry, but you have to leave now."

Benicio stood. He felt something rising in him that at first he mistook for bravery but realized a breath later was just the certainty that he would get his own way. He reached into his pocket and grabbed a sum of money that he'd planted there with a scenario like this in mind. It was just over seven hundred dollars' worth of his father's pesos, a sum calculated to paralyze. Benicio dropped the wad of bills out on the table carelessly, as though he hadn't counted every last one twice. "Just talking," he said. "Just for a minute."

The woman looked down at the blue and purple bills blossoming on the table. She stabbed them with her finger and overturned the pile to make sure it wasn't padded with twenties and fifties. Then she said something in Tagalog that made the men behind her uncross their arms. She led Benicio to one of the curtained doorways at the back wall. "You wait inside," she said, pulling the curtains open to reveal a space about the size of two bathroom stalls. It was hot and dark inside, despite an incandescent bulb that dangled from the ceiling and flickered faintly. As soon as Benicio went in the heavy curtains fell closed behind him. He sat down on the only piece of furniture, a foul loveseat that faced the entrance, and waited.

After about five minutes the curtains cracked open and Solita joined him. She ignored Benicio's objection that he just wanted to talk and jumped roughly on his lap. Her panties rode low on her hips, and the scar tissue on her abdomen brushed his nose as she grinded and lifted. He saw her tattoo again. What he'd thought was a little sun was really a spider—the rays extending from the center were actually furry legs. He was so hard he could feel his pulse in his crotch. She felt it, too, and laughed at him.

"I don't want to fuck you," he managed.

"Then you're in the wrong room."

"I have a question. I just have a question."

She took his chin in her hand and lifted it so they were face-to-face. For a moment he thought they'd hit her, but he realized it was just ketchup in the corner of her lip. "You cost me a lot of money," she said. "They don't let me into the Shangri-La anymore. That means more shifts here."

"I'll fix it," he said. "I'll say I lied about you breaking in."

"They won't listen. White boy makes stink is bad news."

"I'm sorry. Just let me ask my question, and I'll go."

Solita dismounted and squeezed beside him on the loveseat. He felt like he should be relieved, but really he wanted to grab her by the hips and put her right back. He wanted her on the concrete floor of the tank room. He wanted to *be* the spider.

"I saw Howie on the news," Solita said. "I saw you, too. They have cable in our dressing room. For the first time, I'm glad we can't afford it at home. That way June can't see. My poor Howie." She stared blankly at the heavy curtains. "My Howie."

Your June, Benicio wanted to say. My Howie.

"I'm seeing him almost eight years now. June was born in the first year. This is what you want to know?" She didn't give him a chance to answer before going on. "Howie saw my sister for five years before that, but then she died. Cancer, in her breast. Howie was good to her. He paid for everything. Even a specialist in Shanghai. He loved her. Not as much, with me."

Benicio blinked. There were worlds in those sentences. His father in love, if that's what it was. His father grieving, if that's what he did. He stammered. The only way to get through this was to stick to the trail. "June can't be his," Benicio said. "If he was, Howard wouldn't have let you work here. He can be awful, but not that awful."

"Shame on you." Solita scowled at him. "Shame on you to say that, now. Howie is not awful. He is one of the nicest men that comes here. I told you, he gives me some money. But just for June. Enough for school, and clothes, and better food. That's all that matters."

"Can you prove it?"

"Prove he gives us money?"

"Can you prove that June is Howard's son?"

She paused, warily. "Prove how?"

"A birth certificate with my father's name on it? Some paperwork from the christening, or baptism? Tax forms . . . anything written down, really."

She cocked her head and shook it lightly.

"How about pictures. Photos of the two of them or all three of you together?"

"Howie only likes to take pictures . . . he hates being in them."

That this was true proved nothing.

"How can you even be sure it was him? Howard wasn't the only one, was he?"

"No." She straightened. "But he was the only one who paid extra so he wouldn't have to use a condom." This was more information than Benicio was looking for, and she sneered at his reaction. "If you don't want to know, don't ask."

"I don't want . . ." He dropped what he was saying mid-sentence—mid-thought. There was something wrong. The shaking that he felt in his fingers had spread wildly through the air. The ground shifted under them. Music in the main room cut off and was replaced by loud banging. Solita stood, fell, and stood again. She staggered to the curtained doorway, pressed her hands against the frame and looked back at Benicio with big eyes. She yelled at him to move, but by the time he stood the earthquake was over. A full ten seconds passed before the lights went out.

Benicio and Solita felt their way through the curtain and out into the main room. The bartenders had flashlights and the patrons who smoked held lighters above their heads like people at a concert. Two of the big floor-to-ceiling air-conditioners had fallen over, crushing empty chairs beneath them, and bottles of San Mig lay shattered and frothy on the floor. Other than that, the club looked more or less as it had when Benicio arrived. He followed the general flow of patrons and girls to the front door and out into a warm night filled with the sounds of car alarms and howling stray dogs. A crowd gathered in the parking lot to wait for aftershocks but Benicio didn't linger among them. He walked away from the club, out across Roxas Boulevard to the promenade that overlooked the dark bay. Foam splashed against the seawall, haphazard waves butting heads like churned up bathwater.

Benicio sat down on the edge of the crumbling wall, let his legs dangle over the dirty gray water and kept his back to the darkened city. He couldn't believe it. He couldn't believe that Howard would let his baby's mother work in a place like that. Especially when helping her would have meant *nothing*—an imperceptible dent in the figure Hon had written on the napkin. But she's lied before, a part of him cautioned. And she's stolen. So it could, maybe, not be true. A large wave struck the seawall, splashing some oily foam over his feet. As though the ocean itself was calling him on bullshit.

And it wasn't just the ocean—the sky was up to some strangeness, too. The moon looked different than it should have. A bright, clear and unbroken ring glowed all around it, two thumb-to-forefinger lengths on either side as measured by his outstretched arm. There was also something like a cloud, but thicker and blacker than a cloud, rolling in from the east. It swallowed the peaks of ocean-facing towers as it marched past the city and out over the bay. It filled up the sky and blotted out the ringed moon. Benicio watched it for a long time. A single downy flake materialized above and landed on his knee. More followed.

"Ash," Solita said. She'd joined him at the edge of the empty promenade, the beam of her flashlight illuminating a column of falling flakes. "This is like when I was younger," she said. "When we had Pinatubo."

Benicio turned so his legs dangled on the city side of the wall and his back was to the water. She set the light beside him, cupped his cheek in her palms and kissed him. He kissed her back. She brushed welling tears from under his eyes, because he was crying now. Because this ash looked just like snow. And because his mother had been right—he was kissing a skinny muñeca at the ocean while Alice slept. He pulled Solita closer and let his arms settle around her hips. He felt those hips swing. He heard concrete scrape beneath her sandals as she put some weight into the strike. The flashlight went dead as it hit him on the temple. He tried to stop the second strike but by the third he was helpless. Solita turned his khaki pockets inside out. She pulled his shoes off, and his socks, and with a shove sent him tumbling backward like a diver into Manila Bay.

*Chapter 26*

## KILLING KELOG

The television is unbearably loud. Louder than it needs to be to muffle Howard's calls for help. Newscasters' voices ricochet around the room and glance roughly off his skull. He tries to turn the volume down, but Ignacio comes inside and hurts him. He tries to cover his ears, but that hurts too, because one of his ears is a bloody, bandaged hole. Days pass like this. News, and commercials, and news.

On Monday—he thinks it's a Monday—the television begins talking to him. No . . . that's not right. Talking *about* him. He listens to his story break live. He's thrilled, at first. At least people will finally know what's happened to him, because the police, those fuckups, have dropped the ball. But then the coverage becomes exceedingly morbid. Turns out that Ignacio and Littleboy are trying to sell him to the Abu Sayyaf group. The news anchors spell out what this means, exactly, and what it means is horrible. They even bring in this expert who knows all about the particular cultural significance of beheadings.

For the rest of the day Howard cringes as he is invoked in various grand contexts: the War on Terror, southern separatism and potential damage to the tourism sector. The afternoon anchor interviews a Palawan resort owner who is very concerned that his business will be devastated if Howard's kidnapping causes wary vacationers to stay home. The resort owner lists many other local businesses that will also be devastated if his business is devastated. The boatmen's union, the ferry operators, the various markets where his cook buys produce and fish. To say nothing of his seasonal staff, who he'll have to lay off, and who all support family in other provinces and whose families all use their remittances in turn to support other, faraway businesses. It's a whole interconnected system, the resort owner explains. In his delirium, Howard feels very sorry for this man, and for his seasonal staff, and their relatives, and he hopes that things work out for them. Then he yells for a while and elbows the walls and cries.

HE THINKS ABOUT HIS SON A LOT. Then, on Friday—again, it mostly feels like a Friday—he actually hears his voice. It's like Benny's right there in the room with him, talking. Yelling. Howard wonders for a moment if he's hallucinating or maybe dying and hearing Benny's voice on his way to heaven. But that's silly. He doesn't believe in heaven and even if he did he wouldn't believe he'd go there. It's just the TV again. Benny's on TV.

He feels oddly proud of this.

Howard sits up and tries to listen. His son is giving a news conference, but it's hard to make out exactly what he's saying. The damned set is so loud that it all comes out as a booming static ring. Fuckit, he thinks, reaching for the volume knob. He doesn't care if they cut his other ear off. He's going to listen to Benny.

Howard turns the volume way, way down. Down to a normal, human, living room level. Down to where he can concentrate on Benny answering questions. Yes, the local authorities have been incredibly helpful. Yes, of course, he's very worried. Yes, he's praying. His tone is forced, even unconvincing, and Howard doesn't believe for a second that he's really praying. But he doesn't mind the lie. Benny could hardly know he's watching.

Something moves in the other room and the tiles vibrate as the loveseat barricade is pushed across the floor. Howard braces himself. The door opens and he's surprised to see not Ignacio or Littleboy, but the slender, fuzzy outline of Ignacio's wife—the woman who gives him his meals and occasionally changes his bandages.

"I'm sorry," Howard says, his muscles still tense in expectation of a beating. "But my son is on TV. I couldn't hear with it so loud."

The woman stares at him for a while and says: "What the heck? I could use a break, myself. Besides, it's lunchtime. You can keep it down while you eat."

She walks into the room, picks up the bucket with some of Howard's pee in it and exits again. She leaves the door open behind her, and some rooms off, a toilet flushes. The open door distracts Howard, and by the time he turns back to the television his son has quit speaking. There's someone else speaking now. Some policeman.

"So is your son an actor or something?" the woman asks. She's returned with a dish of rice, garnished today with a little eggplant.

Howard gives her a look, and she gets it, and says: "Oh. Of course. Sorry. This is still new to me."

She sets down the rice and then jerks her head a bit, as though casting her eyes about the room. To Howard's sudden horror she steps toward his dirty shirt in the corner, which is hiding the bowl with his contact lens in it. She picks up the shirt, notices the bowl and picks that up also. She begins to walk away with both in hand.

"Water, please," Howard says. "Can I please have that water?"

"This is gross. I'll bring you some fresh," she says.

"Give it to me, please," he says, sitting up on his haunches. He'll tackle her if he has to.

The woman shrugs a bit. "Suit yourself." She squats and puts the bowl to Howard's lips. She tips it up and he tries not to wince as the rancid, salty water slides into his mouth like dead jelly. His tongue probes the liquid, searching out the texture of his soft lens. He pins it against the inside of his cheek and swallows. He nods thanks, worried that if he says anything he might gulp down this last sliver of eyesight.

The moment she leaves he jams fingers in his mouth to scoop out the lens. He puts it delicately in his eye. It feels awful—at once a sting and an unbearable tickle—but for the moment his relief at being able to see again is the stronger feeling. Everything around him is sharp. Things have edges that begin and end. And he can see Benny on the TV, shifting his weight, staring at the floor. The policeman has finished his remarks and now a foxy, not-so-young blonde is behind the podium. She speaks into a cluster of microphones huddling beneath her chin, giving one-word answers to rambling questions. The policeman stares at her and, from time to time, so does Benny.

"This is better," Ignacio's wife says, returning with a bowl of clear, fresh water. She sets it down beside Howard's food, and then sets herself down beside Howard. That's strange. Other than the day when she taped a newspaper to his chest and snapped a photo of him, they've hardly exchanged more than a peep. He wonders if Ignacio knows she's going easier on him. He wonders where Ignacio even is.

"Which one is your son?" she asks.

He looks from her, to the door, which is still open. Out in the living room Kelog the rooster walks to and fro, dragging his spur across the tile, looking strung out. It strikes him odd that he knows the rooster's name and not hers. He's never heard anyone use her name.

"That one . . ." he scooches forward and touches his son's face on the screen, leaving a smudge.

"He's good-looking," she says.

Howard nods, looking at his good-looking kid. He blinks rapidly, trying to focus on Benny's face. There's something else going on there. Something he got a hint of when he heard Benny speaking. His son looks . . . off. Not torn up. But weirded-out. Like he thinks he shouldn't be there. Like he's doing a favor for a not-so-close friend—a favor that leaves him reluctant and chilly. And there is no doubt in Howard's mind, now. Benny knows about Solita, knows—*he's sure*—about her kid. She has found him and told him. Just when Benny was getting over the story of *Howard the scumbag cheat*, just when he was moving past Costa Rica, just when it looked like the two of them could become close again, Solita has fucked it up. Not that Howard blames her. Fucking things up is what she *should* do—no one is going to stick up for her otherwise. Never mind that June probably isn't even his. The timing works, sure, but come on—the kid's darker than even his mother. It's no skin off Howard's back to give them some cash every few weeks. As far as he's concerned he's doing her a favor by letting that shoddy claim of paternity go unchallenged. But Benny, he's sure, will *not* see it that way. Without Howard there to say his piece, Benny will become permanently committed to the weirded-out, distant bullshit they call a relationship. And that won't do at all. They've already wasted too much time on this stupidity.

Howard pushes up off the floor and stands. His knee is still stiff, but he hobbles out to the living room with little trouble. Ignacio's wife rushes after.

"Hey!" she yells. "Hey! If he sees you doing that he'll break your fingers. He'll cut your nose off."

"Ignacio's not here," Howard says. "Is he?"

"He's here." Her voice is wobbly. "Get back inside or I'll call him."

"No . . . he would have come in as soon as I turned the TV down," Howard says. He feels like such an idiot. He's already squandered ten minutes—enough time to have saved his life a few times over. He goes for the nearest door and pulls it open. Closet.

"Which way is out?"

She doesn't answer. She runs into the kitchen and comes back with a wok in her hand, lifted like a clumsy mace. He takes the wok out of her hand. She slaps him on the wound that used to be his ear and he howls, pushing her, roughly, onto the loveseat. He rushes out of the living room, down a short hallway with unfinished walls. There's a door at the end that looks to have natural light leaking under the crack. Just as he's about to reach for it Kelog appears, placing himself with a flapping jump between Howard and the door. Howard looks down at the rooster. It leaps up at him, wings beating his face, beak pecking at his bruises. He tries to push it away but feels a shocking, intense, unreasonable pain. He backs up, trips over his heels and falls ass over head to the floor.

Howard's forearms are covered in a hot mess of deep cuts. Kelog approaches him, talons clicking horribly on the tile floor, cockfighting spur bright with blood. Howard tries to kick the bird as it approaches but it sidesteps, gazing at him with patient evil. Howard feels as though he's losing his mind. "I'm going to kill you," he says to the rooster. "I'm going to break you open with my hands."

He swings out and catches the rooster with an open-palmed slap that sends it tumbling across the hall and hangs a constellation of green feathers in the air. He stands and stumbles after the dazed bird, momentarily more determined to kill it than he is to get out of this apartment. He lifts the wok over his head and is just about to finish it off when he feels another, incredible, unfair, at this point even redundant, pain. Ignacio's wife has stabbed him in the back. Not with a knife, but with something multi-pronged and kitcheny. Like one of those roasting forks. Leaning into the fork, she kicks the side of his bum knee and he knows that's it. Game over. His knee gives out, and he goes down.

IGNACIO AND LITTLEBOY come for him early the next morning. They tie him at the wrists and stand him up. Ignacio switches off the television, and it looms silently in a way that feels very final.

Sweating, fidgeting, grinning, they lead him out of the apartment, into the pre-dawn dark. The residential street is empty save a truck idling by the curb, cab light on and driver's seat empty. Through Howard's crusty lens he sees a big advertisement for chicken feed painted across the truck. A cartoon rooster with boxing gloves on his wingtips poses beside an enormous sack of grain, while all around delirious hens with lipstick on their beaks bustle to get his autograph. Bubble letters below the rooster's feet read: *Feed Your Champion Like a Champion!*

Ignacio and Littleboy open the back of the truck and heave Howard inside. It's no bigger than a small moving van, about ten feet deep by six wide in the rear box, and empty save a layer of dry grain spread evenly over the bed. Howard sits up and looks out the open back. He sees Ignacio's wife standing in the doorway to the apartment. She waves at him, and he waves back, because why not?

Then he sees Kelog. The green bird hops fatly down the steps, its metal spur scraping on the concrete. Ignacio picks it up, coos to it and places it gingerly beside Howard like some kind of fucked-up prison guard. Howard tenses and pulls away, expecting some immediate confrontation. But Kelog ignores him and pecks at the feed spread evenly across the metal bed. It's just a chicken, after all.

Ignacio pulls the rear door down, sealing Howard and Kelog inside. Moments later the engine starts and the truck bed vibrates, making the grain hop like popcorn. The truck lurches forward. Howard knows they can only be going one of two places. Either Ignacio and Littleboy have given up on their plan—who would blame them?—and are taking him to the countryside to cut his throat and bury him, or they've actually found someone to sell him to. Either way, if he's going to save himself, it's got to be now.

"I know what you're doing, and it's a stupid move," he says when the rear door opens again, about a half hour later. The sun still isn't up. He briefly registers the sound of waves, but keeps his eyes fixed on Ignacio.

"Stupid for who?" Ignacio asks, a nervous half-grin still smeared above his chin. He produces a pack of cigarettes and lights one. He offers one to Howard.

"It's stupid for everybody. Listen," Howard sits up, his bound wrists before him in a gesture resembling prayer, and accepts the cigarette. "I get how you're looking at this. You want to sell me. That's simple. That's fine. That happens all the time. *I've* done stuff like that. But listen. From a rational perspective, from a purely financial outlook, it's stone dumb. It's dangerous for everybody. Like I said, I've got money. I've got cash. You really want to sell me? That's fine. But leave the bidding open. Let me buy me."

"Nope," Ignacio says.

"Nope?" Howard shakes a little. The simple ridiculousness of it is maddening. "I'm offering you a guaranteed payday, more than any fucking fisherman can give you, and all you say to me is *nope*?"

"Yup." Ignacio lowers his cigarette so Kelog can puff. He strokes the rooster's green feathers with his free hand and says nothing more. Howard briefly indulges in a fantasy wherein he's rescued and arranges to have Ignacio killed in prison. Tortured, and killed.

"Easy, boy," Ignacio says. "That's the first time I've ever seen you look angry."

"I've been hiding it," Howard says.

"Can't see why." Ignaco stubs his cigarette out on the grain and Kelog pecks at the ash. A moment later Littleboy joins them, holding a length of folded burlap. "Now listen," Ignacio continues. "We're going to put this on you. While you're in here you're going to be nothing but a fat, heavy sack of rice. You do anything that rice doesn't do, like move or talk or fart, then it's just going to scare the shit out of us. I don't know what we'll do. We'll panic. Get me?"

"Yes."

Ignacio puts a finger to his lips. "Hush," he says. "*Rice.*" Then he nods at Littleboy and they roll Howard in the coarse fabric. They lower him off the truck and onto a broad dolly. Howard listens hard as they wheel him down a ramp, ready to shout if he hears the slightest wisp of human noise. Their feet make crunching gravel noises, and then hollow wooden noises. Waves crash like falling bricks. A few moments later Howard is upended and rolls into the bobbing bottom of a boat. The boat dips as Ignacio and Littleboy get in after. They're at a pier—it's got to be Manila Bay considering the length of the drive. There's always someone awake at Manila Bay.

Then, in the distance, he hears it. Unmistakable. A voice speaking Tagalog.

"Help!" Howard screams. "Help! Help me!" He punches through the sack, but catches only air. "Help!"

Ignacio and Littleboy laugh. "It's the radio, genius," Ignacio says. Then he revs the outboard, and with a splash of cold, oily water, they're off.

THE BOAT ROCKS TERRIBLY. Howard lies under burlap in the stern, getting sprayed whenever they hit a wave, which is often. The outboard alternates between a drowning gurgle and rip-roaring in the air whenever they crest a swell. It isn't long before Howard has to hold his head up just to keep it above the collected water. He's so angry he imagines he might have a heart attack or aneurism or something, and the thought of dying on the way is a morbid thrill. He curses. He bangs his feet against the benches and gunwales.

Ignacio pulls the burlap away from Howard's face and glares down at him. "Be nice," he says.

"Let me sit up, I'm going to drown down here."

"Sit up then, what am I, your mother?"

The color drains from Ignacio's face as the boat dips into a trough between waves. Then, as it rises up to the top of the next crest, he turns a shade of green. He sends a mouthful of spit over the side.

Howard sits up, untangling himself from the sack. The boat is small, bangka style, with bamboo outriggers that shudder as they slap the waves. The city still looks nearby behind them, but the horizon ahead is indistinct. Dawn light shines pink on the whitecaps. Ignacio squats by the engine block, white-knuckling the tiller. Littleboy looks ill up at the bow, his knees pressed together, his eyes glued to the bottom of the boat. Only Kelog is relaxed, perched on the stem of the bow like an obscene maidenhead.

Ignacio takes out his cigarettes again and tries to light one. With the boat rocking as it is, it takes a while for him to connect with the lick of flame from his lighter. His hand holding the tiller drifts and they begin to turn, parallel to the oncoming swells. The boat sways, and tips. Ignacio's face goes puffy, and he overcorrects, sending them too far in the other direction. The boat does one complete circle.

"That won't help your belly," Howard says, gesturing at Ignacio's cigarette. "That will make it worse."

Ignacio ignores him.

"Can you swim?" Howard asks. "This boat . . . I don't know."

Ignacio says something in Tagalog and Littleboy reaches across the bench and strikes Howard on the back of his head. He pitches forward into the dirty water sloshing between Ignacio's feet. He stays down there for a moment, trying to rid his expression of satisfaction. Then, as he's about to struggle back into a seated position, he notices something beneath Ignacio's seat. It's a clear plastic container, about five gallons or so, filled to the brim with extra fuel. There's not much space under the aft seat, so the container lies on its side. The nozzle that should be on top is just beneath the surface of the water they've taken on. Howard reaches out quickly with his bound hands and cracks the nozzle open. He sits up and watches gasoline flow out into the saltwater splashing about their ankles. Then he watches Ignacio smoke.

THE MORNING SMOG begins to lift. Birds circle in the haze above. A shoreline becomes distinct ahead. It's a long swim, but Howard's an optimist. Anyhow, he's better in the water than on land.

Ignacio savors his cigarette and Howard prays he takes his time, keeping one eye on the slowly emptying container. Everybody notices the smell and Ignacio peeks back at the engine with a worried look. He says something to his brother in Tagalog—something calming. The cherry burns down, almost to the filter. Ignacio makes to chuck it overboard but Howard grabs his wrist. He pinches the cigarette, fingers burning a little, and drops it into the bottom of the boat. Then he tosses himself overboard.

It's not quite an explosion, but the boat lights up without an argument. Howard's bound wrists make dogpaddling impossible, so he turns on his back and kicks away, like he used to do after surfacing from a dive with Benny, his BCD inflated, his son waving at the hired Costa Rican boatmen and the boatmen waving back cordially. Backpedaling like this, he can see the burning boat. Kelog screams and flames lick up Ignacio and Littleboy's legs, but they seem hesitant to get into the water. Finally they hold hands and jump, kicking wildly to grab hold of the bamboo outriggers. Kelog stays onboard, flapping madly about the hull. His feathers catch, and sizzle, and his owners splash water up at him, trying to douse him. It's no use. Finally he takes off, wings smoking as Ignacio and Littleboy beg him to get into the water. The flames on him grow and trail behind like luxurious feathers. Kelog is a bright lick of green and yellow, flying straight up. By the time the flames burn out there's nothing left of him to fall.

The saltwater has loosened Howard's binding by now, and he's able to get his wrists free. He turns to the island and swims. All his injuries—his bandaged ear, his sliced forearms, his stabbed shoulder—sting in the water, but it has a wonderful, invigorating, antiseptic feel. The island looms large ahead. A rocky beach with palms. The broken hulls of concrete buildings peeking out from a mosaic of lush vegetation. Green cannons pointing straight up at the sky. Jagged coral cuts into Howard's palm and that, too, is a wonderful feeling. His bare feet find rocks, and hedges, and soon he's wading.

And there are people on the beach. Five men stand in a row at the point where the jungle meets the sand. They wear badges around their necks that shine brightly in the morning sunlight. The police have come. Never mind that they're fuckups. Never mind that they're late. They're here, and Howard is happy.

*Chapter 27*

## SAVING HOWARD BRIDGEWATER

Efrem Khalid Bakkar hopes the fire kills them so he won't have to. He stands with Ka-Pow on the rocky Corregidor beach, watching Ignacio's little bangka burn. It bobs in the chop, flames licking out the rudder shaft, glowing from stem to stern. The kidnappers jump overboard and retreat to the outriggers, trying to douse their boat with backward bailing. A single fireball shoots skyward and fizzles. Efrem watches Howard Bridgewater backpedal away from the smoldering bangka. Ignacio makes to follow, but turns back after a few strokes, coughing out seawater and smoke. Reynato points from their boat to his throat, finger a blade. It wouldn't have been different if they'd landed and submitted placidly to handcuffs. Efrem levels his custom Tingin. With two shots he snaps the blackening outrigger struts. Hugging bamboo, the kidnappers float safely away. Efrem mimics Reynato's pantomime, fingerslicing his own throat. From this distance, with this fog, Ignacio and Littleboy look as dead as he says they are.

Ka-Pow recovers Howard, dazed and sputtering, from the shallows. Reynato doesn't look all that thrilled, but says they'll get some food at the Corregidor Island Hotel to celebrate anyway—his treat. He plucks sawtooth blades of cogon grass and has them draw to see who'll hang back on the beach with Howard until the Coast Guard comes to pick him up. On the first draw Efrem comes up short and Reynato has them do it over because Efrem is the hero of the day. On the second draw it's Lorenzo, who throws up such a weepy stink at being excluded that Elvis volunteers just to shut him up.

Despite heavy fog and rough sea, Ignacio actually managed to get his bangka pointed in the right direction. They sank just off the northwest coast of topside Corregidor, and from there it's an easy two-kilometer walk to the tourist hotel at the south dock. Reynato, Racha, Efrem and Lorenzo stroll at an easy pace, emerging from the dense jungle onto a little paved road that meanders from one cluster of war ruins to another. Reynato passes cigars and matches all around, keeping his unlit as always. His mood lightens and soon everybody, including Efrem, is smiling. A trolley approaches with the first morning tourists and Reynato makes a big show of jumping out from behind a crumbling wall and shooting at them with a phantom rifle. Children on the trolley return fire from the barrels of pointed index fingers and squeal with delight when Reynato clutches where his heart would be and falls backward into high grass. He waits for the trolley to disappear before standing and brushing himself off. "Where were you guys? You just let that happen."

To Lorenzo's delight, brunch at the hotel is served buffet style on an outdoor veranda overlooking the bay and the city beyond. They pile plates high and take a table in the corner. Reynato toasts them with a mimosa flute. "You're good at what you do because you do good things," he says. "Here's to all those people worse than us." They clink rims and begin eating. As Efrem chews he watches a television mounted above the buffet. A young newswoman in too much pink talks about the kidnapping as though the kidnapping is still a thing to be talked about. He checks Racha's wrist-fused-watch and sees that it's been over an hour since they left the beach.

"They don't know yet," he says, gesturing at the screen with buttered toast.

Reynato, munching bacon, glances up. The news lady cuts to stock shots—clips of a press conference given by Howard's son mixed with older footage of an Abu Sayyaf terrorist with a rocket-propelled grenade launcher hoisted over his shoulder. The newswoman narrates the montage, outlining perilous possibilities. "Maybe Elvis has no signal on the beach," Efrem says. He takes out his own cell phone and sees he has full bars. "I'll make sure they get the message."

Reynato takes Efrem's phone and pockets it. He dabs the corners of his mouth with a cloth napkin. "Easy does it, Mohammed. You'll get credit soon enough." They regard one another, the hurt and confusion on Efrem's face a little diffuse because he's been feeling it so often lately. Credit is *not* what he was after. Reynato, knowing this, blinks first. He crosses to the television and flips the channel to live cockfighting championships. Racha and Lorenzo, oblivious to the tension, get seconds and thirds at the buffet. They eat with noisy gusto long after Efrem has slid his half-full plate across the table. Lorenzo produces a flask of lambanog from his plastic poncho and fortifies their mimosas. He interlocks elbows with Racha and they sip daintily, braying and spilling. Celebration is a matter of course for Lorenzo at mealtimes, but Racha isn't known to act the fool with him. Reynato eyes him suspiciously. "And what are *you* so happy about?" he asks.

Racha holds both hands in the air, displaying cracked palms and grizzled knuckles, as though that's an answer. He stands and takes his shirt off, turning proudly while people at nearby tables gasp at his sagging adhesions, his missing nipples. He grins and says: "Not a scratch!"

Reynato crosses his arms over his chest. "You must have missed it."

"Nope," Racha says. "I checked two times." He runs his fingers up and down the waxy discolored horror of his torso. "Nothing!"

Concern creases Reynato's forehead. He orders everyone into the toilet where they strip Racha naked and search him for a new wound. As easy as Howard's rescue had been, it was still a mission. Ka-Pow's rules dictate that Racha should have been hurt. That's how his particular bruho magic works—soaking up the evil that finds its way into every mission and keeping it off everybody else. If Racha's come through unscathed it means there's still some evil floating around out there, looking for a place to settle. Reynato questions him while Efrem and Lorenzo probe his unfortunate topography. "You sure you didn't slip on a rock? Step on an urchin? Stub your toe? How's your ankle? How's your instep? Is that blood in your nose? Those look like new shoes, any blisters? Any rashes? Bite your tongue? The path was thorny, any scrapes? Does anything itch?"

But nothing itches. They don't even find a mosquito bite. "Maybe it was that thing last night?" Racha asks. "Maybe the pepper spray counts?"

You know that's not how it works, Reynato snaps. He seems discouraged—even angry. They give up searching and he leads them all back to the table. He says that everyone gets lucky sometimes. Then he takes Glock out of his belt and checks it twice to make sure it's loaded and the safety is off. He shifts in his chair and eyes the exits. He can't finish eating.

Racha, pitying his boss's distress, forks himself in the knee.

REYNATO IS ON EDGE the rest of the morning, and though he doesn't show it, Efrem is too. He gazes out over the bay as they leave the restaurant. Private yachts sway in the wakes of trawlers, but the Coast Guard boats at Sangley Point are still. Back in Manila the police station is quiet. He glances topside and sees Elvis leading Howard into an ancient bunker for shelter from the sun. Howard, filthy as when they plucked him from the shallows, follows in a daze.

Rather than returning topside, Reynato insists they board one of many brightly painted tour trolleys to waste the whole day trundling about ruined barracks and mortar emplacements. They pose listlessly for pictures by a beachside MacArthur statue. They crowd into the Malinta tunnel for historical lectures by animatronic soldiers. They haggle gift shop cashiers to tears. They visit a kitschy outdoor chess set with pieces big as children. Lorenzo challenges Efrem to a game, and cheats, and wins. The tour ends. The sun reddens and dies in the South China Sea. The Coast Guard never comes and Efrem doesn't get his phone back. He peeks at Howard and sees him running from the bunker, chased by Elvis as a horse, pinned by Elvis as a python, carried back into hiding by Elvis as a colony of tremendous ants. They're not saving him *from* anything. They're saving him *for* something. Killing time.

Efrem doesn't speak as they walk back to the topside beach. The moon, low on the horizon, throws long shadows against the ruins. He lags some paces behind the others, and then stops walking altogether. Reynato turns and regards the distance between them without closing it. "Is there a problem?" he asks.

"You're going to kill him," Efrem says. "You're killing Howard Bridgewater."

Reynato cocks his head and grunts. Duckfooted, he walks over and takes Efrem's cheeks in his small palms. "Mohammed," he says. "My friend. What have I done to give you this bad impression of me? You ever see me do a thing like that?" He leans in close. Efrem sees moonlight in his braces. "If I remember right, your tally puts us all to shame."

Efrem steps back. "Don't lie to me."

Reynato steps with him, keeping hold of his cheeks like a bridle. "I lie plenty," he says, "but never to you. I'll admit to some dramatizing, but among you bruhos I'm honest to a fault and I'd appreciate you not saying otherwise." He pauses, looking pained, like a father taken out of his son's confidence. "And I'll be honest now, even though a part of me would rather lie. The smarter part of me, I'm guessing. Especially because we both know I could get away with it. But, what the hell?" He smiles. "I'll keep the streak alive."

Reynato releases Efrem's face and gives it two soft pats. His frayed cigar is bending at the middle and he pockets it carefully. "Sure," he says. "Yes. I am. *We* are. There it is. We're killing him. We're killing Howard. Mr. Bridgewater is fucking doomed." Reynato stares at him, deadpan.

Efrem can't speak for a time. Even after he feels capable of making words, he's unsure which ones to pick. "How is that . . . it isn't . . ." He gawks lamely. "This is *not* sticking up for the unstuckup for."

Lorenzo and Racha howl at this. Reynato hops three steps back, dancing from foot to foot like a child with an answer. "*Right there!* That's it. That's the problem with you, Mohammed." He points, as though the problem is floating in the air—a ghost between them. "With you, and with the whole damn country, as far as I'm concerned. You've seen too many of those moronic movies. You want to talk about the un-fucking-stuckup for? How about *yourself*? How about the people on that island you come from, strangled and half-starved by rich incompetents? Politicians like Charlie Fuentes, who now gets his at-bat, his turn to see how much shit he can break or steal before the voters get wise and replace him with some song-starlet or beauty queen."

"This isn't about my people," Efrem says, wary that Reynato is trying to confuse him. "And it's not about how jealous you are of Charlie Fuentes." Yes, he's noticed—he's not as simple as everybody thinks. "It's about Howard Bridgewater."

Reynato's arms fall to his sides. He becomes less manic, less excited, giving off an air of limp danger. "Howard Bridgewater? The wealthy hotel manager with a suck-my-dick investment visa? The man with a whole embassy full of people out to save his ass? The man who report- ers talk about like he's already died and been sainted, the man whose rescue is the highest priority of a national police force up to its nostrils in some of the worst smelling shit this side of Baghdad? *That guy?* No, sir. People have been sticking up for Howard for his whole goddamn life."

Reynato gets in Efrem's face again, and now all the playfulness is gone. "I'll forgive you the snotty reaction," he says, his voice leaden with menace. "I know that when I just say it flat like that—*We're kill- ing Howard!*—it sounds pretty rotten. Especially given what I've asked of you in the last few weeks . . ." he pauses long enough for Efrem to remember the shabu dealers in Davao, the executed warehouse men, and all those people he struck down anonymously from the high-rise rooftop, surer now than ever before that he's going to hell. "But what you don't appreciate, Mohammed, is that I operate in contexts. I'm not always the freewheeling bruho you know from Task Force Ka-Pow. Nine times out of ten—fuck, more than that—more like ninety-five times out of one hundred, I do things *right*, rigid and upstanding. I'm talk- ing about boring stakeouts. By-the-book arrests reported to superiors in triplicate. Painstaking evidence preservation, even when I know it'll be misplaced and mishandled. I spend whole fucking days deskbound, jumping through silly hoops, explaining to the preteen from tech sup- port why I need write permissions on my C drive, moving my shit from office to office in search of walls without dryrot and ceilings that won't drip on me. Be thankful, Mohammed, that I save you bunch for what you do well. Which brings me to another, say, four cases out of a hundred. When I use rulebenders like yourselves, my own little ends and means committee, to do right things the wrong way. Like with your friends on the list, and Lorenzo's pirate mishap. Maybe we get a little rough, maybe some bills go missing, but it's a net plus. And besides, it doesn't happen every day."

Reynato pauses here, eyeballing his newest recruit. He links elbows with Efrem and begins walking again, slowly. With his free hand he unbelts Glock and aims it casually at the asphalt.

"Which brings me to the last, the one out of one hundred kind of scenario. Every once in a rare while, I break the rules and I break them just for me. That's what tonight is about. I'm not going to contrive some bullshit about Howard Bridgewater being the *real* enemy. I'm not going to try to convince you that the world will be better off without him. For all I know, the world will be worse off without him. But I tell you what . . . Fatty was into some serious problems even before we got involved. And he does *not* get a pass simply on account of being an American and a drinking buddy of that cocksucker Fuentes. Not from me, he doesn't. That's why I . . . why *we* are going to finish that junkie's half-assed plan. We're going to sell Howard to the Abu Sayyaf."

Their footfalls reverberate as they cut through an ivy-draped, ruined barracks. Efrem is dimly aware of being drawn away from the road, out of sight. "They're on their way now," Reynato says, "downright giddy at the thought of kidnapping an American from the very edge of Metro Manila. They knocked off two armored cars in Cebu City just to round up the cash. I won't talk numbers, because you don't have a leg to stand on in terms of negotiating a cut, but I'll say that tonight could make you a rich man, by your standards. By a lot of other people's, too."

Efrem glances up through a moon-filled hole in the concrete roof, out over treetops on the north shore. A boat approaches, nets covering the deck, cabin and running lights doused. Men sleep head to foot in the stern. He recognizes former rebels among them. An old man with a silver beard smokes in the deckhouse. His one hand sits on his white robed chest. The moon reflects in the dark ovals of his sunglasses. Efrem misses a step, nearly pitching into a knee-deep crater in the floor.

Reynato tightens their linked elbows and quickens his pace through the rubble. "I need to know if you can handle this, Mohammed. I need you to visualize yourself helping us or visualize yourself without a weapon, handcuffed for nobody's safety but your own. Visualize a team with shaken confidence. *This* team. Be as honest with me as I've been with you. Do you have a problem with this?"

Efrem answers without hesitating. "No, I don't."

"I knew you didn't," Reynato says, returning Glock to his belt. "I always knew you wouldn't."

KA-POW RETURNS to the topside shore. They collect sobbing Howard from the cave, carry him down a steep pathless slope to the shallows and wait. The fishing boat filled with Abu Sayyaf approaches, near enough now that everybody sees it. Three kilometers out, they kill the engine and coast, silent on the rising tide. Somebody onboard shines a lantern twice. Reynato raises a penlight high and does the same. Then, all in a flash, the boat turns running lights back on. Men appear along the gunwale with long bamboo poles, negotiating with coral and rocks beneath the surface. The Holy Man stands at the bow, his one hand gripping the stem as he stares coastward through dark glasses. Efrem knows he's unrecognizable on the beach, but being this close still dices his breath.

The boat hits bottom a few meters out and men aboard lower palm-fiber ropes and climb down into the shallows. Two of them help the Holy Man over the gunwale while another carries a large sack that he's careful to not get wet. More men come over the side until ten stand thigh-deep in the waves. They brandish bolos and antique rifles. Two wear coconut-fiber belts strung with grenades painted like rotten fruit.

Reynato clicks his tongue as they wade closer. It's five more than they said they'd bring. In a hissed whisper he orders Efrem back up the slope to keep watch, reminding him of the cardinal rule before he goes—*me first*.

Efrem slips away, disappearing into the vegetation beyond the narrow beach. He races up the wooded hillside as quietly as he can and finds a suitable granite outcropping near the top. The stone is cold and wet. It feels good on his belly as he lies flat and steadies his Tingin.

Reynato and the Holy Man shake and banter below. Efrem draws a bead on their clasped hands. He sights his Tingin on the Holy Man. He sights it on Reynato. He wonders if his adoptive mother would be proud of what he's about to do. She wouldn't, he decides. She'd have no sympathy for a rich foreigner who probably deserves it. And even though it was the Holy Man who'd bombed her ferry, she'd call Efrem a faithless, fatherkilling traitor. Because that's what he is. The curse is proven. He really is deadluck. Everyone he's ever touched has passed. Or is about to.

Down below Ka-Pow lifts Howard Bridgewater to his feet. Efrem hears them count down from three before, in one single movement, shoving Howard at the Abu Sayyaf and catching the money sack hurled in exchange. Efrem takes aim at the space between the Holy Man's dark lenses. His fingers shake as he squeezes off a shot. When it's done, the world shakes with him.

*Chapter 28*

## GECKO

Despite the excitement of the evening before, Monique had a good night's sleep at the converted BOQ motel, and woke feeling rested and whole. It was late morning already and Reynato was gone. He'd scrawled a note into the back of one of Monique's business cards and left it beside her pillow.

> *Dear Bruha—*
>
> *If it wasn't an emergency, I'd still be there. Expect good news shortly. Left the car. Room's paid through Sunday. Take the break you need. And don't hurt anybody!*
>
> *—Your Bruho*

She was irritated at his having left her just hours after they were assaulted—or rather felt she should be. But an undeniable sense of relief pushed that perfunctory irritation aside. For the first time since Joseph and the kids left, she had a day that was all hers. Eager to make use of it, she dressed in her wrinkled one-button pantsuit from the day before and left the bungalow-style motel room. Reynato's Honda waited at the far end of the lot, busted left headlight making it look like it was winking. Walking toward it, Monique caught a whiff of the pepper spray she'd emptied the night before and noticed some dried blood speckling the gravel like hearty lichen. The police had searched the bamboo thicket for a good hour and failed to find the scarred attacker. She was strangely unconcerned by this. The whole memory felt surreal, and harmless.

It had been years since she drove stick, but the empty roads afforded her some practice. She had her route all figured out. Heading northeast, she looped around the old Binictican Golf Course where she used to watch her father hit balls into trees. Further north she saw that the commissary was still standing, as was the Kalayaan elementary school that she'd attended off and on during her father's deployments. She stopped in Onongapo for lunch, eating pancit from a cart and feeling conspicuous, like a tourist. Then it was back south to the airport on Cubi Point. She swung around All Hands Beach, cut back up behind the converted BOQ motel and finally stopped at the married officers quarters. Reynato had been wrong. Her house was still there, sulking darkly downhill at a short remove from the other quarters. The windows were boarded up and many of the flagstones had been salvaged from the front walk. Part of the roof had caved in, and waxy leaves climbed out of the hole like smoke from a chimney. Seeing it brought a lingering worry to the front of her mind—that seeing it might not change anything.

Monique parked the car and picked her way down the muddy hill. The front door was unlocked, but humidity had swollen the frame so badly that she had to tug hard to get it open. There was nothing inside. The floor was speckled with sunlight, broken glass and the droppings of a small animal. There was some graffiti on the walls and a used condom so old it looked like snakeskin. Rather than walk through the filth, she cut around the side and found that the back porch was still there, rotting peacefully. Monique kicked dead leaves off the splintered wood and sat, looking out on the same view she'd had as a child. Sagging, vine-heavy woods. A dirt trail that ran from the bus stop on the main road down to the huts and bangka moorings on the water. The same trail had brought the cleaning woman to their home three times a week. It was spotted today, as it had been years ago, with intermittent foot traffic. A teenager walking a bicycle like it was a crippled friend. Two men hauling sacks of something. A woman and child who stared at Monique through the leaves with expressions of concern.

And that was it. Just a tiny wreck of a house and a column of strangers. Could it really be that she'd dragged her family to the Philippines for this? Was this rotten little box really the sense of home she'd been longing for? Monique wasn't stupid—she knew that her memories were idealized and exoticized. Maybe that's why she hadn't pushed harder to come back in the whole year they'd been stationed in Manila; for fear of having those memories invalidated. Maybe that's why Joseph never insisted; because he knew they would be. Still, Monique didn't expect this total emptiness. She could just as well have been on the meticulously preserved movie set of a film she'd enjoyed once or twice as a little girl. It wasn't home. It was hardly familiar.

She was about to get up and return to the car when someone on the trail caught her attention. It was a woman, not ancient but very old, picking her way up in the direction of the main road. Her hair was dyed black but was silver about the roots, making it oddly match her black flats with white soles. She had a walking stick of dried bamboo that she used every other step, as though favoring a good leg. Monique slipped off the porch, cut through the trees and got on the trail, telling herself all the while that this was silly. The similarities were superficial. There was no way this was *her*.

But why couldn't it be? She remembered the cleaning woman cutting fresh walking sticks for each of them whenever they set out on one of their adventures. And there was something in this woman's face, something in her posture that was undeniable. She followed the old woman a short ways up the trail, debating whether or not to say anything. The chances were so infinitesimal—but what the hell? At worst she'd look foolish and that shame would fade by the time she got back to the car.

"Tiya?" Monique called.

The woman kept walking at her irregular pace.

"Tiya?" Louder this time.

The old woman stopped and turned. She put her hand up in a "just a moment" motion and plucked little plastic headphones out of her ears. Frank Sinatra's voice boomed out of them so loud that Monique could hear it from where she stood. The cleaning woman had loved Sinatra! "Can I help you?" she asked.

"I'm sorry. You probably don't . . ." Monique stammered. Not knowing the woman's first name was incredibly embarrassing. "I don't want to bother you, but I used to live here when I was a little girl. And you look—"

The old woman shushed her again, this time with both hands in the air. Her eyes widened like opening mouths. Seeing recognition spread over her face made Monique's knees shake a little. The old woman closed the distance between them and actually put a hand on each of Monique's cheeks.

"My goodness," she said. "My goodness. My goodness. It's you, isn't it?"

Monique choked on her own breathing.

"Anna. You're *Anna.*"

A bird flew noisily through the foliage above, and somewhere in the woods a branch fell. Monique took a step back and the old woman's hands stayed where they were, cupping air.

"You are, aren't you?"

"No. I'm Monique."

"But you look just like Anna. Your hair. Your freckles. She was a beautiful little girl. Her daddy was a geologist and they had a house in Olongapo."

"My parents lived on the base. Just up there." Monique pointed. She didn't know why. "There was a woman who came over three times a week to clean."

"Clean?" The old woman dropped her hands to her sides and wrinkled her nose like a cruel joke had been played on her. "I never cleaned for anyone. You must have me mistaken for someone else."

"I know. I'm very sorry."

Monique turned and walked back up the trail. She cut through the woods to her old backyard. She kicked the porch once and the wood crunched under her feet like slushy ice. She climbed back up the muddy hill, sat in Reynato's car and locked the doors. She'd been wrong about the shame, the feeling of foolishness, fading by the time she got up there.

IT GREW DARK. Monique turned the key in the ignition and flipped on the one remaining headlight. In its beam she could see bats flitting over the treetops, as well as the occasional gangly shape of a flying fox. Her phone was nearly out of battery, but she figured it had enough juice left for her to say what she had to.

"Hey. Baby? Are you all right?" Joseph's voice sounded drowsy on the other end and she realized she must have woken him up. But that was good news. It meant he was sleeping again.

"I'm fine, Joe," she said. "I'm sorry to wake you. I love you."

"I love you, too, darling. What's going on?"

"I just . . . I wanted to tell you that I love you. And that I'm sorry. The last time we spoke I couldn't bring myself . . ." She gripped the wheel with her free hand and turned it; first left, then right. The tires pivoted in the mud below her. "The last time we spoke you said sorry for leaving. You didn't have to. It's not like I gave you much of a choice, with how shitty I was acting. I think that was kind of the point for me. I think I wanted you to go."

The line was quiet for a while. Her battery beeped at her. "I know," he said. "Darling, you sound exhausted. We don't have to talk about this now."

"But we have to talk about it."

"Later," he said.

She heard him shifting; heard the light leafy sound of cotton on wool. He sat up. They were quiet together for a while.

"I know they're still in bed . . . but could I talk to the kids?"

"Why the hell not?" There was a measure of delight in his voice. "Let me get them up."

The mattress springs and then the floorboards creaked. Monique imagined herself tiny, carried in Joseph's palm through the dawn-lit corridors of their distant townhouse. "Your mother." His voice was almost indiscernible—he must have been holding the cordless at arm's length. "Yes, now."

"Mom?" It was Leila.

"Hi, baby. I'm sorry to wake you. I just wanted to say I love you." She bit down on her words to keep them steady. "I love you."

"Mom. Are you okay?"

"I'm fine, baby. How are you doing?"

"I'm asleep, Mom."

"I know. I'm not going to keep you. But you know that I love you, right?"

"Sure. Me too." There was a long pause. "Okay. Good night?"

Monique heard some more shifting and Joseph's tiny voice saying; "Of course she is." Then more footsteps. The creaky door to Shawn's room opening. "Hey, it's your mother. Yes, she wants to."

"Monique!" Shawn sounded like he'd already been awake. "I need to talk to you. You need to tell Joseph about the pipe you found under my bed. It was clean, right? I didn't ever use that stupid thing." Oh well. This was at least a step up from his refusing to talk at all.

"Honey," she said, "I love you. A lot."

"He doesn't believe me about not smoking it. I mean, I did smoke pot, but only at her house, and only twice, *ever*. She just kept giving me the stuff. What was I supposed to do, turn it down? I know I shouldn't have kept it but—"

"Are you listening, Shawn? I love you."

"He won't let me do anything!" Shawn shouted. "You guys made me come back here and now you're fucking up my vacation by keeping me stuck in this damn house!"

"That's enough," Joseph said. He must have snatched the phone back and returned to the corridor. She heard the sharp clap of Shawn's door slamming behind him. Then the sound of Joseph knocking it back open and saying, "Do it again and I take off the hinges."

"Don't be too hard on him," she said. "He's had a tough year."

"If we're not hard enough he'll have a tough decade. Or more." Joseph's footfalls were heavier as he walked back to their bedroom. "Are you sure you are all right, darling? You have got me worried. This sounds a little too much like a call someone makes before doing something stupid."

He was almost right. She was making this call *after* doing something stupid. A lot of something stupid. But at least she was done now. Her battery beeped again. She told him not to worry. She was just overtired, and lonely. He said good night. She said good morning. They laughed at this.

MONIQUE RETURNED TO HER TINY ROOM at the BOQ motel and took a cool, rusty shower. She'd packed some comfy sweats in one of Shawn's backpacks and reached her hand inside to get them. A sudden shock ran up her arm, followed by pain. Something in the backpack had bitten her, hard. She yanked her hand out and about a foot of polka-dotted flesh trailed after. It was the gecko, its mouth closed over her middle and index fingers at the second knuckle. The animal whipped its head from side to side, breaking the skin and sending horrible jolts up her arm. She shook her hand and the gecko shook with her, not letting go. She swung her whole arm and it stayed fastened tight, the gashes in her fingers widening with the pressure. It was unbelievable, even from a documentary point of view, how much this hurt. Finally Monique hopped toward one of the walls and slammed her hand against it. The gecko released her fingers and fell down onto the carpet. It wriggled there for a moment and then stopped wriggling.

Monique stood in a haze above the limp animal. She had no doubt it was Shawn's tokay. It must have been hiding in his backpack when she'd thrown her things in and zipped up. It had been trapped since then, getting hungry and mean. Blood trickled down from the bite on her fingers, pooling at the tips and falling to the carpet in fat drops. She went into the bathroom to clean up. It wasn't the cuts so much as the thought of the animal's spit inside her that was awful. She washed thoroughly, wincing as she worked hand soap right into the wound, shaking from the sting. She wrapped her two fingers in a half roll of toilet paper—the first few layers turning red—and finished the bandage with a dry washcloth and safety pin. Then she sat on the covered toilet, giving the animal time to die if it hadn't already.

When she emerged from the bathroom she saw that the gecko had managed to right itself and move a few inches in the direction of the bed. It was in bad shape. The sharp, snake-like jaw looked like a busted clasp, unhinged from the skull. Both eyes had burst. The three legs that still moved did so in disagreement, as though trying to lead it on three divergent escapes. Monique knew she had to kill it. She considered what method would be easiest for them both.

The gecko had stopped twitching by the time she picked it up by the tail, but she could tell it was still breathing. She left the bungalow-style room and walked out on the moonlit gravel. She remembered some amateur landscaping accented with large stones by the old administration building and headed in that direction. Most of the stones were too big, but she found one roughly the size of a toaster. She laid the gecko on the gravel and worked the stone out of its spot, squatting and lifting. She held the stone over the animal, closed her eyes, and dropped it. She opened her eyes and saw she'd missed—only the tip of its tail had been crushed. She lifted the stone again and made herself look when she dropped it.

It felt wrong to just leave the animal there, crushed beneath a stone, so she dug it a shallow grave in the landscaping. That also felt wrong. The animal was plump in her hands, skin surprisingly warm for a reptile, legs resting on her fingers lightly. On their first day in Manila they'd held a funeral for the cat—the one who arrived from the trans-Pacific flight dead in her carrier. The one who was replaced by Leila's lovebird and Shawn's gecko, now both, oddly, in Monique's hands. Joseph had said some words at the cat's funeral, and Shawn had mocked him for it, and he'd been really hurt. He'd said that the cat was a good cat and that she hadn't suffered. Monique couldn't say either thing about the gecko, so instead of speaking she just looked up. Mount Pinatubo was a dark shape against dark clouds. The moon was fullish and had a ring around it. At first she thought the ring was just normal moonlight, refracted through her tears. But no. It was a ring.

Monique laid the gecko beside the hole and dug deeper, working her good fingers through the mulch and gravel. She was sobbing. She didn't want to be here, alone in a strange place that wasn't—*had never been*—home. She didn't want to be burying her son's pet. She didn't want Joseph to leave her, which would likely happen, when he found out. He was proud. She didn't want the kids to find out. She didn't want Shawn to be so angry or Leila to be so sad. She didn't want this feeling. This sudden tightness around her lungs.

Monique dug madly. She felt strings running down her arms, out her fingertips and into the soil. Right into the hot, dark planet. Something tugged on her; something that would pull her into the gecko's grave. She tugged back, and the parking lot beneath her trembled. She was causing it—of this she had no doubt. She was causing an eruption. She was causing Mount Pinatubo to go from dark to light.

*Chapter 29*

**ASHES**

There's a lot of confusion, a lot of yelling down on the beach. The police—Howard doesn't know if they're really police who act like criminals or criminals impersonating police, and in the end, what's the difference?—fall flat on their asses in the earthquake, guns popping off at the sky. That gets the bandits shooting back. Bullets hit the trembling ground with smacks and splashes. The men holding Howard loosen their grips. One takes a shot to the face, collapsing backward, leaving a specter of red vapor where he'd stood. Howard dives into the wet sand with his hands over his head. Then, when the ground stops moving, he breaks into a jagged, limping run.

He hits the hill beyond the beach and momentum carries him a few paces up, but it's tough going after that. The loamy soil sinks under him and the bramble he grabs at either gives way or is covered in spines. The beach below crackles with cursing and gunfire, and when he glances back he sees muzzle flares sawing through the dark. He also sees a shape, following him. It's the policeman with the gnarly skin—the monster made of scars. His gleaming little revolver bobs in the air and lets out a sound as big as a falling tree when it goes off. Howard feels a pinch in his shoulder, first cold, and then very, very hot.

He keeps climbing. The monster below empties his revolver and Howard feels two more pinches. One of the bullets goes all the way through, pulverizing a little flower in front of him—a pink mimosa. Up ahead he sees a bluish granite outcropping, and he pushes up toward it, hoping for maybe some high leap to safety. Some route that no one without a few bullets in them would follow him on. But the monster catches up to him. He gets in front of Howard and sits down, blocking his path. Slowly, he turns the cylinder of his little revolver, fingering six new slugs home. Howard crawls up toward him.

The next gunshot sounds completely different—like a bullwhip slicing air. The scarred man gasps, his voice coming straight out of his throat, where there's a new hole. He and Howard look up the hill and see a man standing atop the granite outcropping with a long, elaborate rifle in his hands. He's a policeman as well—Howard recognizes him from the beach this morning. The monster skews up his ground-beef face in anger, and charges him. This strange, squat, dark policeman unloads on him, making a butcher's mess of his ribs. A hole opens up in the monster's torso so wide that Howard sees palm tops dancing in the wind on the other side but he keeps going. He tackles the man on the rock, and together they roll in a nightmare tangle of arms and legs down to the fray below.

HOWARD STAYS where he is for a while, slipping in and out. A quiet stretches down on the beach, and soon all the gunshots and voices have faded. The sky darkens, and through his clouded lens Howard sees the moon swallowed up in blackness. Something lands on him. Cement-gray flakes flutter down. It's ash, thick with the sulfur-stink of a burned-down world.

After a while he tries sitting, and can. He tries standing, and he can stand as well. He climbs the last stretch of hill, up past the granite outcropping, and comes out into a concrete pavilion. He finds himself surrounded by old guns from the war, each as big as a lightning-struck oak trunk. Some lie on their sides, a tight cluster of gears rusting at the base of their stems, while others remain aimed straight up, their shocked mouths gulping ash. There's something up here, moving among the guns. He hears footsteps, and heavy breathing. It's a dog. A black Alsatian, big as a pony, dusted with pale flakes.

The dog eyes Howard with ears back and tail swishing. It pants and blood dribbles thickly from its loose lips and large, velvety nostrils. Howard makes to leave the ruined pavilion, and the dog follows him. "Get," he says, but the dog does not get. It matches him step for step.

Together they walk into another patch of jungle, onto a trail marked with yellow blazes for the tourists. The Alsatian rushes when Howard rushes and slows when he slows, always just a step behind in the thickening ash. He feels sorry for the animal. It's hurt, very badly, like he is. It looks a mess, like he's sure he does. He makes a kissing noise. "It's all right," he says, "I won't hurt you." He steps toward it but the dog gives out a shrill whimper and backs away. "That's fine," Howard says. "That's fine."

Together they come to a clearing and the ground beneath Howard's feet changes. He kicks some ash away and sees he's standing on fresh asphalt. A road. That means that somebody will be along. Maybe not in time, but they'll find him, at least. He sits in the middle of the road, and then when sitting gets tiring he lies down. The dog remains standing. It puffs, and shakes its coat to loosen the ash, and then becomes still, and quiet. The dog looks a mess, but it's a beautiful dog, isn't it? It looks so odd, so wonderful standing there in the slowly falling ash. Howard has an urge to call Benny—like he did with the ringed moon and the glowing plankton. Like he always does when he sees something wonderful. He even reaches for his belt loop, but there's no phone there, of course.

Howard closes his eyes, enjoying this feeling of wonder. It pulses inside him. It pours. It trickles out into the ash, into the dark silence, into everything falling.

*Chapter 30*

## MAKATI MEDICAL

The water in Manila Bay tasted foul, so Benicio backstroked. He swam about a hundred yards along the seawall and bumped lightly into the outrigger of a moored fishing bangka. Calling out twice and finding it empty, he climbed aboard, shimmied out along the pointed bow and hoisted his soggy self over the wall and back onto the promenade. Electricity along Roxas was still out and the falling ash had thickened. The crowd in front of the club had dispersed, and those who remained stood under the tacky awning for cover. Edilberto was still parked in the same spot, but all the doors were locked. Inside he saw Berto's feet propped up on the dash and he rapped hard on the glass to wake him.

Edilberto cracked the window open and squinted out groggily. "You're wet."

"Open the door."

"And dirty, too." He pressed his tongue against the backs of his teeth and drew in three little snaps of breath. "Dirty upholstery is trouble for me."

"I'll tell them I made you."

Edilberto leaned across the gearshift and opened the door for him. Benicio's clothes squelched as he got inside and sat. Enough ash had settled on his wet skin that he was caked with grime.

"Bring me back to the hotel. Please."

"Maybe first to hospital?" Edilberto gestured with his chin at Benicio's temple.

He touched his cheek and traced a tickle of drying blood up to the gash that Solita had left in his high-cropped sideburn. It wasn't that deep, but the cut stung, and it was filthy. "Yeah, take me to the hospital." They sat for two minutes in near silence, the only sound being the dry rub of Edilberto's middle and index fingers against his thumb. Benicio understood now that trying to bribe him was a mistake. He'd insulted him, and Edilberto was getting even. But he was pushing it. "I don't have any more money," he said. "I was robbed."

"Robbed? In this kind of place?" Edilberto aped shock. He reached across Benicio's lap and opened the glove compartment, producing a little pad of blank invoices and carbon paper. "You can write a tip-slip, and bill to your room. I get them all the time. No one ever asks why."

Benicio wrote out a tip-slip for another four thousand pesos, tore it out of the booklet and handed it over. Glancing down at the figure, Edilberto balled up the tip-slip and discarded it in the backseat. Benicio took a breath. He signed the bottom of a fresh tip-slip, left the peso amount blank and threw the pad at Edilberto so that it struck him in the chest.

They didn't speak for the rest of the night. Edilberto drove with the wipers on and took Benicio to a gleaming white hospital in Makati where a nurse cleaned his face, swabbed out his little cut with alcohol and closed it with a single stitch. There was some commotion in the hospital—people ran about with worried and intense expressions and the sounds of helicopters carried to and fro through the ceiling—but Benicio thought little of it. He negotiated to have the bill sent to his hotel and went back outside to meet Edilberto.

It was almost dawn when they returned to the Shangri-La. Alice was fully dressed and waiting in the lobby. She saw the car pull up through the big glass doors and raced toward them before Benicio had both feet out. She didn't ask where the hell he'd been. She didn't ask why he was wet and dirty and bandaged. She told him that they'd found his father, that he'd been shot, and they were bringing him to Makati Medical now to try and save him.

HOWARD WAS ALREADY IN SURGERY when they returned to the hospital, and he underwent two more operations before Sunday was over. The doctors said he was disoriented but conscious during the helicopter ride from Corregidor, but he hadn't come back since the first operation. Benicio and Alice made makeshift beds out of plastic chairs in the waiting lounge, and on Monday, when Howard was moved into his own room with a spare cot, they joined him. They napped in shifts all day—or rather Alice did while Benicio tried his best to stay awake all the time. He never left his father's bedside, and spoke only to the nurses who came to change his IV and write things on his chart. The night nurse was especially chatty. She pronounced *Miracle* like it was three words. Her hair was braided so tight it looked synthetic, her forearms were slightly furry and she signed the cross as a kind of punctuation for life—she would have fit in perfectly among his aunts.

"The best thing you can do is take it day by day," she said as he gazed dully at the green peaks of his father's heartbeat. Benicio guessed that measuring things in days meant a week was unrealistic. The nurse tapped her pen precisely on the rigid edge of his father's chart and glanced at the beeping monitors. "How is your wife holding up?" she asked, gesturing to Alice sleeping lightly on the cot.

"We're not married," he said. The nurse replaced the clipboard and made to go. "My father's dying," he said.

"His body may be." She touched the collar of her uniform and he guessed that under the fabric was a dangling crucifix.

"The doctors wouldn't tell me how long."

"That's because they don't know."

"Will they? I mean, when he starts to?"

"It could be sudden," the nurse said. "Or they could know. Nothing is certain. Put your faith in God's hands."

Benicio shifted in his seat beside the hospital bed. He'd released his father's hand when the nurse came in, but now he took it again. "Can he hear us?"

"He hears us all."

"I mean my father."

"Oh. I don't know. I like to think he can." She placed her hand on his and Howard's. They were like a team, getting ready for a game.

"You *like* to think?"

The nurse paused, not quite sure how to take him but embarrassed all the same. She opened her mouth and closed it. She pulled her hand from their modest stack, capped her pen and left. He listened to her footsteps in the empty hall, fading beneath the beep and hiss of life support. Alice sat up on the cot behind him.

"She doesn't deserve that," Alice said.

He was quiet for a while. "No. She doesn't."

The cot squeaked as Alice got up. She crossed to him and draped her arms lightly around his shoulders. She kissed his neck and his ear.

"What do you want to say to him?" she asked.

"I don't know. I've gotten so used to saying nothing." He paused, expecting a gentle admonishment that didn't come. It was a long time before he made a go of it.

"I don't know what this means, but Hon wanted me to tell you that the London thing is figured out." His tone sounded flat and lame in the quiet room. "He came by yesterday. He'd still be here if the hospital would let him . . .".Benicio drifted. He fixed his eyes on the assisted rise and fall of his father's chest.

"I'm glad I started talking to you again. I don't regret stopping, but I'm glad I started again. And I'm sorry if I hurt you." He turned to Alice. "Fuck, it sounds like someone else said that."

"Nope, it was you." She rubbed her hand in slow circles on his back and he shifted his weight a few times to indicate that she should stop. Each breath came close to crumbling.

He tightened his grip on his father's thick fingers and felt the hard wedding band, still coated with coarse flecks of ash. It was loose—

Howard had lost weight. He was quiet for a long time. "I met her," he finally said.

"I can leave," Alice said, "if you want." The back of his head brushed her cheek as he nodded.

She left.

Benicio turned his father's wedding band, slid it off and put it back on again. He remembered the last time he'd held Howard's hand, hardly half a year ago, at his mother's funeral. It was the first time they'd touched, or talked, in years. What had Benicio said to him? Something to the effect of: *I haven't forgiven you yet, but I will.* What the fuck was that? What had he been waiting for? Saying he would meant that he already had. He'd wanted to hug his father right there—a real hug, nothing perfunctory. But there had been something in the way. There was still something in the way.

"I don't know what her name is," he said. "She told me it was Solita. And I met her kid, June. He was about . . . I guess I would have been fifteen when he was born. The winter before we got certified, or maybe the one after. If he's yours. He doesn't look like yours. And if he was, I think even you would have done better by him." He paused to breathe. Under the circumstances, "even you" sounded petty, and mean. "This isn't really fair," he said. "I had all these things to say to you. I'd practiced them. But they're not things you say to someone on a respirator. Who's dying. Or so they tell me." He let out a little laugh that broke in half. He bit his lower lip, hard. "Mom knew," he said. "I was too busy being mad at you, at both of you, to ask. I should have asked her a lot of things." He let his head droop until it rested on the bed. He accounted the way he'd acted to his mother as the worst thing he'd done with his young life. Even confessing this to Howard felt cheap, because Howard probably couldn't even hear it. "She knew everything," he said. "Not just about what happened at the resort, but she knew about Solita, and about the money under your bed, and if June was yours or not. She knew, but nobody asked."

Benicio had to stop there. Thinking about his mother made him cry. He loved her, and his father, too.

LATER THAT MORNING Benicio and Alice returned to the Shangri-La together. They hadn't gone back since Howard's arrival at Makati Med and couldn't go any longer without a shower and maybe an hour or two of sleep in a real bed. As they waited outside for Edilberto to pick them up, Alice touched the cut on Benicio's head and asked if it hurt. "No," he said. He'd taken off the bandage and the single stitch was already halfway dissolved into a little scab. This was the closest they'd come to talking about his disappearance on the night of the eruption.

Edilberto wept as he drove. Alice, warmed by how hard he was taking things, consoled him at red lights. He kept trying to make eye contact with Benicio in the rearview as he said how sorry he was. When they pulled up to the security checkpoint outside the hotel he popped the trunk and hood for the guards and turned around in the driver's seat. He took Benicio's hand in both of his. "Your father was always good to me," he said, holding tight. "He doesn't deserve this. You don't either. I'm so sorry." Benicio felt something moist in the hollow of their clasped hands, and when he looked down he saw that Edilberto was trying to palm him a wrinkled mess of thousand-peso bills. Alice, who'd been watching the security guard roll his mirror around the undercarriage, turned and saw blue notes blossom out of their clasped fingers. Edilberto's wet eyes widened.

"Why are you giving me this?" Benicio asked, doing a passable job of keeping his voice even.

"It's okay." Edilberto pulled his hands back and let the bills splay out on Benicio's lap. It wasn't as much as he'd given him on the night of the eruption, but almost. "It's all right. No problem. I don't need it." He let out a tremulous laugh and turned to Alice. "He's great. I needed some money, and he lent it to me. Last week. But now I don't need it anymore. But he's great to lend it. Very kind."

"Oh." Alice looked from one of them to the other. "That's good."

Benicio collected the bills in his lap, stacked them and folded them once over. "You're sure you don't need it? No problem, if you do."

Edilberto looked relieved and shook his head. He didn't see the guard waving them through with exaggerated, whole-body motions.

When the sedan behind them honked he spun forward and accelerated quickly up the ramp to the big glass doors.

Benicio showered first. Then, when it was Alice's turn, he picked up the hotel phone and called the front desk. He canceled their reservation with Edliberto for the afternoon and reserved another driver. The front desk asked if something was the matter and he said no, they just wanted another driver. Edilberto had done nothing wrong. He said it a few times, but they still sounded wary. "We'll talk to him," they said.

Alice came out of the shower and set the alarm beside the bed for early afternoon. They both got under the covers. Benicio told her that if he made any noises in his sleep, or twitched even, that she should wake him right up. She said she would.

HOWARD HAD A LOT OF VISITORS—CHARLIE, Hon, Monique, the ambassador, an almost imperceptibly limping Bobby Dancer, and Reynato Ocampo in an ill-fitting dress uniform. Only family was allowed into Howard's hospital room, so Benicio and Alice were obliged to take turns receiving people outside the closed door or—in the case of press—in the waiting lounge. By the middle of the week Howard had faded so much that the hospital began keeping his visitors away entirely. This was a small relief.

Just before dawn on Thursday, five days after Howard's helicopter ride from Corregidor, Benicio watched the night nurse taking extra care with her regimen. She left and returned with a doctor. They both left and returned with a priest and an extra chair. Benicio shook Alice awake and took his seat beside Howard. He didn't look any closer to death than he had the day before, or the day before that. The priest produced a bookmarked Bible and dangled rosary beads from his knuckles. "Does your father have a favorite passage?" he asked. Benicio said that he didn't know and the priest opened to Romans and began reading aloud. Something about being buried with Christ, through baptism, into death. Then rising, glory and new life. After a while Alice said that he should maybe go, so he rushed to the last rites, and left.

"I can go too," she said. "Would you like to be alone with your dad?"

Benicio didn't answer, so she stayed there at the edge of the room.

Howard's breathing sounded like diving. The way the regulator reverberated; the slight wheeze when the current rushed against the purge valve. He died at six in the morning, which would have been just about suppertime back home.

*Chapter 31*

## SURVIVING KA-POW

Reynato Ocampo hates hospitals. He hates being watched. Not five minutes go by without doctors and nurses coming into his room at Makati Medical. They stare and write smutty notes to each other on his chart. When it's not them it's his family with adobos and videocassettes, or Charlie Fuentes with insincere condolences, or news crews with unhygienic boom microphones, or his beloved bruha bitching and moaning and breaking his heart. They all make Reynato anxious. Even late at night, when he and Racha are alone in their room, he feels eyes on his skin like a sunburn. Someone peeking in through the third-story window, or kneeling at the keyhole, just watching. Makes it hard to sleep. And when he does sleep his dreams make him wish he hadn't.

Three days of that is plenty. Reynato slips out of bed during the midday shift change, careful not to rip the stitches keeping his shoulder closed. He cradles his arm in a pillowcase sling and walks barefoot, duckfooted, out the door. The young police lieutenant posted to his room gawks at his open-backed gown and bare ass before running to catch up. He asks Reynato what he needs, and Reynato thinks for a bit before saying: "Pants."

The lieutenant's full dress uniform fits Reynato pretty well, just a little tight in the gut and chest. Even though he's eager to get out of the hospital, he goes down the hall for a quick check on fast-fading Howard. Seeing that he isn't dead yet, Reynato chokes up. This goes over well with Howard's tanned manchild of a son, who looks moved and gives overstudied thanks. Returning to the hall, Reynato avoids the near-nude lieutenant getting ribbed by a superior. He rushes to the elevator and heads down to the basement for a parting visit with Elvis and Lorenzo. They're laid out on cold metal tables, stacked alongside all the other corpses recovered from Corregidor.

Four days into it and the medical examiner is still pulling bullets out of them. Reynato's friends lie closest to the door, each bedecked with ribbons, posthumous presidential medals in the nooks between collarbones. Lorenzo came out worse and looks it. His belly unbuttoned, he'd screamed for minutes while his stomach spilled into sand, flowing down toward blue-white waves in red-and-yellow rivulets. His teeth black with ash stains, his jaw locked wide, his chin still scarred from when Efrem hit him with the telephone. Beside him Elvis looks peaceful, more put-together on the table than he'd ever been alive. He must have changed back into a man as he died. The baffled examiner explains that there's not a scratch on him, but there are two BMG slugs in his neck, beneath the smooth skin. Reynato lingers by their bodies. He clutches their hands, but their hands feel gross, so he stops.

Reynato turns to the six terrorists on the other side of the room, naked and washed out under cool fluorescent light. He examines the faces of those who've still got them; the callused palms of those who don't, hoping there's been some mistake. Hoping they really did find Efrem's body, that it's just been misidentified. He can tell the leader by his white beard and stump, but the others are indistinguishable. One near the wall has some potential. Two holes in the upper back that come out just above the heart—more or less where Reynato remembers shooting Efrem. Height and weight seem about right, but it's hard to be sure. Seawater has sucked away his color and left the flesh puffy. His face is a mess from where it got propeller chopped during recovery. It could be Efrem or just a similarly built Moro.

"These the only bodies?" Reynato asks. "Should be four more. Or five."

The examiner does not look up from his scalpel work on Elvis's neck. "High tide carried most out to sea," he mumbles. "Ash in the shallows makes them hard to spot. But crews are still out looking today."

Reynato nods, slowly. "Call me if more come in."

HE RETURNS TO HIS HOME in Magallanes Village that afternoon, where his wife and daughter give him affectionate but concerned hell. They start together but Lorna is louder. "My Lord. My Jesus. My God. Walking out of the hospital? Just *walking* out? I'm surprised you dared come back! This will be the good news . . ." she gestures to his wounded shoulder without touching it. "Did poor Beatrice fly home, did she give up her internship, her sublet, her deposit, just to watch you make me end you?"

"No." Reynato kisses Lorna on the cheek and comes away with foundation-dusted lips. "She's come home to defend me, right Bea-bee?"

Bea sits at the kitchen counter, legs crossed, hands wrapped around a mug of steaming tea. The corners of her bottom lip, heavy with fat, pinch to resist a smile. "I won't help her kill you," she says, "but I won't turn her in when she does."

Reynato gingerly hoists himself onto a stool beside his daughter— moving stiffer and slower than he needs to—and runs fingers under her cool, grapefruit-smelling hair. Lorna trundles behind the counter and serves him green tea in a mug bearing his name, Charlie Fuentes's likeness and numerous inspirational messages. "Enough with the sad face," she says. "I ran out of sympathy when you ran out of the hospital. And those doctors have no manners on the phone. Yelling like I went there myself and pulled you out of bed. I'm not talking to them again, but you should call to tell them you're alive."

He sips tea smilingly. Beatrice works her neck, the base of her skull, into his callused palm. Lorna refills his mug even though he's hardly had any. "Does anything hurt?" she asks.

Reynato points at his heart and his wife and daughter go still. "You're breaking it," he says.

"God forgive you." Lorna takes his free hand in hers and kisses his knuckles. "And if he doesn't, let him at least not punish you too badly." She releases him. "You smell. Did your doctors say if you can shower yet? Did they say if you can eat real food?"

"Didn't say I couldn't." He stands and makes for the stairs. Bea and Lorna try to help him up but he shoos them away. He only makes it a few steps up before calling them back.

Reynato basks in special privileges the rest of the afternoon. Lorna makes a pinakbet with calabaza and lechon, and lets him eat in his bathrobe. Bea finds an extension cord and rolls the television into the dining room. They put on *Ocampo Justice VII*, thinking it's what he wants to watch. Reynato uses his pork-tipped fork to point out inaccuracies in the script, and in Charlie's performance, and his wife and daughter coo and coddle him with questions. They miss punchlines and laugh when they shouldn't. Reynato blushes at the deathless timber of their voices, at how little they know of him, and finds he misses Monique. He wishes she could meet them, but that's impossible, of course.

It's not until dessert—a full-blown halo-halo with purple ube ice cream, whole milk, frosted flakes, sweet beans and Nata de Coco—that the conversation becomes serious. Lorna reveals that she is starting up a fund—with some seed money of their own, or course—to bring Elvis's and Lorenzo's people in from the provinces in time for the funerals. "Those poor, poor men," Lorna says in a lamenting voice, holding her head back so tears won't smear her eyeliner. "Those poor *boys*. A person isn't just a person," she says. "He's everybody who ever loved him." In that case, Reynato thinks, Lorenzo and Elvis were nobodies. His cheeks burn a little at his own dishonesty. He amends his thought: they weren't nobody, they were *me*. "I pray that the American knows how much has been sacrificed for his sake."

"He may never," Reynato says. "The nurses are talking miracles."

"The Lord have mercy. I saw his son on the news last week, a sweet-looking boy. And what about Racha?"

The small, upside-down Reynato in his spoon stares up at him. "I don't think he's going to make it, either," he says.

• • •

AFTER THE MEAL he excuses himself to his study. The room overlooks their machete-trimmed back lawn and is chock-full of documents, tax forms, unpaid bills and those scraps of memorabilia that he hasn't yet sold. All the uniforms he's ever owned—some worn just once—hang on hooks along the walls like shed skins. Medals presidential, congressional, departmental, civil, honorable, charitable and military lie rusting in glass cases on the dusty floor. His desk is decked with framed photographs of him and the last four presidents, none of them as glorious as the shot of him and Marcos playing cards in Malacañang—a shot he destroyed shortly after the revolution. Newspaper clippings of his exploits fill shoeboxes that sit atop and beside a complimentary DVD boxed set of the Ocampo Justice Series—the only perk he's seen out of the whole film franchise in the last five years. He blames himself, of course—he'd been young and stupid enough to make a bad deal during a good year—but he blames the producers, and Charlie, even more.

Reynato eases himself into his swivel chair to catch up on e-mail. His accountant, half his age, has started writing to him in all capital letters. *IT'S TIME TO CONSIDER ANOTHER AUCTION.* Little prick. *W/ FUENTES IN SENATE, INTEREST SHOULD BE HIGH. UR OLD GUN COULD FETCH 10K AT LEAST.* Fat chance. *THAT OR BEA FINISHES DEGREE HERE. UR CALL BOSSMAN.* Reynato's hand strays to the pride of his collection, as though to protect it. His first personal weapon—an old Colt Peacemaker. He spins the empty cylinder and runs his fingers along the barrel, tracing out engraved lettering. Not Truth, from those idiotic movies, but the inspiration behind it. He'd bought the Single Action Army, a genuine west-winning antique, at a trade show in El Paso while on a police exchange arranged by the American Embassy. The trigger stuck and sometimes the hammer did too, but hell, that big heavy beauty was a shitspiller. Just the sight of her sorted cowards from those too dumb or desperate to realize they should be. He'd never sell, and even if he ever did, ten thousand was a flat-out insult. Reynato puts the barrel in his mouth and takes a picture of himself with his webcam. He sends the picture to his accountant—*sooner do this* as the subject line. The response comes minutes later. *SUIT URSELF. DRAMA QUEEN.*

Someone yells in the yard below. Reynato peers out the window and sees Bea wearing a one-piece bathing suit with a little skirt running low about the waist. She's in the pool, floating on an expensive air mattress, waving up at him. "Hi Daddy!" Reynato sets his smile and waves back. He just bought that air mattress a month ago to replace the one she took to the States. The one that now sits in her two-bedroom apartment at Sarah Lawrence. The apartment that she rents alone because her roommate—Reynato knew they were more than just roommates but kept up appearances for Lorna's sake—moved out. The apartment that's as empty now as the loft she's subletting in Manhattan, just a subway stop away from her socially conscious internship. The internship that she's skipping out on now, to be here with him. Because she loves him. Bea shifts positions on the mattress and it suddenly sinks, as if someone pulled the tap. She goes down with it, butt touching bottom, and bursts back to the surface laughing. She waves again and Reynato waves back. He wonders if he can salvage the expensive mattress. With his luck, probably not.

HE SLEEPS BADLY THAT NIGHT, waking once to see eyes in the doorway, twice more to stand in front of the toilet, unable to pee. He leaves the house at dawn, goes straight to the bay and boards the first Sun Cruise boat to Corregidor. He sits in the rocking head, dry-swallowing Vicodin. When they arrive he waits for the tourists to disburse before starting the lonely hike from the south dock to the northwest part of the island. He picks his way through ruins and down densely wooded slopes, tripping through the underbrush in search of the little topside beach where it all happened.

Reynato doesn't find the spot till lunchtime and even then it's hard to tell. The tide has tidied it of shell casings and blood, but Reynato recognizes big trees emerging from the bramble. He sees the rock ledge he'd sent Efrem to. This is the spot where he'd almost died.

He'd known what was happening, of course. The moment the bearded terrorist took one to the face, shattered sunglasses carried aloft on roiled blood, he knew Efrem had turned on them. He'd have reacted sooner if not for the eruption. Reynato fell flat on his butt. Lorenzo fell beside him in a burst of colored kerchiefs and freed doves, grabbing a gut wound, talking in fluids. Everybody shot everywhere. Reynato put two into an adolescent ready to pull the pin on a grenade painted like a mango. The kid went down, groping at his belt, and Reynato gave him another. Next person he aimed Glock at was himself. The muzzle burned when he pressed it to his shoulder. He put a round clean through and collapsed onto the beach.

The pain was bad but he managed to keep the shakes away. Heat flowed out over his shirtfront. Men stumbled across his chest and belly as they ran for safety. Reynato watched them go. He saw wounds bloom on their foreheads like Ash Wednesday crosses. He saw Elvis pitch his arms forward to become a black dog as big as a pony. He saw the dog gallop for the treeline and get skewered through the neck by Efrem's flashing Tingin. He saw Racha square off with Efrem atop the rock ledge, watched as they rolled downhill. Racha filled with holes, Efrem yelling in a language Reynato never heard him speak before. They landed hard on the beach and beat each other's faces with rocks. Efrem scrambled away, took up a dropped rifle and unloaded it into Racha. Racha kept coming. Efrem found another and unloaded that also. Racha swayed and fell to his knees, his remaining eye still full of fight. In the end Efrem had to pile stones on him just to stop him crawling.

And that was it. Efrem stood alone on the beach and Reynato lay near his feet, pretending to be dead among everyone who really was. Reynato felt himself go cold. Volcanic ash drifted out of dark sky and landed on his cheeks and lips. He hadn't known it was the work of his beloved bruha at the time—he'd put this together later, in the hospital, when he started to get over his paralyzing fear. Efrem breathed heavily just above him. He walked out into the water and knelt to wash his dark forearms and face. He didn't turn when Reynato stood and leveled Glock. Not when the first shot hit his back. Not when the second. Reynato watched him fall into the ashy waves. He curses himself, now, for not wading out and dragging Efrem's corpse ashore. To be sure.

But Reynato didn't go into the water. His self-inflicted wound was bleeding heavily, and he had money to hide. He grabbed the sack of bills and rushed into the undergrowth. He followed footprints up the slope—Howard's chubby feet and Elvis's paws. At the top he came to a concrete pavilion filled with meticulously preserved World War II mortars, their twelve-inch mouths gaping up in shocked silence, gulping ash. With some stretching Reynato hurled the money sack down the tallest barrel. He was fading, but he knew that if they found him here the pavilion would be searched, so he kept following the footprints. The ash thickened. The tracks, leading through the sagging jungle and out onto the road, started filling in. Reynato didn't see Elvis till he tripped over his haunches and landed across his big wet neck. They lay eye-to-eye, Elvis's big and bulging, all pupil the way Efrem's would get sometimes. Howard was a few paces down the road, struggling to breathe. A pale bright form stood over him. A woman. A tourist. Flash-light in one hand and old-fashioned film camera in the other, she stood horrified and halogen bright.

DOCTORS AT MAKATI MEDICAL INSIST that Racha's coma is perma-nent. The parts of his throat that make words are still in the ocean somewhere. His mouth is a doomsday mess of gauze, rubber tubing and metal. But none of that keeps him from making himself understood when Reynato visits that evening. He snaps his fingers until Reynato gives him a little pad and pencil.

*You find it?*

"Find what?"

Racha pauses, drumming the eraser against his body cast. *You're playing dumb with a man in my condition? After all we've been through?* He draws a little unhappy face below his lopsided, loopy sentences.

"You mean the money?"

Racha adds horns and little fangs to the face.

"Sure," Reynato smiles despite himself. "I found it."

*All there?*

"Every bit."

*Good. How many ways are we splitting?*

"Just two."

Racha draws a question mark and when Reynato doesn't say anything he writes: *Shit. All of them?*

"Elvis and Lorenzo for sure. Dead as the day before conception. Don't know about Efrem. Shot him twice but I won't be sure till I see the body. You overhearing anything about Howard?"

*He's done. A day more, maybe two. And he won't wake up in between. You're in the clear.*

"You mean we are, handsome." Reynato leans back in his chair, hands clasped over his belly. "And you? They say yet when you can come off the vent?"

*Well, at first they said I'm not going to last the chopper ride to the hospital. Then when I get here they say I'm going to die within the hour. Then when I made it through that they said I wouldn't survive the night—even argued over what critical patient gets my bed when I'm gone! Come morning they're all promising each other that I'm a corpse by midweek. And since then they've more or less stopped coming into my room. I think they're mad.*

Reynato takes the pencil from him, sharpens it and hands it back. "They lack imagination," he says. "You'll be golfing by the end of the month."

*Not so sure.* Racha pauses, his hand twitching. *I feel different this time. I mean, I don't think I'm dying. But I don't think I'm getting better. It's kind of nice actually. The suspense always used to kill me.*

Reynato stays quiet awhile. He tears Racha's notes off the pad so he'll have a fresh page to write on. "I have a question for you," he says, his voice low and quiet. "Since the eruption, have you ever felt like someone is watching you?"

*I feel it all the time. I tell you what, I'm a sight!*

"That's not what I mean."

Racha begins writing something but crosses it out. *You look terrible. I mean really bad. Are you sleeping enough?* A pause. *You think Efrem's still alive.*

Seeing the name in writing sets Reynato's stomach churning. "He might be."

*And you think he's going to kill you?*

"Wouldn't you?"

*No. I mean, I love you. But I know what you're getting at. You're worried he's going to get you. You're worried he's already got you. That he's just waiting for the right time. Well, I wouldn't stress about it. Efrem was never that malicious or creative. If he's out there, then I'm sure he'll take you in a private, dignified kind of way. Like when you're in the shower or something.*

"This isn't a joke," Reynato says, running his palms across his wet cheeks. He can usually tear up at will and now he can't will himself not to. He must be overtired. "Listen," he says. "I've got something to tell you. I've decided to put this whole business behind me."

*Well behind. Far behind. Where's the business? I don't see it. You've got whatever you've got left to look forward to. You could run away with that white girl—the one with the temper. Hey, what happened to her, anyway?*

Reynato doesn't answer. He produces a syringe from his pocket, pricks it into Racha's IV and pushes the plunger home.

Racha's fingers tighten around the pencil. *Why would you do that?*

"I'm sorry," he says, and it's true, he is very, very sorry. "This is more than just a money decision."

*Ba-ha-ha.* Racha's body shifts slightly in bed. The pencil drops and rolls along the floor. Reynato retrieves it and gives it back. *I recognize that taste. That's drain cleaner. Drank a capful of the stuff when I was ten. A bad day for Mom.*

Reynato smiles. Racha was always one of the shy ones, but when you got him alone he had this charming, unexpected, self-deprecating humor. But that's in the past. Reynato knows that if he and his family are to survive Ka-Pow, he'll need the cleanest break possible. "I'll come back every day if I have to," he says.

*You'll have to.*

"I'll set the bed on fire if I have to."

*You'll have to.*

"Why make this hard? I mean, honestly, look at yourself."

Racha doesn't write anything for a while. *It's true. I'm a mess.*

"A big mess." Reynato stands and gives him a squeeze. "Listen, I need to go. I'll see you tomorrow."

*I might not be alive tomorrow.*

"We can only hope."

REYNATO TAKES THE PAD from Racha—evidence, after all—and leaves his room crying like a big, stupid baby. He's almost out of the hospital when, owing to a now unbroken stretch of shit luck, he bumps into Howard's kid. Benicio must be returning to the hospital because he looks showered and clean and guilty for it. "Hey," the kid says, taking him by the shoulders. "You did everything you could have done."

"I know," Reynato says, still dripping from all of his faceparts. "I know." They share a wildly awkward embrace. Then, upon escaping, Reynato continues out to his parked, dented Honda. His beloved bruha's ash still clogs up the filters and brake assembly. The inside still smells of her. A blackened sack of filthy money sulks in the passenger seat—a spot that Monique occupied not one week ago, on their mini-break to Subic. The cynic in Reynato would like to see this change as an improvement. The cynic in him says: You were just using her, so you can't be sad about how it ended. To which the rest of Reynato replies: No one tells me what I can't do.

*Chapter 32*

## DANCER AND DOGS

Benicio didn't know that Alice had bumped up her departure date until he got out of the shower and found her packing. He dried himself in the doorway and watched as she laid out clothes on the bed, folded them into irregular quadrangles and stacked them in her suitcase. "I'll be here for the funeral," she said, a little curtly. "My flight's not till the second.

That's sooner than I wanted, but the week following is booked solid. And I need time to regroup before classes let out. My kids have been with rotating subs this whole time." She sounded mournful at this. And who knows, maybe she was.

Benicio put a robe on and went to go sit on one of the red couches. He was supposed to see a funeral director about arrangements in just a half hour, but for the sake of privacy they'd agreed to meet in his father's adjacent suite; so he had time. "That's fine," he said, even though he didn't really think it was fine. He didn't want Alice to go.

"It'll be good for you, too," she said. "You need time to yourself, with me out of your hair."

"I like you in my hair." He watched as she closed the suitcase, stood it upright on its wheels and then laid it flat again to see how things had shifted inside. "I dreamed about this," he said. "A few days before my father died I dreamed of you packing up your things. But we weren't here. We were back home, in my apartment. The window screens were frozen over. The suitcase was open on the couch. You weren't being careful at all." He took a Fuji apple from the fruit bowl and held it, casually. "You threw clothes in on their hangers, no folding. Your saucepan was dirty on the stove but you just threw it right in also. It got oil on everything." He set the apple back in the bowl. "I think you were leaving me."

Alice looked up from trying to make her suitcase less top-heavy. "Well, I'm not leaving you," she said. "I'm just going home. And that's a weird fucking thing to say, besides." She was mad about something.

"I'm sorry," Benicio said. They looked at one another from opposite sides of the suite. "Just a dream," he said.

Alice quit fussing with the suitcase. "Who's Solita?"

He straightened up. "Did she come to the room?"

"No. She telephoned. It was a few days ago, when I was back here getting clean clothes. She said they won't let her into the hotel now . . . something you did. So I met her outside. Who is she?"

"She's the girl Hon mentioned." He paused, remembering he'd lied at the time about not knowing her. Alice remembered, too. "Dad was having an affair with her. I mean . . . not an affair. He was paying. I met her before you got here, before I knew what happened to him. She's after money."

"She said you're fucking her."

"She's after money."

"A woman who looks like that tells me you're fucking her and you want me to infer the no?"

Benicio stared at Alice. This somehow had the feel of a play fight— Solita was a front for something else. "You know I'm not fucking her," he said. "I was with her on the night of the eruption, but only to talk. Only to ask her about Dad."

"I don't believe you."

"Yes, you do," he said. "If this is about you leaving, you can just tell me. If being here with me, through this, is too much for you, that's fine. You don't need an excuse to bail."

She stared at him quietly, almost coldly, as though weighing options. Then she returned to the suitcase, unzipped the external pouch and extracted something no bigger than a dime. She dropped it into Benicio's hand, and he felt a little sick. It was a stray piece of the birth control packet that he'd destroyed on the night she arrived. "I assumed I'd left them home, at first," she said. "So I filled a new prescription at the drugstore in Glorietta." The anger had drained from her voice. "How's this for an excuse to bail?"

"It's a good excuse," Benicio said. He'd forgotten about the infantile act—it'd happened only minutes before he overheard Solita ransacking his father's room, and he hadn't given the pills a thought since. "That was a creepy, fucked-up thing for me to do," he said, keeping his voice even. He felt that there was a lot riding on the next thirty seconds or so. "I don't have a good excuse. My bad excuses are that I was upset and overtired. And I didn't do it for . . . I did it out of guilt. We'd just had sex, and I felt really good, and I felt really guilty about that. I felt like we should cool it."

"Well, now I feel like we should cool it," Alice said. "I'm not leaving you, but I'm leaving. And you should take your time coming back."

Benicio stood and went to her. "I don't want you to go," he said.

Alice teared up and let him hold her. "I can't do this," she said. "I can't be all you've got."

Then she pulled out of his grip and returned to her suitcase, unpacking and repacking.

BENICIO WAS STILL UPSET when he met with the young man from Crespo Funeral Services in his father's suite. The shy mortician was joined—to Benicio's surprise—by Hon and a somber-looking Bobby Dancer. "I hope we're not intruding," Bobby said.

"You were Howard's friends," Benicio said. "You're welcome." He led them to his father's study where they sat in leather office-style swivel chairs circling the round table. The funeral director glanced nervously from the kitchenette to the balcony doors as he laid out Howard's pre-need contract. Signed in the summer of 1999, it originally stipulated that should Howard die in-country Crespo would restore and embalm the body and ship it back to Chicago for a service and interment. But just four months ago—a month after Ursula's death—Howard had amended the pre-need to stipulate that his remains not leave Philippine soil. He'd ordered cremation and a private service held on a parcel of land he owned near Mainit Point, in Batangas. After the service his ashes were to be scattered in the ocean.

"Which brings me to the problem," the funeral director said, even more nervous now. "Your father's body is still at Makati Medical. The court has filed an injunction barring my people from proceeding with the cremation until a paternity suit is resolved. There's an outstanding petition to collect samples—"

"You know who's doing it," Bobby said.

The muscles in Benicio's face loosened. He walked to the kitchenette and poured bottled water into a tumbler. He emptied it in small sips. When he returned to the study he found that his legs wouldn't bend to sit. "Do I have any options?"

"That depends," Bobby said. "Do you have any idea if Howard is the father?"

"I don't think so. I mean, she's a liar—I've caught her at it more than once. But I'm not sure. He could be."

"Well then, not many," Hon said. "The judge has scheduled an emergency session to hear the petition, but that won't happen until five days after the funeral. If you knew the suit was bogus you could grant the samples whenever . . . but if you don't know, you shouldn't chance it."

"You could contact her lawyer," Bobby said, "and offer them something. They don't know how much money Howard has. They may settle and drop it. Or—"

"Or it could be gas on the fire," Hon interrupted. "They'll see an offer as a sign of weakness, because that's what it is. They'll turn it down, and in the end you'll have a lawsuit. And you'll lose it. Howie was rich, and foreign, and so are you. You've already lost that lawsuit."

"That's not completely foregone," Bobby said.

"The hell it isn't," Hon said. "Benny, I'm telling you, if you do anything that opens the door to the courthouse then you'll make that bitch rich. Don't look at me that way, Bobby, you know she'll steal everything Howie ever had."

Benicio placed his hands flat on the table. "Well, what won't open the door to the courthouse?"

Hon paused. "A talk with the judge. I can arrange it by tomorrow morning."

"Define talk."

"You want me to spell it out?"

"Yes. Spell it out."

"Ten thousand bucks. That'll lift the injunction and buy a clerical error. They'll misplace her petition and won't find it until after Howie's been sent to the crematorium in Sukot and scattered off of Mainit Point, just like he wanted. I'll put the bills in a cookie tin and have it dropped off at the judge's home in Ayala Alabang. He's a friend of mine."

The young funeral director squirmed in his chair. This clearly wasn't a discussion he'd signed up for. Bobby looked uncomfortable as well. But Benicio wasn't about to let this happen. He wasn't about to lose his father to this stranger. "We'll give the judge twenty thousand," he said.

HOWARD'S FUNERAL, held as planned on the first of June, was well attended. Guests carpooled in sport utility vehicles and parked along the mud road, as far away as the Balayan Bay Dive Club. The land was rough, overgrown with ant-swarming bramble and deep-rooted bamboo, but hired men from the nearby village had used machetes to cut a narrow lane through the undergrowth. It led like a hallway down to a clearing by the water where Crespo Funeral Services arranged folding chairs and vases of cut flowers among the wild ones. Camera crews arrived and were turned away, instead setting up their tripods on a hill downshore of the property, getting filthy as they tried to run extension cords through the brush. Charlie Fuentes came with his own little entourage, followed closely by the American chargé d'affaires. Monique introduced Benicio to her bloodshot husband and Hon hugged him and Alice tight, the chill of their first conversation by now completely forgotten. Bobby and Reynato arrived just before the service started and each sat alone in the back. For a moment Benicio didn't recognize either of them—Bobby because his bandages had just been removed, and Reynato because he'd grown a scraggly beard and walked slowly with sunken shoulders.

"Who's that?" Alice asked, following Benicio's gaze. "He looks familiar."

"You met him on your first day here. He's the policeman who almost saved Dad."

"Not him, the other guy." She stared at Bobby with an odd intensity.

"A friend of my father's. I spent some time with him, before I knew what happened. You haven't met him."

"Is his name Robert something?"

"Yeah. Bobby. How do you know?"

Alice looked away from Bobby, as though the sight of him was a little unpleasant. "He was in some of the newspapers I read at the embassy," she said. That was all she said. The specially hired secular officiant took the podium, and they sat.

THE SERVICE WAS SHORT. When it was over Benicio collected his
father's urn and walked down to the beach. He pulled off his suit jacket
and laid it out on the wet, rocky sand. He sat on it and made room for
Alice who squeezed in alongside. It only took about thirty seconds for
him to feel cold water soaking though to his butt and thighs. A small
crowd followed and waited in silence to watch him scatter the ashes.
The minutes became a half hour and they trickled away. Soon the only
one left was Reynato, who'd begun to sob while glancing at the overcast
sky above them.

Benicio opened the urn and put his hand inside. Howard was soft
and coarse at the same time, like the downy flakes that drifted after
the eruption. He pressed his fingers in, knuckle-deep. It was more than
he'd done with his mother. He'd never even cracked the lid of her cas-
ket. For all he knew it was empty or filled with salt. His mother, who
just six months ago had been alive and dreaming up the useless future.
He'd had two living parents then. Five years ago he'd spoken to both,
often and with love. He'd had mild acne and a never-ending boner for
the woman who taught him diving. Benicio tried to add up how much
had changed since then, but he couldn't do it. It was like trying to add
apples and Monday.

Benicio pulled a handful of ash from the urn and looked at it. Seeing the ash, Reynato sobbed louder. It made gray little lines where it
stuck in rivulets to the webbing between his fingers. He poured it back
into the urn, careful not to let a single grain stray. He dusted his hands
off over the open urn and sealed it shut. He stood. Alice looked at him.

"Aren't you going to?"

"No, I'm not." He reached down to help her up. "I'm bringing him
home with me." He left his soaking suit jacket on the beach. He held
Alice by the arm and walked quickly, nodding to Reynato as they left.
He didn't slow until they were back on the road, off his father's land.

ALICE LEFT THE NEXT EVENING. He'd wanted to ride with her to
the airport but she preferred a shorter goodbye in the lobby. Benicio
couldn't say when he'd be coming home—didn't know if he'd make the

July network upgrade or the beginning of the school year at all. Hon thought it best he stay in the country while they figured out the estate and applied for a special investment visa. Alice thought that was best as well. She played it very cool as they waited for her ride to the airport, but once she was buckled into the backseat her resolve broke and she cried a little, and they kissed through the open window.

After seeing her off Benicio returned to his room and found that she'd left something on the bed. It was an old *Inquirer* from earlier that spring with a sticker in the upper-right corner indicating that Alice had taken it from the media center in the embassy. On the front page she'd written a note that read: *He seems like he made it through all right.* Under her handwriting was a headshot of Bobby Dancer. The story was highlighted.

### DANCER AND DOGS ABDUCTED, FOUND BEATEN

Political consultant Robert Danilo Cerrano, aka Bobby Dancer, was found badly beaten and unconscious early this morning in Luneta Park, just ten hours after his mother reported him missing. He had last been seen walking his two male Labradors, both runners-up in this season's showing at the Manila kennel club, some blocks from his family home in Dasmariñas village. Several witnesses reported that Dancer and his dogs were forced by armed men into a purple van and police suspect that these abductors held the young consultant for most of that night. Dancer sustained multiple blows to the side of his head that have resulted in a concussion, a shattered cheek and significant dental damage. Doctors at Makati Medical report that Dancer also sustained injury to his right knee, and that they are treating him for poisoning that occurred when his abductors made him ingest a combination of Fuentes campaign posters, kerosene and other things that this reporter will not mention here. Both dogs were found a short distance from Dancer, castrated and bludgeoned, and both were humanely euthanized on the spot.

Best known as the young mastermind of Senator Amoroso's

sweeping electoral victories in the late 1990s, Dancer
had recently bid farewell to the Koalisyon Demokratiko
ng Pilipinas to join the fledgling campaign of actor turned
senate-seat-challenger Charlie Fuentes. Insiders from the Fuentes campaign have confided to this reporter that former Senator
Amoroso was furious at the departure of her protégé, and one
source who will remain anonymous even went so far as to accuse
the Senator herself of involvement in the attack. The Fuentes
campaign has vowed to see that . . .

Benicio stopped reading and dropped the newspaper back on
the bed. The story wasn't new to him, of course, but the details were.
And God, the details were awful. He'd had enough of awful details. He
wasn't going to think about it.

He looked at the paper again just once before throwing it out, and
then it was just at the file photo of Bobby's face before the attack. The
photo was black and white and very grainy, but still, it looked remark-
ably different from the Bobby who'd been at the funeral. It wasn't
that there were horrible scars—he'd actually healed beautifully. It was
more the fact that the good side looked different once it had been seen
next to the broken side. Handsome as Bobby still was, the symmetry
that existed in this photo was gone, and it wouldn't be coming back.
Even the part that hadn't changed had changed.

*Chapter 33*

## SUMMER

On the morning after the eruption Monique dusted off Reynato's sooty
Honda and drove back to Manila. News of the eruption—*her eruption*—
was all over the morning radio shows. It wasn't so bad, thank God. No
deaths or injuries; only minor property damage. A tremor had run like

a shock down the archipelago's spine, causing Mount Pinatubo, Taal and Mount Apo to expel plumes of ash. Southwesterly winds carried most of the debris into the South China Sea, but areas downwind of the three peaks saw a few inches, including Subic, Manila and Manila Bay and most of Basilan. It wasn't until she got back onto the expressway that they even mentioned Howard's rescue on Corregidor Island. Very few had survived the firefight. Reynato Ocampo, inspiration for the Ocampo Justice films, was in the hospital, but his injuries were not life-threatening. How could they be, after all? He was Reynato Ocampo. The announcer actually said this.

Monique tried to visit him as soon as she returned to the city—because she was concerned, but also because the news hadn't dampened her resolve to break things off with him. The guard at the door turned her away. Her protests of being with the embassy, of being a close personal friend, of having a message for Reynato were all met with the same mute headshake. Finally, after allowing a handful of reporters into the room without similar scrutiny, the guard admitted that he'd been instructed to keep her, specifically, away. He had a picture of her in his wallet—a picture Reynato had taken—with a note on the back that said she wasn't to enter.

Furious, Monique waited for the shift change and snuck past when the new guy was in the bathroom. She understood right away why Reynato had wanted her out. He shared the double hospital suite with a second patient. It was the scarred man. The one with the face like hamburger; the one who had attacked them at Subic Bay; the one she'd pepper-sprayed in the eyeballs and chased into the bamboo thicket. His bed was surrounded by bouquets of artificial flowers, just like Reynato's. The chart tied to the bedrail identified him as Lt. *Racha Casuco*.

"It's not that I didn't want to see you." She turned to face Reynato, who was trying to sit up. "But I was afraid that this would be awkward."

She walked toward him, slowly.

"Aaaaand . . . it is. Shocker."

Still he was being cute? After what they'd both been through? She reached out quick and slapped him across the face. The sharp sound echoed in the tile room.

Reynato ran a finger under his lip and examined it for blood. There wasn't any. "I deserve that."

"I don't need you to tell me." She looked back at Racha, immobile and flower-decked. "You arranged for him to attack us?"

Reynato shifted in bed. It looked like shifting hurt him. "*Me.* He just attacked me. And he wouldn't have hurt either of us. I was just hoping . . . I wanted to make some magic happen. I wanted you to see what you really are. I thought that if he attacked me, then maybe that'd be the kick in the pants you needed. Maybe you'd use your bruha—"

"Don't call me that," she hissed. "I don't need you to show me who I am. I know who I am." Saying this aloud, it felt like she really believed it for the first time in a long time.

"I see that," Reynato said, nodding. "I do. I figure the tremor means you figured it out all by yourself." He paused, regarding her cautiously. She realized that even now he thought he had a chance with her. It suddenly became impossible to comprehend how just a few days ago the sight and smell and sound of him had been so pleasant. "I knew it was only a matter of time until you did, and if you focus—"

"What are you talking about?" she cut him off. "I mean, what are you even saying? I have a life. I have a husband and I have children."

He stared at her for a moment, eyes darting about as he tried to get his bearings. "I have a life, too," he said. "And I share it with people that I love, but who will never know me the way that you do. Just like no one will ever know you the way . . ." he trailed off here, sensing this was a losing tack. "This is what you came back to the Philippines for. Tell yourself it was to find *home*, or whatever, but you came here because you didn't fit in—"

She cut him off again, her voice not forgiving in the least: "Are you for real? You have no idea why I came back. And if you actually think I'm going to *stay* with you, then you don't know half of what you think you do about me."

Reynato reared up in bed, the hope in his face eroding. "Half is a lot, bruha."

"God, enough with the bruha crap." She waved him off. "What are you, five? Is this all just a game to you?"

Reynato laughed and winced and grabbed at his stitches. When he looked back up his expression had completely closed. "Everything is a game to me," he said, his voice irritatingly high. "Why should you be any different?" He spoke slowly, almost sadly, as though inviting her to seek a promised undercurrent of ironic poignancy. But it wasn't poignant—it was just a truism. With Reynato, face value was the only value. Monique felt drenched in revulsion like sea spray.

"Leave me alone," she said, humiliated by how much she'd let this aging infant hurt her. "Don't ever speak to me again." She took a step backward. "You stay away from me and my family, or I'll knock your goddamn house down."

"Oh my goodness. A whole new Monique." He laughed again and put his hands in the air like he was being held up. "I'm terrified." Sarcasm—but she could tell by the tinny ring to his laugh that he really was.

A FEW DAYS LATER Howard died, and a few days after that Joseph came back. The proximity of those events would trouble Monique for years. Howard passing away in the predawn quiet. Joseph, without any kind of announcement, leaving the kids with his sister and returning to Manila early. Howard's funeral on a patch of scrub overlooking a choppy strait. Joseph home, his bags already unpacked, fresh Baguio roses splayed loose over his wilted lap, their leaves and thorns, as well as a few droplets of his own blood, plastered to the bottom of the kitchen sink. She had the odd feeling that these events were mutually conditional. As though if she was to be thankful for one then she must be thankful for them both.

She didn't wake Joseph when she first found him. His worn loafers were propped up on the coffee table and his hands were folded over the roses, making his fingers look like pale wicker. He was still in his traveling clothes—his passport still in his shirt pocket. He stank just a little.

There was no big, warm, enveloping hug when he finally woke up. He pressed his closed mouth to her closed mouth and they started on dinner. The freezer was still full of Amartina's food, and they picked a pair of chops she'd bought at the Cavite market; rubbery white rims of skin and fat still hugging the lean. They defrosted the chops, dredged them in flour and fried them in corn oil. Joseph spread paper towels over a serving platter and as Monique took the dripping chops out of the pan she realized how long it had been since they'd cooked together. She remembered their first apartment in Columbia Heights, one elbow against the wall as she tended a half-size with electric burners. Joseph did prep on the other side of the kitchen. It was so small he could get at the stove, sink and fridge just by shifting his weight.

They ate in silence. Joseph meticulously sliced open a calamansi fruit and sprinkled the sour juice onto his pork. Some round green seeds came out as well and he used the tip of his knife to roll them, one by one, to the rim of his plate. He finally asked where Amartina was—it was a weekday, after all. He asked what happened to the lovebird and gecko—he'd gone to feed them while Monique was still at work and found them missing. She told him that Amartina had quit. She said that there had been an earthquake and the animals escaped. The insufficiency of these answers put him out, and he pouted.

They hardly loosened up after dinner, sitting at either end of the couch, legs in almost perfunctory contact. When it got late, Joseph retrieved a blanket from the linen closet and tucked it under the couch cushions. He went into the bedroom and came back with his pillow. Monique realized that he meant to spend the night out there.

"Don't take this the wrong way," he said, "but I'm going to be completely, brutally honest. I'm mad at you. And I'll need space. Maybe for quite some time."

Mad at her? He had every right, she supposed, but he didn't know that yet. All he could possibly have been mad about now was feeling forced to end his vacation early because she needed him. If that was enough to send him to the couch, what would coming clean about her affair do? Just thinking about it made her queasy.

"That's all right," she said. "Have a good night. I love you."

They did the closed-mouth kiss again and Monique went into the master bedroom, leaving the door open behind her. She undressed and lay down in bed, trying to remember what it was about Joseph that had made Reynato seem like an appealing alternative—someone worth the risk of her life, as she knew it. It wasn't just her wanderlust—her longing for and determination to find a connection in this city. The truth was that Reynato had lived up neatly to the cliché by being everything Joseph wasn't. Confident, direct and singularly at home in the world. Just because she'd ended it with him, just because the thought of him now disgusted her, that didn't make Joseph any more these things. He would still be neurotic. He would still be small and insecure and passive aggressive. Or at least he still *could* be. He could also be other things. He was capable of coming home early because he knew she needed him. And he was also capable of punishing her for it by sleeping on the couch.

After an hour Monique was still awake. She went into the den and saw that Joseph was, too. He didn't protest when she squeezed onto the couch beside him and put a hand on his rising chest. His body filled itself with air, breathing deep and slow, trying to force sleep by mimicking it. She counted his gusts. She matched his rhythm and felt herself begin to drift. Together their breaths surged above them. Monique lifted her hand from Joseph's chest and ran her fingers over it. Their lungs filled, and they emptied.

 *Chapter 34*

## REYNATO WAITS

And what of heartbroken, harried Reynato? He goes home after trying to kill Racha and finds, at bedtime, that sleep is an impossibility. It remains so for the next night, and the next. Reynato moves through the house trying different places and positions—curled up next to Lorna on an imported and as yet unpaid for Swedish foam, sprawled out on the big leather sofa in the living room, atop a pile of pillows in the kitchen, even in the enormous guest bathtub—but everywhere he goes he feels Efrem's eyes skitter over his skin like ants. In his paranoia he's sure that the holier-than-thou gun savant is alive, watching him lather up and shave, wipe himself on the toilet, distract himself with soft-core Internet pornography. *It's guilt*, Racha writes when Reynato returns to the hospital to make a third go at it. *It's a natural thing for you to feel. You're a lousy person. Take it from me; just put the knife down and you'll sleep like a baby tonight.* But Reynato knows guilt, and this isn't it. This is straight-up fear—so intense it infects his blameless family. So deep it wrecks his self-control, leaving him blubbering like a baby at Howard's funeral.

More than a week goes by without proper sleep. Reynato tries hotel rooms and foldout sofas. He tries a sleeping bag under calamansi trees in the front yard. One night he remembers, with sudden hope, the expensive air mattress made into a pool toy by Bea. He finds it in the pool house, shakes it dry and spends half an hour hacking air into it before realizing it's busted. A clean hole, big enough to accommodate a garden hose, runs right through. Reynato fingers the hole. He remembers Bea riding the mattress in the pool, waving up at him. He remembers the way it sank under her so suddenly, as though someone pulled the tap. Stripping down to his briefs, he jumps into the pool, chlorine burning his wounded shoulder through the gauze. He empties his lungs and floats along the bottom, fingering blue tiles. One near the middle feels different. What at first looks like a coin turns out to be the ass-end of a fifty-caliber BMG slug. With some wriggling he works the slug out, surfaces and fits it through the hole in the air mattress. Well. At least it's settled.

Still dripping in his briefs, Reynato goes inside. He treads lightly on the stairs, careful not to wake Bea or Lorna up, and enters his study. It's a mess. The window is riddled with bullet holes. His computer lies in pieces on the floor, all wires and plastic. The hanging uniforms on his wall have all been shot through their left breast pockets. Never mind. Reynato takes a big framed photo off the desk—the one with Erap, third president after the revolution, ousted by a smaller one himself— and writes three words across the back in permanent marker. He returns to the yard, stopping by the kitchen to light his frayed cigar on the gas range.

It's quiet outside. The moon tunnels above through cavern and vault, spilling blue light onto leaves. Reynato stands in the middle of the yard and holds the framed photo over his head. *I Dare You*, it says. He imagines he can hear the airy sound of something falling. Lights on the pool house go dark one by one. Underripe fruit falls from his papaya tree. A passing pigeon lands dead at his angled feet. Reynato is patient. He puffs deep, and waits.

*Chapter 35*

## AFTER THE FUNERAL

Benicio stayed in the Philippines long enough to get a special investor's resident visa, legalizing his ownership of his father's local estate. He sold his stake in the business to Hon at about half the value and listed all the properties at motivated prices. He spent his days in meetings or waiting for them. He tried his best to call Alice only every few days or so. As September rolled into October she wrote to let him know that the school was firing him, but that he should please try to cheer up. He did try to cheer up. On Saturday afternoons he drank mini-bar vodka and laughed his ass off to international versions of *Who Wants to Be a Millionaire* on BBC World. At nights he cried a lot, wishing that he'd been able to do more of it when his mother died and less of it now.

On his last evening in the country he called Bobby Dancer and invited him out to the nearby Café Havana for a drink. Benicio arrived first and sat at a table outside, under newly slung Christmas lights. When Bobby approached he did so without the slightest trace of a limp. His face was finally the same color all over and looked as healed as it was ever going to get.

"I didn't know you were still in town," Bobby said. He lowered himself into a chair, slowly.

"Just for a few more hours. I leave early tomorrow."

"Well, imagine that. I was the first to say mabuhay, and now here I am to bid you pamamaalam. That means farewell." He summoned a bereted waitress over. "What are you drinking?"

"I wasn't, yet."

"Well, why not go out how you came in? We'll have two lambanogs," he said. "I wish I'd known you were still around. Charlie had this thing yesterday honoring the two surviving policemen who rescued Howard. I mean, they used to be surviving. One of them is missing, and the other died last weekend."

"I'd heard."

"I would have invited you, for sure."

"I'm not sure I would have come," he said. "But thanks." The waitress returned with their drinks and Benicio took his from her hand before she had a chance to set it down. He took a long sip of the mouthwash-tasting lambanog, holding it in his cheeks before swallowing. "I wanted to tell you something," he said. "I hope you didn't get the wrong idea before the funeral. I did what I did so we could have the service. But I'm giving—I've given her half of everything. It wasn't about the money."

"Wasn't it?" Bobby asked. "Then why not give her everything?"

Benicio laughed at this. Then he saw that Bobby wasn't joking. "Maybe it was a little about the money. But it was also about my dad. Whatever he had with her, he was *my* dad. I wasn't about to give him up."

Bobby ran his finger around the rim of his glass. "So you don't know, then, if Howard is the father of her kid."

"I don't," Benicio said. "But whether he was or not, he treated her wrong. She and the kid will be taken care of. They're rich now, by most standards. I think it's worked out as well as it could have."

Bobby looked down at the table and nodded, seeming to consider this. "You look like shit," he said.

They shared a moment of quiet, and then they both laughed. "Well, you look great," Benicio said.

"I know, right?" Bobby sipped his drink and made a face at it. "Word is out among the barboys. Dancer is back."

"Any pain?"

"Nope. I don't think so, at least. It's hard to remember what I felt like before. But I think this is normal." Bobby shook a cigarette from his pack, lit it and took short drags. "It was a really nice service. I hope it wasn't weird—Charlie can't go anywhere without making an entrance."

"It wasn't weird," Benicio said. Looking at Bobby, he found it impossible to keep the article he'd read from springing up in his mind. The conjecture that they'd made Bobby watch as the tops of his dogs' heads were cracked open with hammers. The evidence that he'd been forced to swallow hunks of their testicles along with shredded campaign posters and kerosene. "Actually, that's a lie," he said. "It was very weird. There were four TV crews on the hill. Nothing about it wasn't weird."

Bobby smiled. "Well, I hope you don't blame us. You're implicated. You brought as much weird along with you as you found here. Or like, forty-sixty at least." His cigarette wasn't a quarter done but he crushed it into the ashtray. "Do you know when you're coming back?"

"No. I mean, I'm not. Not ever. No offense."

Bobby's expression turned quizzical. "Well . . . since this is our last conversation, where's my incentive not to be offended? I'm good at marching off in a huff. I've done that shit before."

"It's not the city. It's who I am here."

"Who are you here?"

"I'm . . ." Benicio crossed and uncrossed his legs. He found the sudden edge in Bobby's voice disconcerting. "It's like my father. He was a different person, not just here but whenever he left home. A worse person. He cheated on my mother here, years before she died. He had this whole hidden life that he never told us about. I mean, for all I know June really is his kid, and he let June's mother work out of a filthy goddamn brothel. It could be that June's not even the only one."

Bobby leaned back in his chair. "Wow. I see you're taking this whole consequence-free last conversation thing to heart."

"Sorry. I don't mean to unload on you."

"No, it's fine. But as long as those are the rules—Manila didn't make your father shitty. People are who they can afford to be. When your father was here he could afford to be Mr. Playboy. Maybe at home he could afford less. That doesn't mean he was different. And it's the same with you—you can afford to be Mr. Goddamn Generous. You can afford to spend a fuckload on peace-of-mind, because you've got a fuckload to spare. But don't tell me, or yourself, that leaving will make you better. Whatever you see peeking out right now, whatever it is you don't like; well I've got news for you. *That's Benicio.*"

Bobby turned halfway around and drew a rectangle in the air with his index finger to signal for the bill. Benicio fumbled in his pocket and placed some cash on the table. They waited in silence. When Benicio spoke his voice was dry and pitchy. "I never said it wasn't."

TWO DAYS LATER HE WAS HOME, unpacking while Alice boiled noodles in the kitchen. He carried his dive bag to the bathroom, filled the tub with cold water and prepared to rinse out the gear he'd only used once. The black velcro and rubber hoses were crusted over with a thin layer of grit that dissolved as he lowered everything under the clear surface. He cleaned the gear the way he'd been taught—purging mouthpieces, keeping the dust-cap tight, filling the BCD with water and shaking it above his head to rinse it from the inside out. He added his wetsuit and fins to the tub, holding them under the surface, submerged to his forearms. Spray from the tap rushed over his fingers and left little bubbles that clung to his arm hair. It reminded him of the dives with the Costa Rican instructor. The way you could be made a beginner again by the current.

Benicio pulled the water-heavy gear from the tub and slung it over the bar above. He ran his hands along the wetsuit legs, squeezing them dry as best he could. He'd owned this same suit for almost ten years and there was hardly a rip or tear in it. He remembered the long procession of colors and brands that his father had gone through; how he'd torn each new wetsuit with his expanding belly and clumsy bottom-scraping. How the constantly replaced gear gave him a different look on almost every trip. Once, when Benicio was seventeen, he actually lost track of who his father was. It was a gentle drift dive with a hefty tour group from Arkansas. At sixty feet Benicio noticed an outline in the sand—a flounder, big as a loveseat—and grabbed at what he thought was his father's wrist to point it out. But it was a stranger. She pulled her hand back and shot him beady annoyance through her prescription mask. Benicio swam out ahead of their party and looked back at them. The divers were all big, bright shapes. He couldn't pick his father out.

He only found him at the end, when they all floated atop a high ridge of coral to decompress before ascent. Howard was hugging the base of a barrel sponge, kicking his feet out now and again to keep himself stationary. Near the base of the sponge was a crust of dead coral, and sprouting from that was a single blue-and-yellow Christmas-tree worm no bigger than a child's thumb. Howard waved his hand in front of the worm and—*shump!*—it retreated into its hole. He waited, rapt. The worm remerged, its short little tendrils splaying out one by one. He waved his hand and again it shot back inside.

Howard looked up at Benicio with delight. With wonder. He pointed to the worm—which was emerging yet again—and signed *OK*, which meant "not dying" but also "this is good." Benicio returned the *OK*. The master unsheathed her dive knife and banged it against her tank to get everybody's attention. She thumbed up at the surface for them to ascend. Howard drifted away from the barrel sponge, but Benicio lingered there for a moment, staring at the tiny animal. He didn't get what was so special about it. But he sensed, at least, that it *was* special. Then, with a kick, he floated weightlessly away. He looked straight up to keep his airway open. He felt his breath expand. Up above Howard was already near the surface—his arms extended, like they'd been trained, so those above would see him coming.

ABOUT THE AUTHOR

Alexander Yates grew up in Haiti, Mexico, and Bolivia. He graduated from high school in the Philippines, where he returned to
work in the political section of the U.S. Embassy after receiving a
BA in English from the University of Virginia. He holds an MFA
from Syracuse University. His short story "Everything, Clearly,"
appears in the 2010 edition of *American Fiction: the Best Unpub-
lished Short Stories by Emerging Writers.*